MARTYR

MARTYR

RORY CLEMENTS

THORNDIKE
WINDSOR
PARAGON

This Large Print edition is published by Thorndike Press, Waterville, Maine, USA and by BBC Audiobooks Ltd, Bath, England.
Thorndike Press, a part of Gale, Cengage Learning.
Copyright © 2009 by Rory Clements.
The moral right of the author has been asserted.

LIBRARY OF CONGRESS CATALOGING-IN-PUBLICATION DATA

Clements, Rory.
   Martyr / by Rory Clements.
      p. cm. — (Thorndike Press large print reviewers' choice)
   ISBN-13: 978-1-4104-1900-2 (alk. paper)
   ISBN-10: 1-4104-1900-2 (alk. paper)
   1. Secret service—England—Fiction. 2. Drake, Francis, Sir, 1540?–1596—Assassination attempts—Fiction. 3. Great Britain—History—Elizabeth, 1558–1603—Fiction. 4. Large type books. I. Title.
   PR6103.L45M37 2009b
   823'.92—dc22   2009018503

BRITISH LIBRARY CATALOGUING-IN-PUBLICATION DATA AVAILABLE

Published in 2009 in the U.S. by arrangement with Bantam Books, a division of Random House, Inc.
Published in 2010 in the U.K. by arrangement with John Murray (Publishers) Ltd.

U.K. Hardcover: 978 1 408 45924 9 (Windsor Large Print)
U.K. Softcover: 978 1 408 45925 6 (Paragon Large Print)

Printed in the United States of America
1 2 3 4 5 6 7 13 12 11 10 09

*To the memory of my father,
who knew more than most about
overcoming adversity*

Chapter 1

Rose Downie sat on the cold cobbles, cradling a swaddled baby that was not hers.

She leaned her aching back against the wall of the imposing stone house, close to its arched oak door. Under any other circumstance, nothing could have brought her near this building where baleful apprehension hung heavy in the air like the stink of tallow, but the man who lived here, Richard Topcliffe, was her last hope. She had been to the court of law, and the justice merely shook his head dismissively and said that even had he believed her — and that, he said with a scowl, was as unlikely as apple blossom in November — there was nothing he could do for her.

The constable had been no more helpful. "Mistress Downie," he said, "put the baby in a bag like a kitten and throw it in the Thames. What use is it alive? I promise you, in God's name, that I will not consider the

7

killing a crime but an act of mercy, and you shall never hear another word of the matter."

Now, outside Topcliffe's house in the snow-flecked street, close by St. Margaret's churchyard in Westminster, Rose sat and waited. She had knocked at the door once already, and it had been answered by a sturdy youth with a thin beard who looked her up and down with distaste and told her to go away. She refused and he closed the door in her face. The intense cold would have driven anyone else home to sit at the fireside wrapped in blankets, but Rose would not go until she had seen Topcliffe and begged him to help.

The bitter embers of sunlight dipped behind the edifices of St. Margaret's and the Abbey, and the cold grew deeper. Rose was fair, young, no more than seventeen with a face that, in other times, sparkled with smiles. She shivered uncontrollably in her heavy gowns and clutched the baby close to share what little warmth she had. Occasionally she lifted a large, well-formed breast from her garments to feed the infant; the milk was free-flowing and rich and her need of relief was almost as insistent as the child's hunger. Steam rose from her breast in the icy winter air. The child sucked at her with ferocity and she was thankful for it. Monstrous as she considered the baby, some instinct still made her keep it and feed it, even though it was not hers. The day moved on into darkness, but she was as immovable as stone.

CHAPTER 2

John Shakespeare stayed up late into the night, and when, finally, he crept into bed he slept fitfully. Like all Englishmen in these terrible days, he was fearful for the safety of his Queen and country. At night these anxieties spilled out in dreams and he awoke bathed in sweat.

Before dawn, he was out of bed breakfasting alone at his long table. He was a tall man, six foot, but not powerfully built. His eyes were hooded and dark and carried the cares of the world in their depths. Only when he smiled, and that was rare enough these past few months, did he appear to shake off the worries that permanently clouded his face.

His maidservant, Jane, was bleary-eyed in her lawn coif and linen nightdress as she lit the fire. He liked to see her like that, unkempt, buxom, and still warm from her bed, her breasts loose and swaying beneath the thin material. He guessed from the way she looked at him that she would receive him with warmth, energy, and generosity should he ever climb the stairs to her attic room and slip under the covers with her. But there would be a reckoning. Such nectar always came at a price, be it the parson's knock at the door demanding the banns be called or the wail of a babe that no one wanted. And Shakespeare was too cautious a fox to be so snared.

Jane served him three small hens' eggs boiled hard the way he liked them, good manchet bread and salt butter, some Dutch cheese, common saffron cakes which she had bought from the seller the day before, slices of spiced rump beef, and a beaker of small beer. The room was lit by beeswax candles that guttered in the draft through the leaded window. This winter of early 1587 was cold and Shakespeare ate well to fill his belly and stir life into his limbs.

While Jane cleared away the remnants of the meal, he knelt briefly and said the Lord's Prayer. As always, he said the words by rote, but today he laid emphasis on *lead us not into temptation*. He was twenty-eight; time to be married. These feelings — urges — were too powerful and needed an outlet other than those to be found in the comfort of a single man's bed.

At first light, his man, Boltfoot, was waiting for him in the paneled anteroom of the ancient house. He was talking with Jane but she scurried away to the kitchen as soon as Shakespeare entered. Shakespeare frowned; surely there was nothing between them? He shook his head dismissively. No, a young woman like Jane would never see anything in a grizzled former mariner with a clubfoot.

The building that John Shakespeare called home was a handsome four-story wood-frame house which had creaked and moved and bent sideways with the passing of the years. At times Shakespeare wondered whether it might fall about his ears, but it had lasted two centuries thus far and was conveniently close to Mr. Secretary Walsingham's fine city house in Seething Lane. Though not large, it served as office and home for Shakespeare.

"Is Slide here?"

"Two men, Mr. Shakespeare," Boltfoot said. "Slide and a constable."

"I'll see Slide."

Boltfoot Cooper was like an old oak, thought Shakespeare, the sinews and raised veins of his face weathered and rutted like bark. He watched his servant as he turned toward the door, his body short and squat, his left foot heavy and dragging, as it had been since birth. He was in his early thirties or so he believed; his mother had died of childbed fever and his father could never recall the year or month of his son's birth to tell him. Somewhere around 1554 seemed most likely.

"Wait. What does the constable want?"

Boltfoot stopped. "Says there has been a murder." His voice, brusque and deepened by years of salt air in his time as a ship's cooper, revealed him to be from Devon.

"Just that? A murder? Why come to me? Why not fetch the justice or the tipstaff?" There was an unmistakeable edge of irritation in Shakespeare's words. At times these days he felt as if he would seize up like rusted iron, that the pressure of responsibility laid on him by Walsingham was simply too great for one man.

"Says the woman killed looks highborn," Boltfoot replied. "Soft hands. Says there are papers and strange letters and the house where she was found was burned down. He's scared."

Shakespeare sighed in resignation. "Tell him to wait while I see Slide."

Harry Slide bowed low as he entered the antechamber, sweeping his sable-edged cape aside with extravagance, and then, as he rose, extending his fingers like the neck of a swan.

"All right, Slide. You're not at court now."

"But I *am* in the presence of greatness, am I not? The magnificent Mr. John Shakespeare. I have a hundred marks says you will be a minister of the Crown before too long."

"If you had a hundred marks, Harry, I doubt you would be here."

Shakespeare eyed Slide's glittering clothes, his taut collar and stiff doublet with gold and black slashes in the Spanish style. With such expensive tastes, it was hardly surprising he was always impoverished. "So, what can you offer me?"

"I hear *everything,* as you know, Mr. Shakespeare. Today I heard that the Archbishop of Canterbury was caught in the vestry on Sunday last with his cassock around his waist swiving a member of his flock."

Shakespeare raised a disapproving eyebrow. Such irreverence could cost a man his life or, at the very least, his ears.

"Nothing very strange about that, you might think," Slide continued. "But the next day he had her for dinner with carrots and some garden mint."

14

Shakespeare couldn't help laughing out loud.

"At least she was a ewe, not a ram, so I suppose that's all right. Isn't it?" Slide said. "I'm afraid I am not sure of the teaching on such matters in the new church."

Shakespeare laughed again. He was grateful to Slide for lightening his mood. There had been much darkness lately — plots against Her Majesty, a pending death sentence hanging over Mary, Queen of Scots. "You will get yourself hanged if you do not take care, Harry Slide."

"Perhaps. But for the present, could I interest you in the whereabouts of two priests of the Society of Jesus . . ."

Shakespeare suddenly paid attention. "Two Jesuits? Garnet and Southwell?"

"The same."

"Well, yes, of course, that would be a big catch. Do you have them?"

"As good as in the net, Mr. Shakespeare."

"Tell me more."

Slide was a slender man with open features beneath fair locks. It was said he could charm eels out of rivers or bees from their hives. Even those he betrayed — and there were many — found it difficult to dislike him. "I want a hundred marks for my information."

15

Shakespeare knew the man was dissembling, that he did not as yet know where the notorious Jesuits were hiding, but if anyone could find them it was Slide. He claimed to know what was going on everywhere in the capital and swore he had one or more informers in every prison in London and Southwark. Shakespeare didn't doubt it. Slide had played a major part in exposing the recently foiled plot to murder Elizabeth and replace her on the throne with the Scots Queen. It was the Scots Queen who now seemed likely to have the shorter life, for she had shown herself to be up to her slender royal neck in the conspiracy against her cousin. Tried and condemned to death, Mary now awaited her fate in the bleak confines of Fotheringhay Castle in Northamptonshire. All that was needed was a stroke of Elizabeth's quill on the death warrant.

Mary's plight was in no small part thanks to Harry Slide, for he had infiltrated the conspirators, and followed their every move on behalf of Walsingham and Shakespeare. The guilty men — Babington, Ballard, and the rest — never stood a chance. Their short lives had ended in torment and butchery at Lincoln's Inn Fields, hanged by the neck but not allowed to die, their bodies sliced open, entrails drawn from them, beating hearts tossed carelessly into the cauldron, then their carcasses quartered and spread about the capital. Finally, their heads were thrust onto pikes and raised above London Bridge to warn other would-be traitors.

If Slide felt anything for these hapless, tragic men, whom he had come to know so well and whose friendship he had encouraged, he did not show it. He was an expert in the art of projection, feigning sympathy with a cause to draw its adherents to their doom. It might be impossible to trust Slide but, like a sharp kitchen knife that could slip and cut you, he was necessary. And, as far as Shakespeare was concerned, he was good company.

"You will have to tell me more before I can even *think* of parting with such a sum for a couple of Jesuits."

"Well, I have sound knowledge that Southwell is living close by the city."

"Where exactly?"

"I will know within forty-eight hours."

"And Garnet?"

Slide grinned disarmingly and shrugged his well-padded shoulders. "Garnet is not here, I think. Gone traveling among his flock of traitors in Norfolk, I believe."

"Well, that halves the price to start with."

"Mr. Shakespeare, I have expenses . . ."

Shakespeare took his purse from his belt and removed two coins. "You mean you have tailors, vintners, and whores to keep happy. Gaming debts, too, I don't doubt. Three marks now and twenty-seven more if you bring me to the Jesuit."

Slide took the coins and jiggled them jauntily in his hand. "You are a hard man, Mr. Shakespeare."

"Luckily for you, I'm not as hard as I might be, Harry, or you'd spend half your life in the pillory. But keep alert as always. We need intelligence."

"Your will be done, O master."

Slide departed with another sweep of his expensive cape.

The constable could not have been more of a contrast as he bent low beneath the oak lintel of the door. He was big, with long-bowman's arms that bulged through the woolen smock beneath his oxhide jerkin, and yet he was shaking with something akin to terror. He smelled of fire.

Shakespeare called in Jane, to bring ale to calm his nerves, and then the man blurted out his story of a woman found murdered. Shakespeare listened intently. It was a grim tale and one that Walsingham would expect him to investigate without delay.

The three of them — Shakespeare, Bolt-foot, and the constable — took horse and rode through the busy morning streets up through the Bishop's Gate, beneath the piked heads of thieves and murderers.

Ten minutes later they arrived at Hog Lane, close to Shoreditch and just north of the theaters where the old Holywell Priory had stood before Great Henry pulled it down. Their horses stood in the cold winter air, steam rising from their flanks and hot breath shooting from their nostrils. In front of them was a burnt-out house. The depressing stench of soot and burnt straw hung around them. Blackened debris lay around the horses' hooves on the hard, icy earth.

Shakespeare huddled into his black bear cloak, a very welcome gift from the New World presented to him by Walsingham at Christmas last. It was a generous gesture and typical of Walsingham in his dealings with those he loved or for whom he felt responsible. He had taken Shakespeare into his employment nine years earlier, when he was a young lawyer newly arrived in London from the Midlands. Shakespeare's master at Gray's Inn, Paul Ballater, was a friend of Walsingham and had recommended his pupil for the post, thinking the younger man more suited for practical work than endless dry books. "I see you looking out the window when your mind should be on precedent law, John," Ballater had said. "Take my advice and go with Walsingham. You will find no better patron in all of England." Shakespeare had seen the truth in this and had not hesitated in accepting the post. He had suffered few pangs of regret, though Walsingham — the world called him Mr. Secretary — was an unbending driver of men.

The constable brought him back to the present. "I believe this fire was set deliberate, Mr. Shakespeare," he said. "When it caught, at midnight, the house and thatching suddenly went up into flames. I am told it was as if a taper had been put to powder, sir. George Stocker, the bellman, was here very quickly."

"Where is he now?"

"At home not far away, sir, abed. He sleeps by day."

"Fetch him."

The burnt house stood in a row of a dozen or more frames that had clearly been thrown up quickly in three or four acres of uncultivated land. Shakespeare recognized it as part of the expansion outward from London into what was recently open country to the north of the wall, past Spital Fields toward

20

Ellyngton Ponds. The encroachment was everywhere. The ruined house had not been well built. It looked hastily erected by the landowner, and Shakespeare guessed its purpose was to house incomers from the shire counties; there was good money to be made providing lodging for skilled men who had any sort of work. The city was growing fast with men moving from all parts of the country and from over the water, either seeking wealth or escaping persecution in France or the never-ending war in the Spanish Netherlands. London could no longer contain all those who would live there.

Under the eaves of the stabling near the house, four vagabonds, all of them men and sturdy beggars by the look of them, lay beneath woolen rags on the bitter ground, sleeping off a night of strong ale. They looked like the sort of people no one wanted, the sort who could not get a bed without thieving the wherewithal, and later, most likely, swinging on the fatal tree at Tyburn for their trouble.

"Wake them up, Boltfoot. But keep them here. I want to question them."

Boltfoot dismounted from his horse and approached the gang. With his good foot he kicked them one by one in the ribs and pulled them to their feet, ordering them not to move on pain of a flogging. They moved stiffly in the cold but made little protest; the sight of Boltfoot's short-muzzled caliver — a light musket — slung around his back and the cutlass hanging loosely from his right hand was enough incentive to keep all four standing obediently in their tatters, shivering.

The bellman, George Stocker, arrived with the constable from the direction of Shoreditch. He was still adjusting his smock, having been raised from his slumber, and his bell clanked as he walked. He was a well-fed man with a belly like a pig ready for the shambles.

"Tell Mr. Shakespeare what happened, George," the constable ordered.

Stocker removed his hat. His beard was thick and full of goose grease and his brain was clearly as slow as only a bellman's could be. He grunted some indeciperable greeting, then began his story. "I did ring my bell hard and loud, sir, and called out. Folk came from out their beds in the houses around, sir, and drew water from the well in pails. We did douse it quite quickly, sir . . ."

Stocker glanced at the constable, who nodded. "Go on, George. Tell the master what you told me."

"I did find . . . Sir, I do not know whether

I should say this for it feels like a sin to talk of it."

"I believe you found a body. Is that right?"

Stocker tensed and looked down at the rough earth beneath his paltry-shod feet. "There was the body of a young woman, sir. Unclothed, sir. And most terrible dealt with."

"And what else, bellman?"

"Papers, sir, with writing on, I know not what."

"You can't read?" Shakespeare asked.

"No, sir."

"And you, Constable? Can you read?"

"No, sir. Though my wife's brother knows some reading. Should I fetch him?"

Shakespeare ignored the question, slid from his gray mare, and handed the reins to the constable. "I'm going inside. Hold my horse and stay out here with them." He nodded toward the beggars. "Come, Boltfoot."

The neighbors had done a good job of dousing the fire; London was a city built largely of wood, and fires were frequent, so every husbandman had to be proficient at fetching and carrying pails to douse them. The walls of this house were still standing, though blackened. Shakespeare allowed the bellman to lead the way through the gaping hole where the door had been kicked in. He was conscious of the time. One of Walsingham's post riders had arrived late the previous evening saying Shakespeare was wanted at Barn Elms by midday on a matter of urgency. The Principal Secretary would not wait.

Shakespeare looked around the gloomy shell of the house. It was remarkably intact, given the ferocity of the fire described by the constable. Something caught his eye on the sodden floor. He picked it up. It was a paper, wet and unreadable. Then he saw that there were more papers lying around amongst the burnt stubble of thatching. Some of the papers had distinguishable words and all of them were unfolded, which almost certainly meant they were new printed. He signaled to Boltfoot. "Gather them all up."

There were other things, too: type sorts for printing. But no sign of a press. "All of it, Boltfoot, the type sorts, too. I will examine it all later. Perhaps we can discover the letter foundry where it was made. Now, Mr. Stocker, where is the body?"

Above them the roof was burnt away and the sky hung a brilliant gray where the ceiling should have been. A few flutterings of snow began to drift down.

The staircase was intact, though charred, and they ascended it to the second floor, where, in a jetted chamber at the front, they found a woman's corpse, naked and bloody, stretched obscenely on a large oaken and canopied bed. A kite was pecking at her eyes but flew up through the skeleton of purlins and rafters as they approached. The bell-man gripped his hat in his hands as if he would wring it dry, and averted his gaze. Shakespeare understood why he would wish to do so and why the constable had seemed so shaken.

Her throat had been slit until her head was almost separated from her body. The pink of the woman's skin had turned a ghastly blue and the blood a coagulated red like dark rusted iron. Her head hung limply with a gaping wound like a second mouth, but that wasn't what caught the eye. It was her splayed legs and her woman's organs that commanded attention.

Her belly had been torn open and her womb exposed. A fetus, perhaps three inches long, had been pulled from her and lay above the wound, still attached by its cord. Shakespeare shuddered; its little head seemed perfectly formed. Pulling his eyes away from the tiny body, he approached the bed and examined the woman's face.

Though twisted and contorted by her death agonies, he knew her features. He turned to the bellman. "Leave us, Mr. Stocker. Wait outside with the constable."

The bellman needed no second bidding to leave this charnel house; he was gone like a hare from a hound.

"What do you make of it, Boltfoot?"

"Most profane, master."

"Do you recognize her? She's a Howard. Lady Blanche Howard." The dead woman was, in fact, as he knew well, a close cousin of the new Lord High Admiral and commander of the English Navy, Howard of Effingham. She had been brought up in his household when the plague took her parents. The Lord Admiral was known to treat her as his own daughter.

"Yes, sir."

Shakespeare was silent for a few moments. He looked closely at the body and then took in the surroundings. What was a woman like Blanche Howard, a cousin of the Queen, doing in a place like this? Though far from the worst sort of tenement, this house was a long way from the palaces and great country houses to which she was born.

"This is a bad business, Boltfoot."

Shakespeare had seen Blanche at court from time to time, and thought her to be about eighteen or nineteen. She had seemed typical of the younger women of the nobility who made their way to court and fluttered about like butterflies or attended the Queen's chamber until their parents made a match for them and they were consigned to their husband's country estates. Were there rumors about her? Was she married or betrothed yet, and if not, why not? He thought he recalled hearing that she had fallen in with some of the more loose-living, wanton elements, but there was nothing unusual about that. The young ladies of the court were not exactly known for their purity. Shakespeare suddenly felt the cold of the morning through the thickness of his long fur cloak and doublet. He held out his gloved hand to Boltfoot, who handed him the papers he had gathered.

"Is that all of them?"

"I believe so, master."

"Check again. And start a fire outside."

Shakespeare shuffled through the papers. They were all the same, new printed. The scattering of type sorts seemed to suggest this had been the site of an unlicensed "wagonback" press, an illegal printing works that could be transported relatively easily from hiding place to hiding place. It also seemed certain that whoever was printing here had left in a hurry, in too much of a rush to gather up the remaining papers and type sorts. What kind of infamy had Blanche Howard found herself involved in here? And, more importantly now, with *whom* had she been involved, and who had killed her?

He took the best preserved of the papers and held it away from his eyes under the snowy light. It was headed "God's Vengeance On The Bastard Usurper." After a short preamble, it read:

Whereas previously we have discussed the deceits, dissembling, lying, flattering, complots and secret practices of the said monstrous Earl of Leicester and his designs for the crown of England, let us not neglect the wretched sins and wickedness of that same Virgin by which he would have succeeded in his foul and corrupt aims. Withal she had the pox, this great sovereign lady, daughter of the harlot Boleyn and murderer in heart of her father's true-born daughter, yet it was not God's visiting on her but a base man, with the aid of his complice, the self-same Mother Davis of whom we have heard, that brought her abed. And a strange pox it was that swelled her belly and brought forth another bastard of her abominable line, wet-nursed by the sorceress Davis and brought to her majority in great secrecy. . . .

Shakespeare shook his head dourly. "That same virgin" was clearly the Queen. The curiously phrased tract seemed to suggest that she and Leicester, her favorite courtier, had had a child together. And that the child had been suckled by the notorious — almost certainly nonexistent — sorceress known as Mother Davis. It was a preposterous accusation, but certainly not the first time that such a publication had suggested the Queen had secretly given birth to Leicester's baby. The problem was, the more such allegations appeared, the more they came to be believed by the gullible among Elizabeth's subjects. That was why it was necessary to stamp down so hard on these libels.

This was turning out to be a very bad day indeed. Shakespeare read on. There was more of the usual diatribe against Leicester, with additional accusations against Walsingham and Archbishop Whitgift. Finally, it came to the Scots Queen, Mary. The threat in the paper was clear: should sentence of death be carried out on her, then the "bastard usurper" — Elizabeth herself —

would die, too. Shakespeare's jaws tightened.

Outside, Boltfoot had a fire going. Under the watch of the constable, the band of beggars shuffled closer to get some of its heat. Shakespeare gazed at the bleak scene with a dispassionate eye: these vagabonds were a sorry lot, but he couldn't take chances; they must be held until he had time to question them. One of them put his hand up and tried to say something. He was a tall, rangy man with bird's-nest hair and a bright red jerkin that had seen better days.

"You will get your chance to speak later," Shakespeare said curtly. He turned away to toss the libelous pamphlets on the fire. He kept one paper, the least damaged by water, and thrust it into his doublet, along with a corner of a damaged one which was printed with a good sample of typefaces.

"Boltfoot, make sure all these burn so that not an ash survives. Ensure no one reads them. Then go through the house again, every nook and cranny. If you find more of these papers, burn them. If you find anything else, hold it for me. Then enlist the constable and bellman and any other respectable neighbors you might need. Get the body to the Searcher of the Dead at St. Paul's and inform the coroner. Take the vagabonds under guard to Bridewell, where you will have them set to work. It will do them good. Leave sixpence for their food. Also, inquire who owns this house. We will meet in Seething Lane at dusk."

Boltfoot motioned toward the beggars, singling out the one who was tallest, in the frayed red jerkin. "Mr. Shakespeare, that one says he would speak with you."

"I know, Boltfoot, but he will have to wait. I must hasten to Barn Elms."

Shakespeare remounted and was about to spur his horse toward Bishop's Gate, when he heard the clump of hooves on hard earth. He turned and saw four horsemen approaching. He stopped. They came on fast, halting in a fury of stamping hooves, rearing, twisting necks, and flying manes. Shakespeare recognized their leader instantly: Richard Topcliffe, the Queen's Servant.

"What is here, Mr. Shakespeare?" Topcliffe drew his horse alongside, so he and Shakespeare were face to face.

"A murder," Shakespeare said slowly and deliberately. He fixed his eyes on Topcliffe's and held his gaze. "It need not concern you."

Topcliffe's brow clouded like an approaching storm. "I decide what concerns me, Shakespeare. The Queen's life and the

31

security of her realm concern me, and anything pertaining to these matters. Answer me: who has been killed here?"

"You will find out in due course."

Topcliffe was silent a moment, as if considering his response, then he said slowly, "Would you *cross* me, Shakespeare?" When Topcliffe spoke, in his distinct Lincolnshire tone, it was more like the growl of a wildcat from the menagerie at the Tower than a human voice.

Shakespeare breathed deeply. He and Topcliffe had clashed over the recent Babington conspiracy to murder the Queen. Some of the accused had ended up in Topcliffe's hands at the Tower. He had brought torture to bear and muddied the waters. Shakespeare, who had been deeply involved in breaking the plot, had wanted to interrogate the prisoners. He was convinced that more could have been elicited from the plotters by gentler means than torture, including the names of other conspirators; Topcliffe, who had done his grisly work with the full authority of the Queen, had simply broken their bodies on the rack. When Shakespeare protested, he and Topcliffe almost came to blows. Only the intercession of Walsingham had kept them apart. Now Shakespeare could smell Topcliffe's brutish animosity. It was a stench beyond sweat. Shakespeare held his ground. "Talk to the Principal Secretary. I report to him, not to you."

Topcliffe jumped from his horse. He was a man in his mid-fifties with the raw physical power of a fighting bandog. In his hand he carried a silver-tipped blackthorn stick, heavily weighted at the silver end like a cudgel. He strode two steps to Shakespeare's horse and casually wrenched him from the saddle.

Shakespeare was dragged by his prized bear cloak like a sack of beets. He scrabbled against the hard ground as Topcliffe pulled him toward the house. Shakespeare gained a foothold and stumbled to his feet. Undeterred, Topcliffe reached out and took hold of the nape of Shakespeare's neck and pulled him like a reluctant schoolboy, then stopped abruptly in his tracks.

Boltfoot had the slender octagonal muzzle of his ornate caliver full in Topcliffe's face, primed and ready to fire.

Topcliffe weighed up the position for no more than two seconds, then laughed and dropped Shakespeare. He smacked the silver end of his blackthorn into the palm of his hand menacingly. "I'll have you, John Shakespeare. I'll sup on your blood. And you, Boltfoot Cooper." He left them and swept into the house.

Shakespeare dusted down his suit of clothes. They were muddy and damaged and he was angry. He followed Topcliffe through the doorway. Boltfoot stayed outside, his caliver leveled at the remainder of Topcliffe's band, all still mounted and looking very little concerned.

In the second-floor chamber, Topcliffe stared down at the corpse of Blanche Howard for a moment, then grasped her hair and lifted her head to get a closer look at her dead face.

"Who is she?"

"You'll find out when Mr. Secretary or the Council sees fit to tell you."

"The Council!" Topcliffe snorted with disdain and flung the near-severed head back on the stained mattress. He turned to Shakespeare and rested his broad hands on his hips. "If we waited on the Council, we'd have a Spaniard for our sovereign."

"I know what I must do, Topcliffe."

"Do you? I believe you are a boy trying to do a man's job, Shakespeare. And do you really think I don't know who she is? She's a Howard. Now, where are the papers?"

"Papers?"

"I am told there are papers here. Give them to me."

"There were papers here, but not now. I have had them burned."

"All of them?"

"Yes, *all* of them, Topcliffe." Shakespeare had to restrain himself from folding his arms tight around his chest where the paper was secreted.

"If I find you lie to me, I'll have your head, Shakespeare. I know about your father's little secret. And are you any different? You say so — but so do many."

Shakespeare's skin rose in bumps. "You know nothing of my family, Topcliffe." But clearly he did, and the words worried him.

He had entered the service of Walsingham believing that the new religion, this Church of England, was the *true* religion; that the Roman way, with its sale of relics, its superstition, its cruel Inquisition and burnings of flesh, was the corruption. In his soul, he could only fight for this English version of Christianity if he believed in it utterly. And yet family loyalties tore at him, for his father still clung to the old religion in private, breaking the recusancy laws by not attending the parish church on Sundays. Such knowledge, in the hands of Topcliffe, was like a charge of gunpowder in the fingers of a child playing with flint and steel. It could go off at any moment and ruin his father. And it would do very little for his own prospects in the service of the Crown.

Topcliffe spat at Shakespeare's feet. "I know what I know and you know that I know it. And I'll tell you this: the Howard business is Queen's business and I'll deal with it. I know what's happened here. Southwell, the Romish girl-boy, has done this. It's all his ilk know to do with a woman. I will find the Jesuit Robert Southwell, and then you shall see the murderer. I will hang, geld, and bowel him myself. I will wash my face in the blood from his heart and there will be much merriment."

CHAPTER 3

The tide was still rising when Shakespeare reached the steps just upstream of London Bridge. As he waited for a tiltboat, taking precedence ahead of the bustling throng with his cry of "Queen's business," he thought of what Topcliffe had said of his father and felt unnerved. Yes, his father had been fined for recusancy — refusing to attend his local parish church — and yes, the old man did still hold to the old ways; it had caused endless arguments between father and his eldest son and, finally, a rift that might now be irreparable. Shakespeare felt an immense sadness. He still loved his father, but thought him wrongheaded in his stubbornness and the cause of unnecessary misery to his whole family.

Now Topcliffe was suggesting that the father's recusancy might somehow reflect on the son. It was obvious to Shakespeare how dangerous such words could be in days like these, when the merest hint of popery could result in a midnight call from the pursuivants, the feared band of heavily armed men who did the bidding of government officers such as Topcliffe.

And what of Topcliffe's belief that the Jesuit Robert Southwell was the killer? Yes, Southwell was a wanted man, perhaps the most hunted man in England, but did that make the priest a murderer? Perhaps Topcliffe had some information of which Shakespeare knew nothing.

As he stepped into the tiltboat, the smell of the river was rank as the incoming currents pushed up shit and rotting animal bodies from Deptford, Greenwich, and beyond. But it was a good strong tide and it carried the boat speedily upriver on its swell toward Surrey and Barn Elms, country home of Sir Francis Walsingham.

Dismissed in characteristic fashion by Walsingham as "my poor cottage," Barn Elms was in fact a fine manor house on a bend of the river, with extensive acreage, both gardens and farmland. In summer the soaring hundred-foot elms that gave the estate its name shadowed the house in fair dappled light, but now they were leafless and dark and hung like black crows over the land. The stabling was remarkable;

seventy good-quality horses boxed in fine brick-built quarters that a working man would not be ashamed to call home. Keeping the stables running smoothly was a full-time operation, with a master smithy and his apprentices working all hours to keep the horses shod, while servants fed, worked, and groomed them. There were ten or more permanent post riders, cantering day and night with messages to and from Westminster, London, Greenwich, and farther afield. This was the hub of Walsingham's intelligence network, which stretched to every capital of Europe and even to the bazaars and seraglios of the Turk.

By the time Walsingham received John Shakespeare in his office, he had already heard of the death of Lady Blanche Howard and had sent word by messenger to court so that her family, the Privy Council, and the Queen might know of the crime.

Walsingham's room was simple, with little furniture or ornamental plasterwork, reflecting his own austerity. This was a room for work and planning, full of books, letters, and vellum parchments in piles and on shelves. In these papers, he stored information from all corners of the world, even the Indies and the heart of the Spanish colonies. Walsingham was privy to it all; he knew what each piece of correspondence and document contained and where it was amid the seeming chaos. He had two large oak tables, one of which was covered with maps and charts, some of them plundered from Spanish ships, others made by his own cartographers. The other table was clear apart from his writing materials and quills.

Walsingham, dressed as always in dark, sober clothing and the most modest of ruffs, sat stiffly, plagued by his back and his kidneys. He had a small silver cup at his side. He nodded at his chief intelligencer. "This is bad, John."

Shakespeare bowed low to him. He knew better than to ask after his master's health or indulge in other pleasantries. Instead, he removed the paper from his doublet. "There is worse, Mr. Secretary." He handed him the paper. "This."

Walsingham read the paper quickly, then looked up.

"Does anyone else know of this?"

"Not what it says, I think. The constable and bellman could not read. Topcliffe turned up; he had heard of it, but by then I had burned the others. I did not tell him of this."

"Why not, John?"

"I considered it to be for your eyes only."

Walsingham looked gravely at Shake-speare. His dark, molten eyes could see into men's secret corners. "Your cloak is muddy and your clothes torn. If you are not care-ful, you will be dressed as dully as me."

Shakespeare laughed at Walsingham's typically self-deprecating humor. It was pointless dissembling; Mr. Secretary always knew everything. "I was pulled from my horse."

"By Topcliffe?"

Shakespeare nodded.

"There is bad blood between you, John. I won't tolerate that. The farm that is riven will fall into disarray; its crops will fail and its beasts sicken and die. We fight a com-mon enemy. With the Spaniard beating at our door, threatening us with her ships out of Lisbon and Parma's armies out of the low country, we have no time to fight one another. England's survival depends on our diligence."

"I know that . . ."

"But you don't like each other's ways. Topcliffe thinks you weak. He doubts your commitment to the cause of Christ and England. You think him cruel. Well, I know he is wrong. I know that you are not weak, merely . . . *earnest.* But I say this to you, John: needs must in these times when we

41

face a cruel enemy. Topcliffe is effective and the Queen honors and admires him and he *will* be allowed to go about his business in his own way. If you cross him, it will be at your peril. As for your man with the caliver, I think he has made an enemy for life. . . ."

Shakespeare smiled almost imperceptibly. "I don't think that will cause Boltfoot Cooper too many sleepless nights. A man who has gone around the world entire with Francis Drake and has fought and bested hunger, tempest, and the Spaniard is unlikely to fear the likes of Richard Topcliffe."

Walsingham's voice did not rise, but the tone stiffened. "Perhaps not. But you *will* take care to obey my wishes. Answer me this, John: why do you think I chose you as my assistant secretary and chief intelligencer?"

"Sometimes, I confess, I do wonder."

"I chose you, John, because I saw something of myself in you. Not that we are the same; you have less . . . *rigor* . . . in religious matters. But you are diligent, John; you are fiercely loyal. And, most important, you worry a lot. It is your anxiety — *our* anxiety — that leads us to take care of the detail of the work we do. And it is the detail that will achieve results. This is not a task for those who think to solve matters of state with an impassioned speech and a grand gesture. We must toil away in the dark like moles. Each inch of the way through the tunnel will be torment to you, John. If it is not, then I have greatly misjudged you. And remember this always: what we fight for is *worth* fighting for. The enemy would destroy everything we *both* believe in."

Shakespeare was left in no doubt as to the serious purpose of what the older man said. He bowed low once more to the Principal Secretary of State in acknowledgment. "I understand, Mr. Secretary. But I must protest that I have never disagreed with *your* methods. I realize that when the security of our sovereign and realm are at stake, extreme measures are necessary. And if that includes torment of the body to obtain information, then so be it. But I cannot stomach a man who breaks men — and women, at times — for the pure pleasure of it."

Walsingham silenced him with an angry wave of his hand. "Enough. I will hear no more concerning your feelings on the subject of Mr. Topcliffe." He signaled for Shakespeare to sit and his voice eased. "There is more, John. I wish I had endless funds to hire an army of true Englishmen to fight this war of secrets, but these are straitened times and we must live within our means. You will continue your inquiries into the affair of Blanche Howard. I fear that far more is at stake here than the death of one woman. Discover her familiars. Had she turned Papist? Who has done this to her and why? What is the meaning of the text and who was behind it? Jesuits? Get Slide involved; use his network. He owes his neck to me and he'll likely know who's behind this. Find this Robert Southwell, too. He's dangerous. Is he responsible for the death of Blanche Howard? I hear Topcliffe thinks so. It would not be the first time a Southwell helped do away with a Howard. Did not this Southwell's father, Sir Richard, come forward as chief accuser against Henry Howard, the Earl of Surrey, and bring him to his death? There is no love between these families, John."

"But this is different."

"Is it? Let us find out, shall we? Within weeks, God willing, the Scots devil will lose her head and then we shall see a reaction. Then the powder will ignite. We must all be prepared. Every scrap of intelligence, every disloyal word in the ordinaries and inns of London and beyond, must be scrutinized. There must be no more attempts on the life of our sovereign Majesty."

Shakespeare felt his stomach knotting like cable around a capstan. At times it felt as if the whole future of Elizabeth and her subjects rested on his shoulders alone. How could he, one man, stand against the threat of the so-called Enterprise of England — Philip of Spain's growing armada of ships now being assembled with the aim of invasion of England and destruction of the Queen?

The enemy was everywhere: London and the counties seemed to be awash with priests sent from the seminaries and colleges of Rome, Rheims, and Douai. Their aim? Sedition, insurrection, and the perversion of men's souls. The common or garden priests were a poor lot. It was the Jesuits, disciplined and determined though few in number, who threatened the stability of the realm: the Devil's army of the Counter-Reformation.

"There is another matter, John," Walsingham continued, his voice quiet, as if the walls would hear him. "The matter of Sir Francis Drake."

"What of him?"

Walsingham sipped sweet Rhenish from his small silver cup. His face was half in shadow in this weak wintry light. There was a fire in the hearth, a single small log glowing without enthusiasm; it did little to dispel the chill. He rose and fetched a paper from a pile near one of the tables, and handed it to Shakespeare, who saw instantly that it was encrypted in a Spanish code.

"Berden waylaid that in Paris. It was on its way from Mendoza to the Spanish King."

Shakespeare was aware that any communication between Mendoza, the Spanish ambassador to Paris, and King Philip was of extreme importance. No one had done more to undermine Elizabeth and the English state than Don Bernardino de Mendoza; he had been expelled from England three years earlier for his endless conspiracies, and even as he left under armed guard, he turned to one of the Council and taunted him that he would return as a conqueror. As for Berden, Shakespeare knew of him as one of Walsingham's top intelligencers in the field. There would be no reason to doubt the authenticity of this intercept.

"I assume you have had it deciphered?"

"It is a subject close to your own heart, John. Phelippes has broken the code and finds this message: 'The dragon slayer has been dispatched to England.' It goes on to ask for funds of seventy thousand ducats to be made available in the event of a successful outcome. This note is a warrant for murder, John. It tells us an assassin has been sent to England to kill Drake. We have no way of knowing when he was sent, how long he has been here, or how far his plans are advanced. But there is no question as to the import of the message and the seriousness of the position."

Shakespeare nodded assent. He knew that Thomas Phelippes, Walsingham's cipher expert, would not have made an error in discovering the meaning of such a paper. It was his breaking of the Queen of Scots's intricate code that had convicted her of treason. And now, if this encoded message was to be believed, a killer had been contracted to murder Sir Francis Drake. All Spaniards feared Drake and called him "El Draque," meaning Dragon. His title was Vice Admiral of England and yet his repute far exceeded mere titles. In a country of superb mariners — Walter Raleigh, Martin Frobisher, Thomas Cavendish, Humphrey Gilbert, Richard Grenville, John Hawkins, and Howard of Effingham — Drake was peerless. And he was driven by hatred of the Spanish. It was a loathing born of the cruelties meted out to his friends and comrades-at-arms long ago, in 1568, when they were taken by the Inquisition at the debacle of San Juan d'Ulua in the New

World. The names of those men still gnawed at Drake's soul, and he thought of them often: fellow Devonian Robert Barrett, burned to death in the auto-da-fé at Seville; William Orlando, dead in the same town while festering in a dungeon; Michael Morgan, tortured, whipped almost to death, then put to the oars as a galley slave; George Ribley of Gravesend, garroted and his body burned at the stake. This was what infused Drake with feral courage and kept hot his bitter enmity for the Spaniard. It was a hatred that was fueled by every Spanish outrage that occurred: the 1572 massacre of men, women, and children in the Dutch town of Naarden; the slaughter, rape, and sacking of Antwerp. These events seared themselves into Drake's memory and kept his rage burning like molten iron. His enmity was returned in kind by King Philip II, who had long since decided Drake must die.

All in England knew that no single man was more important than Drake to the survival of the realm. If anything could prevent an invasion by the rumored armada, it was the fighting skills and strategic brilliance of the Vice Admiral. During twenty years at sea, he had proved his courage and seacraft time and again, capturing scores of

Spanish galleons and storming ports with irresistible ferocity.

No one was in any doubt that Spain's invasion fleet must be beaten at sea — for if it disgorged its battle-hardened troops on English soil, all would be lost.

England's land forces were woefully ill-prepared. They would be swept aside and slaughtered within days. And then the terror would begin: the dread Inquisition.

Soon, villages, towns, and cities would be ablaze with the burning bodies of tens of thousands of Protestant "heretics." No one would be safe from torture and execution.

Shakespeare shuddered at the prospect. He knew what was at stake from his own experience.

As a junior intelligencer in Walsingham's service five years earlier, he had helped break another Spanish plot against Drake. The money on offer to kill him then was twenty thousand ducats. Shakespeare had worked to identify the conspirators. It was a simple and amateurish plot: Pedro de Zubiaur, the Spanish agent in London, had recruited a merchant named Patrick Mason to persuade an old enemy of Drake's to kill him. This enemy was named John Doughty, the vengeful half-brother of Thomas Doughty, who had been executed before his very eyes by Drake on his round-world voyage. A little judicial torture and Mason had named names. As far as Shakespeare knew, Doughty was still rotting in the Marshalsea prison.

And now King Philip was raising the stakes. Seventy thousand ducats would tempt desperate men.

Walsingham continued: "Philip plods with feet of lead across the world's great stage. It is easy to make merry at his expense when he complains like a girl child about Drake and Hawkins and the rest plundering his treasure. But though he plods, he does have weight behind him, thanks to his riches from the New World. And he can *crush*. I would say that, at sea, my good friend Drake is more likely to die of scurvy than fall to the sword or pistol of a hired killer, but now that he is on land, fitting and supplying the fleets in the reaches of the Thames, he is an easy target. In the shipyards by day he is *vulnerable,* John, and at court by night he can scarcely be safer. He's in danger, just when we need him most. Santa Cruz, King Philip's admiral, is like to sail with his fleet this spring or summer. My spies tell me he conspires to meet up with the Duke of Parma's armies in the lowlands and carry and protect them as they cross the sea to England. With Drake out of the way, their passage would be a thousand times easier."

Shakespeare hesitated. Everything he knew of Drake by repute suggested he would not need anyone's help to survive. He had been fighting and defeating Spanish fleets for nigh on twenty years now. "Surely Drake can look after himself," he said at last.

"Can he, John? At sea, yes, of course. But on land, in the teeming shipyards, full of foreigners of every hue and creed? Who will spot one man with an arquebus or crossbow among the hundreds at work? Drake needs protection — and *you* will provide it."

Shakespeare ran a finger around his ruff. He felt hot, despite the lack of warmth in this cheerless room. "And Lady Blanche Howard?"

"And Lady Blanche. And all your other duties. We are all stretched like bowstrings. That is the way it is. Anyway, it seems to me you have the perfect servant to assign to Drake — your former sailor, Mr. Boltfoot Cooper. I believe he already knows Sir Francis rather well."

Shakespeare almost laughed. There was nothing to be gained from arguing. Walsingham must know that Boltfoot had parted on bad terms with Drake, having protested

51

that he had been cheated of his fair share of the colossal plunder taken aboard the *Golden Hind* from the Spanish treasure ship *Cacafuego.* He had also said that after three years at sea in Drake's company he would never board a ship again and certainly not one of Drake's. No, Boltfoot would not be happy to be in the Dragon's company once more.

CHAPTER 4

Night had come and gone when Rose Downie was startled awake. Topcliffe was standing over her, prodding at her with his blackthorn. She scrabbled to her feet, heart pounding. Her hands were stiff with cold, clutching the baby. The child chose that moment to wail; its piercing, monotonous cry, like the howl of a cat, sent shivers down her spine, but Topcliffe merely smiled.

"Is it baptized in our church?" he asked, and touched its strange face, with its curious, un-human eyes.

Rose Downie felt fear in her heart but she needed this man. Her friend had told her that he knew everything about everyone in the city, that he would help her as he had helped others, but that he would demand much in return. "My own baby was baptized, sir, by the Bishop of London himself, but this is not my baby."

"Then you have stolen this one."

"No, sir, *mine* has been stolen. This . . . *creature* . . . was left in its place."

"Let me see its face by the light." Topcliffe bent down toward the face of the child in the gloom. He pulled back the swaddling bands from its head and looked intently at it. The child's face was small and round, its eyes spaced widely. Too widely. There seemed to be no chin to speak of and the ears were curiously low. Any mother, Topcliffe thought, would want to disown such a thing. "Come in with me. My boy Nicholas tells me you have had a long vigil here. I'll beat his arse raw for leaving you out in weather like this."

He pushed back the oak door to his home. Rose hesitated, fearing to enter. The hallway was lit by the flame from a candle, which cast strange shadows in the breeze from the open door. She stepped forward into the unholy gloom.

On a dark-stained coffer lay a large gilt-bound book, which, though she could not read, she recognized as a Bible. Topcliffe took Rose Downie's right hand from the baby and held it down hard on the book, as if to ensure there was solid contact. "Do you swear by Almighty God that the baby you are holding is not yours?"

Rose felt colder inside the house than

outside in the winter wind. There were strange smells in this place; it held the chill and smell of a slaughterhouse. "I do swear, sir; it is not my baby. My baby, William Edmund Downie, has been taken from me. Please help me, sir. I believe that only you can help."

"Where is your husband, Mistress Downie?"

"He died, sir. He was out with the trainband at Mile End Green by Clement's Inn after church a month past, and his hagbut did explode."

Topcliffe touched her arm with seeming compassion. His hand remained there, keeping her close to him. "I am sorry to hear that, Mistress Downie. England has need of such men. Such a thing should not befall a pretty wife."

Tears welled up in Rose's eyes at the memory but she refused to weep. She had been heavy with child and he was late home from practicing firing his arquebus and wielding his pike. He, like thousands of other good men, had been doing his duty, she knew, training week after week out in the open countryside or within the brick walls of Artillery Yard. He had volunteered himself for service as part of the Carpenters Company contingent. It was men like her husband who would stop the Spaniard. That day, she had waited for him on the road, but instead of his jaunty step and broad smile coming toward her, she saw six other members of the trainband approaching, pulling a handcart with what, at first, she took to be a dead animal. Then she saw that it was his bloody remains and she collapsed fainting. Later, they told her his arquebus had misfired and exploded in pieces, ripping open his throat. They had been wed less than a year, by the Bishop who would later baptize their child. Her husband's name was Edmund and she called him Mund. He was such a fine man, a yeoman carpenter with shoulders as wide as his smile. On the day of their wedding, they had scarcely been able to wait for the Bishop to give his blessing before retiring to their room to tear the clothes from each other's backs. When Mund died, she felt that her life was over. She hungered each night for his body over hers. But instead of the joy of him, she had nothing but tears. And then the baby came a week after his death and she began to find a little life again. He was a boy and he was perfect in every way. His name was William Edmund, but she called him Mund, like his father. He would be the new man in her life.

"Come further into my home," Topcliffe said, his arm moving around her shoulder, "and have a draft of beer, for you must have a thirst to slake."

If she had been asked to tread through the portals of hell, she could not have been more scared, yet she could not say no to this man. She knew his repute as a brute, but she also knew that he had power. Her friend Ellie May from the market had told her she must go to him, for he was reputed to know all there was to know in London; he could see into souls and was privy to dark secrets that no one else could know, Ellie had told her.

In his teeth, stained mottled amber, Topcliffe clenched a long wooden stick, which he drew on every so often, and then blew out smoke. She looked at it astonished, as if he were breathing sulfur from the fires of Satan, for she had never seen such a thing. He laughed at her bewilderment. "It is a pipe of sotweed, from the New World." He called in a servant to bring drink, then another to stoke the fire in the hearth and — as the man crouched to the grate with bellows and logs — cursed him for letting it go so low.

He asked her questions. How she survived, where she lived. She told him she was a malkin — a kitchen drudge — in the buttery of a great lady. She had left service when she married Edmund, but on his death she had been received back into the household in her old serving job.

As she talked, Topcliffe smiled at her with his hard, dark teeth. Eventually he put down the sotweed pipe. "Well, Rose, I should like to help you if I can. We must find the mother of this changeling you have brought us."

Again he put his arm around Rose Downie's shoulders, drawing her to him. "We must look after Her Majesty's subjects, must we not, especially the widow of a fine young man who died for his sovereign. Tell me, Rose, where was your baby stolen?"

She recalled the day precisely. It was a week past, when the child was just twelve days old. She had gone to the market for cheeses and salt pork. Her son was swaddled and she held him in her arms. But there was a disagreement with the stallholder and she had put the baby down for just a short moment because her arms were full of groceries and she was counting out the farthings to pay for them. The argument became heated and the short moment of leaving little Mund in a basket by the stall became a minute or two. She was still angry when she went to pick him up, but then her anger turned to horror, for her baby was no longer there. In his place was this monster, this creature, this Devil's spawn.

"Well, we must find little William Edmund," Topcliffe said. "But first, let us become better acquainted, Rose."

His arm was strong around her now, and he pulled her down. She did not resist, as if she half expected this as part of the price. In one movement, he lifted her kirtle and smock, turned her with a strength she could not defy, and, without a word, entered her with the casual indifference with which a bull takes a cow.

CHAPTER 5

In the crypt of St. Paul's, the Searcher of the Dead stood in his bloodstained apron over the unclothed carcass of Lady Blanche Howard. For a long while he was silent. With his strong hands he moved her poor head this way and that with practiced gentleness, examining her wounds; he did the same with her paps and with her woman's parts; he held up the scarce-formed baby, still attached to her womb by its cord, and looked at it from all sides. He ran his fingers through the woman's flaxen hair and he explored inside the pits of her arms, the backs of her legs, and the soles of her feet.

The stone walls of the crypt glistened with trickles of water. The Searcher parted the legs of the cold body and examined further. He removed objects and put them to one side dispassionately. He moved his face near the fair V of her womanhood and sniffed.

Above them, in the nave of the great

cathedral, the throngs of people went about their business, dealing, conspiring, laughing, fighting, robbing each other, or simply passing the time of day. But down here, the only sound was the shuffling of soft leather soles on stone and the occasional drip of water from the walls and ceiling. Shakespeare stood back and watched. The Searcher, Joshua Peace, was so intent on his work that he seemed unaware of his presence. Shakespeare liked Peace; he was a man of knowledge, like himself, the type of man to shape the new England now they were almost rid of the superstitions of the Roman church.

Peace was of indeterminate age, perhaps late thirties but he looked younger. He was slim but strong and his head was bald on top, like a monk's tonsure. He sniffed some more, around her mouth and nostrils, then stood back from his work and met the eye of John Shakespeare. "There is the smell of fire on her, and also the lust of a man," he said. "And not just that smell, Mr. Shakespeare — there is the three-day smell of death."

"Three days?"

"Yes. Three days at this time of year, the same as a day and a half in summer. Where did you find her?"

"In a house that had been burned out, toward Shoreditch."

"Well, that explains the smell of fire. From the smell of her skin and mouth, I can detect no poison. I take the cause of death to be the slash of a butcher's blade or some such to the throat. Tell me, was there a great deal of blood around the body?"

Shakespeare thought back to the horror of the scene he had encountered, then shook his head, surprised. "No. She was on a bed and there was some blood staining on the sheets, but very little."

"Then she was killed somewhere else, or in another part of the house, and taken there. She would have lost a lot of blood with these injuries." The Searcher held up two objects — a piece of bone and a silver crucifix. "These were inside her, thrust in most unkindly. I think the bone is a relic, a monkey's bone passed off as the finger of a saint, for all I know."

"What was it doing there?"

"You will have to ask her killer that, Mr. Shakespeare. All I can tell you is that the girl was about eighteen, certainly no older, and in good health. As to the child, it was twelve weeks gone, a boy. From the spread of blood about her person, I feel certain that the wound which ripped it from her belly was inflicted after death, which may be some small comfort to her family."

Peace pushed his arms underneath the body and lifted it so that the bare back was visible. "Look at this, Mr. Shakespeare."

Shakespeare moved closer. Her slender back, from nape to lower back, had two red raw lines, which made the shape of a cross. At the house in Shoreditch, where she lay with her front exposed to the sky, he had not seen this.

"What is it? What has caused this?"

Peace ran a finger down the bloody stripes. "It seems to be a crucifix, crudely cut after death."

Shakespeare stared at the wounds as if by staring he would go back in time to when they were inflicted. "Is there some religious significance?"

"That is for *you* to answer, Mr. Shakespeare. There is something else, too . . ."

As Peace spoke, carefully laying the body back on the slab so that her wounded back was no longer visible, the ancient door to the crypt was flung open. Two pikemen marched in, taking up positions either side of the doorway. They were followed by a man of later years, probably in his fifties. His hair and beard were as white as the snow outside, and his eyes were keen. He was tall and lean, with the languid air and fine clothes of the nobility. Shakespeare recognized him immediately as Charles Howard, second Baron of Effingham and Lord Admiral of England. Howard looked first at Shakespeare, then at Peace, without saying a word. He stalked forward to the body of his beloved adopted daughter, Blanche, lying on the Searcher's stone slab, for all the world like a carving on a sarcophagus. For two minutes he stared at her face, then nodded slowly before turning on his heel. In a moment he was gone, closely attended by his pikemen.

Shakespeare caught Peace's eye. "I suppose there really was nothing to say."

"No. Nothing. Now let me show you this one other thing." Peace lifted her hands and showed Shakespeare the wrists. They were marked with a raised weal. "That is a rope mark, Mr. Shakespeare. Whichever brute did this to her tied her up most cruelly."

Shakespeare looked closely at the marks, then winced with the thought of the suffering this poor girl had endured before death. He shook Joshua Peace by the hand. "Thank you, my friend. Consign her body to the coroner. You know, in quieter times it would be a fine thing to pass an hour or two with you and a flagon of Gascon wine at The

Three Tuns."

"Yes," said Peace. "And let us drink heartily to quieter times."

Outside, up in the daylight, Shakespeare was surprised to find the Lord Admiral and his pikemen waiting for him. It was snowing properly now, dropping a carpet of white around St. Paul's, but if Howard of Effingham felt the cold he did not show it. He stood stock-still, like a soldier, his colorless face set and hard.

"My lord . . ."

"She was with child?"

Shakespeare said nothing. There was a sadness in the old man's voice that needed no response.

"Who did this thing to her?"

"I intend to discover that, my lord. Could I ask you about the people she knew? Do you have any idea who the father of her child might be?"

Howard breathed deeply. "You are Shakespeare, Mr. Secretary's man, I believe."

"I am."

"This is a tragic business. Tragic. I loved Blanche as if she were my own child. She was part of me. But it is also delicate, Mr. Shakespeare. There is the family to think about."

"I understand. But you must want to find

her killer."

"I do, I do." The Lord Admiral hesitated. "Let me just say, there were people in her life of late of whom I did not approve. . . ." He stopped.

Shakespeare needed to probe deeper. He needed every crumb of information this man could provide, but he began to realize it was not going to be forthcoming.

"These people . . ."

The admiral looked distraught. Momentarily he reminded Shakespeare of a lost puppy he once chanced upon in his schooldays, which he had taken in, much to his mother's disapproval. "I really can say no more."

"Do you, at least, know anything of the house in Hog Lane by Shoreditch where her body was found?"

"I am sorry. I know nothing of such things."

"My man Boltfoot Cooper has made inquiries but he failed to discover the landlord or tenant of the building."

Howard said nothing. He stood like a rock.

"Perchance, in a day or two you might talk with me, my lord?"

"Perchance, Mr. Shakespeare. I can promise no more."

"One last question. Was she a Roman

Catholic?"

It seemed to Shakespeare that Howard of Effingham clenched his teeth. He did not answer the question but nodded to his pikemen, then turned and walked to his horse, which was tethered nearby. To Shakespeare, his reaction spoke more than a printed volume could.

As Howard rode away eastward, some apprentices threw snowballs at Shakespeare and one hit him. He laughed and gathered up some snow, crunching it hard together in his gloved hands before flinging it back at the boy.

It was Friday, a fish day. Many days were fish days, as a means of boosting the fortunes of the fishing fleets, but that was no hardship for Shakespeare, who enjoyed fish in all its forms. Soon it would be Lent and then every day would be a fish day. Jane, his maidservant and housekeeper, had given him smoked pike instead of flesh for his breakfast this morning, and he would have some eel and oyster pie before bed.

The trees were decorated white as Shakespeare walked through the streets of high houses, their shutters thrown back to let in the air. Thick wood smoke belched from their chimneys, adding to the permanent city stench of ordure until the mixture clogged the nostrils and the lungs. Summer was the worst, particularly here, near the confluence of the Fleet and the Thames and close to the Fleet and Newgate prisons, where the rotting flesh of dead convicts might be left uncollected for weeks on end; at this time of year, thankfully, the stink retreated to a background whiff.

An endless procession of carts, drays, and wagons, laden with farm produce, barrels, and building materials, trundled nose to tail in both directions, their horses' iron-clad hooves turning the new snow to slush, slipping and stumbling in the endless potholes. There was barely room for them to pass on the narrow streets, and they often ground to a halt, setting the carters to shouting and swearing. At times, blows were exchanged before a beadle interposed and brought some order.

In a few minutes, Shakespeare had followed the road out of the city, over the Fleet river (if such a putrid ditch was deserving of the name "river," he thought), soon turning left toward the high, forbidding walls of Bridewell. Every time he came here, he found it difficult to believe that such a dark fortress could ever have been a royal palace, yet barely sixty years ago, Henry — the great Henry — had entertained his Spanish

Queen at dinner behind these walls. His son, Edward the Sixth, had handed the dreary place over to the city fathers for the housing of the poor. And now it was little more than a prison for the city's harlots, gypsies, and vagrants.

A squadron of eight armed men, pursuivants, marched past him with a prisoner, their boots stamping through the snow. They came to a halt, throwing their prisoner to the ground, and their sergeant, whom Shakespeare recognized as one of Topcliffe's men, hammered on the massive Bridewell door. Almost instantly it was opened by the gaoler, clutching his clanking keys.

"A priest of Rome for you, gaoler," the sergeant said.

The gaoler grinned, revealing a couple of brown, broken teeth, but mostly diseased gum. "And very welcome he is, too, Master Newall, for his friends will pay well to feed him and keep him alive. They are all welcome here, all your Popish priests."

"Well, don't forget our agreement."

"A mark for each, catchpole. Bring them on! Never have I fared so well. Last month they brought me a vicar of the English Church. He starved because no one brought him a crust of bread, and why should *I* feed him? The Anglicans are like vermin here.

Bring me Romans, catchpole, for they do garnish my table."

Newall pulled the priest to his feet and handed him, manacled and shackled, to the gaoler. "Mind you work him hard. Get him making nails or stripping oakum to caulk Her Majesty's ships. And flog him soundly, gaoler, or I shall take him off to the Marshalsea or the Clink, where he should be by rights." The sergeant spotted Shakespeare and grinned. "I'm sure Mr. Topcliffe wishes you good cheer, Mr. Shakespeare."

Shakespeare ignored Newall, whom he knew to be of small wit and too close-coupled to Topcliffe for comfort, and walked past the squadron. He nodded to the gaoler, who knew him well, and went through the doorway. He was immediately knocked back by the stink of human dung and sweat. Before him in the first large courtyard and in the cloisters was a swarming mass of the lowliest of humankind. Here were hundreds of beggars, whores, doxies, and orphans. Many had come to London in search of a better life and had been brought here by way of punishment and hoped-for redemption. It was a vain hope. Shakespeare saw their dull eyes as they toiled on the treadmill or performed one or another of a dozen unpleasant tasks set them by the gaoler to pay for whatever food he might consent to give them. The gaoler pushed the newly acquired priest forward into the crowd, where he was seized by a taskmaster.

"Some vagabonds were brought here yesterday by Boltfoot Cooper," Shakespeare said at last, when the sergeant and his squadron had gone. "I will see them."

The gaoler's brow creased in puzzlement. "Of course, I do remember them, Mr. Shakespeare; they were Irish beggars or some such, I believe. But they were taken away this morning on your orders, sir."

"I gave no such orders, turnkey."

"But, Mr. Shakespeare, I saw the warrant that the two men brought. It had your mark on it."

"My mark? Can you read, turnkey?"

"Why, yes, sir, enough. Your men said the vagabonds were to be taken to some other gaol as criminals, as I do recall. They had your mittimus from the justice. I have seen many such warrants."

"You say my men took them?"

"Aye, sir, and did leave me a shilling for my trouble."

Shakespeare's blood rose. How dare Topcliffe cloy away his witnesses?

The gaoler grinned, his mouth hanging open like a Bedlam loon. "But tarry a while,

Mr. Shakespeare. You be just in time for the Friday floggings. If you'd care to stay and take some wine with me, we can observe them together."

Shakespeare did not dignify the offer with a reply.

CHAPTER 6

Tramping through the slush in his fine leather boots, with a winter cloak of crimson worsted and white fur, the man called Cotton could not fail to catch the eye of the goodwives, procurers, and water-bearers crowding the muddy, cart-thronged thoroughfare of Long Southwark. Though he was slight and lean, he was striking. Beneath his black velvet hat, embroidered with crimson beads, his hair and beard were golden-red and trimmed short. His gray eyes were at once intense, good-humored, and watchful. He walked briskly, with the confident air of a gentleman who knew his place in the world. For a man who might have wished to go unremarked, he was brazen and conspicuous, but that was the very quality that made him invisible to searchers and pursuivants; they were looking for men in hoods and dark cloaks, loitering in shadows and doorways, and they failed to see what their eyes alighted on so easily.

The weak afternoon light was fading fast as he made his way with purpose southward, past Winchester House, St. Mary Overies, and the inns and bawdy houses, toward the high walls of the Marshalsea prison, where he was immediately given entrance in exchange for a coin.

The gaoler clapped him on the back in welcome. "Mr. Cotton, sir, it is good to see you again."

"And you, gaoler."

The gaoler, a big, long-bearded man with a heavy woolen smock and wide leather keybelt strapped tight around his great belly, grinned broadly at Cotton as if waiting for a reaction.

"Well?" he said at last. "Do you not notice something about the place, Mr. Cotton?"

The man called Cotton looked around the dark walls of the entrance chamber. It all seemed as bleak and cold as ever.

"The smell, Mr. Cotton, the smell. I have reduced the stench of the prisoners' dung."

Cotton sniffed at the air politely. It was still putrid, but perhaps slightly less so than usual. "And how have you effected this, gaoler?"

The gaoler once again clapped his shovel-sized hand on Cotton's back. "Pails with lids, sir, pails with lids. I have struck a deal with Hogsden Trent, the brewer of Gully Hole, for his old and cast-off kegs. I cuts them in half and fashions a lid for them, then sells them on to the prisoners, Mr. Cotton. No more shitting in the straw, sir. No more pissing against the wall."

For a moment, Cotton envied the gaoler his simple pragmatism; it stood in sharp contrast to his own otherworldliness where the day-to-day functions of eating, sleeping, drinking, and defecation were but furniture to God's great purpose. He and the gaoler walked through the echoing, tallow-lit passages, past cells where, occasionally, prisoners moaned and shouted, until they arrived at a solid wooden door, strengthened with thick iron straps, on which the gaoler was about to bang his enormous fist. Cotton shook his head, almost imperceptibly. "Leave me now."

The gaoler lowered his fist, bowed, and backed away. Cotton was waiting for him to go when he heard his faint whispered voice from the shadows: "Bless me, Father. Please . . ."

Cotton hesitated only a moment, then made the Sign of the Cross and spoke the words the gaoler so wanted to hear: *"Bene-*

dictio Dei Omnipotentis, Patris, et Filii, et Spiritus Sancti, descendat super vos et maneat semper . . ." There were many like him in England in these days, men and women who pledged loyalty to the new church in public, fearing persecution and a fine if they failed to attend Sunday service, yet who hungered after the old Roman ways in their souls. Cotton watched until the gaoler, warmed by his benediction, slid away down the passageway, then he opened the door a few inches, revealing a large, low-ceilinged cell with bare brick walls. In a building rich in human misery and squalor, it was surprisingly clean and well kept. More surprisingly, there was a table in the middle of the room, with six chairs, two on each of the long sides and one at each end. The table was laid with platters of cold food and a flagon of wine. Cotton stepped in and quickly clanged the door closed behind him. Three women and two men stood at the far end of the table, the women's faces drawn in fear and anticipation. Cotton smiled at them. He made the Sign of the Cross again. *"Dominus vobiscum,"* he intoned.

The five who faced him, all dressed in fine clothes, crossed themselves and replied, *"Et cum spiritu tuo."* The strain fell from their faces. They moved apart to reveal a small covered altar, complete with the Sacred Vessels — a small silver chalice and paten — and good candles, which were already lit and cast a warm, flickering glow over all the cell.

Cotton moved forward and was welcomed by each of the five in turn; he held each one by their hands and kissed their cheeks and blessed them. One of them held his eyes longer than the others; the one with the secret to pass on. As the man greeted Cotton, he clasped him and held his arms tight, so that he stayed, held in his embrace. Cotton tensed, disgusted by the stink of the young, captive priest, whom he knew to be called Father Piggott. Piggott and the other man, Plummer, were priests sent covertly from France by the English college at Rheims, where the pair had studied. They were held here as prisoners, though their movements were not greatly restricted. Piggott and Plummer had been caught by the magistrate Young and sent here untried, but they were fed well by their friends and not ill-treated by the gaoler.

"So fine to meet you, Mr. Cotton," Piggott said, his voice thick and unctuous. "I have a message for you to pass on, an important message."

Cotton felt sick. He unclasped Piggott's

talon-like fingers from his arm and found that he was shaking. Stepping back, out of Piggott's reach, he nodded tersely, took a deep breath, steadied himself, and prepared to say Mass.

With an extravagant sweep, Harry Slide slapped a broadsheet down on the ale-soaked table. "You owe me a penny for this, Mr. Shakespeare, and more."

They were in a partitioned booth in the Bell tavern in Gracechurch Street. A good fire was blazing in the hearth and the windows were steamed over. From beyond the paneling came a din of noise as a group of city merchants celebrated the arrival of a carrack from the Indies. It was clear from their very loud and drunken voices that the vessel had come laden with spices and silver, having been away more than a year and feared lost. They had ventured a large amount of money and now their faith had paid off, their wealth increased many times over. This evening they were happily drinking away a small part of their profits while being entertained — if that was the correct word — with a ballad sung with feeling but little joy by a shabbily dressed young troubadour, plucking at his lute in a corner by the kegs. Outside, the sky was cloudless at last and sharp with cold, turning the slush of day to a thin sheet of ice.

"Don't worry, Harry, you'll get more. A lot more."

"Well, *there's* a change of tune, Mr. Shakespeare. Yet I would be more content if the minstrel would change *his* tune, too." He cupped his hand to his mouth and shouted out, "Something cheery, minstrel, for pity's sake!"

John Shakespeare tugged at his short-cropped beard and sighed. "The truth is I need you, Harry." He reached over and touched his arm by way of emphasis. "I need you to assist me as an employed man. There is much to be done, not just the Jesuits. My hands are full. Will you help?"

Slide took a long sip of Gascon wine, dark red and sweetened with sugar, and considered the proposition. It was one thing bringing intelligence to Mr. Shakespeare and Walsingham when he had a juicy morsel to sell, but it would be quite another thing being a hired hand, a journeyman intelligencer. He was not, however, in the least surprised that he was needed. "Would this be something to do with Lady Blanche Howard?

"So you know about that?"

Slide threw up his hands with palms

exposed to the ancient beamed ceiling. "The whole of London knows about Blanche Howard." He nodded at the broadsheet lying on the tavern table. "Have a look at that."

Shakespeare picked up the paper and felt the prickles rise on his neck.

The broadsheet was titled *The London Informer.* Printed on one side, under the heading "Horrible Tragedy of Lady Blanche Howard," and the secondary heading "Murdered by Foul Priest," it proceeded to give intimate details of her injuries and the manner in which she was found. It then went on with a rambling discourse, referring mischievously to Howard of Effingham's sisters, Lady Douglass and Lady Frances, suggesting they might not have been so enamored of Blanche as their brother. *"Friendly reader,"* the tract concluded, *"we must tell you, though it pains us so to do, that they may well have just cause for their reluctance to don the drear weeds of mourning. How else could it be, when we know that the Lady Blanche had already hazarded her place in God's Kingdom by her monstrous associations with lewd Popish beasts, one of which, the notorious Southwell, late of Horsham St. Faith in Norfolk and the traitors' colleges of France and Rome, had brought her with child and, fearing for his own mortal life, has taken hers with a cruel dagger. This Southwell is thought abroad in London, given solace, food, and lodging by those who wish harm to our Sovereign Lady Elizabeth. He is the foul murderer, with cross and relic and blade, and we beg you all, our fellow English men, if ever you happen upon him or his confederates, to spare no mercy but to bring him to the hangman's righteous rope."*

"Where did you get this, Harry?"

"It's Walstan Glebe's rag. He had a bundle of them over by Fishmongers' Hall, selling them a penny each."

So this was Glebe's work. Shakespeare knew of him. He was a rat from the sewers, a pedlar of dirt and dissimulation. Before taking up his profession as broadsheet writer, printer, and seller, he had scratched a living stealing the odes of others to sell as his own. Swooning lovers had paid him money for poems to woo their fair ladies, for which he had merely copied out the work of other scribes and poets and handed it over as his. His crime had come to light when a red-faced swain had gone to the magistrate complaining that his intended had laughed at him for reciting to her an ode that was already common currency. For his pains, Glebe had been branded by hot iron on the forehead with an *L* for *Liar.* Now he wore his hair low over his forehead and had acquired a reputation for printing the most seditious and salacious broadsheet in the city.

"What do you make of it, Harry?"

Slide's lips turned down uncertainly. "I don't know, Mr. Shakespeare. You tell me. Does the paper speak the truth? I thought you should see it."

Shakespeare gave it consideration. He had to concede that it was generally accurate, surprisingly so given Walstan Glebe's history, though he had no way of knowing what Lord Admiral Howard's sisters, Lady Douglass and Lady Frances, thought of their adoptive sister. Was there bad blood between them? What *was* interesting was the suggestion that Lady Blanche had got mixed up with the Jesuits. Was this Topcliffe's voice? Most of the other information certainly could have come from him or, indeed, from the constable or bellman.

But one thing puzzled Shakespeare: the line that read *"He is the foul murderer, with cross and relic and blade."* The cross and relic had not been discovered until the Searcher of the Dead, Joshua Peace, had extracted them from the corpse. Peace would have told no one, of that Shakespeare was certain. So how did Glebe know about them?

At last the mournful minstrel took a break from his singing and playing. Harry Slide cheered and clapped with painful irony. Shakespeare found himself laughing. Harry did that to you. Shakespeare knew a little about his past, or at least the story he chose to tell: his father had been a lawyer who lost a fortune gambling at cards, cockfights, and horse races. When he ended up in the Clink for debt, he hanged himself, leaving nine-year-old Harry and his mother destitute. She scratched a living working for a tailor and bought Harry an education. It had not been the easiest of childhoods, but there were plenty who fared worse. So why did Harry seem so . . . half-formed? It was as if some of his soul were missing, that he could draw men in with his seeming good character, only to betray them. Shakespeare downed the last of his wine and felt its warm sweetness course down to his belly. "We need to talk to Mr. Glebe, Harry. Can you find him?"

"I can find anyone, given time."

"We don't have time. Find him quickly. And what are your thoughts about the connection with Southwell? Is he in any way involved?"

"It is possible, of course . . ."

"But you have doubts?"

Slide nodded.

"Well, make inquiries about him. Bring him in. He can't be allowed to remain at large any longer. Mr. Secretary wants him in custody, as, I know, does the Queen. Let us lock him away as safe as the crown jewels. Use your best connections to discover the truth about this murder. Three marks a day, Harry, with twenty-five more for bringing me Southwell and a further twenty-five for finding the killer of Blanche Howard."

Slide was silent a moment as he thought the deal through. What it came down to was that he needed the money to see him through this chill winter. He smiled that winning smile. "Of course, Mr. Shakespeare. A most generous offer. Consider me your man."

CHAPTER 7

At seven, long after dark, the Marshalsea gaoler lumbered along to the cell for Cotton and the three ladies. "I must lock up now, Mr. Cotton," he said apologetically.

The six dinner guests had almost finished their own feasting and were sipping wine together and discussing the dark plight of England. All were fearful that Mary, Queen of Scots, the great hope of their Catholic cause, might soon suffer a martyr's death. Even now they prayed for a miracle to save her and raise her up instead to her rightful place as anointed Queen of England.

They had, for a short while, been able to forget their anxieties; the Latin Mass said by Cotton had suffused them with a fleeting joy, especially the three women, the Lady Tanahill, Lady Frances Browne, and Mistress Anne Bellamy. They were from three of London's leading Church of Rome families, and all of them were suffering harshly in these times when the ironclad gauntlet of the state could beat down their door at any hour of day or night. Lady Tanahill's husband, a onetime favorite of the Queen, was now in the Tower, having been arrested while attempting to leave the country to meet up with Church of Rome leaders abroad. The Countess was left at home with their small child, who had never yet seen his father. Her heart was heavy, yet the still, loving presence of this man Cotton brought comfort.

As Lady Tanahill looked at Cotton talking animatedly of his belief that the true church would rise again in England, she made a decision: she would invite him to be her private chaplain, to live in her home and bring the Sacraments to her daily. But she would not mention it here in front of these others. The arrest of her husband, betrayed by a priest they had befriended, had taught her a bitter lesson in trust.

Piggott and Plummer wiped the last hunks of bread around their trenchers and ate greedily. The food had been hearty, with good joints of mutton and fowl even though it was a fish day. "May as well be hanged for a sheep as a fish," said Plummer, laughing. And the wine was sweet.

Cotton, along with Plummer and Piggott,

remained in the cell while the three women left together. After the women had gone, Plummer said farewell to Cotton, clasping his hands and urging him to be strong in the faith. Then Piggott again embraced Cotton, holding him in a screwlike grip. Cotton flinched. Piggott's breath rasped and his coarse black beard, ill-covering his pox-pitted face, scoured Cotton's cheek as he spoke low into his ear so that Plummer could not hear him, only Cotton.

"Tell our friend this, Father Cotton. Tell him Cogg. Cogg of Cow Lane outside the city wall by Smith Field. Cogg has what he desires, Father Cotton. Cogg will see our friend right."

Again the proximity of this man made revulsion well up within Cotton, and he wrenched himself free. For a few moments the two men stood eye to eye, until Cotton looked away. He took his leave of Plummer, then left the cell and slammed the door hard without looking again at Piggott. A family of fat rats scuttled ahead as he followed the gaoler once more through the dank corridors to the great door. He was still shaking from his encounter with Piggott as the gaoler clapped him yet again with his giant's hand and whispered conspiratorially, "Pails with lids, Mr. Cotton. Pails with lids."

He walked over the bridge into London, slipping and sliding through the icy, deserted streets. By the time he arrived at the riverside house where he lodged, he still felt uneasy. Piggott had worried him, and he did not like his message.

For a few moments he waited at the end of Dowgate, near the Tower, looking around him back down the streets of tall houses with their leaded windows heavily curtained or shuttered. Only the merest flickerings of candlelight were visible. He was looking for movement and shadows, listening for footfalls. When he was sure he had not been followed, he went to a side door of the house and banged twice. The door was opened to him almost immediately and shut again the instant he stepped in.

It was a large and very new wood-frame house, a work in progress but already part-occupied by its owner, Thomas Woode, a widower in his thirties, and his two young children, Andrew and Grace. Woode's wife had died of consumption when Grace was little more than a year old and Andrew was three. Now they were four and six and the building of this house was his way of forgetting the past and forging a new future for the family.

The children's governess, Catherine Marvell, stood at the door. She was a slender creature with remarkable blue eyes, unblemished skin, and long dark hair, pulled back from her face. It was a face that was now fixed with a look of horror.

"*Pax vobiscum,* dear Catherine," Cotton said, and held her hands between his own. She was shivering. "What is it?"

"Have you not heard?"

"Heard what, Catherine?"

She spoke low, though there was no one to hear. "Blanche is dead, Father. Murdered."

"What?"

Catherine Marvell closed her eyes, as if she would blot out the imagined vision of Blanche that would not leave her mind. "By Shoreditch. Her body was found most horribly wounded in a burnt-out house." And then she whispered even lower, with urgency, "They say she was with child, Father."

He tried to hold her in his arms, to comfort her like a father would a daughter, but she backed away from him. Cotton understood. The touch of another human being is not always the best remedy for grief and horror. Lady Blanche? Who could or *would* have done such a thing to so beautiful and loving a woman? Cotton himself had brought her to the Holy Roman Church. Was this a cause of her death? She had never, as far as he knew, harmed a soul.

They stood awkwardly in the entrance hallway, neither knowing how to deal with such news.

He tried saying words to console her, but they sounded trite and unworthy. Still, he attempted to soothe her, though he wondered whether it was *he* that needed the soothing more. Cotton wanted to stroke Catherine's long dark hair, but he feared his touch would be unwelcome. The Jesuit colleges had removed him from the physical world of human contact, and ofttimes he missed it, the touch of a hand or the brush of a cheek.

She led him through to the hall, where logs were burning and crackling in a wide, stone-surround hearth and a man dressed in servant's clothes was waiting for them. The room was large and high-walled, hung with rich tapestries of blue and gold, displaying the wealth of the owner. Everything seemed new, the green oak beams vibrant with color in the brilliant light of dozens of candles.

The man who waited was lean and tall. He stood close to the fire, soaking up its heat. Unlike the fine dress of Cotton, he wore simple clothes in dark colors, the livery of a senior household valet or butler, though he was nothing of the sort; his hair was cut short and he was clean-shaven. He had a modest ruff, a black doublet over a white shirt, black, knee-length breeches in the Venetian style, and white hose.

He bowed his head. He did not smile. "Good evening, Father Cotton," he said, slowly and deliberately. His voice was faintly accented.

"Good evening to you, Father Herrick."

"What news of your day?"

"A fair day, Father."

There was a stiffness between the men. They were not friends. Cotton had been ordered to help Herrick and he would do so; that was as far as the relationship went. It had started with a letter from Rome, signed by Claudius Aquaviva, general of the Society of Jesus, requiring Cotton to welcome Herrick to England and to help the priest find lodging and put him in touch with important Roman Catholics so that he could begin his mission in safety. Cotton had bowed to Aquaviva's command, but felt uneasy.

At first he had asked Thomas Woode, the owner of this house, if Herrick could stay for a night or two. Woode had not objected though Cotton could see he was unsure about having another priest under his roof. Two priests doubled the risk, and if he was caught harboring priests, particularly Jesuits, Woode's very life could be at stake.

Cotton had intended to find somewhere else for Herrick to stay almost immediately, but somehow that hadn't happened and so he had remained here, posing as a serving man and going about his spiritual mission in his own way. It was a situation which, Cotton realized, both Thomas Woode and the governess Mistress Marvell wished to end, and soon.

Catherine Marvell stepped back into the doorway. "Can I bring you refreshment, Father?" Her words were directed at Cotton, and pointedly to him alone. With her master out at a livery company banquet, the house creaked between these three disparate people. Upstairs, the children of Thomas Woode slept in their little beds.

Cotton shook his head and smiled. "No, thank you, child. I have supped well. And you, Father Herrick?"

"Perhaps a little food before bed . . ."

Catherine nodded and turned away in silence. She clearly had no wish to prepare food for Father Herrick. "And do you have word for me, Father Cotton?" Herrick said when the two men were alone.

Cotton hesitated. There was something very wrong here. During his eight years of training for this mission, he had met many curious men, not all of them holy. There had been ambitious men, fearful men, angry men, spies sent by Walsingham, and, of course, many devoted men. But this Herrick — Cotton realized that was not his real name — was different in a worrying way. How, exactly, did this stranger fit into the Society of Jesus and its cause? Herrick was not forthcoming about the mission he had undertaken, though he mentioned he had served the cause in the Netherlands and even hinted at time spent in the New World saving heathens for Christ. "Let us sit down, Father Herrick, and take a little wine together while we wait for Catherine to bring your supper. It has been a long, cold day."

"I think you know I do not take wine, Father Cotton. I know, too, that you would wish I were not here in this house. Yet we both work for the same great cause. . . ." He spoke perfect English but for that faint accent. Only the trained ear could tell its origin as Dutch Flemish, for he was the product of a Dutch father, a musician at the court of Queen Mary, and an English mother.

"Do we?" Cotton asked, and regretted the question as soon as it was asked. "I am sorry, Father. That was unforgivable of me."

Herrick's expression betrayed nothing, but he chose his next words precisely. "Whatever you *think* you know, Father Cotton, I can assure you I know more about you than you do of me. Most vitally, I know you have the information I need, the meaning of which is not for you to think on. This is required of you by our superiors in Rome, and you *will* obey their wishes."

The harshness of Herrick's words stunned Cotton. For a minute he did not speak. A voice inside told him to say nothing, to refuse, for no good could come of it. But his Jesuit training had taught him total obedience, even at the risk of torture and death, and it was quite clear that Aquaviva wanted him to give Herrick everything he required. In this case, that was the name and address of the man Cogg. Who this Cogg was or what he did, Cotton had no way of knowing, but he feared that it had little or nothing to do with the Holy Roman Church.

At the doorway Catherine Marvell had re-appeared, holding a tray of cold food for

Herrick. Now, she shrank back, watching the two men.

Cotton spoke quietly to Herrick: "Cogg. Cow Lane."

The ghost of a smile crossed Herrick's face. His lips moved. "Thank you, Father Cotton. *Pax vobiscum.*" Then he turned to the doorway where Catherine stood rooted to the spot. He made the Sign of the Cross. "Bless you, too, child."

CHAPTER 8

They made speedy headway toward Deptford. The watermen had an easy job maintaining four or five knots downstream with the receding tide. Shakespeare sat in the back of the tiltboat, beneath the canopy. A salt wind billowed from the side and blew the hat from his head. It caught the edge of the tiltboat, but Boltfoot Cooper grabbed it just before it bounced into the choppy gray waters.

Boltfoot grinned into the spray as he handed back the hat. "Paying your respects to our sovereign nonpareil, Mr. Shakespeare? I believe she is in residence."

Shakespeare ignored him. The Queen was indeed at Greenwich Palace, beyond Deptford. With its sweeping lawns and its views of the river, crowded with the towering sails of great galleons, it was the loveliest of her homes, a palace of dreams divorced from the commotion and dirt of nearby London.

Yet in these noisome days, the palace was, thought Shakespeare, probably the least pleasant place in the realm. No one would wish to be in the presence of the Queen as she wrestled with her conscience over the death warrant awaiting her signature. Shakespeare had no intention of going to Greenwich Palace if he could avoid it, and he did not envy the courtiers and Privy Councillors who were with her day by day. Having met Elizabeth Tudor on several occasions, he felt fortunate that she had not taken a greater interest in him. Though he revered her as his sovereign, he liked to keep his distance; those who caught her eye lived a life between heaven and hell depending on her moods, which were as changeable as the weather: one moment sunshine and balm, the next, thunder and rage. These days, her sunny spells were not in evidence; nothing but black clouds and the boom of cannon fire. He quite understood why Walsingham was protesting illness and staying at Barn Elms — anything to keep away from their monarch in these gloomy times when she was consumed by indecision, torn on the one hand between her desire to be rid of her treacherous, scheming cousin and, on the other hand, her reluctance to do away with a fellow prince and thus bring down the wrath of the Roman Catholic world on England.

The rowers held a steady course, battling the current as they passed the dangerous West Ferry at the tip of a thumb of land where Kent bulged into the river, then turned southward. The waters eased and they ran smooth toward their destination, Deptford, where Drake was said to be overseeing work on ships of war of which he hoped to win command. Give him the vessels, he said, and he was confident he could take on the Spanish King and conquer him anywhere. Even if Philip did, as rumored, have the largest invasion fleet ever seen — up to two hundred great ships — carrying tens of thousands of troops.

The dockside at Deptford was a madness of shipping. You could scarcely see the shore for the forest of tall masts and their weblike rigging. The gaunt spars of the berthed vessels were as bare of sails as the trees on land were now leafless. Dozens of large ships, galleons and barks, were moored here, their great oak bulwarks and castles towering over the houses onshore. There were also pinnaces and dozens of smaller craft. From the river it was a stirring sight. As they came closer, it seemed thousands of men were at work among the long line of shops, riotous inns, ship chandlers, cooperages, sailmakers, spirit sellers, caulkers, pitch men, timber merchants, joiners, and carpenters that lined this stretch of river.

As the tiltboat pulled up at the stairs by the naval yard, it was immediately clear from the shouting and commotion that something was afoot. On the shore, a throng of men was grouped around something prone on the pebbles. Disembarking from the tiltboat, Shakespeare told the watermen to wait for him. Though they knew he was on Queen's business, they began to argue with him, saying they were due to wind up their day's work, but Boltfoot silenced them by producing his razor-sharp dagger and drawing it lightly across his throat in warning.

On the shore, the crowd was growing larger. Shakespeare strode down from the Strand across the gravel and mud to see what was there at the water's edge. Through a gap in the crowd he thought he saw a giant man in black lying there twitching.

Shakespeare pushed his way through the jostling crowd, receiving angry elbows for his pains. As he got closer, he saw that it was not a man but a huge black fish or sea monster, twenty-five feet or more from nose to tail. It seemed to be alive, for it was moving slowly, its fins flapping gently against the ground. A couple of apprentices were laughing and kicking it, trying to get a reaction out of it.

"That'll make a few fish suppers," said one young journeyman with the work apron of a joiner around his waist.

Shakespeare felt a curious pity for the huge beast. Its gray-black skin shimmered in the cloudy light. It was encrusted with barnacles. Seaweed growths straggled from its great belly. He moved forward and tried to stop the apprentices kicking it. They laughed at him and carried on, their fellows joining in.

"It's an omen," someone said. "A sign of evil tidings."

"I think it's a Spaniard," said the journeyman joiner.

"It's King Phil himself," said another, standing beside him. "Big fucker, isn't he?"

Shakespeare turned to Boltfoot Cooper. "Put the fish out of its misery."

Boltfoot still had his dagger in his hand. He moved forward and knelt beside the crippled animal, stroking its huge forehead. He seemed to whisper something to it, then thrust upward through its exposed white underside. As he withdrew the long blade, a rush of blood poured out. The animal thrashed for barely a minute, with Boltfoot cradling its enormous head, then died.

" 'Ere, he's killed the King of Spain!"

"Good riddance to him. Romish bastard. Now let's get the Scotch whore topped."

"It was a leviathan," Boltfoot said quietly to Shakespeare as he stood up, wiping his blade on his kerchief. "I saw many of them in the southern seas. Sometimes they'd follow us in our wake. Twice the size of that one there, some of them. Fifty foot or more."

Shakespeare felt a hand on his shoulder and turned sharply.

"Hello, John. I thought that was you."

Shakespeare found himself staring into a face he knew well. "Harper!"

"At your service. I was told to expect you."

Captain Harper Stanley was a proud man with a high ruff that looked preposterously uncomfortable to Shakespeare. He had a broad brown mustache that tapered horizontally into points above an equally pointed beard. He was just a little too tall for a naval man; he'd have to stoop belowdecks, for there was little headroom, even for the most dwarfish of men.

Shakespeare smiled warmly as they shook hands. He had always liked Stanley. "We're looking for the Vice Admiral."

"He's at Greenwich. Let me take you to him." Stanley turned to the two mariners who accompanied him and ordered, "Impound that whale. Have it rendered to lantern oil and set aside the jawbone for carving."

Captain Stanley led the way. As they passed the weatherworn carcass of the *Golden Hind* — Drake's ship that had encompassed the globe, now laid up forlorn behind the Royal Dock for all the world to come and gawp at, tread upon, and carve keepsake pieces of wood from — Shakespeare cast a look at Boltfoot. His eyes were held determinedly ahead as though he could not bear to look upon it.

"Seen a ghost, Mr. Cooper?" Captain Stanley inquired with a light chuckle. "Flogged on the fo'c'sle, perhaps? I'll wager there are some bad memories for you there, sir."

Boltfoot grunted a denial and walked on, dragging his clubfoot forward.

Stanley took them to a ship's boat and ordered the coxswain to take them to the palace. As they settled on the benches, he said at last, "What is your concern here, John? Sir Francis received your message

yesterday afternoon that you wished a meeting."

Shakespeare tried to reconcile this confident fellow with the callow young ship's
officer he had met five years earlier while
investigating the Spanish plot by Zubiaur,
Mason, and John Doughty against Drake's
life. Harper Stanley had not been on the
Golden Hind but had entered Drake's service
in 1581 — the year after the ship's return
from its great three-year voyage around the
world, laden with treasure stolen from the
King of Spain's ships. Stanley had arrived
from the northeast of England with letters
of recommendation, which Drake had studied dubiously. The Admiral was not keen on
gentleman sailors but liked Harper Stanley's
persistence and had taken him on. Nor was
he disappointed. Harper quickly proved
himself an able mariner and won rapid pro-
motion.

When the John Doughty plot was revealed,
Drake was as unconcerned as ever. He had
nothing but scorn for the King of Spain and
any attempt he might make on his life.
Grudgingly, he had assigned Stanley to help
Walsingham and Shakespeare with the
inquiry into the conspiracy, but wanted
nothing more to do with it himself.

Shakespeare had wanted to know more

about the events behind the plot. Why had John Doughty been so set on revenge for his brother? It was then that Harper Stanley produced Boltfoot Cooper to give Shakespeare a description of the trial and execution of John Doughty's brother, Thomas.

Boltfoot had already left the sea and had his own reasons for disliking Drake, but he was a fair witness. Though taciturn at the best of times, the former seaman spoke freely of the unhappy events of July 1578 at Port St. Julian, as if he had something to get off his chest.

Shakespeare had interviewed Boltfoot Cooper in the antechamber of Walsingham's house in Seething Lane. Cooper, who had settled to work away from the sea in a large London cooperage, seemed ill at ease in the high-chambered room with its great leaded windows. He spoke quietly at first to explain how he had entered Drake's service. "I had been pressed by the Devon sea-captain John Hawkins when I was an apprentice cooper, about twelve or thirteen, I'd reckon. It was an illegal act because I was bound to another man. Hawkins assigned me to the *Judith,* under the command of Mr. Drake, and I stayed with him thirteen years in all."

"And your main role was cooper, making barrels?"

"Yes, but Mr. Drake would often have me help the carpenters with mast repairs and careening. And when there was action, I fought alongside the rest of the men. I know that he did like me and trust me, and I suppose I looked up to him as a father. He was always a fair man . . . in those days."

"And latterly, Mr. Cooper, you were with Sir Francis — or Captain-General Drake as then was — on his venture to the Magellan Strait and through to the Pacific Ocean?"

"Yes, sir."

"And so you knew Thomas Doughty and his brother, John?"

"Yes, sir. For myself, sir, I did not like Thomas Doughty. He thought he was the Captain-General's equal, yet he was not, by no means. He and the other gentlemen aboard the *Pelican* were nothing but idlers. They had no respect for the men below-decks and we had none for them. They lorded it over us, taking our plunder, then tried to bribe us to betray the Captain-General. The Doughtys were like wasps in a nest, whispering together. Before entering the Plate River in South America, I refused an order from Thomas Doughty to climb the rigging to spy out the coast. It wasn't his place to give me such an order when the Ship's Master and the Captain-General were both aboard. Mr. Drake would never have given me such an order, because he knew about my foot and the problems I would have in climbing. But Thomas and John were pigs. They must have known that I could not climb, but when I refused Thomas Doughty's order, John Doughty took a length of cable and started whipping my head, sir."

"I'm very sorry to hear that, Mr. Cooper."

"He was laughing, sir, as if it were a jest."

"Finally, as we now know, Drake had had enough of being undermined by Thomas Doughty. He put him on trial before a jury of forty men at Port St. Julian, some hundred miles north of the Magellan Strait, and sentenced him to death."

"We called it Blood Island, Mr. Shakespeare. It was where the Portuguese sea captain Magellan had put down a mutiny and hanged a man some sixty years ago or more, before he went through the strait that now bears his name. I am not a superstitious man, but there were some believed that place was haunted. We did find the gibbet where Magellan hanged a mutineer, with black bones and shreds of old clothing beneath it still."

"And the execution of Thomas Doughty?"

"That was strange. I seen men go to their

deaths before, but never so well as Mr. Doughty. His death was the making of him. He chose the axe rather than the rope, which was his right, and Drake gave him two days to prepare himself. In those last days, he made peace with Drake, and they did dine together in Drake's tent."

"And where was the brother, John Doughty?"

"John held himself apart, went down to the rocks at the water's edge and sat there. He wasn't laughing *then.* When the execution was taking place, the Captain-General made the whole fleet's company assemble to witness it, and John Doughty was brought forcibly to watch. His arms were held on either side as the axe fell on his brother's head. John Doughty didn't blink, sir. I was watching him to see what he would do or say, but he did nothing and so I knew . . ."

"You knew what, Mr. Cooper?"

"I knew that one day he would seek revenge."

"Thank you, Mr. Cooper. You have been a great help. But before you go," Shakespeare said, "I believe you are no longer on speaking terms with Sir Francis Drake. Is that right?"

Boltfoot grunted. "There's many as won't talk to Drake now. For he is a rich man from the spoils we took from Spanish ships, especially the *Cacafuego* off the coast of Peru. It had twenty-six tons of silver, eighty pounds of gold, and thirteen chests full of coins — it took six days to unload it. And do I look a rich man? Yet we braved the same storms and endured the same scurvy. He is a great man, a fair man at sea, but on land Drake is something else. I will say no more on the matter, if it please you, sir. But take this, Mr. Shakespeare." He held out a piece of aged wood, shaped like a small tankard, which he removed from his pocket. "I did pull down Magellan's black and rotted gibbet and carved out many such cups on the long way home for my shipmates, as remembrances. I tell you this, though, I did never give one to John Doughty."

Five years later, Shakespeare had the cup still, though he never drank from it. He also had the services of Boltfoot Cooper, for Shakespeare had seen that he was not happy in his new life building barrels for brewers. Shakespeare had also seen some quality in Boltfoot, a steadfastness that would repay loyalty a hundredfold. So they made a contract a few weeks after their first meeting, and Boltfoot had worked for Shakespeare ever since.

Now Boltfoot sat with the coxswain while

John Shakespeare spoke with Captain Harper Stanley at the back of the ship's boat. "It seems there is another plot to do for Drake." Shakespeare said it quietly. "I want Boltfoot to guard him."

Stanley laughed. "Boltfoot? Are you moon mad, John? Drake won't let Cooper shadow him!"

"That is my fear. It was Mr. Secretary that suggested it. You're close to Drake, Harper. How *can* we protect him?"

"Does he really *need* protection?"

"Mr. Secretary believes he does. I admit I am worried, too. The Spanish were quite serious about it at the time of the Doughty conspiracy and it was chance alone that foiled their plot. There is evidence that they mean this time to get the job done. I fear they have found someone more adept in the bloody arts than John Doughty."

"Well, they won't have an easy time of it. Drake is always with people who would hazard their own lives for him."

"Where does he lodge?"

"At court, usually, with his pretty young wife. Sometimes he will stretch the hours by staying aboard ship at Gravesend when he journeys there. When he is here at Deptford he spends much time in meetings with my lord Admiral Howard who, you must know, has a house here on the Green. But if you ask me how we can protect Drake, I would say only this: get him to sea as quickly as possible."

CHAPTER 9

On the first floor of a broad tenement house in Cow Lane near Smith Field, Gilbert Cogg was sweating profusely, which had less to do with the heat from the fire and more to do with his three-hundredweight girth and his exertions with a girl named Starling Day.

She had come to the door of his workshop asking for employment in his bawdy house. He told her he would not employ her without sampling what she had to offer, and said she could have sixpence and a tankard of ale. She asked a shilling. After a brief bout of bargaining, they had agreed upon ten pence. She had earned her money well, half-crushed to death beneath his prodigious weight. As he pounded greedily into her hungry body, his enormous bed threatened to break its boards and joists and collapse through to the ground floor.

But it survived, as did Starling Day. Now

they lay together on the dirt-gray sheet. Cogg was panting as if he would soon breathe his last. His belly and chest heaved and sank like a ducking stool. Starling rolled over and slid out of the bed. Her body was thin from lack of nourishment, having walked from Nottingham to escape a marriage in which she had been beaten one time too many. Though the ribs in her chest looked like a washboard, her bruises had faded and she was still womanly. She would have been pretty had she had the opportunity to take more care of her hair. She dressed quickly, watching Cogg as his breathing eased. At last she held out her hand to him.

"What would that be then, my pretty bird? Sixpence I do believe?"

"Ten pence, Mr. Cogg. You did agree ten pence."

"Did I now? Did I so?"

"You did, sir, Mr. Cogg."

With difficulty he shifted himself upright off the bed. Standing naked in front of her, his member now flaccid and barely visible beneath a belly that hung down low like a sack of turnips, he pushed his stomach forward with evident satisfaction and grinned as he gave it a hearty slap. "You don't get a belly like that without some hard eating and drinking, my girl."

"No, Mr. Cogg."

"It's living so near the shambles, little Starling, that's what does it. The slaughtermen and butchers bring me offal and offcuts and in return I helps them with little things. Money for the rentman, pretty favors from friends like you. You name it, Cogg provides it. I provides fine favors for gentlemen, too, so those as works for me never knows who they might meet. You want fine sotweed? Cogg can get it. You want a prime view of a hanging, drawing, and quartering? Cogg provides."

"I had heard you were a generous man, Mr. Cogg. I was told you might be able to give me work."

"Well, we'll see, won't we? You're new to Romeville, my girl, but you've already got some nice Boleynish tricks there. I reckon you could do with some feeding up, though. So I tell you what, I'll give you a whole shilling this time so you can buy yourself some pies and perhaps you'll come to see me again on the morrow and we'll see what we can do."

"I'd like that, Mr. Cogg. Thank you, sir."

He handed her a coin and squeezed her breasts, then clasped her face to his in a fetid kiss. Starling knew better than to pull away.

"And do you have a lodging, my pretty bird?"

She shook her head. There was a time when she would have cried in her misery, but those days were long past. Nights in the open or huddled beside the other poor and dispossessed in barns and byres had hardened her.

"Well, get yourself to the vaulting house right by the Bel Savage, my girl, and tell them Cogg sent you. Talk to Parsimony Field. She's my best girl. She'll look after you and find you a comb to pretty yourself up a little. A cot, too." He slapped her behind as she left, knowing that the shilling was a fine investment that would pay him many times over.

Cogg was still naked when Miles Herrick arrived soon after the girl had gone. Swiving gave him a strong appetite and he had just sat down to devour the remains of a fat and fresh turkey cock that a farmer's son from Suffolk had given him in exchange for a night with Parsimony. Most customers banged on his workshop door, but Herrick appeared in the chamber while Cogg was licking his fingers and chewing on some crisp, fatty skin from the wishbone.

The man stood there watching him, a dark shadow in black clothes. Cogg recoiled in shock, then jumped up from his three-legged stool, knocking it backwards into the hearth.

"Who are you?" he demanded, trying to gain his composure as he scrabbled for his breeches and shirt.

"I was given your name."

"So you just walk into a man's chamber when he's at his repast?"

Herrick smiled. "I think I just watched your repast leave by the front door. A fine but skinny wench, Mr. Cogg. It is Mr. Cogg . . . isn't it?"

"It is, sir, yes, but who, pray, are *you?*" Cogg was half-dressed now and trying to impose his authority on the situation.

"I bring you gold, Mr. Cogg. And I believe you can supply a certain item in return."

Cogg pulled the stool from the fire. "That depends on just who I am talking to."

"My name is Herrick. Miles Herrick."

As if a taper had been lit behind them, Cogg's eyes brightened. "Ah, yes, Mr. Herrick. I had been expecting you." Suddenly all was clear. Cogg's manner changed; here was the prospect of good money. He had been thinking of how to squeeze this orange ever since the commission had been agreed.

"Let us go down to my workshop, if it please you. It is more of a place to strike deals."

He led the way through the doorway, his bulk barely managing to negotiate the narrow frame, then down a flight of thirteen wooden and ominously creaking steps to a large shoplike area that took up the front half of the ground floor of the wide-fronted building. He opened a door to the rear and showed Herrick through.

The back room was a cluttered heap of boxes and barrels. A layer of dust covered many of the trunks and crates. The ceiling and corners of the room were clothed in cobwebs. "Whatever you want, Mr. Herrick, I'll guarantee you'll find it here."

Herrick's eyes flicked around the dimly lit room. He looked at Cogg, who was panting like a dog in summer.

"I tell you, Mr. Herrick," Cogg continued. "As a boy I used to dig marl. From the age of eight until I was twenty, day after day after day, I dug the same thick white-gray clay in the depths of a dark pit in the shire of Northampton. Backbreaking work that left me strong as a bull. The farmer treated his swine better than he treated me. But one day I just upped sticks and walked to London, where I got work slitting pigs' throats in the shambles. I had my eyes on a better life, though, so I'd get things for people, like the foreman, who had a taste for chewing Moorish hemp. I'd go down to the docks and buy things from the mariners and sell them on: strange foods and odd carvings, knives taken from Indians and Mussulmans, medicines from the ends of the earth to cure the ague, wenches of every hue, not all of them Christian, wild beasts such as you'd never find even at the Tower menagerie. I can find you liquids that flame to burn down a house and perfumes that will poison with a sweet smell. Whatever a man could desire, Mr. Herrick, Cogg gets it for him."

"You *know* what I want, Mr. Cogg." Herrick's voice was cold. "The question is: do you have it?"

Cogg waddled ducklike among the crates and barrels. "Oh yes, Mr. Herrick, you had a very special request, as I recall. Not one of Cogg's easier undertakings. A long-muzzled gun with a barrel exactly two feet eight inches, using a strange firing mechanism: a snaphaunce lock, I think. . . . Is that a Hollandish word, sir? You do sound a little Hollandish, if I might say so. I believe there is a bit of common or garden flint in the gun's cock, which sounds strange to me, but if that's what you want. Most clients want wheel-lock pistols, sir, gold-damascened and small as you like to proudly display at the waist . . . or to conceal up a sleeve."

"So you have it?"

"Cogg doesn't fail, sir. You said you wanted the barrel rifled, fine rifled. And provision of a fine powder, using good willow coals, the best I could discover in all of England. There were to be twenty-four balls so crafted that they would be a perfect fit for the barrel. Would that be the sum of your requirements, Mr. Herrick?"

"Let me see it."

Cogg raised a hand, a bulbous white thing with five protuberances like outsized maggots. "Mr. Herrick. I have, indeed, had the gun made. By a gentleman called Mr. Opel, a Germanic living here in England. He told me he had never made such a fine weapon. Reckoned it could kill at a hundred and fifty yards. Said he had never heard of a gun that could find its target at more than fifty yards. So this gun, Mr. Herrick, what would it be for killing? A deer? A man? It is a very curious shape, to be sure, and sadly lacking in ornamentation."

Herrick's eyes pierced Cogg's. His voice lowered but did not soften. "I was told you didn't ask questions."

Cogg raised his hand again, this time defensively. "My apologies, Mr. Herrick. I meant no offense. The use of the gun is entirely your concern. But it is such a remarkable piece, sir, that I would like to know about it. Maybe there is a market for such articles? Would gentlemen want such a weapon for hunting? Tarry, Mr. Herrick, sir. Take some Spanish wine so we can talk a while and drink to the Spanish King's death."

In a movement of elegance and speed, Herrick went forward and his hand was at Cogg's fat neck, crushing his windpipe. Cogg writhed but the grip was like an iron vise. Then, as suddenly as the assault began, Herrick released Cogg.

"I do not want your wine, I do not want to talk with you. Bring me the gun, for which a price has been agreed."

Cogg sat down heavily on a low crate and fought to regain his breath. For a moment he had thought he would die, so powerful was the hand that held him. Gilbert Cogg retained much of the strength he had as a young man, but this stranger's power was of a different order. His common sense told him that Herrick could kill him with casual ease and that he would do well to hand over the gun at the price agreed. But his instinct told him never to pass up an opportunity to make ready money. And now in this game of cards with Herrick, he held the kings, because he had the gun still, and Herrick would be pressed to find it without him.

"Remind me, Mr. Herrick," he said, his voice rasping from the assault on his throat. "What was the agreed price?"

"Nine marks, Cogg, as well you know."

"In gold?"

"In gold. Four sovereign coins."

Cogg knew he should stop now, take the money offered. There was a good profit in it already: three marks for him, six for Opel. And yet he could not stop. He knew this weapon was worth far more to Herrick than nine marks. It was one of a kind.

"Mr. Herrick, this weapon has cost me far more than anticipated. My man Opel has worked long hours to a standard never before seen in the gunmaker's art, using new methods to meet your requirements. I have had to pay him more than double the fee we did agree."

Herrick smiled then. "How much, Cogg? How much will it take for you to be silent and for me to walk out of this room with no more cheapening?"

Cogg's mouth wrinkled, his shoulders

wobbled. At last he spoke, in his most reasonable voice. "Can we say thirty marks, sir?"

"And that is your last demand?"

Cogg rubbed his pudgy hands together. "My *very* last."

Without another word, Herrick took the purse from his belt and counted out thirteen gold sovereigns and two crowns. Cogg took the coins. The gold glinted at him from his white palm. He looked up at Herrick. "And now, if you will excuse me, sir, I require privacy while I retrieve your piece for you. I'm sure you understand."

Herrick shook his head. "No. Get it now."

Cogg hesitated a moment too long. Herrick's hand shot forward and slammed the fat man's head down hard onto the top of a large cask, then, with his right hand clasped on the nape of his neck, he pulled Cogg's left arm up by the wrist. "Where is it?"

Cogg grunted as if he were trying to speak. But the words, if there were any, were too indistinct for Herrick to make out. In a single motion, Herrick snapped back Cogg's wrist. There was an audible crack as the bone shattered. Cogg screamed.

Herrick pulled his head off the cask and rammed his gloved fist into the screaming mouth to silence it. Blood spattered from

Cogg's loosened teeth down his unkempt beard. Herrick had his dagger out now, clasped in his left hand. Blood from Cogg's mouth dripped over its black bone handle. The dagger was thin with a point like a needle. He held it to Cogg's right eye, the tip touching the black center. "Another sound, except for the words I want to hear, and I will prick out this eye, Mr. Cogg."

Cogg knew now that he was going to die, but the thought of his eye being pricked and the fluids therein bursting forth was too much to bear. "I'll get it, right away, Mr. Herrick."

Herrick released him. Cogg's hand hung loose from his arm, the bone protruding through the skin and flesh at the wrist at an unspeakable angle. Like a bullock at the slaughter, he stumbled through the boxes and barrels, falling over them in his haste.

The weapon was concealed beneath floorboards near the back of the house by a door that gave out onto a small courtyard where chickens clucked and pecked. With his one working hand and a jimmy, Cogg prized up the loose boards and brought the weapon out. It was in two parts, a plain thing, wrapped in jute sackcloth that did no credit to its fine craftsmanship. His fingers trembled as he lifted the gun. It was heavy and difficult to balance with just one hand. He turned. Herrick stood in front of him, the thin dagger loose in his right hand. He slid it into its sheath and gently took the gun from Cogg. The sacking was tied at both ends with coarse string, which he quickly slipped off.

The gun did not look much like a gun. One part was a bare wooden stock, triangular but curved on the shortest of the three sides. The stock had two joiners' hooks to attach it to the front of the weapon, a dark metal barrel, and the snaphaunce mechanism. Herrick clicked the two pieces together, then examined it closely, turning it this way and that, peering down the muzzle, testing the lock and pan cover, cocking the hammer and letting it fall against the frizzen. The action was smooth. At last he looked up. "Where are the balls and powder?"

Cogg saw his last chance. "I kept them separate, Mr. Herrick. They are at the front in an old cabinet where I keep smaller things."

"Remember your eyes. Nor will I stop with the pricking out of your eyes. I will slice off your pizzle and stones and you will go to your death a girl if you make just one little error."

Cogg shuddered, but there was one thing he had to try. Herrick dismantled the gun and replaced it in its sacking. He followed Cogg through to the front room. It had a ware-bench, like a shop, and behind it a tall wooden dresser with cupboard doors at the top and little drawers below. The pain in Cogg's broken left wrist was almost beyond enduring. As he pulled open one of the cabinet doors with his good hand, the packages were revealed on a shelf: the black powder wrapped in a large purse of leather, the balls in a bag of jute cloth. As he picked up the balls and powder he turned and threw them into Herrick's face, then launched himself at him in a last desperate effort to survive, as hopeless as a chicken running from the farmwife's blade.

Starling Day stopped halfway down Cow Lane. She knew now that Cogg would take her on as one of his whores, so why did she have to wait another night to hear it? Why couldn't she do a deal with him today and start work immediately? She needed the money badly, for she wanted clothes and food. She also had debts, for which she would suffer if she did not repay them by the week's end. She had learned about Cogg from her cousin Alice, who was already whoring at his bawdy house by the Bel Savage.

At first Alice had not been pleased to see Starling; she was less than a year older and they had played together as children, swimming in the stream in the summer and stealing coal from the slack tip when winter froze the land. Perhaps Alice was ashamed of what she had become. But when she realized that Starling intended to enter the same line of work, she warmed to her. "I never understood what you saw in that pig Edward," she said when Starling told her about her husband's viciousness. "I'd rather die of the French pox in London town than live as a beaten goodwife with a drunken coal hewer for a husbandman in Strelley." Over drinks in the Bel Savage, she had told Starling where to find Cogg.

"This is the way things are with him, Starling, so listen well. He's as fat as six men stuck together, but never laugh at him or shy away from him. He likes Paris tricks, so use your tongue like this." Alice rolled and curled her tongue to show just what Cogg wanted. "His terms are half and half, but you'll have to pay him for food and lodging, too. It doesn't sound the best bargain this side of Cheapside, but Cogg always gets us a good price. Keeps us free of the pox, mostly, which is what the men want. You'll learn how to look at them, see if they're diseased — and tell them to piss off if they are. Cogg's got ointments of herbs from the apothecary to keep us free of it. Told me he paid for them with the eyes and tongue of a hanged woman. But remember this: if you do get the pox, you're out, and then it's the lowest stews in Southwark or back to Strelley."

Retracing her steps, Starling was about to knock at Cogg's front door when she heard a noise from inside. Voices. It seemed as if he had another visitor — but this was a man's voice, not another girl. She turned the door handle and found it was open, the lock sheared away from the wood. Whoever was in there with Cogg had done this; she was sure the lock had been secure when she left. Starling slipped into the front room. She heard footfalls at the top of the steps and quickly hid herself, crouching behind a workbench and boxes.

The man she saw with Cogg was tall, dressed darkly, clean-shaven. She felt a chill of unease and wished she had not entered this house again. As she watched him follow Cogg through to the back room and heard the whump of violence and Cogg's shrill scream, she trembled in fear.

She knew the smell of violence too well. It stank of the sleeping room at the cottage she once called home. Each night, when her husband returned from the coal mine, his face and hands and clothes black, he would eat whatever food she had scavenged or grown, drink strong ale, then hit her. Every night. Every night of the year, without fail. Some nights he would make her lie flat on the straw, her wrists tied to the rough-hewn bed leg with his leather belt as he beat her with the broken haft of an old hayfork. And then, inevitably, he would occupy her, brutally but briefly, as if only her pain could bring him pleasure. Every daybreak when he went off to be wound down the well into the pit of the earth with his little tallow lamp and coal pick, she would pray for the walls to cave in and bury him. And when that didn't happen, she stopped believing in God and took the road for London.

Huddled behind the workbench, Starling could hear her heart. Did that mean the man in dark clothes could hear it, too? She saw the two men return to the front room. Cogg's left arm hung limp at the wrist, broken, blood dripping where the bone protruded through the skin. She felt no pity for him. She felt no pity for any man. The other man was carrying something. It looked like some sort of tool, but she had never seen its like before.

Cogg took something from the cabinet behind the ware-bench and threw it at the other man's face. It was a pathetic effort, evaded easily, and as Cogg lunged toward the man, the dark-clothed one swiftly side-stepped him and pushed Cogg forward so that he fell to the floor, flat on his face. The stranger sat on him, his legs straddling his huge back, and pulled Cogg's straggly hair. Then, with a thin, black-handled dagger, he stabbed twice at the fat man's face, the blade descending each time into the eyes and through to the brain. To the hilt. Cogg didn't scream, but gurgled and thrashed and grunted with the urgency of an animal that suddenly finds itself prey.

The dark-clothed man stood. He wiped the blood and brain from his blade on a rag and sheathed it before dropping some gold coins into his leather purse. He then picked up the objects that had been thrown at him, slung the unidentified tool over his shoulder, and left as quietly as he had arrived.

Starling waited long minutes behind the workbench. Cogg's feet were twitching but she knew he was dead. At last she came out from her hiding place and went over to him. He was no use to her now. She spat on him.

Then she spat on him again. Somewhere in this house, she realized, there must be a goodly stash of gold. Cogg had been a wealthy man.

CHAPTER 10

They found Drake pacing a wood-paneled anteroom at Greenwich Palace like a man demented. Boltfoot had seen him pace like this many times, on the quarterdeck when the wind wouldn't rise.

Francis Drake, Vice Admiral of Elizabeth's navy, was a short, thickset man of forty-six. His sharp little beard was still fair and golden but now flecked with gray. His hair was a darker red, graying also, curled and combed back off his broad and deep forehead. His eyes retained the vital blue of his youth. He wore court clothes, a brilliant green velvet cape over a green and silver-wrought doublet, all tailored at great cost by Gaston de Volpere of Candlewick Street, along with an outrageous ruff, as wide as a serving platter. His blue eyes could twinkle with amusement but now they were angry, like the dark blue of the stormy sea that was his home.

He was angry, very angry, and nothing the two people with him in this small official room could do or say could calm him down. His young wife, Elizabeth Sydenham, had tried to soothe him without success and now sat on some cushions with a book of poems, trying to shut out the raging torrent that foamed from her husband. His constant companion, Diego, the slave he freed in the Spanish Indies and who had since circumnavigated the world with him, stood at a window, gazing idly out at a bark drifting slowly downstream toward the estuary. He had seen these rages so many times before, and they had long since ceased to frighten him. Drake glared at the new arrivals — Shakespeare, Stanley, and Boltfoot — and stopped his pacing.

"In God's faith, this is a sorry affair, Stanley. She won't see me. There was a time when I would be admitted to her presence eight times a day; now, when we need her most, she closets herself with lady's-maid poltroons like Davison and Burghley. This realm will be a Spanish colony before summer's end if she continues this way!"

"Sir Francis," Captain Stanley said, bowing briskly. "May I introduce Mr. John Shakespeare, an assistant secretary to Mr. Secretary Walsingham."

The furious cloud momentarily lifted from Drake's brow. "Ah yes, Mr. Shakespeare, I have been expecting you."

"It is an honor to meet you, Sir Francis."

"Likewise, likewise. A good man, Walsingham. England would be lost without him. I love him like a brother. Now, what exactly is his concern?"

Shakespeare viewed the tableau before him with fascination. The great, heroic mariner, in a rage because the Queen refused to see him, his wife so busy in her poems that she scarce looked up at the new arrivals, and a blackamoor dressed like a fine English gentleman and affecting disinterest in the proceedings. What glue held these three disparate creatures together?

Catching the direction of Shakespeare's eye, Drake broke in before he could speak. "Forgive me, Mr. Shakespeare, I have not introduced you to my wife, Elizabeth . . ."

Elizabeth's delicate, heart-shaped face lit up in a guileless smile that seemed to cast sparkles in the fat sapphires, rubies, and pearls that adorned her neck and fingers. Shakespeare bowed to her and she held out her delicate white hand for a kiss. Drake, meanwhile, was moving swiftly on: ". . . and my very good friend Diego, who probably hates the Spanish even more than I do."

Boltfoot Cooper had been hanging back, behind Shakespeare and Stanley, but now Diego caught sight of him and strode forward to shake his hand. "Boltfoot, it is good to see you."

"It is good to see you, too, Diego."

"I saved Diego from the Spanish in Nombre de Dios," Drake continued, addressing Shakespeare and Stanley and ignoring Boltfoot. "I think they had an idea that a hanging would make their saints look favorably on them, and Diego was to be the day's entertainment. Luckily, he has a strong neck, because he was already dancing the hempen jig when we cut him down. Been my fine companion ever since. He is a master of tongues who has helped me many times talk to my captives when we have boarded ship or taken a town. How many languages do you speak now, Diego?"

"Four."

"Four! English, Spanish, Portuguese . . ."

"And Mandingo, my own tongue."

"Tell me again, Diego, what would you like to do to the Spanish King?"

Diego laughed, too, as if he had heard it all before a thousand times. "Chain him up, brand him, sling him and two hundred other Spaniards into the stinking hold of a slow carrack across the western sea, set him to work on a Caribbean plantation for ten years. And then I'd hang him."

Drake clapped his hands. "And may he burn an eternity in hell, the way he has burned so many others." At last he turned to Boltfoot Cooper. They were both short, squat men and they stood toe to toe, neither man blinking. "And you, Cooper, what in God's name are you doing here? Why aren't you shaping your staves, bending your hoops, and fashioning your faucets some-place?"

"He is in my employ," Shakespeare said.

Drake put an arm around Boltfoot's shoulder. Boltfoot stood sullenly and stiffly as if in the grip of a tropic snake. "I know, I know," Drake told Shakespeare. "He works for you and Mr. Secretary. You're a ship-wreck of a man, Cooper. You should be building casks, which is what God put you on earth to do, not promenading around London with your caliver and cutlass like some landbound pirate!"

"And you're a common thief, Mr. Drake."

Drake took his arm from around Bolt-foot's shoulder and pushed him in the chest. His face had turned to ice. "I've killed men for less, Cooper."

Boltfoot stood his ground. "You were not the only man to journey around the world,

Mr. Drake. I was there with you near death from ship's fever, hunger, and the bloody flux. Where is *my* share of the treasure?"

"Why, Mr. Cooper, you have had gold."

"Enough to keep me from starving, maybe, Mr. Drake. You feed us a pension in dribs and drabs as it pleases you, and you turn us into beggars for what is rightfully ours. Where are the riches you promised us?"

"I will hear none of this. Mr. Shakespeare, please remove your man."

Boltfoot was not so easily silenced. Rarely had Shakespeare heard him say more than a dozen words together at a time, and now he was in full flow. "Do you not recall that gold Will Legge and I found in the chest of the master's cabin aboard the *Capitana* and gave to you? Six and a half pounds that you had not seen. You cut us a wedge twenty-nine ounces and marked it with our names and pledged it to us when we reached England. Where, then, is that gold now, Mr. Drake? Will and I have seen none of it."

Drake was near foaming with anger. "God's faith! You are the vilest knave that ever lived, Boltfoot Cooper. I tell you, you and all the men have had your share and more. Did I not write your names in glory?"

Shakespeare decided it was time to intervene. "Sir Francis, if I may speak with you a while in private —"

"I'll run you through, Cooper, you base scoundrel —"

"A brief word or two, Sir Francis?"

Drake snapped out of his tirade and turned toward Shakespeare. "Get me away from the company of this monstrous, dissembling, perfidious, lame bilge-scum of a man. Come, Mr. Shakespeare, Mr. Stanley, let us adjourn and take some wine. Diego, you stay with Cooper." He nodded briefly toward his wife. "M'lady . . ."

Drake strode ahead of them into the adjoining room, the slight limp he carried from a leg wound sustained in his raid on a Spanish mule train at Nombre de Dios still evident fourteen years later. The three men sat at a table and Drake hammered it with his fist. "The Queen will not hear me. She affects to despise me for the lack of pearls, gold, and emeralds brought her from the Spanish Main this last year, but she knows I wreaked terrible harm to the Spanish King. And if she'd give me the commission of ships I need, I would go and sink this king and his enterprise forever."

"Sir Francis . . ."

"I know, I know, Mr. Shakespeare, you have something to say. But hear me out. I am the one man in England who can save this Queen and this realm from the foul Antichrist of Rome and his Spanish toy dog . . ."

"That, Sir Francis, is why I am here." Shakespeare knew as well as any the boastfulness of Drake. It was common knowledge in England and throughout Europe, and those who did not fear him and admire him sneered at him for it.

And yet he had much to be boastful about. Some said the total plunder taken on his three-year round-the-world voyage amounted to five hundred thousand pounds. Much went to the Queen and her treasury, yet Drake himself was left one of the wealthiest men in the realm.

He had won it through courage and cunning and remarkable attention to detail. However distant the sea, he never allowed his ships to fall into disrepair. Despite hunger and illness, he would drive his vessels ashore to be careened — clearing the hulls of barnacles and weed — so that they remained trim and swift and strong.

Never did he shy away from a fight — either with the Spaniards or native peoples. Yet neither did he kill unnecessarily. When he took prisoners, he treated them with courtesy and mercy — a thing rarely true of the Spanish.

Back home, he had for many years been the star in the Queen's firmament, always welcome in her presence with his vivid tales of a world beyond these shores. Yet now, when England needed him most, he found himself washed up and out of favor. And he could not contain his rage.

He eyed Shakespeare warily.

"Tell me then, sir. Why *are* you here? Some threat to my life, I am told."

"A threat that Mr. Secretary takes exceeding serious, Admiral, coming as it does from a ciphered message between Mendoza and the Spanish King."

Drake laughed, a long crashing wave of a laugh. "The Spanish King kill me? I will nail his ears to the flummery altar in his Escorial palace before he kills me, Mr. Shakespeare."

"We believe Mendoza has found a seasoned mercenary, a paid assassin, to do his work for him. The price on your head, Sir Francis, has increased considerably."

"Well, well, and what are the Spaniards offering now? Twenty thousand ducats it was last time, I do believe."

"It is now seventy thousand."

Drake clapped his hands, like a river fisherman who has just landed a twenty-pound pike. "They will be offering ten times seventy thousand before I am in my grave, Mr. Shakespeare. What say you, Captain Stanley?"

"I agree entirely, Sir Francis. But perhaps it would be prudent to hear Mr. Shakespeare out. The world knows you are invincible at sea, but now you are ashore, you are not so safe."

"Indeed, sir. And do I seem *afraid?* Is John Doughty at large again with his wooden sword to scare me into my mother's bed?"

This was going to be difficult. Shakespeare understood that it was vital to play to Drake's vanity. "No, Sir Francis, you seem anything but afraid. And that, we believe, is the card Mendoza and his hireling will play. Because you are so very visible at Deptford, at Gravesend, and at court, you are a tempting target — dare I say an *easy* target — for a determined killer. I understand that you do not fear for your life and never have, but we must all fear for the life of Her Majesty and for the future of England. If you should fall to a Spanish ball, bolt, or blade, we will all be lost."

Drake stood up and started pacing again. His face was florid now, a hot red. He was silent a while, then he turned sharply toward Shakespeare and Stanley. "So then, what does my friend Mr. Secretary propose?"

Shakespeare sighed. "He wants me to protect you."

"And how would you do that?"

"Firstly by asking you to curtail your movements. To make yourself less visible, surround yourself at all times with trusted lieutenants. When you board a ship to inspect its caulking and provisioning, spend as little time on deck as possible. When you are at court, avoid the public areas. When you are in the dockyards or chandleries, keep a watchful eye at all times and do not tarry long in one place. Take no chances, Admiral. Your apparel" — he nodded toward Drake's brilliant velvet gown — "is very visible."

Drake's brows knitted in amusement. "You don't think I wear a cloak like this outside court, do you? I'm a mariner, Mr. Shakespeare, I dress in sea clothes. So how else would you protect me if God wills it otherwise?"

This was the hard bit. Shakespeare took a deep breath. "I would assign Mr. Boltfoot Cooper as your personal guardian, Sir Francis."

Drake exploded with laughter. "Cooper! My personal guardian!"

"He is very handy with his caliver and

cutlass, Sir Francis. He knows your ways . . ."

"Never. In God's faith, never."

Shakespeare played his final card. "Mr. Secretary Walsingham, your friend, requests this of you. He understands your reluctance and the bad blood, caused I am sure by Mr. Cooper's avarice, but he begs this one indulgence."

Drake began pacing again. His right hand was gripped on the hilt of his sword, but the weapon stayed firmly in its scabbard. "Boltfoot Cooper protect my life? I have sailed tempests and seen strange sea monsters and been at one with God on the empty ocean, but never have I heard such a thing. What say you, Stanley?"

"He has courage, sir."

"Aye, I'll give you that. Cooper has courage. He was always a fine man in a fight with the Spaniard. Never did he hold back when the powder was burning hot."

"I vouch he is indeed a fine man, Sir Francis. I would swear before God that he is loyal, true, and strong."

"Well then, be done with it and give me the knave. I'll remind him what it is to be Drake's man. But he is under *my* command, you understand, Mr. Shakespeare."

"I understand, Admiral."

Drake's eye suddenly twinkled. "I think I will set him to making casks for the fleet. That is a far more useful occupation; it is well-barreled water, ale, and salt pork that keeps a man alive at sea."

Shakespeare had to intervene. "Forgive me, Sir Francis, but I think not in this instance. Your own life is what will keep your men alive at sea on this occasion."

Drake gave Shakespeare a hard look, thought a moment, then changed the subject. "And tell me, what has happened to John Doughty? Is he hanged yet?"

"I fear I do not know, Admiral. The last I heard he had been consigned to the Marshalsea, but that was four or five years ago. God willing, he has died of the plague . . . but I mean to find out."

CHAPTER 11

Starling Day could scarce contain her fear and excitement. What could she do with all these riches? Where could she hide them? And what of the body?

She sat on a trunk looking at Gilbert Cogg's corpse. In the palms of her open, spread hands was a bar of gold which, though she had never seen its like before, she knew to be worth riches beyond her imagining. Upstairs, in a coffer, hidden behind a barely visible door in a low cupboard to the side of the hearth, there was yet more gold, much more gold, along with silver and stones set as jewelry. Much more than she could reckon.

She clenched her fingers into talons over the gold as she tried to concentrate. She had to get the treasure out of this house quickly. Unless she moved Cogg's body, it would soon be found. But there was too much treasure, and too heavy. Her mind kept drifting. How would she use this wealth? Fine clothes, a great house, good wine and food. But how could she buy all this and ensure her sudden wealth went unnoticed? Her dearest wish would be to return to her home village, Strelley, and parade in finery in front of her cruel husband and his witch of a mother to show him what she had become, but that would never be possible.

Alice. She would have to bring her cousin Alice in as her confederate in this. She could not cope with this alone. And anyway, there was more than enough to share; they would both be left wealthy. She looked again at the body. It was the size of a two-month heifer, more than three times her weight. She would never be able to move it alone. Perhaps, together, she and Alice could shift it. In the meantime she would have to cover it with something. She knew that Cogg had many visitors and he could be discovered at any moment.

The body was uncomfortably close to the front door. There was a bolt on the inside, which she had slid into place. Two people had already knocked on the door since she had been there, both eventually leaving disappointed. How long before someone broke in? She feared, too, that if someone looked closely through the window, they would glimpse the corpse.

Starling went back upstairs and took the covers from the bed where she had endured Cogg's grunting, slathering weight. There was a carpet bag there, into which she put the gold bar she already held and a second one. Then, after concealing the rest of the hoard as well as she could, she brought the bag and the bedcovers back downstairs. She used the bedcovers to cover Cogg. Then she shifted the table so that the huge mound of his body was less visible from the window near the door.

She waited, listening for footsteps with trepidation. Finally, she slid back the bolt and wrenched open the door. Her heart thumped in her slender chest. She looked right, left, then shut the door behind her and moved quickly down Cow Lane, clutching the heavy bag to her breast, hunched forward into the cold, cold wind.

It was a brisk ten-minute walk through the mud and slush to the Bel Savage by Fleet Prison, hemmed in between the ditch and the western wall of London. The tavern was one of London's most famed, attracting a fine crowd of lawyers, merchants, market traders, whores, and those who merely wanted to get knockdown drunk. There was always good entertainment to be had: lively minstrels and players staging entertainments. The tenement next door to it was well maintained considering its purpose as a bawdy house for the selling of women's bodies. Downstairs was an anteroom, where customers — many of whom spilled straight out of the Bel Savage with a bellyful of ale or brandy befuddling their better judgment and keeping them from their wives and homes — could come to consider their purchase. Upstairs there were a dozen rooms, each with a bed and a fire and each shared by two whores for sleeping but with a different purpose when customers were to be entertained.

Alice had just finished with one of her regulars, a balding, half-blind old retainer from the Earl of Leicester's great mansion just along the Strand. He was so decrepit it had taken him an hour to get started and another hour to finish. Starling pushed past him into Alice's second-floor room and slammed the door shut with her shoulder. She dropped the bag with the gold bars on the far side of the bed in case anyone entered unannounced, then clenched her fists and let out a silent scream of joy. "Alice, something has happened which I must tell you. We must be quick."

Alice finished washing herself and began dressing. "That bastardly gullion. He took two hours and paid me for one. He's getting worse." She pulled her blouse about her breasts. She was more rounded than Starling, her skin was clearer and more luminous, and her hair was fairer. Cogg had made sure she was properly fed with meat from the market at Smith Field and had plenty of ale.

"Alice, forget about him. You must listen to me."

"What, cousin, have you won at the cockfights?"

"Better. Oh, Alice, riches beyond your imagining." She clasped her cousin in a hug. "Look in the bag, but hurry. I'll stay by the door."

Alice went beside the bed and opened the bag. As she looked at the gold bars she could not at first work out what she was seeing. Then she thrust in her hands and pulled one of them out.

"Leave it in the bag, Alice. Someone might come in."

"Starling, *where* did you get this?"

"It was Cogg's but now he's backed, good and proper."

"Cogg? Dead?"

Starling nodded furiously. "Dead, Alice,

murdered . . ." She saw the horror in her cousin's face. "No, no, no, not by me." Hastily she gabbled out the sequence of events as they had unfolded at the house in Cow Lane. Alice listened, still unbuttoned but her clothing forgotten.

"I need you," Starling said at last. "We've got to hide Cogg and get the gold out of there to somewhere safe. I'll give you half of everything."

"Starling, this is dangerous. You'll get us both strung up at Tyburn."

"It's our one chance, Alice. You've got to help me."

Walking from the river stairs by London Bridge back to Seething Lane, John Shakespeare felt uneasy. He kept turning, certain he was being followed, but he could make out no one suspicious among the rowdy throngs of merchants, clerks, and apprentices who crowded the streets, nor among those driving the slow, ox-drawn wagons, laden with produce from Kent.

He had left Boltfoot at Greenwich with Drake. Boltfoot had been discomfited and Shakespeare felt bad, realizing the other man was in for a hard time staying close to his former captain twenty-four hours a day.

As Shakespeare left the palace, there had

been a great excitement along the royal jetty. He saw Robert Beale there, among a group of courtiers, just about to get into a state barge. Beale was Clerk to the Privy Council and brother-in-law to Walsingham. Shakespeare knew him well.

He greeted Beale with a wave. "What news, Robert?" And then he saw that Beale was white and drained and distracted.

"The best and the worst, John. I would say more but cannot."

"Has she signed the warrant?"

"I can say no more." And with that Beale stepped into the barge and disappeared from view.

Shakespeare felt his heart pounding. This sounded very much as though the Queen had signed the warrant for the execution of Mary Stuart. But Elizabeth could change her mind a dozen times within a day. If it was to be done, it would have to be done quickly before she thought better of it. And what if the head fell? The reaction from the Catholic world could be bloody and swift. This sobering thought occupied him on the long journey back upriver against the tide. He reclined beneath the canopy on cushions and pulled a blanket around him, closing his eyes as the watermen strained their sinews to their oars. He thought, too, of his father and his refusal to attend church, and worried again. Did Topcliffe really have influence in the Midlands?

At his door, Jane was waiting anxiously. "Someone has been here, master, while I was out at the market."

"Well, did they leave a message?"

"No, master, I fear we have been robbed by them."

It was then that Shakespeare saw the door was broken around the lock. He went in to his anteroom. It looked undisturbed.

"Your solar, Master Shakespeare, I fear they have disturbed your papers and books."

Shakespeare went upstairs to his solar, the light-filled room that he used for working. His papers were strewn all over the floor; cabinets and tables were overturned. There was damage to the wall paneling, and boards had been ripped from the floor as if someone had been searching for something. Topcliffe. Shakespeare slammed his fist against the wall in frustration and anger. He turned and saw Jane.

"I'm sorry, Jane. A cup of wine, I think." He could see the shock and incomprehension in her face. "And one for yourself if you wish it." He liked Jane. He liked her openness, the generous proportion of her breasts, her moon face framed by auburn hair that always crept untidily from beneath a lawn coif, the way she carried herself. She had come to London from the county of Essex, the eldest daughter of a family of twelve girls and no boys, and she had been with him two years now. She was easy to live with, but he knew this was not the perfect position for her; she was hungry for a husband and would find none here in this house, unless she took a liking for Boltfoot Cooper, which was about as probable as a man growing wings and flying. She was accustomed to a big, noisy, peasant farm household, full of shouting and tears on a daily basis; this house was quiet and contemplative, with just the three of them.

There were times when Shakespeare wondered whether she entertained hopes she might be his one day. Yes, he liked to gaze upon her body. What man would not? But a marriage had to be based on more than common lust. He would tire of her and they would resent each other.

He started picking up papers. He wondered if Topcliffe had been looking for the paper he had found near Blanche Howard's body. The constable's runner or the bellman had probably told him that Shakespeare had ordered them burned; perhaps he suspected that a sample had been kept.

Later, as Shakespeare sat with his wine, having cleared up the papers and righted the furniture — the damage to the paneling and boards would have to be repaired by a joiner on the morrow — Harry Slide arrived. He looked disheveled and slipped in quietly with none of his characteristic fanfare.

"Well, Harry?"

"Not at all well, Mr. Shakespeare. I have not felt so bad in all my life."

"Are you ill, Harry? Sit with me by the fire and take some warming hippocras."

As Slide seated himself awkwardly on a bench by the fire, shivering, his face turned. By the candlelight Shakespeare saw that it was bruised and bloody. He looked like the loser in a Bartholomew Fair bout of the heavyweights. His nose was cut and his eye blackened, while his expensively barbered fair hair, normally swept back to good effect, now looked ragged. His neat beard was rusty with caked blood. "Harry, by the Lord, what has happened to you?"

"I was set upon, Mr. Shakespeare. My purse was cut from me. He came at me from behind. Before I could draw my sword I was flat down on the ice, being kicked in the face. Look at my clothes." Slide pulled off his cape, which was relatively unscathed, to reveal his fine yellow doublet, torn and muddy.

Shakespeare rose and called to Jane to bring warm water and towels to wash his wounds. "Where did this happen, Harry?"

"Holborn. I'd been in a few ordinaries and taverns, asking the gossip. It was gullish of me to be caught like that. . . ."

Jane returned with water and began washing Slide's face. Shakespeare poured him a large goblet of spiced wine.

"At least I discovered where to find Walstan Glebe," Slide continued. "It seems he has a press not far from where I was drinking. Fleet Lane. I'm told he's not always there — the fox has many lairs — but he could be about tomorrow morning, early."

"Are you all right, Harry?"

Slide sipped the wine. "Well, my head feels as if the headsman had taken an axe to it and caught it a glancing blow, but I'll survive."

"Yes, Harry, please do survive. Stay here tonight. Jane will make you up a bed."

"I shall take you up on your offer, Mr. Shakespeare, but first I have other things to tell you."

"Yes?"

"It may be nothing. But I was told of a curious dinner at Marshalsea two nights past. Two priests were there, already in custody, and they had four visitors and together they broke bread and took fine wine and one of the priests said Mass."

Shakespeare had heard of such things happening before. The Marshalsea and the Clink seemed very easygoing with their captive priests. It was not something that concerned him greatly. "And do you know who any of these people were?"

Slide smiled and immediately regretted it; too painful. "Well," he said, "the priests were not important. Piggott and Plummer. Piggott is a poor creature who deserves hanging. Plummer is my source. He long since discarded Romish ways, but it pays him to stay in prison; the Romans give him money for food and I give him more for information."

"What of the others?"

"Three gentlewomen. All of them from known Romish families — Lady Frances Browne, a young girl called Anne Bellamy, and the Lady Tanahill."

Shakespeare was surprised. "Lady Tanahill? She is living dangerously, considering her husband is in the Tower. And the Bellamy girl has already lost two brothers to the rope for association with the Babington plotters." His mind went back, briefly, to the previous autumn, when Anthony Babington and others were executed for plotting to kill the Queen.

Slide nodded. "But it is the sixth and last member of this happy band that most interests me. His name was Cotton and he is a Jesuit priest."

Shakespeare's brow creased. "Another Jesuit?"

"Yes, Mr. Shakespeare. Another Jesuit. Most assuredly, from what Plummer says."

How, Shakespeare wondered, had *a Jesuit* slipped in without Walsingham's knowledge? His spies in Rome and the other English colleges abroad knew the names and movements of all the English Jesuits, or so it was believed. Walsingham had known Southwell and Garnet were coming to England even before the two priests set sail from France. This was grim news if it meant there were now *three* Jesuits at large in England. Walsingham would not be happy to hear that. Even less happy would be the Queen. She did not like Jesuit priests at large in her realm.

"There is, of course, one other possibility," Slide said through the corner of his split lip. "It occurred to me that Cotton is unlikely to be his real name. He may, perhaps, be the very man we are looking

155

for: Robert Southwell."

"What did he look like?"

"I am told he was well dressed. Golden hair, lively gray eyes, a confident air. And I do know that this Southwell is said to be a handsome man. A priest told me that when he was at Douai, everyone called him the 'Beautiful English Youth.' "

"Well, Harry, it is imperative we find out the truth of this."

Slide rose painfully to his feet and rubbed his neck. "There was one other thing, Mr. Shakespeare . . ."

"Yes?"

"The man who kicked me, as he was leaving, he said something."

"What did he say?"

"It was difficult to make out. My ears were ringing, but I thought he said, 'There's more where that came from, Slide.' I'm sure he said 'Slide.' How did he know my name? If he was just a cutpurse, Mr. Shakespeare, how did he know my name?"

CHAPTER 12

Shakespeare and Slide took horse and were across London and through the City wall by the New Gate just before first light. Their destination was Fleet Lane, where they hoped to catch Walstan Glebe off guard.

"Over there," Slide said at last. "That's the place."

Snow was falling. The horses' hooves were silent on the empty road. As they stopped, Shakespeare jumped down nimbly from his gray mare. He handed the reins to Harry Slide, who had awakened feeling stiff and battered. He looked haggard but still insisted on going along. "You wait here with the horses, Harry. I'll go in alone."

"Call out if you need me."

"Don't worry. I will."

It was a tall wood-frame house with an exaggerated overhanging second story that blanked out much of the rising eastern light. There was no sort of lock, so Shakespeare went straight in. The entrance hall was empty. He went through to another, larger room, where he found a printing press, surrounded by boxes of type sorts. The press was a rickety device that stood against one wall to the height of a man. Shakespeare had a pretty good idea how it worked; the lead type would be set letter by letter into forms along with woodcut pictures, on an easel, like an A-shaped two-sided lectern. It would then be tightened into each form with quoins — wedges — and inked before being inserted into the bottom of the press, where paper would be placed above it. The press would be screwed down a sheet at a time for printing. Nearby lay a pile of broadsheets entitled *The London Informer,* already printed, the ink dried, and waiting to be distributed. Shakespeare looked at the papers and found himself stifling a laugh.

"Amazing Sea Monster in Thames," said the first line. Underneath, it said, *"Behemoth is evil omen, avows soothsayer."*

Clearly, Walstan Glebe had a refined knowledge of his customers' reading requirements, but the printer had missed what Shakespeare believed to be the tastiest news of the day: that Mary, Queen of Scots was about to be relieved of her head.

Shakespeare climbed the steps to the

second floor, where he found a shut door to a chamber. From outside he heard a chorus of snoring. He unhooked the latch and went in to find a large, canopied bed with what looked like a solid mass of bodies in it. Stepping farther into the shuttered room, he could tell that there were three people in the bed — two female and one male. The man was in the middle and most of the snoring was his, although his friends were contributing plenty of noise, too. Shakespeare leaned over one of the females, a buxom doxy lying on her back with her mouth sagging open and her hair splayed out in a dark frame to her face, and shook the man. He opened an eye groggily.

"What is it?" the man managed to say.

"Get up. Queen's business."

"Queen who?"

"Queen Elizabeth, and if you don't like the idea of a day in the pillory, I suggest you move. Now!"

The man struggled up immediately and tried to get his bearings. "What is this?"

"My name is John Shakespeare and I am here on Queen's business. Get out of bed, Glebe."

The man yawned and scratched his head. "You've got the wrong person. My name's Felbrigg."

Shakespeare leaned across the bed again and grabbed the man's thick, tousled hair, wrenching it upward. An angry red *L* was revealed on his forehead.

"*L* for *Liar,* Glebe. You were branded for stealing the work of other men. I know all about you."

Shakespeare released his hair. Glebe shrugged his bare shoulders and grinned like a grammar school boy found out for copying a fellow scholar's work. "All right, all right. Give me time to cover myself."

The two women were stirring. "What's going on?" one of them mumbled.

"Nothing. Go back to sleep."

"You've woken me up now, sweeting."

"Well then, get your clothes and piss off. And take your sister with you."

"You're a real charmer."

Glebe turned to Shakespeare. "I'm sorry, Mr. Shakespeare. A rough night and strong ale, I'm afraid." He was out of bed and had started pulling on a shirt and breeches. He nodded back toward the two women. "Not bad for a cold night in February, those two. I can fix you up if you're interested."

Shakespeare was in no mood for frivolity. "Come downstairs, Glebe. You're in trouble."

In the press room, Glebe stood with his

shoulders drooping, scratching his balls.

"A case of the French welcome, Glebe?"

"Me and everyone else I know, Mr. Shakespeare."

"That might say a lot about the sort of people you know." Shakespeare gestured toward the press. "I take it this has been licensed by the Council through Stationers' Hall."

"Of course, Mr. Shakespeare."

"You have been branded a liar, Glebe, and you are still a liar. If you don't cooperate with me fully and unreservedly, this press will be closed down and your broadsheets destroyed. Not only that, but I will bring the full weight of the law down on your head for sedition. Which, to my mind, is another word for treason."

"Mr. Shakespeare, this is a gossip sheet, harmless news for the people of London. There is nothing treasonable here. Look, sir." Glebe held up a copy of his pamphlet. "The whole world wants to know about this great fish. It is the talk of the city. What harm is there here?"

Shakespeare tore the broadsheet from his hand, crumpled it into a ball, and tossed it to the floor. "I'm not interested in your whale story, Glebe. It's the murder of Lady Blanche Howard that interests me. Where did you get your information for this pamphlet?" He pulled the offending broadsheet from his doublet.

Glebe suddenly looked worried. He spread his hands beseechingly. He was a man of about thirty, short, with a pinched face, sharp teeth, clever eyes, and a knowing smile. But now his brow furrowed. "It is the talk of the town, Mr. Shakespeare. Every tavern, inn, and ordinary from Westminster to Whitechapel is alive with word about the Lady Blanche. A tragic tale, to be certain, sir. I merely listened and wrote down what I heard."

"There is a line in the broadsheet blaming the Jesuit priest Southwell for the murder with what you describe as 'cross, relic, and blade.' What does that mean and where did you get your information?"

Glebe looked past Shakespeare as if he could not meet his eyes. "Why, Mr. Shakespeare, again it is the gossip that this lewd Popish beast is the killer. Surely you have heard this yourself?"

"I may have heard the suggestion, but I know of no evidence. That is beside the point: what do the words 'cross, relic, and blade' mean?"

Glebe hesitated, as if he did not entirely understand the question. He seemed to be sweating, despite the cold of the morning. "Mr. Shakespeare?"

"The cross, man. The relic. What information do you have about these things?"

"Why, sir, I have no information about such things. I meant them only in the sense of a metaphor; that is, they are symbols of the devilish Roman practices at work here. What could you have thought I meant, Mr. Shakespeare?"

Shakespeare was becoming increasingly irritated. He did not believe a word Glebe said; the man was as slippery as a pan of slow-worms. "And what of this imputation against Lady Douglass and Lady Frances, that they do not mourn their cousin's murder?"

"That's what I heard, Mr. Shakespeare."

"It is tittle-tattle. You have already been branded. For listening to such idle talk, you can expect to lose your ears. And for repeating it, I could easily recommend you have your tongue pulled out by its root and fed to the kites. I have heard enough from you, Glebe. We will continue these inquiries at Her Majesty's pleasure. You are under arrest. Come with me."

Glebe put up his hands, palms facing Shakespeare as if he would push him away. "Tarry, sir. Just say what you want to know and I will tell you true. I pledge it."

"You know what I want, Glebe. I want to know who mentioned a relic and cross to you. I want to know who mentioned the name Robert Southwell to you. Furnish me now with this information or tonight you will sleep locked away with thieves and murderers and may be questioned under duress."

Glebe's narrow eyes were flickering. Shakespeare knew he had him where he wanted him: desperate and afraid.

"Mr. Shakespeare, I want to help you but what can I say? These are just things I heard in a tavern booth. Idle talk among apprentices and merchants, sir. The lifeblood of London. Everyone wants the news. I could sell *The London Informer* twice over, sir."

"Glebe, I don't believe you. You're coming with me."

"All right, I'll come. But let me attire myself properly first. It's bitter out there."

"Just get your cloak and boots."

Shakespeare heard a low whistling behind him and spun around. The two wenches from Glebe's bed, sisters if he were to be believed, were standing at the bottom of the steps not three feet from him. They did look alike, as sisters would. They were healthy, plump girls, and they were both naked from head to toe, thrusting their goodly-sized chests out toward him.

Shakespeare stood looking at them a moment too long. They *were* alluring in a base kind of way, and he was stirred as any man might be. He turned back just in time to see Glebe making off through the back room. Shakespeare stepped forward to pursue him but found the two women either side of him, rubbing themselves against him, trying to kiss him, holding his arms, restraining him, tickling his stones through his breeches. Angrily he pushed them aside and forged ahead after Glebe. But the printer was gone.

The two women cackled with laughter.

"There will be a price to pay for this," Shakespeare told the women in a fury, and immediately felt foolish.

"A price, love? We're free. Anytime you like." Again, they fell about laughing and Shakespeare realized it was a lost cause. He would send men later to break up the press, but there was little else to do here. The women disappeared upstairs with much hilarity, presumably to get dressed, while Shakespeare searched the room. He found a print of the poems of Aretino and some woodcut prints illustrating its bawdy verses.

There was also a pile of almanacs containing the preposterous predictions of the French fraud Nostradamus and an account of Sir Walter Raleigh's recent venture into Roanoake in the New World. Shakespeare took copies of each of these, along with the most recent *London Informer* broadsheet, and carried them outside to where Slide was waiting with the mounts.

"Was he there, Mr. Shakespeare?"

"Don't ask, Harry. Don't ask."

CHAPTER 13

Job Mallinson sat in the court room at Stationers' Hall by St. Paul's and looked out of the tall window onto the company's bleak winter gardens. He held his hand to his bandaged jaw as if somehow this could relieve his pain of the toothache that had afflicted him all night. In other times, when his head did not throb like a smithy's hammer beating iron on an anvil, he was known for his good humor and amusing tales. Now he simply sat and shivered and wished the day away. He had decided to come here because he could no longer bear his wife's ministrations. She had given him salves for his wounded mouth, but they did little to help and, anyway, her talking doubled the pain. A walk to Stationers' Hall through the brisk air seemed the best way to take his mind off his predicament.

A liveried manservant came in and spoke with him. He hesitated a few moments, then nodded in assent, and the servant disappeared, only to reappear a minute later with John Shakespeare.

Mallinson rose to greet him and the two men shook hands. They had met before, first at a Guildhall banquet celebrating the setting sail of John Davis's expedition in quest of the northwest passage, and then two or three times since on state business when seditious materials had been discovered.

"I am sorry to see you have some ague about the face, Master Mallinson," Shakespeare said, indicating the bandage.

"Tooth," Mallinson said, as well as he could.

Shakespeare, realizing that Mallinson would find conversation difficult, came straight to the point of his visit. "Mr. Mallinson, I need information about some newfound prints that have been discovered." He held up the scrap of paper. "Is it possible to identify which press has been responsible for printing this?" Then he held out a copy of Walstan Glebe's broadsheet. "And could it have been printed by the same press that produced this?"

Mallinson examined the papers. As Warden of the Assistants with the Stationers' Company, he was steeped in all things to do with printing, yet he knew his limitations.

In a faint voice, he said, "Yes, I think it is possible, but I am not the man to help you. You need one with more expertise in such matters." He winced as he spoke, and a trickle of blood seeped from the corner of his mouth.

"Is there someone here who might be able to help me then, Master Mallinson?"

Mallinson shook his head, then closed his eyes. He breathed deeply, steadying himself to speak once more. "No, Mr. Shakespeare, not here. But there is a man who might be of assistance. His name is Thomas Woode. He is a book merchant and an agent of Christophe Plantin's printworks of Antwerp. Woode has made much money by his printing of playbills, for which he possesses the monopoly. He has a house close by the Thames at Dowgate. You cannot miss it, sir, because it is scaffolded. If anyone can help you, Thomas can. He is a good man."

"Thank you, Master Mallinson. And I wish you well of your tooth. One more thing: get your men to break up an illegal press in Fleet Lane. It is run by a scurrilous fellow called Glebe."

Mallinson attempted to smile, but it was more like a grimace. "Oh yes, Mr. Shakespeare. I know of Walstan Glebe. We have been looking for him for quite a while. It will be a pleasure for our men to break his press into a thousand pieces."

Starling Day and her cousin Alice were drinking and singing in the Bel Savage. They were certain they had covered their tracks. Half an hour earlier, in Cogg's bawdy house, they had given a piece of their mind to Parsimony Field and had sauntered out, laughing and jeering. Now they were buying drinks for the off-duty girls and anyone else who happened to be in the tavern.

Parsimony, who was not only Cogg's best girl but also ran the whorehouse on his behalf, had been struck dumb by the audacity of Starling and Alice. None of the girls had ever dared tell her to fuck off before, and if they had they would have been beaten senseless for their pains; Parsimony was tall and strong enough to hold her own against a lot of men, let alone women, and she had the backing of Cogg. But she had been caught off guard by the pair of them, Starling and Alice, talking to her like that. After regaining her composure, she followed them into the long bar of the Bel Savage and watched them getting more and more drunk by the minute.

"Come on, Arsey-Parsey, come and have

a drink with us," Alice called, catching sight of her. "I'll buy you a beaker of nightshade cordial, ducks." And she thrust two fingers in the air as a salute.

For a moment, Parsimony considered going up to the pair at the bar and dragging them by the hair back to the stew. But she wasn't sure she could manage it with both of them, and she didn't want to risk humiliation in front of the other girls. Cogg would expect her to act, however, so she must do something. He wouldn't want to lose two whores, that was certain.

As she watched, the taproom became more and more raucous. In unison, Starling and Alice turned their backs on Parsimony, lifted their skirts, bent forward and exposed themselves full-on in her direction, then farted and collapsed onto the sawdust-strewn floor, laughing. When they got up again, Parsimony noticed something she hadn't seen before: Starling and Alice were both wearing jewelry — necklaces and bracelets — which looked very much like gold, not the gaudy base metal that whores usually wore. Parsimony knew then that she had to get to Cogg straightway. He would want to know about this. There was something bad here, a stink as bad as a basket of six-day-dead mackerel. Slipping out of the tavern, she gathered up her skirts and, though not dressed for the cold weather, ran to Cogg's place in Cow Lane.

He wasn't there and he hadn't locked up. Parsimony was puzzled. Cogg never went out; with his great girth, he couldn't move. She went up to his bedchamber. There was a platter of almost-finished food, chicken bones or something, and the bedclothes were awry. She sat down on the bed and tried to gather her thoughts. He *should* be here. She couldn't remember the last time he went out anywhere. He couldn't even make it to the whorehouse by the Bel Savage these days, which was why the girls came to him. He had slowed down a lot this past year. Something *must* have happened to him.

Parsimony twiddled the ends of her pretty hair in her fingers. She had been with Cogg since her bricklayer husband ran off to be a player and writer of plays when she was sixteen. That was seven years ago. She had liked the life of a whore from the start; swiving for a living seemed like easy money and, at times, enjoyable, too. She liked the mariners best, the ones just returned from long voyages; they were free with their pay, liked a laugh, and had strong, weather-hardened bodies. More to the point, she and

Cogg had a good understanding. In return for managing the stew, he let her keep twice as much as the other girls. She reckoned by working for him she could have enough set by to start her own trugging house before she was twenty-five.

She stood up and began looking around in earnest and soon found his body downstairs, packed into a large barrel that had contained hides and furs from the Baltic lands. The skins had been pulled out and shoved into a pile that looked at first sight like a great sleeping bear. The barrel had been tipped on its side so that Cogg's three-hundred-weight corpse could be pushed inside. It didn't fit; it was only because the opening was turned toward the wall that she had not spotted his blubbery naked feet immediately. It was clearly not a method of concealment that was intended to last long.

So they had killed him. The dirty, cross-biting, light-heeled trugs. They had probably robbed him, too. Well, she'd do for them. And she knew how.

The question was: where *was* Cogg's fortune? Had they found it all and stolen it, or was some of it still here? She spent a few minutes searching, but found nothing, then hurried back to the Bel Savage for fear that they would have skipped away.

She threw open the door to the taproom. It was thick with wood smoke and the fumes of ale. Starling Day and Alice were insensible from drink, snoring on the taproom floor, their dresses awry and their limbs splayed. The other girls stood around drinking with their money and making merry with some traders.

For a moment, Parsimony stood there unnoticed. Then one of the girls spotted her and nudged her neighbor. There was a sudden silence as they ceased their carousing and looked at Parsimony fearfully, sensing the anger in her eyes. She strode over and slapped one of the girls hard on the face, then told them all to deal with Starling and Alice sharpish. "Get them back to the vaulting house and stand over them," she said in a cold voice that she knew would be instantly obeyed. "Don't let them out of your sight. I want a word with them two foul cozeners when they're awake. Break the ice on the cask in the yard and chuck a pail of water over them. It'll be nicely chilled."

CHAPTER 14

"Have you seen that play yet?" Denis Picket asked over a gage of booze in the Falcon post inn at Fotheringhay.

"No," Simon Bull replied. "What was it called again?"

"*Tamburlaine.* A good lark, Bully. Lots of fighting. Lots of laughs."

"Where's it on, then?"

"The Curtain, Bully."

"Oh, right. And it's *Mr.* Bull to you, Denis."

"Sorry, Mr. Bull."

"So what's it about?"

"Turks, I think. Lots of battles and killing."

"Not for me then, Denis. I don't like all that bloodshed they put in their plays these days." Bull glanced around the room and noticed the eyes of the regulars turning away quickly, as if they had been caught staring at him. He was used to that and didn't give it a second thought, but he was worried about his assistant. Denis Picket was young, good at his job at the shambles by all accounts and he'd done his share of rope tricks, but he'd never had a job as big as this one. He didn't want to make him any more jumpy than he already was.

"Where's Digby staying, Mr. Bull?"

"Up at Apthorpe, with the gentry. Mr. Secretary wanted us to go there, but old Mildmay wasn't having it. Thinks we're too common. But I can tell you, Denis," and here he reduced his voice to a whisper, "I've lopped types every bit as noble as him. We're all one when our heads are on the block."

"So what you done with the axe, then, Bully?" Picket asked at last.

Bull put the index finger of his very large right hand to his lips. "It's in my trunk, Denis, but keep it down. Don't want to worry the locals. And it's Mr. Bull. I won't remind you again."

"Sorry, Mr. Bull."

Less than a day earlier, Simon Bull had been at his house outside Bishopsgate when Walsingham's man Anthony Hall arrived with news of the commission. There had been a bit of haggling over the price, but in the end they had agreed on ten pounds in gold, plus travel costs and good board and lodging for Bull and his assistant. There had been some dispute over the usual access to clothes and jewelry removed from the body of the intended, but Bull had stood firm and Hall had finally agreed they could decide about such things when the time came. No point in upsetting the headsman before he had done his hideous work, was there?

"Now, Denis, how about one more quart while I gets some food inside me? Then it's bed and a good night's sleep. We got to be up early, son."

"All right, Mr. Bull."

"Good lad. I fancy a couple of pigeons and a good bit of beef. Would you mind seeing if they can do something like that for us?"

"Certainly, Mr. Bull."

"And some good fresh bread and butter to mop up the sauce would go down well, too."

"Yes, Mr. Bull. I'll see to it."

Starling Day was awakened by the sting of Parsimony Field's hand across her face. *Slap, slap,* back and forth from side to side, hard.

She recoiled from the blows. "Please, Parsey, lay off," she begged, her voice weak but desperate.

"I'll lay off when you tell me where the gold is, Starling Day." Parsimony hit her again. "You're in trouble up to your scrawny chicken neck."

Starling was bound to the four corners of a bare straw pallet on a wooden bedstead. Her head was spinning from the drink. Her backbone against the unforgiving wood was causing her agony. She felt the bile rising, turned her head to one side, away from Parsimony, and vomited.

"If that'd gone over me, I'd have killed you."

Starling closed her eyes. In her boozy delusion, she was back in Strelley, tied to the bedpost, being beaten by Edward. She had thought that was all behind her. Gradually the events of the night before came back into focus. They had hidden the gold and jewels (except for a few necklaces and bracelets to pretty themselves up) and then gone back to the bawdy house to collect Alice's few pitiful things. Something in them, some rash boldness, had made them give Parsimony Field a piece of their mind and then go to the Bel Savage for one last drink before disappearing forever. After all, why not? Arsey-Parsey had no idea what had been going on at Cow Lane, and she couldn't restrain the both of them. But the drink had taken hold and now they were paying the price.

Starling wanted to clutch her beating head, but she couldn't because her wrists were tied to the bedposts. Why had they stayed for that one last drink that turned into fucking twenty? Half a day ago the world was looking good; now it was a blocked-up jakes of a place again. They had to get out of here and quick.

Parsimony's fist came smashing down in the center of her face. Starling just managed to turn her head sideways before the blow struck or her nose would have been broken for certain. But it hurt. It really hurt. Parsimony hit like a man.

"All right!" she screamed.

"All right what?"

"All right, I'll show you where the fucking gold is."

"Yeah? And what fucking gold would that be?"

"You know what gold. Cogg's gold. We'll split it three ways. You, me, and Alice."

Parsimony sat back at the end of the hard bed. "Let me think now. Is that a good deal for me? By my reckoning you'll be lucky if I don't turn you in. Because if I did, your chicken neck would be in the halter at Tyburn scaffold before morning and I'd be there cheering the hangman on. The way I see it, you owe me, Starling Day. You owe me your very life. So it's three-quarters for me. You and Alice can share the rest any way you like."

"But I never killed Cogg!"

"No? Looks like it to me and I reckon the Justice might agree. Dead body found in barrel; deceased's worldly wealth found in possession of Starling Day. How's that going to sound to a jury?"

"All right, all right. Half to you. But you won't get nothing if you turn me in or if you do for me. Now just untie me. Please, Parsimony. And for what it's worth, I *didn't* do it. I didn't kill Cogg. But I saw who done it."

"I'll think about that, Starling Day. I will. I'll give that a lot of thought. But first I'm going to get meself some nice breakfast. How does that sound to you?" Parsimony stood and turned toward the door.

Starling panicked. The thought of being left here like this was too awful. "No — wait. Why don't we just go and collect the treasure now, eh? There's loads of it, Parsey, plenty for all of us. It's like he plundered a Spanish galleon or something."

"Yeah? Let me think about it."

Starling wanted to be sick again. She writhed on the bed.

"I know," said Parsimony. "I've got a better idea. Why don't you tell me where the gold is and I'll go and get it? Then when I've got it, I can untie you. Does that sound fair?"

"Parsimony, I'm begging you! I can't stand this a moment longer. I'll be fit for Bedlam if you leave me like this."

"Simple then, isn't it, dove? The sooner you tell me where to look, the sooner you'll be a free woman."

Starling Day may have been at the end of her tether but she knew that if she told Parsimony how to get Cogg's jewels, she'd never let her go. She'd either kill her herself or lay information with the constable to set her on to the road to the gallows.

"You got to set me free first, Parsey. I can't tell you nothing tied up like this. And where's my cousin?"

"Oh, don't worry about her, my dove. She's having a lovely sleep upstairs."

The words chilled Starling. "You haven't done nothing to her, have you, Parsey?"

Parsimony's mouth was set hard. "What if I had? It'd mean more for you and me, wouldn't it?"

■ ■ ■ ■

"Do you know what, Bully . . ."

"Mr. Bull, please, Denis."

"Do you know what, Mr. Bull? Last summer I worked killing dogs when the weather got hot."

"I didn't know that, Denis."

"I hated that line of work, Mr. Bull. We rounded 'em up every day by order of the City corporation and then did away with them any way we could: drowning, strangling, cutting their throats, smacking their heads between stones. I understand it's necessary because they carries the plague, but I didn't like killing dogs."

"A job's a job, Denis."

"You're right, of course, but I was brought up with dogs. Good creatures. I always trained 'em good, too, to get rabbits and hares for the pot."

Simon Bull looked at the boy and shook his head. They were dressed the part now, standing all in black with butcher's aprons and masks, strong like proper headsmen, their muscles rippling. Bull's enormous hands rested gently on the haft of the long-handled axe. He knew he was a terrifying sight; he had stood long hours in front of

182

the looking glass perfecting the pose. Best that way; if the intended wasn't intimidated, all sorts of trouble could ensue. Once he'd had to chase a young noble all round the scaffold, trying to catch him, like a farm-wife after a fowl. A nasty business, that; bits of body all over the place, blood everywhere. Today would be easier.

They were at the side of the black velvet-draped platform. It had been hastily erected, the hammering reverberating around the hall these past two days in preparation for this blood-drenched little ritual.

"We've been here more than three hours now, Mr. Bull. I'd have had more breakfast if I'd known I'd still be here at ten o'clock."

"We'll sup again soon enough, Denis."

There was a murmur and they turned. Mary, the Scots devil herself, came in, dressed in black velvet, her head held high. Behind her, weeping, walked six chosen attendants in pairs, three men and three women.

"One of the dogs, a mastiff it was, looked at me with these sad eyes, Mr. Bull —"

"Shh, Denis, not now," Bull said in a low voice as the murmur of the two hundred people in the hall subsided. They were a strange, solemn bunch, some shuffling awkwardly, others standing stock-still.

Steam rose from their rain-drenched riding clothes as the fire in the hearth roared out its scorching heat. Their eyes were all fixed to the front, straining to make out the features of the black-clad woman against the black backdrop of the stage as she climbed the steps. Armor-clad halberdiers guarded her and supported her at each elbow. She took her place in the black-draped chair that had been placed there just for her. Bull's eyes followed her. He didn't look at her face but rather her apparel and the things she carried. There would be good money there. She held an ivory cross and at her throat was a chain of beads attached to a cross of gold. At her waist, she wore a rosary. Her clothes were dark and somber, but they had quality and would fetch him a good price. The black velvet gown could be cut into small fragments, squares of an inch or two, to be sold as relics. On her head she wore a cap of white cambric, trailing a white linen veil. Such things would sell very well. Even her kerchief, a burnished yellow that seemed to glint in the firelight, would fetch a pound or two. His man in Cheapside would pay him a pretty penny; the Papists would give well over the true value to get their hands on such items.

Mr. Beale, the Clerk to the Council, who

had traveled up here to Northamptonshire with Bull, Picket, and Walsingham's servant George Digby, read out the warrant citing the condemned's conviction for high treason and conspiracy against the person of Her Majesty. Then Shrewsbury took over the proceedings. "Madam, you hear what we are commanded to do?"

"Do your duty," Mary replied in a quiet voice that quavered only slightly. "I die for my religion."

Denis had an itch on his nose and scratched it. His back ached from all this standing around and his stomach was a hollow pit that needed filling. He just wished they would cease all the chatter and get on with it, but then some vicar or bishop got up and started speaking, while the condemned droned on in Latin.

At last Mary slipped from her chair onto her knees, and her rising voice cut the Dean of Peterborough short. "I shall die as I have lived, in the true and Holy Catholic faith. All your prayers can avail me but little." She held her ivory cross above her head and called on God to convert England to the true faith and for Catholics to stand firm.

She seemed disinclined to cease her ramblings, praying for England, for Elizabeth, for the Church of Rome. Bull nudged Picket and spoke quietly in his ear. "This is it, lad. Let's speed things up a bit."

Together they stepped forward and knelt down in front of Mary in the time-honored tradition and asked for forgiveness for what they were about to do. She readily gave them absolution. "I forgive you with all my heart," she said firmly. "For I hope this death shall give me an end to all my troubles."

Bull rose from his knees and started to remove her gown. She shied away from him, then seemed to laugh, maiden-like, saying, "Let me do this. I understand this business better than you. I never had such a *groom* in my chamber."

Bull backed away. No matter. If the lady wanted to be coy with him, that was her choice. The clothes would all come to him anyway. Two of her three ladies took over now, fluttering and weeping as their dainty hands undid her stays and removed her black gown to reveal her satin underbodice and kirtle, all crimson like a wound. There seemed to be a gasp from the witnesses of the hall, but perhaps it was the soughing of the wind in the chimney.

Removing the gold cross and beads from about her neck, she asked Bull whether she might be allowed to give it to her maid and that he would be paid more than their value in gold. He shook his head and prized the crucifix from her fingers, placing it in his shoe for safekeeping. Then he took her ivory cross, too, and her rosary and handed them to Picket.

Unbidden, as if suddenly deciding she wanted no more delay to the proceedings, Mary gestured to her ladies and one of them bound her eyes with her kerchief, with a knot at her neck, a target for the axe. She stretched forward and rested her chin on her hands, over the edge of the block. Bull nodded to Picket, who stepped forward and pulled her hands away so that her arms stretched out in front of her, held gently in his.

She was speaking now, Latin once more, first a psalm and then, over and over, she commended her soul to God's hands: *"In manus tuas, Domine, commendo spiritum meum."*

Bull raised the heavy, double-edged axe high above his head. It hovered there, at the top of its swing, for an eternity, then fell in a great arc into the back of her skull. The sound of sharp steel cracking bone, like the thud of the butcher's cleaver, shattered the silence. Bull looked down through the slits in his mask at the gory mess below. Shit, he'd missed her neck. Quickly, he raised the axe again and brought it down once more. This time his aim was true and the blood spurted forth in a fountain.

He knelt down beside her to reach into the gore to pick up her severed head but saw that it still wasn't severed. Gristly tendons still attached it to the body. With the edge of his axe he sawed through them, then clasped his blood-greasy left hand around her hair and held it up high for all to see.

"This is the head of Mary Stuart!" he bellowed. Only it wasn't; it was her auburn wig. Her head, all gray and shaven, had rolled forward across the platform. Luckily, no one could see behind his mask, for now he closed his eyes in the closest thing Simon Bull ever came to embarrassment. At last he remembered his lines and took a deep breath. "God save the Queen," he said with conviction.

It had been a bad day for Simon Bull and it got worse. As they were clearing up and stripping the body, the clothes were taken from him to be burned. He was deprived, too, of the crosses and beads he had taken from her. Walsingham would decide what would happen to them in due course. When Bull, feeling cheated, protested that the effects were his right to keep, someone muttered about "not having any relics left to make a martyr of that bloody woman."

Finally, there was the dog, a little terrier, all spattered with gore, that scuttled out from the dead woman's clothes as they were cut from her body to be taken outside and burned in the courtyard. Picket's eyes lighted on it first and his masked face broke into a smile. "Hello," he said, lifting it up.

"Put it down," Bull said sullenly. "If we can't keep a cross, they won't let us keep a dog, will they?"

Reluctantly, Denis Picket put the dog down and it ran, whimpering, to the now naked corpse of its mistress. Picket eyed it with something akin to yearning. "You know that mastiff I was telling you about, Mr. Bull? I couldn't kill it. Still got him at home and a fine creature he is. I call him Bully, after you —"

"Well, then, Denis, you should have called him *Mr.* Bull, shouldn't you, lad?"

"You're right, Mr. Bull, I'll do that. From now on, I'll call him Mr. Bull."

CHAPTER 15

Bonfires lit the damp night sky. On every street corner and in every tavern, minstrels played merry tunes and people braved the rain to dance, drink, and rejoice. The murdering, adulterous witch of Scotland was dead. After nineteen long years, England was free of her malign presence. By midnight, the pitch black sky was howling, the flames of the bonfires fanned into a firestorm before finally dying down to sodden embers in the early hours when the revelers sank, drunk, into their beds.

Thomas Woode was shaking. While others sang and danced and drank, he sat alone at his table. And when the rest of London was snoring, he stayed awake. He had bitten the last of his nails to the quick and was now nicking pieces of the hard, stubby flesh at the end of each finger. In the gray rain of dawn, his white teeth glimmered in the light of three good beeswax candles, each burnt down to an inch. Their flames flickered and leapt briskly in the drafts that rushed up from the river and in through the gaps at the edge of the leaded lights in his private office in Dowgate. Rain slapped at the window in squally gusts.

This night past he had done without a fire; it would have been improper for him to have warmth when the butchered body of Mary Stuart lay cold in a box. He tore off his ruff and hurled it across the room. He picked up a quill, sliced the tip with his desk knife, and dipped it in the inkhorn. Hurriedly he wrote onto a scrap of parchment, then scratched the words out again. He needed to compose a business letter to Christophe Plantin in the Gulden Passer, the great Antwerp printers and bookworks where so much of his own wealth emanated. The words would not come. He was bone-tired; this was not a time for mundane business dealings.

He heard a scurry, a knock at the oak door. "Come in."

It was the governess, Catherine Marvell. Woode was wealthy, a merchant of the class that now owned London, but he did not keep a big household. It simply wasn't safe to do so; not with his secrets. Maidservants came in during the day to see to the housework and cooking, as did carpenters and masons for the construction, but at night it was just him, Catherine, the children, and their two guests, the Jesuit priests Cotton and Herrick, who wore the clothes of serving men in case anyone should call on the house. It was *their* presence that endangered his family.

Thomas Woode knew that everyone in the house was in mortal danger, and it troubled him. Harboring priests sent from abroad amounted to treason in the eyes of the law. London was full of spies and betrayers who could track the priests here at any time and inform the heavy-booted pursuivants of their whereabouts. But Thomas Woode was obligated to accommodate these men; it had been his wife Margaret's dying wish that he bring up their children in the true faith. They needed instruction and they must hear the Mass regularly. Margaret also wished him to support the persecuted Church in whatever way he could. He had agreed to her requests because he loved her and because she was dying. How could he refuse her in such circumstances? Yet he regretted it every day. He would *never* have taken this path of his own accord. There were times, if truth be told, when he doubted his own belief in God.

There were practicalities to be observed. Yes, Cotton and Herrick could come and go as they pleased; when they went out they would wear the garb of tradesmen or gentlemen. When they were at home, they remained hidden by day. Only by night, when the household staff had gone home, did the priests venture out of the room they shared to eat and converse with the family, dressing as servants.

"Catherine, it is good to see you."

"Master."

"A sad day."

"Yes, master."

"We must take comfort in the certain knowledge that she is in a better place."

Thomas Woode had never met Mary Stuart, yet he had revered her. Yes, his faith sometimes faltered, yet he was certain that if there were to be a religion, the Roman Church of Mary was the only possible way; he saw the Anglican church of Elizabeth and her ministers as a sacrilegious imposter, a false religion, a manifestation of power rather than spirituality. When he imagined Mary of Scots, he pictured her with the face of his late beloved wife. He smiled wanly at Catherine. "These are bad days. The people sing and dance, but the ports have all been closed down and the prisons shut to all but official visitors. Pursuivants march the streets, searching and questioning anyone they don't like the look of. Even the ordinary people play their role, pelting stones at anyone they take to be foreign."

Catherine's dark hair hung in soft waves. The shrug of her shoulders was almost imperceptible. "Well then, let us stay strong."

Woode found her a strange creature; the fire in her belly was most uncommon in a young woman. While he was mourning a queen others reviled and grieving for the future of this and every Catholic family in the land, Catherine spoke of *strength.* And he had to concede that she *was* strong. Her strength had helped bring new life back to this family since the dark days following Margaret's death. The children had grown to love her.

"How is the boy?"

"Making mischief as ever," Catherine answered. "The fever has subsided. It was nought but a winter sweat."

"That is good, good."

She looked up and he saw that her startling blue eyes were still bright. In her hands she held a cup of fine Gascon wine, unsweetened. She put it down on his worktable, close to his right hand.

"Thank you, Catherine."

She breathed deeply, composing herself. "Might I speak plain with you, Master Woode?"

"Why, yes, Catherine. My door is always open to you. Please, sit down. What do you wish to speak on?"

Suddenly she laughed. It was a laugh of release, not of humor. "You will think me a fishwife or a gossip, Master Woode. Coming to you with tittle-tattle."

Thomas Woode was in his mid-thirties, his sandy hair graying around the temples. He felt himself ageing; his eyes and brow were lined. Yet he was still a well-formed, handsome man. He looked grave. He drank some reviving wine.

"I do not know how to say this without causing offense or showing myself cowardly and lacking in fortitude," she continued. "I would say nothing for my own sake, but I fear the danger to Andrew and Grace."

Woode rose and went to sit beside her. He held her hands and squeezed them gently. "Speak plain, Catherine. You are like a mother to my children. Nothing you say can seem out of place to me."

She was silent a few moments. "It is Father Herrick," she said at last. "I have . . . doubts. In plain speaking, I do not like him and I do not trust him, Master Woode. I fear he is not what he purports to be."

Woode felt the prickles rise on his neck. The sudden thought that a traitor, a spy, was here in this house was simply too terrifying. "You think he is one of Walsingham's men?"

Catherine shook her head. "That is *not* what I think. Not necessarily, though it is possible." She wrung her hands together as though kneading dough for bread. "I think he may be something else."

Thomas Woode smelled her warmth, the salt scent of her stirring him, something that had not been there with any girl or woman since the death of his wife three years ago. "You must speak openly, Catherine. What you say will not go beyond these walls."

How exactly could she explain her doubts about Herrick? It seemed to her that when the priest had first met her friend Blanche at the Bellamys' house, Uxendon Manor, where they both worshipped, he had looked at her not as a man of chastity should do. Blanche had liked Herrick, that was clear. His feelings for her were less clear.

There were Herrick's strange comings and goings, the calculating looks Catherine sometimes caught when he thought she wasn't aware of him at a meal or during

196

Mass. His eyes followed Blanche in an unseemly fashion; was he thinking of her carnally? She suspected that Father Cotton might share her doubts, although he had not said as much. Now she needed to convey these misgivings to Master Woode.

"I know it is sinful to speak ill of the reverend Father, but . . . let me start at the beginning. When Father Herrick came into our lives, we welcomed him as is meet and proper. You, Father Cotton, and I went out of our way to bring him to the attention of our fellow Catholics, and many welcomed him into their homes to say Mass, or visited him here. One of those he became close to was Lady Blanche, who had been brought to the true faith by Father Cotton and subsequently became my friend. It is the nature of that closeness that came to concern me. Father Herrick was very . . . familiar with her. I noted it more than once in the way that he touched her. You may think me too free with my opinions, and I will confess that is true. You may even think me lacking in Christian charity, but it seemed to me that Father Herrick's great interest in Blanche coincided with his learning of her connections to Lord Howard of Effingham."

"He was sent by the Society of Jesus,

Catherine. There can surely be no doubt about *their* motives."

Catherine smiled. "No, of course not. But hear me through. When I heard Blanche had died in this cruel manner, the face of Father Herrick came immediately to my mind, as in a dreadful dream. In my dream it seemed there was darkness in him, Master Woode. Now that must make me seem even more the village idiot and you may wish to send me to Bethlehem Hospital. I set no store by dreams myself. Yet this vision haunts me. Even in my waking moments, it is an image I cannot dismiss. Why does it haunt me so?"

"A dream, Catherine?" Thomas Woode raised a quizzical eyebrow. He stood and walked the room, slowly. These imaginings of Catherine disturbed and bewildered him. He was exhausted from his night without sleep and he could not think clearly. He needed to rest his head on the pillows and sink between the cool, clean sheets of his bed.

"Yes, master. But not *just* a dream." She had not wanted to speak of it, as if somehow it were her shameful secret, but now it was necessary. She took a deep breath. "Last week, as you know, the children and I went to the menagerie at the Tower. Andrew began complaining of a stomach pain, so we came home. As we arrived back at Dowgate, he was asleep in my arms and Grace was quiet and subdued. I could hear noises from upstairs. I thought it was one of the maidservants, but then I recalled it was a Holy Day and they were all off work. As I opened the upper floor gallery, I saw two people, Herrick and a woman. I turned away quickly, trying to shield Grace's eyes, but the child had already seen what I had seen. 'What are they doing, Mistress Marvell?' she asked me in her innocence. I didn't know what to answer. They were both without clothes. Herrick was stretched out, facedown on the floor, and his back was red with weals. The woman's right arm was raised. In her hand was a knotted scourge, about to come down on Father Herrick's back. The woman turned and saw us, her hand hovering, not completing its stroke. She smiled at me. I pulled the children away and ran to my room with them. Later, Father Herrick came to me. 'Mistress Marvell,' he told me, 'I had not expected you back so soon.' I asked him what in God's name he had been doing. He looked at me as if I were slow-witted. '*Pax vobiscum,* child,' he said. 'I am sorry you have witnessed this. As I am sure you understand, I was exorcising my sins through the offices of that poor sinner.' I fear I laughed. 'Father Herrick,' I said, 'I am afraid I do not believe a word you say.' A darkness crossed his eyes and I worried that I had overstepped the mark. I thought for a moment he might kill me, so I went on, 'Of course, I understand it is a private matter and none of my concern.' Father Herrick hesitated, as if weighing up what he should do. In the end he bowed. 'Thank you, Catherine. I see you are a woman of the world. I will trust you not to mention this to Master Woode. He may not understand the severity of our Jesuit ways.' I did not argue then. I just wanted him to go away. I told him I would not mention it to anyone. But now I think you need to be told this."

Thomas Woode spoke firmly. "I am shocked, Catherine. Shocked and deeply sorry that you have been exposed to such abomination under my roof. I will ask Father Herrick to depart this very day. There is a safe house for priests of which Father Cotton has knowledge. I will ask Father Cotton to take him there. As to Father Cotton himself, he will be leaving us in the next forty-eight hours. He has been offered sanctuary elsewhere. It will be more convenient for him, and safer for us. It has become too dangerous for either of them to stay here. I must confess, Catherine, it will be a great relief to me, too. I can scarce sleep for worry while they are here."

Catherine rose from the settle. "Thank you, Master Woode." She lifted the latch to let herself out of the room. But she did not feel completely reassured. It wasn't enough for Herrick to be leaving. A dangerous man was dangerous anywhere.

CHAPTER 16

Four men sat around the long table in the library of Walsingham's mansion house in Seething Lane. Mr. Secretary had at last recovered enough from his long, debilitating illness and was back in London from his country retreat of Barn Elms, where he had stayed these past weeks.

"I think it is the falling of the Queen of Scots' head that has taken the weight off Mr. Secretary's sh-sh-shoulders," Arthur Gregory, an assistant secretary, whispered in John Shakespeare's ear as they waited for Walsingham. "It was a very *convenient* illness . . ."

"Not so good for my Lord Burghley," said Francis Mills, another of Walsingham's secretaries, who heard the remark. "I am told the Queen has quite cut him dead. Burghley implores and begs and whimpers like a puppy to be allowed back into her presence, but she won't see him. She won't even read his letters. Burghley has never known its like."

Shakespeare sat silent, as did the fourth man, Thomas Phelippes. All four of them had been summoned here urgently but had now been waiting an hour for Walsingham to appear. All were aware that the Queen was in a thunderstorm rage over the axing of her cousin Mary Stuart. She blamed everyone but herself for the death, as though it were not her own name scratched on the death warrant. William Davison, one of her two Secretaries of State and the man who brought the signed warrant before the Privy Council to act on, had been taken to the Tower and was being threatened with the rope. Her Lord Treasurer, Lord Burghley, meanwhile, looked likely never to be spoken to again. Of her senior councillors, only Walsingham had somehow escaped the worst of the censure, because he was away ill at the time of the decision to proceed with the execution. "And yet it was *his* hand behind this deed," said Mills, laughing. "Walsingham was the one who brought this thing to pass with his machinations. Signor Machiavelli would have been proud."

The room descended once more into silence. Tension was palpable. Each man here at the table was racked by the demands made on him in these difficult days, for they were at the heart of Walsingham's intelligence operation.

Mills was a tall man, slender, of middle years with small, sharp eyes and a short white beard. He was of equal rank to Shakespeare, though unlike Shakespeare he was not active in the field. His talent was interrogation, particularly of the many priests sent over from Europe and captured.

Gregory had brown hair and a pinkish tinge to his skin and eyes. He spoke slowly and deliberately and sometimes stammered his words. He had been brought to Walsingham's attention because of his remarkable ability to reveal invisible writing on a supposedly blank paper and to open a sealed letter and reseal it without anyone being the wiser. This had enabled Walsingham to monitor letters going in and out of the French embassy, which had been the conduit for all Mary Stuart's intimate correspondence.

Phelippes was, in many ways, the most important member of the team. Proficient in at least six languages, he was short and ill-favored physically. He wore thick-glassed spectacles on his pox-holed nose, and his lank hair hung yellow and wispy about his sallow face. But whatever the deficiencies of his features, the inner workings of his mind were a thing to dazzle. He was the cipher expert who had broken the Spanish codes and the coded letters between Mary, Queen of Scots and the Babington plotters. Phelippes was methodical and dedicated to his work. He would spend hours and days poring over a new cipher, analyzing the frequency of symbols to discover which were "nulls" — meaningless additions to fool the code-breaker — and which were likely to be the most common words and letters used by those involved in the correspondence. So far, no code had eluded the alchemy of his extraordinary mind. He had another skill, too: the ability to forge any writing style. It was this ability that eventually won Walsingham the names of Anthony Babington's fellow plotters; for it was Phelippes who had forged Mary Stuart's writing to ask Babington for those names. The result had been bloody retribution meted out at Tyburn for Babington and thirteen other young men in front of a cheering crowd.

The door opened. Walsingham stood a moment looking at his assembled officials, then walked unsteadily to the head of the table. He was pale and Shakespeare thought he looked less well than when he had last seen him at Barn Elms. Mr. Secretary smiled little at the best of times, but now his face was grim. His dark eyes were fixed ahead of him as he took his seat. He was not going to engage in small talk.

"I have brought you all here today on matters which concern the very future of our Queen and the realm of England." He held up a letter. "Mr. Phelippes already knows the contents of this missive. It contains powerful and incontrovertible evidence that the Spanish fleet will sail on England by summer. Our information is that sixteen new galleys of more than one hundred tons are being readied in Santander. Fourteen more of similar tonnage in the Passage of Gibraltar. In Laredo, there are eight new *pataches,* which I believe are what we call pinnaces; in San Sebastian, six galleons of three hundred tons and four of two hundred. In Bilbao, six more *pataches;* in Figuera, four new barks of a hundred tons. More being built in the river at Fuenterrabia; in the estuary at Seville, eight great galleons of three hundred tons and four *pataches;* in St. Mary Port, two more galleys and four *pataches.* Add it up, gentlemen, then add the total to possibly two hundred ships already at the Spaniard's disposal: carracks, galleons, galleasses, galleys, hulks, pinnaces, zabras, armed merchant vessels. I do not wish to weary you with naval detail, but the picture is clear. Philip is amassing the greatest fleet the world has seen. And its intent is plain: invasion of England and the death of Her Majesty."

The room remained silent. No one doubted the stark figures. All present knew the extent of Walsingham's network throughout Europe and Asia Minor. He had at least four permanent spy bases in Spain itself. Nor was Mr. Secretary one to exaggerate or become excitable; if Walsingham was worried, so should they all be.

"What this means is we must get Vice Admiral Drake afloat and sinking Spanish shipping as soon as possible. We must delay Philip for as long as we can while we strengthen our own fleets and land defenses." He looked pointedly at Shakespeare. "I trust I make myself clear."

Shakespeare nodded. "Yes, Mr. Secretary. Abundantly clear."

"So Drake's safety is paramount. But it is no longer enough simply to protect him, although I am sure Mr. Boltfoot Cooper will do a workmanlike job in that wise. You all know there is an assassin sent by Ambassador Mendoza to kill Sir Francis. It is now vital that this man be hunted down like a rabid fox and disposed of before he can do harm. This assassin must not be allowed to get close to the Vice Admiral. And if he has associates, they too must be rendered harmless."

Shakespeare ran a hand through his hair. *Easier said than done, Mr. Secretary,* was his immediate thought. *Easier said than done.* London churned with gossip and intrigue, but one man sent alone, with no known connections, was every intelligencer's worst nightmare.

"I know what you are thinking, Mr. Shakespeare, but if you have any doubts about the serious nature of the threat we face, there is more." Walsingham turned to the man to the left of Shakespeare. "Mr. Mills, your report on the Dutch connection."

All eyes looked to Mills. He bowed softly like a player taking center stage, then cleared his throat. "For this," he said, "we must go back almost three years, to July the tenth in the year 1584, when William, Prince of Orange, was murdered in Delft. His death was the most outrageous act of political violence of our age. As I am sure everyone in this room knows, he was killed with three shots from a pistol fired by a Roman Catholic named Balthasar Gérard, a traitor in the pay of Philip of Spain. Gérard was captured almost immediately and put to death in a manner which makes hanging, drawing, and quartering seem a pleasant morning's outing by comparison. He was hung from a pole, the *strappado,* suspended by his hands which were tied behind his back. He was whipped until his body was an open wound. Salt was rubbed into these wounds. Gérard was rolled into a ball, his limbs lashed together so he could not move, and he was left like that for a night. After this, he was again hung at the *strappado.* Weights of two hundredweight or more were attached to his feet, almost ripping the joints of his arms from their sockets. The pits of his arms were branded with hot irons and a cloth soaked in alcohol was slapped on his body wounds. Pieces of his flesh were torn, to the bone, from six parts of his body with pincers; boiling fat was poured over his back; carpenters' nails were driven under the nails of his fingers. His right hand — the hand that fired the shots — was burned off with a red-hot iron. He was then boweled alive; his heart was cut from his body and thrown in his face. For good measure, he was quartered and beheaded. His death must have been blessed release to him. Four days this torment took, gentlemen. Four days."

Mills paused for the effects of his unrelenting description of Balthasar Gérard's punishment to sink in with his audience. Then he continued. "I would ask you to excuse the gory facts of this story. You may well think all this is by the by and certainly no less than he deserved for so horrible a crime. And I would agree with you. But there *is* a reason for all this; I am trying to have you imagine the state of mind of this wretched man. Curiously, Balthasar Gérard was extraordinarily brave in his own way. He did not cry out or beg mercy. We know from the authorities in Delft that even in the worst of his agonies, he seemed quite calm and was not given to screaming much. But we also know that at times he became delirious and spoke as if talking in his sleep. He would not have been aware of saying anything. But what he did say in his delirium is revealing and could be of crucial importance to our own investigations. He said repeatedly, 'We have slain Goliath, praise God. Oh my friend, we have slain Goliath of Gath.' " Mills paused for a sip of ale.

"The common belief is that Gérard acted alone, but I can tell you now that he most certainly had an accomplice. The Delft civil militia do not even rule out the possibility that there was a second gunman, out of

210

sight, perhaps, or missed in the confusion. Did all three balls really come from the one wheel-lock pistol? Why did Gérard say '*We* have slain Goliath'? Why not '*I* have slain Goliath'?"

Walsingham broke in, his voice at once powerful and frail. "This is where it becomes tenuous. If there *was* a second gunman, and I happen to believe there probably was, how does that help us? What clues could there be to his identity? And why have I come to the conclusion that this may well be the same man sent here by Mendoza to kill Drake? Mr. Mills . . ."

Mills took another sip of small ale to wet his throat. "There was in Delft at that time another murder committed, of a whore whose name is of no concern. You might well think that there could be no possible connection between the killing of a loose woman and the murder of a prince, and one of the finest princes in all Christendom at that. But there are compelling reasons to believe there was some link between the two cases." He paused again, looking in turn at the four seated men, all of whose eyes were trained on him. "Gérard was a foolish, hotheaded young man. There were those who thought such a one could not have succeeded at his foul task alone. Inquiries eventually proved that while planning his crime, Gérard had lodged at an English-owned tavern in Rotterdam called The Mermaid, which, as the name suggests, was a bawdy house. He was not alone in lodging there at that time. He was seen with another man, a man whom the women there remember quite well. This other man, a Fleming, had a taste for the women of the house and paid generously for their services. But his ways were strange. He asked the women to beat him. Such women are accustomed to unusual requests, including acts of violence, but this man went too far. After being beaten by one of the women, he turned on her, tied her up and hurt her badly; she feared she might die. Her bawd, the landlord of The Mermaid, flung the man out of the tavern. Balthasar Gérard left the same day. A week later a whore was discovered murdered in Delft, only a few miles away. She had been beaten to death in a tenement lodging that had been rented by two men, one of them answering to the description of Gérard, the other very much like his Flemish companion from The Mermaid in Rotterdam. The woman's injuries were similar to those suffered by the injured whore at The Mermaid — a severe beating that went too far and her wrists bound to the bed with ropes. One report says he cut her, that religious symbols were carved into her body. No more was seen of either man until Gérard turned up less than a week later with his pistols at the Prinsenhof, the residence of William the Silent, where the Prince was murdered ascending the stairs. My assumption — and I believe the evidence is compelling — is that this second man was there, too. Or if not actually there, was certainly involved in the detailed planning of the killing. One way or the other, you may be certain Balthasar Gérard did not act alone."

Shakespeare leaned forward. In his mind he had a chilling vision: the corpse of Lady Blanche Howard, lying cold on a slab in the crypt of St. Paul's, the Searcher of the Dead turning her over and revealing her back with the crucifix cut into it. Was it remotely possible that the man who inflicted these wounds on Blanche was the same as the man in Delft who murdered a prostitute and was accomplice to the assassination of William the Silent? But first, though, there was the connection with the killing of William of Orange and the plot against Drake. "So you think this second man could be the so-called 'dragon slayer' sent to kill the Vice Admiral?"

Walsingham signaled Phelippes to speak. "Thomas, if you will . . ."

Phelippes pushed his metal-rimmed glasses up his nose and consulted a paper on the table in front of him. "Here," he said in his thin, birdlike voice, "I have a message decoded last autumn, shortly after the Babington plotters came to trial. At the time we were not at all sure whether it was important or even what it meant, although it was clearly about the Spanish plans to send an armada against us. This code was on its way to Philip, but this time the message was from the Duke of Parma rather than the Spanish ambassador Mendoza. I will read it to you: *'What of Delft in the clearing of the seaways? One man with the eye of a falcon might be worth a hundred ships in the enterprise of God.'* The word *Delft,* I suggest, refers in this instance to the assassination of Prince William. And the words *clearing of the seaways* are self-evident: the Spanish want their fleet to be able to proceed along the Channel with no hindrance from the likes of Sir Francis Drake. If you accept this, then the meaning of Palma's message is clear: *'Let us send the Delft assassin after Drake.'* "

"Thank you, Thomas," Walsingham said. "Now, John" — he turned to Shakespeare

— "you will need a description of this man and everything that is known of him. As Mr. Mills said, he is a Fleming. We have descriptions of his person from the authorities in Delft and Rotterdam. He was a man of uncommon height, above six foot, slender but strong, habitually clean-shaven — though that could mean nothing, for he may have affected a beard since then. He has a cold eye, almost black, is pale of skin, and he frequents whores. In Rotterdam he went by the name Hals Hasselbaink and claimed to be a Lutheran. It may not be much, but it is a start and it is more than we had. Get Slide out into the stews; go to them yourself if needs be. This Fleming obviously has tastes which must be satisfied. Ask around. Have any women been attacked in such a way?" He paused and looked around the table. "In particular, keep your thoughts on the weapon used in the assassination at Delft. I cannot emphasize enough my fears over the use of the wheel-lock pistol. The Queen is very concerned. Such weapons are too easy to conceal and especially lethal when used at close quarters. If King Philip's hired killer is to use a pistol, there is every chance he has acquired it here. Go to all the gunsmiths. In the meantime, I must insist that everyone in this room redoubles their vigilance. The death of the Scots she-devil changes everything and nothing. It will undoubtedly provoke a reaction from our enemies at home and abroad. Gentlemen, be prepared for the worst and hope for the best."

Shakespeare was about to tell Walsingham of his suspicions that there might be a connection between the murder of William the Silent and the killing of Lady Blanche Howard, but before he could utter a word, Walsingham was up from his chair and out of the room. Shakespeare sighed and snapped his quill.

"He is expected at Greenwich," Mills explained with a smile. "Mr. Secretary has a state funeral to organize. Our sovereign lady is communicating once again. As the Mussulmans are wont to say, the dogs bark, the caravan moves on."

CHAPTER 17

Shakespeare knocked at the door of the house in Dowgate. He thought he heard noises inside, but no one answered. He began hammering impatiently and finally a woman came to open it.

She looked at him with one eyebrow raised, as if in wonder that anyone could beat at the door quite so angrily. "Forgive me for being so tardy, sir. I was putting the children to bed."

Shakespeare grunted but did not apologize. "I am come to talk with Mr. Thomas Woode. Are you Mistress Woode?"

"No, sir," she answered in a clear, low voice. "There is no Mistress Woode, unless you mean my master's three-year-old daughter, Grace. I am Catherine Marvell, governess to the children. I believe Master Woode is in his library."

Shakespeare suddenly took note of her look. Was she making jest at his expense?

She was dark-haired with an oval face. At a time of year when skins were pallid and gray, hers was clear and had some hue. Her blue eyes met his and then she laughed at his somber formality. He bristled. "Tell him John Shakespeare wishes to speak with him on Queen's business." His voice was stiff. He began to feel foolish. Too late, he tried to smile but he was aware that it might have appeared as a grimace.

Catherine Marvell bowed and again he got the uncomfortable feeling that there was some mockery. "Certainly, sir. Please come through to the anteroom while I find out if Master Woode is available to see you."

Shakespeare stepped into the welcoming warmth of the hallway. It smelled of fresh-hewn oak and fine beeswax candles. On the walls were four or five portraits, probably of old family members. One in particular was more prominent than the others: a young woman with fair hair, wearing a dark gown and looking solemn. She had a pure white coif on her locks and a cross about her throat. She looked, he thought, very devout, like a nun.

Catherine Marvell returned after a few moments. For some reason, he found himself wishing to repair the damage wrought by his aggressive knocking and tone, but was tongue-tied. She led him through to the library. Thomas Woode rose immediately from his table.

"Mr. Shakespeare?"

Shakespeare shook the man's hand, which he noted was tremulous. "Indeed, sir, I am come from Mr. Secretary Walsingham. And you are Thomas Woode of the Stationers' Company, I believe."

"Your servant, Mr. Shakespeare. Catherine tells me you are here on Queen's business of some nature. May I offer you refreshment? Catherine, perhaps you would bring us some of the best claret."

"Certainly, Master Woode. Can I just remind you that the children are abed and would bid you good night."

"Of course, of course, in a few minutes." As Catherine left he turned to Shakespeare. "Now, how can I assist you, sir?"

Shakespeare did not wait to be asked before taking a seat at Thomas Woode's table. He looked around him and observed his surroundings: fine wainscot paneling on the lower portion of the wall, bookshelves full of weighty tomes, a white ceiling pargeted with Tudor roses. A rich tapestry on one wall, a Turkish carpet on another. An Italianate painting of the Virgin and babe. Thomas Woode was a wealthy man, of that there was no doubt. "A fine house you are constructing here, Mr. Woode."

Woode sat at the end of the table and put his hands flat on it. "It is for the children more than anything. I had planned it these ten years past but lost the will to proceed when the Lord took my good wife, Margaret, three years ago. At last, though, I realized my children needed a good home. I had more to think about than just myself."

"I am sorry about your wife. Is that her portrait in the hallway?"

Woode smiled a gray, sad smile. "I loved her deeply. We had known each other since childhood. Our parents were friends. When I lost her, I very nearly lost the will to live. But who are we to question the ways of our Lord?" He paused, suddenly uncomfortably aware that he was straying into private grief in the presence of a complete stranger. "God rest her soul," he said softly.

"From her portrait, I would say she was beautiful. Please, forgive my intrusion." Shakespeare laid out the paper and the type sorts retrieved from the burnt-out house in Shoreditch two days earlier. "I am told by Job Mallinson at Stationers' Hall that you are the man who knows most in England about the provenance of letters and papers. I want you to tell me what you can about this paper and these type sorts."

Thomas Woode did not need to look closely at the paper or the sorts; he knew them all too well. He felt the prickles of hair rise on his neck as he gazed upon them. He picked up the paper and looked at it this way and that in the light of a candle. He brought out a goldsmith's loupe from a drawer and held the paper and the type sorts up close to his eye, one by one.

Shakespeare waited and watched him, saying nothing. Catherine came back with two stoups of wine. Shakespeare gazed at her as she moved with quiet grace to the door, closing it soundlessly behind her. At last Thomas Woode put down his loupe.

"And this," Shakespeare said, taking out the broadsheet. "Could this have been printed on the same paper and by the same press?"

Woode looked at it quickly.

"Well, Mr. Woode?"

Woode nodded slowly. "I can tell you a great deal about these papers and type sorts, Mr. Shakespeare. Can I ask you where you found them?"

"No, I fear not. It is part of an investigation into a most grievous felony; I can offer you no more than that. But I can say that the broadsheet was bought from a street seller."

Woode moved the broadsheet to one side. "Well, there is no connection. The broadsheet is poor stuff, but it most certainly has not been made with the same paper or press as the other scrap and sorts."

"Then concentrate on the scrap, sir."

Woode held the scrap of paper between them so they could both see it clearly. "What I can say first of all is that this is inferior-quality paper and very bad printing. See how brown and stained it is? The paper has been made using turbid water, almost certainly at a mill downstream of a town. The manufacture of paper needs a lot of very clear, pure water, Mr. Shakespeare, which is why paper mills should always be built on the higher reaches of rivers, upstream of towns where so much accumulated filth is dumped and so much river traffic stirs up the sediment. Muddy streams will stain the paper brown, as this has been stained. The other requirement of good paper is good-quality rag, which, as you probably know, is the raw material of our industry. Good rags are hard to come by, which is why so many of us scratch our heads wondering what alternative material might be used. But as it is, we have nothing but rags and I can tell you plainly that whoever manufactured this paper did not have access to a good supply of them. That might, of course, lead one to think that the papermaker was either very bad at his craft or, more probably, that he was working outside the law with whatever materials he had available."

Shakespeare tapped his fingers on the table. He studied Woode with a stern, impatient eye. Did the man take him for a fool? His hackles were rising; first the girl had laughed at him, now this. "That could very well be the case."

If Woode saw the way Shakespeare was looking at him, he did not betray it, but continued his theme. "Now let us consider the typefaces used on this piece of paper — and these, I can tell you, correspond with the selection of type sorts you have brought me. They are old and worn, which is why the print quality is so poor. Some of the letters are so degraded that you cannot, for instance, tell a *D* from a *B*. Type sorts are made of soft metal and invariably wear down at an alarming rate, which is why the great printers, such as Plantin of Antwerp — for whom I am an agent — replace them frequently. They are very expensive and often it is difficult to get enough of them.

To my mind, the use of such old, thinned sorts would reinforce the suspicion that this was printed outside the law. Furthermore, we have here a curious selection of fonts from letter foundries all over Europe. You see these roman types? They are from Rouen and are commonplace in England. But they are mixed up with others, such as this black-letter, which I am certain is from Basle. No printer would use these together in the same line unless he had no option. For one thing they look odd — Gothic simply doesn't work with roman — but mainly, they will have been made to a different gauge and will have to be filed to size by the printer, an extremely time-consuming task. There are other fonts, too, some of them from Italy. It is a curious collection, like the sweepings of a printer's floor, Mr. Shakespeare."

Shakespeare drank some wine. It was remarkably good; clearly Thomas Woode had good taste as well as wealth. Unfortunately, the man was a dissembler, too. "Can you, then, venture to suggest who *did* this printing?"

Thomas Woode put his hand to his furrowed brow, his soft gentleman's fingers flicking the gray at his temples. He seemed to be deep in thought, as if trying to work out who had made this paper or who had done this printing. But the truth was, he knew the answers to these questions very well: he had supplied the typeface and press himself and the paper had been made by the old monk Ptolomeus on the Thames by Windsor. Who else could have made such a poor job of it? At last Woode sighed and shook his head. "All I can say with certainty, Mr. Shakespeare, is what I have already told you: this was not printed by a licensed printer. I would venture to suggest a wagonback press, the sort that can be lifted and moved from hiding place to hiding place at a moment's notice, possibly concealed beneath hay bales or canvas as it is transported. As to the paper, it would probably have been made near a town on the Thames or the Medway. A river setting not far from London. No one would bother to carry such a poor product any great distance, however malign their intent. Further than that, I'm afraid I can't really say. It certainly hasn't been produced by any of the recognized papermakers or printers licensed by the Council through Stationers' Hall." He sighed and met Shakespeare's gaze. "I apologize for my inability to be more specific, but I hope I have been of some use to you."

Shakespeare gave Thomas Woode a hard

look. He didn't believe a word the older man said. Woode was lying to him and he wasn't very good at it. When Shakespeare spoke, his tone was curt. "You must come across many different printers, Mr. Woode."

The heat was rising in Woode's breast. It suddenly occurred to him that he was performing his part badly, very badly. He was under suspicion of something, but what? This agent of the state did not trust him and that was dangerous. He rose and went to the hearth to damp down the fire. "Sir, I pride myself that I know all the legitimate printers in London and the counties close by. I can tell you for certain that none of them is responsible for this shoddy work. Are you sure that it was printed here in England, that it was not smuggled in by a colporteur?" Woode felt a bead of sweat at his brow. If only this man would go. He was not made of the stuff of martyrs; he did not wish to die for his religion as others were prepared to do. He was merely the son of a successful printer who had learned his trade well and become even more successful than his father. Apart from his Roman Catholicism, he would be of no more interest to the state than any other wealthy merchant in this affluent city. Yet here in this house, not far from this man sent by Walsingham

— who could order torture and organize execution of anyone he wished — were secreted two renegade priests who could, with their discovery, bring him and his family to their doom.

At first, he had shrunk from the task of telling Herrick he had to go; he had feared the priest's reaction. But in the end he had approached him that morning after they had breakfasted. Woode explained his fears for the safety of his children. Herrick merely shrugged his shoulders, smiled, and agreed it was time to move on. It had been good of Woode to have him here at all, he said, and he would be gone on the morrow. This, too, was to be Cotton's last night under their roof. He already had another lodging to go to, in the house of a great lady, who wished for a resident chaplain. In some ways it had been Cotton who unnerved Woode the more; he so blatantly *yearned* for a martyr's death, as if life were nothing and the life hereafter the be-all. It was a way of thinking Woode could not comprehend. He would have given anything to have Margaret back with him, alive, in *this* world.

And now . . . what if Shakespeare should order in the pursuivants? It would be all too easy to find the priests. They would be here only a few more hours, but a lot could go wrong in that short time. Thomas Woode needed to get Shakespeare out of here.

"I am sure of nothing, Mr. Woode. That is why I have come to you, for some answers," Shakespeare said. "Yet I feel you are not being straight with me. Why is that? I came to you with one thought in mind: to use your extensive knowledge of the print, but now I find myself wondering whether there is not something more to you than meets the eye. I have to tell you, sir, that I am not in the habit of delving into the recesses of men's souls, but nor am I willing to walk away and ignore the fact that you, for whatever reason, are holding something back from me."

"Mr. Shakespeare, sir . . ."

"Spare me your protestations, Mr. Woode. I would have you tell me more about yourself and your circumstances. Some might imagine your business to be suffering since the fall of Antwerp to Parma's army. But you and I know that Mr. Plantin is favored by the Spanish King and that his business not only survives but thrives under the Spanish occupation. Why do you think he is so well looked on when many other Antwerp merchants have been forced to flee in the face of a pitiless enemy?"

Thomas Woode mopped the sweat from his brow with a gold-trimmed kerchief.

"This fire is overzealous, Mr. Shakespeare. Of course I will tell you everything I can. It is not my intention to hold anything back from you or Mr. Secretary. But please forgive me one moment while I attend to this fire." He went to the door and called out. "Catherine, please come."

She reappeared in the room, her eyes keen.

"Catherine, please see to the fire. It is quite burning up myself and Mr. Shakespeare here."

Shakespeare gave her an inquiring look, as if to ask her whether she, too, found the fire hot, then said, "I am fine, thank you, Mistress Marvell. I find the heat quite pleasant. Perhaps Mr. Woode is growing ill with the sweating sickness . . ."

"Fie, Mr. Shakespeare, you will find enough heat in the next life, I am sure. Let me turn it down a little in this . . ." Catherine went to the hearth and tried to reduce its heat. Shakespeare watched her, then turned to Woode. He noticed he, too, was watching his governess intently and not, perhaps, in the way a master looks at a servant.

"You were saying?" he prompted.

"I just wish I could be of more assistance . . ."

"And about yourself. You have standing in

the Stationers' Company?"

Thomas Woode could not help himself preening somewhat. "I am indeed a member of the board of assistants. It is true I have standing in the company. I have worked hard over many years to earn the right to don its livery."

"And has your Roman faith never been a hindrance to you?" It was an arrow shot in the dark, based on nothing more than a painting of the Virgin, and Shakespeare felt a pang of guilt for even asking it, yet he needed some response here, some reaction. Woode froze like an ice statue.

Catherine hardly missed a beat. She turned from the fire, poker in hand. "Mr. Shakespeare? I wonder what your motive is for asking such a curious question?"

Shakespeare was taken aback. He stared at her questioningly, his brow crossed. "Mistress Marvell?" was all he could find to say.

"Well, sir, you are invited into this house seeking assistance and then you pry into matters seeming unrelated. Are these *Walsingham* manners?"

"My motive, Mistress Marvell, is to seek out some truth in this house. I think there is much dissembling here."

"And this from a guest who accepts our

wine and hospitality?"

Shakespeare turned back to Woode. "Your governess has a sharp tongue on her, sir. I am surprised you entrust your children to her care."

"I think much of her care, Mr. Shakespeare."

"And do you think enough of your neck to answer my question? Would you deny your faith?"

Woode couldn't think. His mind was a pit of confusion. Did this Walsingham agent have some prior knowledge of his religious persuasion? Or was it simply a guess? Was it safer to admit it or try to equivocate as the Jesuits were taught? Once again, Catherine stepped forward boldly.

"I would not deny *my* faith, Mr. Shakespeare. I am of the Romish faith and proud to be called so. But you will find me, also, a loyal subject of Her Majesty the Queen. I fear that being a loyal subject is not always a great help, though, is it? Did not Father Edmund Campion honor and pray for our Queen even as her men were tearing him apart like wild dogs?"

The words stung. It was the contradiction at the heart of all John Shakespeare's work. He understood this well and could not escape it. And yet he knew that fire had to be used to fight fire, that this fragile reformation was susceptible to those who were determined to bring wholesale torment and bloodshed to England's shores.

"You seem lost for words, Mr. Shakespeare."

"I am just glad to hear that you are a loyal subject of the crown, Mistress Marvell. To that end, I assume you accept Her Majesty as supreme head of the Church in England and would die to protect her from foreign potentates or the Pope himself. Nor will I ask whether you go to church as required under law, because I consider that a matter between you and your parish. No, I do not wish to delve into souls, though others might. But," and here he addressed Woode, "I will not be *lied* to. If you have any information about the printing of that paper — or even, perhaps, the writing thereof — you will reveal it to me. And I promise you it were better to do so now, to me, than to others who might come after me. Do you understand my meaning, Mr. Woode?" Shakespeare's voice was as cold as a Norse winter, but it was a curious rage, tainted with fury at himself for being led down this path and at finding himself in barbarous argument with this Catherine Marvell. He realized suddenly that he *liked* these people.

He could tell that Thomas Woode was a goodly person. And as for Catherine Marvell — well, there was something about her that moved him and disturbed him as a man, not an investigator. He was angry, too, because he feared for them should they ever find themselves in the hands of those with fewer scruples.

Woode was visibly trembling now. "I understand you very well, sir," he replied. "But I swear to you that I have told you all I know. And no, my faith has not been a hindrance to my career, for I have not advertised it. As for Christophe Plantin of Antwerp, yes, he too is a Catholic, but more than that he is a great craftsman, an artist, and he is a threat to no one, least of all England. Why, he is renowned for printing the Bible in Dutch. So far as I know, he was not considered an enemy by William of Orange, and I do not see why he should now be considered an enemy by you or Mr. Secretary Walsingham or anyone else." Woode paused to draw breath and, perhaps, for effect. "And I, like Catherine, am a true subject of the Queen."

Shakespeare rose from his chair, frustrated and with a gnawing sense of impotence in the face of this man's contradictions. "Then I will leave you, Mr. Woode. But I will be back and I pray you may not live to regret it."

As Catherine walked Shakespeare to the front door, Woode watched him in a kind of terror.

"You had better look to your master, Mistress Marvell," Shakespeare said so that Woode could not hear. "I fear he will choke on his own self-righteousness."

"Better that than die of hypocrisy."

Shakespeare turned to look at her. "You do have a viper's tongue in your head, mistress."

"Aye. And an adder's teeth."

Thomas Woode looked at her with fearful eyes. What was she saying to Shakespeare? Did she have any idea how dangerous this man could be to all of them? There could be no more delay; Cotton and Herrick would have to go, this very evening, because if Shakespeare returned with the pursuivants to tear down their walls, there could be no protection for any of them.

CHAPTER 18

Parsimony Field weighed the gold in her hands. Its brilliance and weight sent a chill of amazement and fear through her. The question was: how to turn it into coinage — and quick? She was well aware that possession of such treasure could be a death sentence.

It had not been easy securing it. Despite threats, Starling Day wouldn't talk and Alice was dead, choked on her own vomit. Time had been running out because Parsimony knew that Cogg's body would be found by someone else soon enough and then all hell would break loose. Put like that, there really had been no decision to make; she'd have to cut Starling free and make a proper deal with her.

When she returned to the chamber where Starling was stretched out, she found that her breath was coming short and fast. The young whore had been struggling against her bindings since Parsimony left and was becoming more and more frantic. Parsimony watched her from the door, knife in hand, and saw the rush of horror in the girl's eyes.

"Don't worry, dove, I'm not going to kill you. I'm going to set you loose. But I warn you: one wrong move and I'll fill you full of little holes."

As Parsimony cut the ropes, Starling closed her eyes, clearly convinced the knife would slide into her flesh at any moment. "There, that wasn't so bad, was it?" Parsimony said at last.

Starling rubbed her wrists, scarcely able to believe she was free. She sat up on the bed, astonished to be alive.

"Well?"

"Thank you, Parsey. I mean it, thank you. I thought you were going to do for me."

"Would I harm my best girl? Come on, let's do it. Half and half, you and me."

"And Alice . . ."

Parsimony winced at the name. "Dove, I'm really sorry, but your cousin's done for, drowned in her own puke while she was asleep." She reached out and touched Starling's hand. "Honest truth, dove, I'm truly sorry."

Starling looked at her for a moment. Had

she killed Alice? Not that it mattered now; for better or worse they were in this thing together with one less person to share the loot. The thing to learn was never, ever to turn her back on Parsimony Field. Once Parsey had her mucky grasp on the treasure, Starling was sure she would be as good as dead if she didn't move sharpish.

They spent the day looking for a tenement lodging. They had to get away from the Bel Savage whorehouse; it would be the first place anyone who knew Cogg would look for them and the treasure. Eventually, they found a place across the river in Southwark. It wasn't much, just a room with a window out onto the street, but it was in one of the better roads where they were less likely to be burgled. Once they had the stuff safely stashed away, they had to sell it. Then they could go their separate ways. But first they had to retrieve the gold and jewels from Starling's hiding place.

The churchyard behind the ruins of St. Bartholomew the Great was a ghostly place at night. Starling led the way. There were still revelers about in Smith Field, drinking to the death of the Scots Queen, but the celebrations had been going on a long time, so the watchmen had been ordered to clear the streets and impose a curfew. Any drunks found were to be beaten home with clubs; the government wanted no disturbances at this sensitive time when invasion or insurrection were real fears. Starling and Parsimony dodged behind a wall at the northern end of Cock Lane. They stayed there, crouched down with the spades they had bought hours earlier. When the way was clear, they darted across the great six-acre square. They heard the cry of a watchman calling after them but sprinted on regardless until they were safely at the far side by the rubble where the old church's nave had been pulled down fifty years ago.

"Where now, dove?" Parsimony said, panting.

"Round the back."

The problem now was to dig up the stuff without being seen. Starling and Alice had buried it in a new-dug grave where the earth was fresh-turned. They had planted it two feet down, probably a couple of feet above the interred corpse. Starling and Parsimony worked by moonlight; they didn't dare use pitch torches for fear of being spotted by the watch.

The earth was heavy and cloying. They took it in turns to dig. Starling hit an old stone from the demolished church nave and the spade clanged loudly. "Keep it down!"

Parsimony whispered. "Do you want to get us strung up?"

"We must be there near enough," Starling said. "We didn't bury it too deep." Suddenly she got down to her knees and scrabbled in the earth with her hands. "Here it is," she said, grasping hold of the handles of the carpet bag. She yanked hard. "Here, Parsey, we got it."

Something in the glint of Parsimony's eye, silvery black in the moonlight, told Starling she had let her guard down again. Just as Parsimony lunged forward, Starling side-stepped, and managed to trip her, flailing, into the cold, damp earth.

Starling dropped the bag and leapt on Parsimony's back, pushing her head down into the mud as though to suffocate her as, she was sure, Parsimony had choked Alice. It would be a fitting end for her.

But Parsimony was stronger and wrenched Starling off. Thrashing about in the thick, wet clay, they hit each other, tore hair, twisted limbs, and scratched. They fought to the point of exhaustion. Eventually neither could raise another punch and they lay back, panting for breath on the soft ground, side by side, their clothes filthy and torn.

"By God's little finger, dove, I never

thought you had it in you to put up a show like that."

Nor had Starling known she had the fight in her; she rather wished she had had half as much fight a while back in Strelley when she was being beaten as black as coal by Edward. "It's my one chance, Parsey, and you're not taking it off of me."

As they lay there, gasping, a kind of respect arose between them. More than that, they both began to come to a realization; they really *did* need each other. It would be impossible to conceal and sell all this stuff alone. Maybe, just maybe, they could work together.

"What about it then, Parsey? Shall we do this thing together? We could even buy a place with this plunder."

"Go into business together?" Parsimony thought for a moment. "I've always wanted my *own* stew. You seem a likely partner, dove."

"We could have a palace of a place."

"Get the gentry coves in. Bit of gaming, too. Be the best place in town. All we need do is find ourselves a good broker and turn this little lot into coin. What a place we will have!"

Starling laughed. "We could call it Queens — because we'd be like a couple of queen bees. You and me, mistresses of the game."

Parsimony struggled to her feet and brushed herself down as best she could. "Or we could call it The Queen's Legs — we never close! You know, dove, it's a shame you didn't get to know Cogg better. He'd have loved you. You're just his type, you are. Who was it who killed him? It looked like his eyes had been poked out."

"It was a horrible man in dark clothes. He had a funny voice. Cold as a Christ-tide frost he was. He had this thin, black-handled skene that he used on poor Cogg. Stabbed him twice as I saw — once in each eye, up to the hilt, into the brain. Kill you as soon as swive you, that one, I reckon."

Starling was standing now, the carpet bag gripped in her left hand. She looked at it and then, in a moment of trust, held it out for Parsimony to take.

Parsimony took the bag, fished out two gold bars and felt their weight; they dazzled her in the moonlight. Then she put them back in the bag and shook her head. "No. You carry it, dove."

Starling nodded. "One more thing, Parsey. That killer — after he put his skene through Cogg's eyes . . ." She paused, wide-eyed, remembering. "He crossed himself like a fucking priest."

CHAPTER 19

Walking along Deptford Strand among the bustle of sailors, sailmakers, carpenters, shipwrights, and whores, no one would have noticed Miles Herrick in his workmen's jerkin with the tools of his trade slung in a bag over his shoulder.

It was a crisp, bright February day, almost springlike. The last of the snow had melted or been washed away by the rain, and suddenly there was a new fire in men's bellies. The world seemed brave and worth getting out of bed for. Herrick looked around him and examined the houses and shops that fronted the riverbank. His eye fixed on a chandlery, an ancient, leaning building of three stories with small windows. A sign outside said *Room to let.* That would do. He ducked into the shop. It was thick with lung-clogging sotweed smoke. Through the fug, among the cordage, the sail gear, the galley pots, the barrels of hard biscuit, dried peas, and salt beef, and all the other essentials of a voyage to sea, he saw two men in conversation; strong working men who seemed to be arguing over some detail of a shipwright's plans of a caravel, spread over a trestle. As he approached they stopped talking and turned his way, pipes of sotweed in their mouths, belching forth smoke like autumn bonfires.

"Are you the master of this chandlery?" Herrick asked the taller of the two men, who seemed the more assured. "I am looking for lodging and saw your sign. Is the room still free?"

"It might still be free of *tenants*," the taller man replied, "but it would certainly never be free of *charge.*"

Herrick smiled thinly at the man's attempt at humor. He took his purse and loosened the drawstring. "I can pay well. I am here from the Low Countries, looking for work with armaments." He enjoyed the irony; the word *armaments* made him sound plausible. He knew, too, that such a claim would never be checked on.

"Well, you have come to the right place. There is plenty of work to be had. The admirals will be glad of another armaments journeyman. Come with me and see the room."

The room was on the third floor, under the pitch of the roof. Exactly what he required. He heard rats or birds scuttling behind the plasterwork, in the eaves. There was a bare palliasse and a small table and three-legged stool. Nothing else. But there was a small casement window that gave out over the river. Herrick stood at this window a long moment, then turned back into the room. God's work. *Thy will be done.*

"I will take it."

The landlord reached out his hand and brushed some cobwebs down from above the low door. "My name is Bob Roberts. I will supply you with blankets and a pot to piss in. Two shillings and sixpence a week, but you can have it for half a crown."

Herrick put his bag of tools on the floor as casually as a goodwife depositing a basket of laundry, and shook hands with the landlord to seal the agreement. "I am van Leiden. Henrik van Leiden."

"Well, Henrik, come down and share a stoup of ale with us and you can pay me the first week's rental," the landlord said and turned to leave. "And if you need any names of captains for work, I will happily help you."

"What of Drake, the greatest of all captains?"

The landlord laughed. "Aye, what of him? Work for him? Drake will give you no rest and no pay."

"So he is in these parts?"

"Every day. Never have I seen a captain put so much into preparation. If the fleet is not ready for the armada, it will not be for want of Drake's efforts. But beware, after a few days in his employ you might wish yourself an oarsman slave, manacled and thrashed daily on a Spanish galley."

Herrick smiled. "I understand. But it would be a great honor to make his acquaintance."

"Then I wish you well, Henrik, but beware. Drake will press you into service as soon as shake your hand."

As the door closed behind the landlord, Herrick stepped once more to the window. The sill was three feet above the floor. The window was two feet wide and three and a half feet top to bottom. It would be perfect for his purpose. He crossed himself, then knelt and prayed.

CHAPTER 20

The face of Catherine Marvell haunted John Shakespeare. What was she? A Catholic governess, probably a recusant, in a household of secrets. What was her true connection to Thomas Woode? Was she more than a governess to the man? She was certainly familiar in his presence. Shakespeare kicked his horse with a violence that, on another day, would have made him ashamed. He would dismiss the woman from his thoughts.

He rode on to the bridge to Southwark. He was still full of unreasoning anger. He was angry with Thomas Woode for his foolish lies; he was angry with the intruder who had broken down the door to his home and ransacked the papers in his solar; he was angry with himself, though he was not sure why.

When he got home, Slide had been waiting. He had brought with him another copy of *The London Informer,* which carried a lurid story describing the last minutes of Mary, Queen of Scots. Shakespeare read the story slowly. It told him nothing that he didn't already know: grisly details of the head rolling out of the hand of Executioner Bull. That did not surprise Shakespeare; Bull was incompetent at the best of times. He read on; the blood-red martyr's garb she wore; tittle-tattle about the dog cowering among her petticoats; a few lines on the great rejoicing of London and the fears of a Spanish invasion fleet being dispatched at any moment.

"How did Glebe get this paper printed?" Shakespeare exploded, tearing it into pieces and throwing them to the floor. "I thought his press had been broken up by the Stationers' Company."

"Perhaps he had access to another press, Mr. Shakespeare."

Shakespeare growled. "Well, find him, Harry. I want Walstan Glebe locked up and fettered until I have questioned him."

Slide bowed. He would, of course, do his best, he replied, and he was quite sure it was only a matter of time before Glebe was apprehended.

"And I want the Jesuit Southwell incarcerated. You said you could deliver him, so where is he? You've been paid in advance, Harry. Bring him in! Mr. Secretary will want my own head on a platter if we don't have Southwell soon."

Slide took Shakespeare's rage without flinching. He still looked battered from the attack he had suffered. The cuts were clotting to scabs and the bruises turning yellow, but he looked a mess. He assured Shakespeare, however, that he was well enough. He didn't, though, mention that his leads to Southwell had gone cold; that would have done nothing to calm the storm.

"I want you to get out into the stews, Harry. Find out if the bawdy baskets have been lashing any strange clients, or have been berayed unkindly in their turn. Have they entertained any Flemings or men with Dutch or German accents? Ask everyone you know. If there are any strange or curious customers about, I want to know — and I want to know quickly. Keep asking about Blanche Howard, too. Was she moving in dissident circles? Was she close to any foreign men, particularly Flemings? I think there is some connection here. Return to me with information as soon as possible."

"Consider it done, Mr. Shakespeare."

"And Harry, what do you know of a Thomas Woode, merchant? Is there any talk about him?"

"Well, of course I have heard of him. He is wealthy, though not ostentatious. A little bit puritanical, on the Presbyterian side, I would think, the way he lives. Perhaps he is of the same persuasion as Mr. Secretary."

Shakespeare laughed without humor. "I think not, Harry. Woode is of the Romish persuasion. Mr. Secretary would not be amused at a suggestion that he shared anything in common with Mr. Woode."

"Ah . . ."

"But find out what more you can. Anything in Thomas Woode's past, any contacts he has with merchant strangers. Who are his friends? And he has a governess for his children, one Catherine Marvell; find out what you may about her."

"Of course, Mr. Shakespeare." He hesitated a moment, then added, "Forgive me, sir, for bringing up such a delicate subject . . . I do realize that this is not the meet and proper time to make such a request, but I am sore in need of funds."

Shakespeare bared his teeth. He was about to say something that he suddenly realized he could well regret; he needed Slide now. Badly. He could not afford to lose him. And clearly, he had to have gold. "All right. How much?"

"Fifteen marks. If I am to go to the stews, the apple-squires and whores will not talk without sweetening. You must know that, Mr. Shakespeare."

"Indeed. Forgive me, Harry, but I fear my knowledge of the ways of bawdy houses is scant. I am sure, though, that you are well versed in such matters and could educate me over a quart of ale some day. But not now." He opened his purse and counted out coins, then handed them to Slide without ceremony. "I expect results, Harry. And I expect them *fast*. Go."

Now, an hour after that conversation, Shakespeare reined in his horse by the Marshalsea. He told himself he would have to go back to Dowgate later this day, to talk once more to Thomas Woode, bring the merchant in for interrogation if need be. He also had a curious compulsion to see Catherine Marvell again. Had he been thinking more clearly, he might have recognized the symptoms; age twenty-eight, a time when most men were settled into comfortable marriage and fatherhood, and still in need of a wife. All he could think was that he was a poltroon, a fool for a girl with whom he had scarcely even talked. And there was nothing he could do about it.

■ ■ ■ ■

The Marshalsea gaoler was a giant of a man, yet when Shakespeare announced he was there on Queen's business, he thought the man seemed uneasy.

"I would see John Doughty, Mr. Turnkey."

The gaoler looked genuinely puzzled. "I do believe I know no one of that name, sir."

"Come, come. Doughty had plans to kill Sir Francis Drake. He has been here these five years past, I am certain."

The gaoler shook his head. "No, sir, for I have been here myself for three of those years, and I do not recall ever having a prisoner of that name or similar."

"Let me see your records."

The gaoler gave Shakespeare a bewildered look.

"You do have a black book, I take it, man?"

"Of course, sir. But how could that help if the prisoner you seek isn't here?"

"Let's just have a look, shall we."

The gaoler's room offered little respite from the gloomy atmosphere of the prison. He had a table, two stools, a fire, and the tools of his trade: bunches of great keys, lashes and canes, brutish manacles and deadweight chains. He reached up to a dusty shelf and brought down a tome, which he dropped with a thud on the table next to his half-eaten trencher of food.

Shakespeare turned the thick pages of the black book back to the year 1582 and the time when Doughty should have been brought here. There it was: *Doughty, John, for conspiracy to do murder; close confinement.*

"Here is our man, Mr. Turnkey."

The gaoler clanked his keys nervously. "Never did hear of the man, Mr. Shakespeare, sir. You'd be welcome to look in all the cells and talk to whomsoever you please, but I defy you to find someone of that name here."

Shakespeare looked the gaoler in the eye. Despite his unease, the man was telling the truth. So what *had* happened to Doughty?

"Do you have any prisoners who have been here five years or more, someone who might recall this man?"

"Aye. I think I could help you there. Davy Bellard is the man, sir. Been here fifteen years or more for counterfeiting. As fine and clever a man as you could meet, Mr. Shakespeare."

Bellard was a short fellow with long, unkempt hair and beard that had evidently not been trimmed during all his years of incarceration. But his eyes were still bright and alert. "Yes, I do recall John Doughty," he said. "Angriest man I ever did know, Mr. Shakespeare. Wanted to kill the whole world for the injustices suffered by him and his brother. I made the mistake of laughing at him, I'm afraid, and he tried to kill me." Bellard lifted the tattered remains of his shirt. "See there, that scar? He had a buttriss for paring horses' hooves which he had somehow got hold of. Stuck me with it. Lucky for Davy Bellard, his aim was poor and the blade glanced off my ribs. I avoided John Doughty after that. He was a man beyond reasoning."

Shakespeare examined the scarred-over wound. It had been a jagged gash and very unpleasant. "So what happened to Doughty, Mr. Bellard?"

"That's the curious thing, sir. We thought he would be hanged for certain. Conspiring to commit a murder must be a gallows offense, or so we did believe. But if he was hanged, we heard nothing of it. One fine summer's day, a few weeks after he arrived, he just weren't here anymore. He might have been moved to another prison, but I couldn't say. Nor would I know whether he was strung up or set free. It was a mystery to us all and still is, sir. Not that we gave it much thought, to be honest. I, for one, was glad to see the back of John Doughty."

"Thank you, Mr. Bellard." Shakespeare handed him a shilling. "What is your sentence?"

Bellard glanced around to make sure the gaoler was out of earshot. "Ten years, sir, but don't tell the gaoler, sir, or he might kick me out. I do well here, sir. I don't want to leave."

Shakespeare managed a smile, the first one of the long day. "Fear not, Mr. Bellard, your secret is safe with me. And if you hear anything of any interest to me within these four walls, then I would be pleased if you would somehow get the information to me at Mr. Secretary Walsingham's department."

Bellard tapped the side of his nose conspiratorially. "Intelligencing is it, sir?"

"Something like that. In particular, I would like to know of any Flemings you might have word of. And any Jesuits . . ."

Shakespeare took his leave of the prisoner and asked the gaoler to take him, separately, to see Piggott and Plummer, the two priests of whom Harry Slide had told him. It was a long shot, but Shakespeare was more than a little interested in the guests at the Mass and dinner of which Slide had told him.

There might, just, be more information to be had from these men. If they could lead him to the Jesuit Southwell, it would be one rod off his back.

Plummer was first. "Ah, Mr. Shakespeare. Harry Slide has told me of you."

"And he has told me of you, too, Mr. Plummer. You give him information from time to time, I believe."

"Indeed, I do, sir."

"I would know more of this Mass that was held here. Yourself, Piggott, three ladies — Anne Bellamy, Lady Frances Browne, and the Lady Tanahill — I believe."

"And a Jesuit called Cotton."

"Are you sure that was his real name?"

Plummer scratched his privies as if he had the French pox — which, for all Shakespeare knew, he might well have had — and made a face as if he were in extreme discomfort. "Now, how could I possibly know that? If you ask my opinion, I would say it was highly unlikely that he was using his real name. Few of us sent over from the English colleges do, you know."

"I understand. Could he, then, have been Father Robert Southwell?"

"Mr. Shakespeare, how could I possibly know? I have heard of Southwell. He is a poet and was renowned among the Popish fraternity for his saintliness even before he came to England last summer. But I was not at Douai or Rome with him, so I have not made his acquaintance."

"We have a description of Southwell from his younger days. It is said he was not tall, nor of a very great weight. His hair a flame-golden color and his eyes green or blue. Could that have been the man Cotton?"

Plummer did not have to think hard. "It most certainly could have been him, Mr. Shakespeare, though I would have said his eyes were gray."

"And did he give you any inkling of his movements? Where he lodges? Who he sees?"

The priest shook his head. "No, nothing. These Jesuits are cleverer than that."

"And the ladies at the Mass, did they know him?"

"I think the Bellamy girl knew him, but not the other ladies, though I would say that they seemed much taken with him. As was I. He was an uncommon man and likeable. I could see how he could attract people to him and bring them into the Roman faith. Mr. Shakespeare, he would draw them all in."

"What of your colleague, Piggott?"

"I don't like the man. I don't trust him

and he doesn't trust me. Piggott was quite familiar with Cotton, clutched him to his foul, pox-ridden breast and whispered secrets in his ear. If you want to know more of Cotton, you had best speak with him. Piggott is your man for that. I think he could be dangerous."

"And the three ladies at the dinner?"

"Simpering, stupid women who would rather be occupied by God in heaven than enjoy a decent fucking here on earth, Mr. Shakespeare. I fear they are all on a mission to die, for which I am sorry, for they are harmless fools posing no threat to the state."

Shakespeare made to leave. "I will see you are recompensed for this, Plummer. Keep your ears and eyes wide. I want word of a Fleming, one with a taste for being beaten by women, and beating them in turn. And tell me one more thing: the gaoler seemed mighty nervous when I arrived. Why do you think that might be?"

Plummer scratched his stones once more and then put his hand down the back of his woolen smock to rub his neck. "Fleas, Mr. Shakespeare," he explained. "The place is alive with them. I fear they live on the rats, which are as fat as well-fed cats. Yes, the gaoler. A good man, runs a good prison here except for the fleas. But he has a little secret:

can't quite let go of the old faith. And you know, sir, there is another thing that might have set his nerves on edge; you were not our only visitor today."

"Really? Who else has been here?"

"Richard Topcliffe. Like you, he was asking questions about our little supper party and Mass. I am happy to admit to you, sir, that he scared me half witless."

Every muscle in Shakespeare's tall, lean body clenched. "Topcliffe?"

"He, too, seemed most interested in the ladies and Cotton. Threatened me with the rack if I did not speak plain, so I told him everything I could without demur."

"Did you mention the work you do for Slide?"

"No. I am not such a cony as that. But I did mention that he might get far more information from Piggott. I fear Father Piggott may now be even less kindly disposed toward me. . . ."

"Thank you, Mr. Plummer. Feel free to use my name if you ever feel you are in danger and need assistance. But you may find it does not work miracles with Richard Topcliffe, I am afraid."

Plummer put that thought away. He took Shakespeare's hand and held it. "Thank you. And I hope I have not given you my fleas to take home."

Outside the cell, the gaoler was waiting, and walked Shakespeare the few steps to Piggott's dungeon. The priest was in a corner of his cell, hunched into himself like a wren in a hard frost. He did not move or utter a sound when Shakespeare entered and clanged shut the door.

"Mr. Piggott?"

Piggott did not move.

"Mr. Piggott, I will talk with you whether you wish it or not."

Still no movement. Shakespeare grasped the collar of his coarse woolen smock and pulled him up sharply. As he did so, Piggott's head flopped into view and Shakespeare recoiled in shock; it was a bloody pulp. His nose looked broken, his eyes swollen red dumplings with pinpricks of light. The man tried to sit up, but groaned as if his ribs were cracked.

Shakespeare moved his hand forward to help him, but Piggott shied away as if he would be hit. He tried to speak, but no human sound came from his mouth. Shakespeare went back to the door and ordered the gaoler to bring water and rags to wash the wounds, and try to find bandages.

The gaoler was reluctant to comply. He stood there, dumb and inert.

"If you have any sense, gaoler, you will do as I say. Or perhaps you would like me to put out your little secret? I am sure Mr. Topcliffe would like to hear of your Romish leanings." It was a low trick, but it worked. The gaoler looked shocked for a moment, then lumbered off. He returned hastily with all that Shakespeare required, save the bandages. "Now clean the blood from the prisoner."

The gaoler gaped at Shakespeare as though he were mad. Why would anyone wish to clean the blood from a prisoner's face? But when he saw the scowl in Shakespeare's eye, he sighed in submission and advanced on Piggott, grumbling as he roughly wiped the clotted blood away. When he was at least partially clean, Shakespeare handed the gaoler two pence and told him to go to the nearest apothecary for muslin bandages to wrap Piggott's injured chest.

"I cannot leave my post. It is against the law and my terms of employment."

"Then send one of your turnkeys. Do I have to remind you this is Queen's business? Would you have me draw your neglect to the attention of Mr. Secretary Walsingham?"

"It seems everyone is on Queen's business today," the gaoler grumbled as he trundled off once more.

"Now, Piggott, we are alone," Shakespeare said in a low, urgent voice as he stood over the prisoner, who, he had to admit, did not look much better cleaned up. He was an ill-favored individual with heavily pitted skin and thinning, lank hair. "Be straight with me or I will have you in the Tower this day, where you will be confined to Little Ease before questioning under duress. This is a matter of state and I will be answered." Little Ease: a cell so small that a prisoner could neither stand nor lie down, nor even sit properly. "Little Ease, Mr. Piggott. Discomfort so severe that you would beg for the backbreaking pain of the pillory in exchange."

Piggott picked a stray clot of blood from his nostril. He looked like a dog that had been whipped to the point of death. "Don't worry." His voice was a hoarse whisper. "I'll tell you everything I told Topcliffe." He winced with pain and put a hand to his injured jaw.

"Well?"

"I told him I had a message to pass on. It was a message for a priest, a priest whose name I do not know. All I know is that he is lodged with Father Cotton."

"And what was the message?"

261

"Cogg. Cogg of Cow Lane. Just that and no more."

"And who gave you this message to pass on?"

"I . . . I do not know."

"I could have you on the rack this day, Piggott. Do you know what the rack does to men's bodies?"

Piggott nodded sullenly. All men knew that the rack could pull bones from joints, that it could tear muscles and tendons irrevocably so that the racked man would never walk or use his arms again.

"So answer me. Who gave you this message to pass on?"

"It was a Frenchie. I do not know his name. He came to me here and said he was sent by Dr. Allen. He may have been from the embassy of France. In truth, Mr. Shakespeare, I do not know. That was enough for me. He gave me money, two marks. Such money is the difference between life and death in a place like this."

"And what did you consider the message to mean?"

Piggott was in so deep now, all he could think of was staying alive. He would sacrifice the Pope, Cardinal Allen, and the English College at Rheims for the slim chance of life. His voice grew even lower and seemed to scour his mouth. "I took it to be the whereabouts of a weapon of some manner. A dag, perhaps. That is the way to kill princes these days, I believe."

Oh yes, thought Shakespeare, a wheel-lock pistol is certainly the way to murder princes; it had worked with William the Silent and now Elizabeth feared it would work its evil on her. A wheel-lock pistol could be ready primed and was small enough to be hidden in a gown or sleeve. That was why wheel-lock pistols — dags — were barred from the precincts of royal palaces. "Is that merely your surmise? Or do you have some reason for believing this?"

Piggott shook his head wearily. "Surmise, Mr. Shakespeare, merely surmise." He turned his head once more to the wall and slumped back into his fetal position, the only sign left of life being the fast and harsh sound of his painful breathing.

CHAPTER 21

Two heavily armed men stood at the doorway to Cogg's property in Cow Lane. Shakespeare dismounted and approached them. "Is Topcliffe here?" he demanded.

They looked at each other, winked, then turned back to Shakespeare and smirked. "No entry," one of them said with studied nonchalance.

"Do you know who I am?"

"You could be the King of Sweden's monkey for all I care. No entry."

"I am John Shakespeare, secretary to Sir Francis Walsingham. I am here on official business and I will be admitted."

"Try it if you like. Best of luck."

Shakespeare stepped forward. The two men immediately moved closer to each other to form an impenetrable wall. They wore thick doublets of oxhide, garments that would deflect most knife blows. They carried skenes and wheel-locks in their belts and swords in scabbards, which they did not bother to draw. Both were strong of arm and broad of chest. "If you do not let me pass, you will answer to Her Majesty's Principal Secretary. Do you understand what that means?"

"Look, whoever you are, do you think we're worried about you or bloody Walsingham? We answer to Mr. Topcliffe and he answers directly to the Queen. Do you understand what *that* means? Now then, which of them two would scare *you* more?"

At that moment the front door opened. Topcliffe stood there. He glowered at Shakespeare, then diverted his attention to the two guards. "Get a handcart," he ordered. "We've a body to move."

The more vocal of the two guards bowed obediently, then shuffled away.

"Topcliffe," Shakespeare said, "what is going on here?"

Topcliffe was about to turn back into the building, but he thought better of it and stopped. "What's it to you, Shakespeare?"

"You know very well, Topcliffe. I am in the middle of an official investigation."

"And by God, you are slow. Would you have found Cogg without me? Would the foul priest Piggott have talked to you if I had not softened him first? I doubt you could find a cunny in a whorehouse."

"Topcliffe, we've got to work together on this. We may not employ the same methods but I know we share the same ends — the security of our Queen and country."

"And what sort of milk-livered country will that be with the likes of you fighting for it? A country of men who would rather kneel and kiss the feet of the Antichrist than wash their hands in the blood of the Queen's foe. I would rather spill every last drop of Popish blood than see a single hair on her body harmed. Would you? Which church does your father go to of a Sunday, Shakespeare? Tell me that." Topcliffe spat at the ground between them. "Come in then, boy. Come and see what we have found and explain to your Walsingham why you always follow where Topcliffe leads."

Shakespeare's heart was pounding with rage, yet he swallowed his pride and stepped into the building. A large body lay beside a barrel, its head a mask of caked blood. Flies feasted and buzzed.

"Stabbed through the glaziers," Topcliffe said. "Looks like a pig, don't you think? Get him down the shambles and turn him into pies, no one would know the difference."

"Who is that? Cogg?"

"Oh yes, that's Cogg all right. Whoremonger, broker of stolen goods, wild rogue with a taste for meat and venery."

"I take it you knew him?"

Topcliffe put his heavy boot square on Cogg's dead chest and leaned forward so that Shakespeare could smell him. "He could get you anything you desired. He was dangerous but he had his uses, Shakespeare. Sometimes. He didn't always choose his friends wisely, as you can see. But we know who did this to him, don't we?"

"You think it's Southwell?"

"I *know* it's the boy-girl. And I know *why.* A dag. Southwell bought a dag from Cogg to kill our Queen and then tried to cover his tracks by killing him. We both know the Popish beast Southwell did this, but you will flounder like a fish in a bowl while I will catch him and make sure he departs this life in great pain and torment, wriggling like an eel as I remove his pizzle and sweetbreads and hold them, dripping, before his bulging eyes. And I will do so *before* he harms our Queen."

Shakespeare had much more to say, but held his counsel. He knew that it would all be so much wasted breath. It was impossible to talk to Topcliffe; he was set in his brutish ways. Like a terrier with game in its jaws, nothing would prize him from his belief that the Jesuit Southwell was on a killing spree, with Elizabeth as his ultimate target. For one brief moment, Shakespeare had a flicker of doubt. Perhaps Topcliffe was right in this? The moment passed. Yet he had to ask one more question. "Topcliffe, you took my witnesses. Where are they? I must talk to them."

"What witnesses would they be?"

"You know very well. The vagabonds from Hog Lane. You removed them from Bridewell where I had sent them in custody."

"Vagabonds? Gypsies? I know nothing of any gypsies, Shakespeare. And if I did, I'd rack them, every one, then hang them. I'd clear our country of such foul slurry."

"Are you denying that you had them removed?"

Topcliffe said nothing, merely looked at Shakespeare with scorn, then turned back to his work.

There was nothing Shakespeare could do on the matter. He had no way of proving anything against Topcliffe. And even if he did, who would care? Most people in this town would consider the disappearance of four vagabonds a good thing and shake Topcliffe by the hand for it.

Shakespeare wasn't certain what he was

looking for, but he searched the house, impeded at times by Topcliffe's men, who delighted in trying to trip him and bar his way. After an hour, he left and set off for Seething Lane. He badly needed to see Harry Slide again. Something had been nagging at Shakespeare since his visit to the Marshalsea. How exactly had Topcliffe heard of Piggott, Plummer, and the Mass said by the Jesuit priest Cotton?

Slide was waiting for him, but he wasn't alone. He had with him a constable and Walstan Glebe, publisher of *The London Informer.* Glebe was bound by the hands and was being restrained by the constable. He tried to protest at his detention, but Shakespeare would not listen. He ordered the constable to wait with Glebe in the antechamber, then took Slide through to the solar, now nearly restored to the condition it was in before being ransacked. "Harry, before we talk about Glebe, I've got to ask you something. How did Topcliffe know about the Marshalsea Mass?"

Slide looked genuinely shocked. "Topcliffe knew?"

"Oh yes. He got in there before me. He beat Piggott halfway to death. Have you been dealing with him?"

"Mr. Shakespeare, no. Never. I have never

dealt with Topcliffe."

"Only I couldn't help but wonder about your injuries . . ."

"In God's name, no. No. That was as I told you. I was robbed and beaten in the street by an unknown attacker."

"So I would be wrong in wondering whether Topcliffe beat the information out of you as he beats everyone else to get what he wants?"

Slide shook his head vehemently.

"So how do you think he knew?"

Harry Slide sat down. He looked utterly distraught, but Shakespeare knew all too well how he could dissemble. Walsingham had once said that if Slide ever gave up intelligencing, he could get work as a player with Mr. Burbage at the Theatre, so clever was he at playing a part. Slide shook his head. "*Anyone* could have told Topcliffe. The gaoler, one of his turnkeys, a visitor, prisoners. They come and go, Mr. Shakespeare. The Marshalsea is not the Tower. It is as tight as a goodwife's sieve."

Shakespeare sat down beside Harry Slide. He wasn't by any means certain that he believed the man, but he was sure he needed him. "All right. Leave it at that. I will accept your denial. But let me tell you, Slide, that if ever you *do* consult with Topcliffe, you will make an enemy of me, and an enemy of Mr. Secretary, who prizes loyalty above all else. Now tell me what you know about Cogg of Cow Lane."

A painful smile at last forced its way on to Slide's yellow-bruised face. "Gilbert Cogg! The fattest, greediest felon in all of London, Mr. Shakespeare. But a jovial fellow."

"A dead fellow now. Murdered. Stabbed in the eyes with some thin blade."

Slide did not look surprised. "Ah, a sadness. Not a great shock, however. Cogg dealt with many dangerous people. He loved gold more than anything. More than meat, drink, or lechery. Gold and rare stones were always his things and I know he would do anything to acquire them."

"Such as supply a pistol to a hired Spanish killer?"

Slide's eyes finally met Shakespeare's. "So that is what this is all about. Is there some connection with Piggott?"

"He was the intermediary. Whoever organized Cogg to supply the weapon got the message to his killer that it was ready via Piggott. So now we have a killer loose with a weapon, the like of which we can only imagine. To stop a determined man with a wheel-lock, we would have to keep Drake hidden away in his cabin, seeing no one until the Admiral is safe at sea. I fear that is most unlikely. And with Cogg dead there is no witness to identify the assassin."

"What of the Jesuit Southwell?"

Shakespeare laughed humorlessly. "Is he the killer? Everything we know about him suggests not. Tell me this though, Harry: if Cogg was so wealthy, where was his gold? I searched his house thoroughly. Topcliffe did, too. There was no sign of it."

"Cogg *was* wealthy. Maybe Topcliffe did find it and has kept it for himself. Or maybe he kept his treasure banked elsewhere. He had a whorehouse beside the Bel Savage, much to the irritation of the city aldermen. They found it far too close for comfort, though many were not above making use of its services."

"Take me there one day, Harry. It might be an education. Sometimes I think I have lived far too innocent. But in the meantime, go there and make inquiries. The geese might know something. First, though, let us speak with Mr. Glebe and see if we can't find some reason to give him a spell in the pillory. A spattering of eggs and a back that aches beyond enduring might make a better man of him. Where did you find him?"

"Back at Fleet Lane. He was trying to take apart his press to get it out of there. Evidently your friends at Stationers' Hall were slow off the mark."

In the antechamber, Glebe hung his head sullenly. His hands were bound but he could use his fingers as a comb, teasing his thick, wiry hair into a fringe to conceal the branded *L.* He looked up as Shakespeare and Slide entered the room, then thrust his bound hands in front of him. "Please, untie me, Mr. Shakespeare. I am not going anywhere."

Shakespeare nodded and the constable proceeded to cut him loose. He picked up a small bell from a coffer and rang it. Jane quickly appeared. "Some ale, please, Jane." Slowly he began to pace the room. Glebe's eyes followed him expectantly. Finally Shakespeare turned to him. "Well, Glebe, it seems your days of beslubbering reputations are over. At the very least I have you on charges of illicit printing and resisting arrest. With your previous record, I think the very least you can expect is the loss of a hand, both ears, and ten years with hard labor —"

"Mr. Shakespeare —"

"Have you anything to say to me before I consign you to Newgate and let the law take its course?"

"What can I tell you, sir? All I have done

is repeat gossip that I have heard in the taverns and alehouses."

Jane returned with ale. She poured beakers for Shakespeare, Slide, and the constable but hesitated before giving any to Glebe until Shakespeare nodded his assent.

"No, Glebe, that is *not* all you have done. Someone who knows about the murder of Lady Blanche Howard has spoken to you. I think a spell in Newgate and the thought of what is likely to befall you might concentrate your mind. I do not have time to listen to your denials."

Glebe looked even more sour, as though he had swallowed unripe medlar fruit. "Sir," he protested, "what have I done wrong? I merely wish to exercise my rights as a freeborn Englishman. Are we slaves? Have you forgotten the Great Charter?"

"This is nothing to do with slavery. You know as well as I do that all printed works must be licensed. You have not done so and you will pay the penalty. Had you co-operated with us, we could have let you go about your business, but this matter involves the murder of a cousin of the Queen — and we need to find out who did it. Once you are in the cage, there will be no way out, Glebe. No appeal. I am sure you understand."

Glebe shrugged his sloping, rounded shoulders. "I have nothing more to say. Do your worst."

For a moment, Shakespeare was caught off guard. He had expected Glebe to crumple and talk. Surely a man who had known the stench of his own burnt flesh, and the pain associated with it, might wish to avoid further internment and possible mutilation?

"So be it. Take him to Newgate, constable. Make sure he is shackled to the floor and given nothing but porridge and water. And tell no one he is there."

CHAPTER 22

The *Elizabeth Bonaventure,* a royal ship of six hundred tons with thirty-four guns and a crew of two hundred and fifty men, slipped away from the quay at Gravesend on the tide and made sail with the wind. It was a chilly morning, just past break of day, and a brisk breeze stretched the ship's pennants bravely and churned the gray surface of the Thames.

The sailors set to work, coiling ropes, scrubbing down the decks of all the land detritus that had collected in port. Behind them, growing more and more distant, the smoke of London spiraled hazily into the sky. Gradually the river grew broader and the great ship moved elegantly onward through the swift, turbulent flood on her way down to the sea. As the wind freshened, it whistled through the shrouds and sails, casting a curious spell that, for a while, rendered all aboard silent in their toil.

Boltfoot Cooper rested his left arm on the polished oak bulkwark and watched Vice Admiral Drake from a distance of not more than forty feet. He kept his right hand on the hilt of his cutlass, which was thrust loosely through his belt. At last, in the early afternoon, they reached the gaping mouth of the river and flew before the wind into the narrow sea.

"Cooper!" Drake's gruff voice rang out above the wind. "Drag yourself here, man!"

Boltfoot moved resignedly toward his former captain. He had vowed never to take orders from him again, nor ever to set foot aboard another of his vessels.

"Report to the carpenter, Mr. Cooper. There will be plenty of work to do on the spars and casks. Make yourself useful. I don't need watching like a babe out here."

Boltfoot stood his ground. "I am ordered to remain with you at all times. Who is to say that one of this crew is not a hireling of Spain?"

"By the bones of the deep, Mr. Cooper, would you disobey an order of your captain? I'll have you hanged at the yardarm."

"My captain is Mr. Shakespeare and my admiral is Mr. Secretary Walsingham, as you know, sir. I am answerable to them and to them only, save the Queen and God."

"Huh! You have a fine spirit this cold morning, Mr. Cooper. Take a tot of brandy." Drake turned to his lieutenant. "Captain Stanley, be good enough to ask the galley steward to bring us a bottle of Aquitaine liquor."

Stanley, thought Boltfoot, looked a little bit disgruntled, as if it were not his place to call upon a steward to serve them, especially with Boltfoot and Diego in close attendance. But though Harper Stanley might have felt slighted, the lieutenant did not complain. When the brandy arrived, Boltfoot insisted on tasting Drake's first, for poison. Drake scowled at him. "You think me as womanly as a Spaniard, Mr. Cooper?"

Boltfoot glared back and grumbled, "Marry. If it were mine to choose, I would poison it myself."

"And I would gladly make *you* drink it, Mr. Cooper!"

Diego clapped Boltfoot on the back. "Do not listen to him, Boltfoot. I think he loves you. Let us drink a toast to the *Elizabeth Bonaventure*."

"Is she not yare, gentlemen?" said Drake. "Mr. Hawkins has done a splendid job here. Low to the sea, fast and responsive. She has the narrow waist of a wanton. It will be a rare Spanish galleon can match the *Lizzie* when we have the weather gauge. Now, Mr. Stanley, bring forth the Master Gunner and let us prepare to have some sport with the ordnance. We will soon be upon the target hulk."

They were moving on a broad curve northward, close to the tidal sands of Pig's Bay near Shoebury Ness. A coaster with coals from the north tacked southward past them and disappeared slowly into the Thames. The *Lizzie* had been Drake's flagship sixteen months earlier on his Caribbean raid. She was already a quarter of a century old on that voyage, but John Hawkins had streamlined her and made a new ship of her. Since then, with advice from Drake, he had made more adjustments to improve her speed and maneuverability. Sleek, fast, like a wisp in the wind but with the firepower of a dragon, the *Lizzie* was a Spanish galleon commander's nightmare.

At last, a boy at the top of the mainmast called out, "Hulk ahoy." And soon they all saw it, a weathered old vessel stuck fast in the sand with nothing left but its hull and a broken skeleton of spars and masts, dating back to the turn of the century or more.

"We will take six turns, Master Gunner. First turn long range, five hundred yards," Drake announced. The Master Gunner, a broad-shouldered man of thirty, bowed to his Vice Admiral and went straightway to the gun deck, where he began issuing orders.

As they came around for the first turn and as the great cannons boomed and recoiled on their four-wheeled carriages, the smoke of gunpowder choked out the sun, like a crackling bonfire of greenwood in autumn. Boltfoot kept his eyes on Drake and remembered the long sea days of the circumnavigation in the great oceans with a curious nostalgia that he had thought never to feel again.

In his mind's eye, he could see the vastness of the open sea, when you knew there was a God in heaven and that He was very close. On a clear day, the ocean was a glory to behold. The rolling waves, higher than the bowsprit of the *Golden Hind,* reaching as far as a man could see, north, south, east, and west; immense in their splendor. As the *Hind* descended from one wave into a long, dipping trough, the next wave rose like a tall, gray cathedral before them and the ship itself began to rise to meet it, before falling once more down a wall of water into an enormous, foam-wracked trough. Such days had terrified many mariners, yet Boltfoot loved them; until this moment, he had forgotten how much.

"Regrets, Mr. Cooper?" Drake bellowed, just after the second boom of the *Elizabeth Bonaventure's* guns, as if reading Boltfoot's mind.

Yes. That you cheated me out of my plunder, Boltfoot thought, but said nothing.

The ship continued its long sweeps across the hulk, turning with grace and speed, its bow low and eager to please, then firing with increasing accuracy from different ranges, crashing the hulk into splinterwood. Finally, when the supply of balls was exhausted and the hulk had all but disappeared beneath the sea, Drake ordered the master to take them home. "We will make for Deptford, where you will land me. Then you can take her back to Gravesend with Captain Stanley."

They arrived back soon after a limpid sun rose the next day, the *Elizabeth Bonaventure's* sails gleaming in the low eastern light. Boltfoot had stayed the night outside the great cabin in the sterncastle, taking turns with Diego to sleep in a hastily raised hammock. This was also the way it was working now at Drake's home in Elbow Lane and at court when they stayed there. Despite his reservations about being protected, Drake was allowing Boltfoot and Diego to camp outside the chamber he shared with his wife.

The *Lizzie* dropped anchor in midstream, some way from the landing steps at Deptford. The coxswain, Matthew, lowered the captain's boat and brought it into position. When the oarsmen were all at their stations, Drake descended the rope ladder, a small, indistinct figure against the vastness of the sleek, oiled oak of the bulwarks and the pitch-blackened hull below. Boltfoot followed him.

Herrick, in his room above the chandlery on the Strand at Deptford, had been awake and watchful since first light. He had seen the *Elizabeth Bonaventure* from some way off. She was every inch a royal ship, proudly bearing flags with the white cross of Saint George and silken pennants of gold and silver, flying thirty yards or more from the masts. And then, as she came closer, he could see the rose shield of the Tudors adorning the low race-built forecastle — the same diminutive structure that made the ship so vulnerable to boarding yet, at the same time, as nimble and quick as a wild cat.

For a moment Herrick found himself admiring her lines. She was majestic and it occurred to him that if the English had many more such ships, they could trouble, if not match, any armada that Philip could muster and put to sea. He resolved that when this Holy mission was done with, he would go to Mendoza in Paris with information on what he had seen here. His Spanish masters should know the truth about this English fleet.

From the bag he took the two pieces of gun; the mechanism and the barrel in one piece, the stock separate. They clipped together easily. He primed the weapon with the fine willow powder and rammed home one of the balls into the muzzle. It fitted perfectly. Herrick removed his sighting stand from below the bed. It was short, no more than two feet. He had crafted it himself from wood he had found discarded outside the dockyard timber merchant's lot nearby. At its top was a notch he had cut, on which he could rest the muzzle.

He opened the little window and looked out. Beneath him the early-morning throng was going about its business. No one looked up. Herrick took his pillow cushion from the bed and put it on the floor close by the window, where he placed it beneath one knee, crouching low so that his head would not be visible from the street below. He had a clear, unimpeded view of the landing steps where Drake would soon land.

He could see the cockboat now, rowed hard and in time by four oarsmen. The coxswain stood, directing their strokes. In the back, the captain sat in splendor, talking to a dark-skinned man to his left. On the other side of him sat a thickset man who looked for all the world like a broadsheet version of a pirate. Herrick studied the captain in the middle. Was this man definitely Drake? If his information was correct that Drake would come ashore from the *Elizabeth Bonaventure* this day — and Herrick had no reason to doubt it — then this had to be him. He took the portrait from his doublet and studied it briefly. This captain fitted every description of Drake he knew: the proud, puffed-out chest; the stocky stature; the jutting, sharp-cut golden beard; the curled, flame-red hair; the arrogance. Herrick discarded any doubts. This was Drake.

The cockboat was about two hundred yards away. Herrick rested the barrel of his snaphaunce musket on the makeshift stand, its muzzle protruding not more than an inch over the sill of the window.

He knew it to be a remarkable weapon. Before coming here to this eyrie in Deptford, he had taken the gun, concealed in his bag, out to the woods past Islington ponds.

There he had expended three-quarters of the twenty-four specially manufactured balls in target practice. The musket was as accurate as claimed by its maker, Opel. He knew he could easily hit a man's head from a hundred yards, probably one-fifty, and possibly even two hundred. With such a weapon ranged against them, no prince or captain-general would ever be safe again.

Herrick lined up the sights of the gun on his target and squinted down the barrel at Drake. He could take him now, while he sat in the back, literally a sitting target. But he held back; the boat was swaying in the choppy swell. Herrick could wait. He had been here at this window for sixty hours now, watching the Strand, the river, and the moored ships almost every moment of daylight, barely breaking for food or drink. Wait until Drake was closer to shore but not yet landed, that was the thing. This was the place, his man had assured him.

Drake's head was in his sights now, as big and lush as the watermelons in the market at the bottom of the Capitoline Hill, near the English college. He let the muzzle drop and lined up on Drake's chest. Aim for the biggest target — the body, not the head.

They were close enough now. The boat was in calmer water and there was no obstacle between the muzzle of Herrick's gun and the body of England's greatest mariner. Herrick held the stock hard into his shoulder to minimize recoil, then pulled the trigger.

The explosion in the small, enclosed room was deafening. The recoil threw him back. Smoke billowed from the muzzle. Herrick set the weapon on the bare boards of the floor, then looked from the window, trying to make out the boat. There was a mass of confusion and the vessel was rocking madly. The oarsmen were all now standing; they seemed to be crowded around Drake. Was he dead? He had to be dead. There was no time to lose; Herrick had to move fast. He couldn't get back to London by boat. The river would be shut down immediately. He had a horse liveried at a tavern stable inland, half a mile to the south, toward the gabled manor house Sayers Court. His plan was to ride to Southwark, where there was a safe house, and stay there until the hue and cry died down. Perhaps a week, maybe more. The ports were all closed anyway since the death of Mary, Queen of Scots, and the searches of any foreigners trying to get across the Channel would now be redoubled. He must keep his head, stay low and wait.

He dismantled his weapon, threw it back in the bag, and stowed it beneath the bed. No need of it now. He had no other belongings, merely the clothes he stood in, the wheel-lock pistol at his belt, his thin-bladed skene and rapier. He shut the door of the room behind him and walked down the creaking staircase to the shop below.

Bob Roberts, his landlord, was there, standing at the doorway. He turned and smiled broadly at Herrick, clutching the base of his fume-belching pipe. "There's quite a to-do out there, Mr. van Leiden," he said, carelessly blowing smoke in Herrick's face.

"What is it, Bob?"

"Hard to say. Looks like someone's been hurt." Roberts looked curiously at Herrick. "Are you all right, Mr. van Leiden? I heard a noise from upstairs. Thought you must have fallen out of bed."

Herrick laughed. "That I did, Bob. That I did. And now I must take my leave of you and try again for some work. I will see you at dusk." He stepped out from the doorway intending to hurry to the stables. But first he would join the throng at the waterfront, to make sure Drake was dead.

Boltfoot Cooper was drenched. He stood

on the quayside, his eyes focused on a small window. Just before the shot rang out, Boltfoot had caught a dull glint from that window, in the middle of the row of shops and suppliers at the back of Deptford Strand. The dull glint had become a puff of smoke, swiftly followed by the familiar sound of a charge of gunpowder exploding. At that moment, Matt the coxswain moved to the side with the landing hook to pull the boat into the steps when she came alongside. The coxswain took the bullet in the lower abdomen and crumpled down and backwards into Drake's lap.

Boltfoot's eyes turned briefly from the window to Matt, then back to the window. As the puff of smoke cleared, a face appeared. It was clean-shaven, as pale as a carved marble bust, and it was peering hard toward them. After the initial shock, the oarsmen and Diego clustered around Matt, lifting him off the Vice Admiral's lap and laying him down in the bottom of the boat where they could tend to him. Drake immediately took control of the situation. Boltfoot scrambled out of the boat, dragging himself through the water to the steps, which at this high tide, were below the river's surface.

Boltfoot pulled himself up the steps onto

the quay, his clothes dripping wet. Crowds were now milling around, trying to see what had happened in the cockboat. After a moment standing on the quay getting his bearings, he pushed his way through the throng and looked across to the window he had seen. The face was no longer there. He started to stride toward the building. He was surprisingly quick, despite his clubfoot. His cutlass was now drawn and hanging loose in his hand at his side. The chandlery where he had seen the face at the window was sixty to seventy yards away. There was a man at the doorway now. He was bearded and looked for all the world like a casual onlooker. Another man appeared beside him. He was clean-shaven, like the face at the window. It *was* the face at the window. Boltfoot's pace quickened.

Herrick's eye caught Boltfoot's as soon as he stepped out from the doorway. He recognized him instantly as the piratical figure sitting beside Drake in the cockboat. His cutlass was drawn and he was coming straight toward him in a difficult, loping stride, one leg dragging as if it were injured. Had the sailor been hurt in the melee when Drake was hit? Herrick switched plans; he would not go to the waterfront. This man was coming for him. Swiftly, Herrick turned right and ducked down an alley, barging past a waterseller, knocking the great conical butt from his shoulders to the ground. The butt was well hooped for strength and did not shatter, but the water flowed forth. The water-bearer cursed, but Herrick was already gone.

Boltfoot appeared in the alley as the water-bearer was lifting his ungainly butt back onto his shoulders.

"Where did he go?"

The water-bearer, a gray-haired man with a stoop, pointed down the alley and indicated that the fugitive had turned right at the end. "And give the whoreson a bloody nose from me!"

Boltfoot had unslung his caliver and was priming it. He loped on. At the end of the alley he turned right and saw the back of the intruder, perhaps thirty yards ahead of him. It was an impossible shot, but Boltfoot knew he would never catch the man on foot. He stopped, knelt, held the wheel-lock gun in his right hand, resting on his left forearm, took aim as well as his heaving lungs would allow, and fired.

Herrick felt a searing pain in his side, just below his left armpit, and arced forward. But he did not falter. His right hand clutched at the wound. His fingers were wet with blood but the wound would not stop him. At most, he reckoned, the ball had torn a bit of flesh and skin but had ricocheted off his ribs. He was lucky. He ran on.

The alleys were dense and mazelike, with jettied overhangs from the crowded buildings. Many of the buildings were in some way connected to the sea trade that was the essence of this town: sailors' lodgings, alehouses, stews, chandlers. Herrick pushed on, loping like the wolf evading a shepherd whose lambs it has just slaughtered. He was fit but his chest and lungs hurt. At last he came out of the main part of Deptford. He ran across a dirt road, then another, narrowly avoiding a horseman who had to rein in sharply. Ahead he saw the stable and slowed to a walk. One of the ostlers was just leading his mount out into the cobbled yard.

"Good morrow, Mr. van Leiden. Fine timing, sir. Your mount is ready for your morning ride."

Herrick caught his breath. He took the reins from the groom and accepted his cupped hands as a step-up, then swung himself onto the horse. *Slow down now,* he told himself. *Slow down. Don't arouse more suspicion.* He managed to smile at the ostler and found a coin for him in his purse.

"Thank you, sir." Then, "It seems you have hurt yourself, Mr. van Leiden."

"I fell and caught my side on a piece of iron. I think it was an old spoke from a carter's wheel."

"Too much of the falling-down juice, is it, sir?"

Herrick laughed. "Something like that." Over the groom's shoulder he saw, in the distance, the advancing figure of the limping gunman who had just shot him; his awkward running style was unmistakable. Herrick dug his heels into the horse's flank, shook the reins, wheeled around, and was gone.

CHAPTER 23

The muffled beat of drums hung in the air like the distant thunder of war. All roads through the city of London were blocked to traffic. Every street was thronged with somber crowds, come to honor their valiant knight and poet, Sir Philip Sidney.

He had died of the black rot following a shot in the thigh when he and his troops were ambushed by the Duke of Parma's Spanish forces at Zutphen in the lowlands the previous October. His body had been embalmed and brought back to England in a ship with black sails, and for months he had lain in state at the Minories, close to the Tower, awaiting England's first ever state funeral for a nonroyal.

Now the day had arrived. Sir Philip had been Walsingham's son-in-law, and Mr. Secretary was paying for the extravagant procession with funds he could scarce afford. It was an occasion of symbolism: the laying to rest of a champion of the Protestant Reformation. Seven hundred official mourners followed the cortege as it wove slowly through the streets of London from Aldgate to St. Paul's. At the head of the procession, dominating all, was the catafalque, laid over with velvet and flags and surrounded by close members of the Sidney and Walsingham families. The great of the land were there, including Sir Philip's uncle, the Earl of Leicester, looking tired and wan as though the fight had left him, and Leicester's stepson, the Earl of Essex, new-blooded hero of the lowlands war. Of the ruling elite, only the Queen herself was missing; still raging over the execution of Mary Stuart, it was said, in her privy chamber at Greenwich Palace.

The crowd applauded the funeral cortege with tears rolling down their cheeks, their emotions heightened by the recent news of the attempt on the life of their other great hero, Drake. Many called out tributes for Sidney, this most loved son of England; others called for vengeance on Parma, King Philip, and Spain.

John Shakespeare watched awhile. The sight of Topcliffe, up with the vanguard of mourners, was too much for him. Their eyes met. Topcliffe seemed to smirk through his brown teeth, bared like fangs. Shakespeare turned away; there was work to be done. He needed to see Catherine Marvell and Thomas Woode again, and he had to travel to Deptford to talk with those who had encountered the man who'd tried to shoot Drake. He had another task at Deptford, too: to try to talk once more with Lord Admiral Howard when he returned from the funeral. There must be more he could learn from him about Lady Blanche. As Shakespeare walked toward Dowgate, the scent of hot chestnuts roasting in a brazier enticed him and he bought a few, then strode on, peeling and eating the chestnuts as he went. The muffled drums, all draped in black, beat out their deathly march, fading slowly into the haze behind him.

Catherine was at home but Woode was not. She did not seem pleased to see Shakespeare. "I am surprised you are not at St. Paul's mourning the heroic Sir Philip," she said. "Everyone else in London seems to be."

"Do you not think him heroic, Mistress Marvell?"

"Oh, indeed I do, sir. He was a very perfect, gentle knight. It is the timing of his funeral that interests me, however. The day was chosen by your own Mr. Secretary

Walsingham, I do believe. How curious that it should come so close after the dispatching of the Queen of Scots. . . ."

Shakespeare had, of course, heard the scurrilous mutterings about the choice of dates. In fact he had wondered about it himself, for this great funeral of Sir Philip Sidney was indeed a most convenient way of deflecting public interest from the execution of Mary of Scots. It was one thing to have such thoughts; however, quite another to voice them openly as this Catherine Marvell was doing. "You should beware your tongue, Mistress Marvell, lest it attract unwanted attention to this household."

"Have they passed a law now making it a capital offense to call myself Catholic?"

Shakespeare bridled. "You may call yourself what you wish, so long as you attend your parish church and do not harbor priests come here from abroad. For you must know that it is a treasonable crime for a Popish priest to enter England."

"Well then, Mr. Shakespeare, I must take care not to harbor any Popish priests."

"As for the Scots Queen, I am surprised you have tears to spare for her. Was she not an adulteress? Did she not kill a husband in cold blood? Do you doubt she meant to murder the Queen of England?"

"I will let God be the judge of that, yet I do believe she died a Christian."

This was a bad start. Shakespeare had no desire to cross swords with this woman. He stood there awkwardly, like a grammar school boy, looking at her, not sure what to do or say next. He did not want to play the heavy government agent with her.

"I am sorry, Mr. Shakespeare," she said at last, a smile lighting her blue eyes. She wore a long dress of fine burgundy-red wool and matching bodice. Her ruff was simple and her long dark hair was uncovered. The whole effect was to accentuate the unwavering character in her eyes and mouth and the slenderness of her figure. "I am sure you did not come here to be berated so. It is unforgivable to leave you on the doorstep in the cold. Please, do come in."

He thanked her and stepped into the warmth of the house. From within, he heard the sound of children laughing and playing.

"That is Mr. Woode's children. Would you like to meet them? Perchance they have been harboring priests."

Shakespeare found himself smiling. "Your sense of comedy may well prove your undoing, Mistress Marvell."

"Well, that is who I am, I'm afraid, sir. If speaking my mind leads me to Tyburn, it will say a powerful lot more about you and Walsingham than it will about me. I am sure of that."

Shakespeare sighed deliberately and dismissively, the way his old schoolteacher used to do whenever a pupil gave a poor excuse for being late on a winter's morning. "That, as you know well, mistress, is *not* the point. And you must know that it is not I who would bring you to the headsman's axe. There are . . . *others* . . . others less understanding, less mindful of your welfare."

"Yes, I realize that. But you are in bed with them, Mr. Shakespeare, and you cannot so easily distance yourself from your bedfellows."

"Nor you, mistress. For you must know that the Romish priest Ballard conspired to kill our sovereign lady. You must know that the Pope himself has condoned the Queen's murder and sends seditious young men from the serpents' nest of the English college in Rome to undermine her realm. Are these *your* bedfellows?"

Catherine's eyes burned bright. "I have *no* bedfellows, sir. I am a maiden. Come, let us go to the children. They have better conversation."

She led the way through to the nursery.

The boy, Andrew, immediately ran to her and threw himself into her arms. He was a hefty six-year-old with fair hair like his father and the same broad brow. The girl, Grace, looked to Shakespeare like a younger version of the portrait in the hall of Woode's late wife. Grace also ran to Catherine, dragging a wooden doll along the timbered floor by its one remaining limb. Catherine put her arms around each of them and crouched down to their level to hug and kiss them. Suddenly the children noticed Shakespeare and drew themselves closer into their governess's arms.

"Andrew, Grace, this is Mr. Shakespeare. Will you please greet him as you should."

"Good morrow, sir," the boy said firmly as he had been taught.

Shakespeare bowed down and shook his hand. "And good morrow to you, Master Andrew."

Grace merely turned her head away coyly and would say nothing.

"Never mind," Shakespeare said. "I'm sure she has far more important things to do caring for her doll than talking with tedious adults."

Catherine removed the two children gently from her arms and patted them. "Go and play while I talk with Mr. Shakespeare, please."

The children ran off across the room, as far from Shakespeare as they could get. "Now, can I offer you some refreshment, Mr. Shakespeare? Perhaps some hot spiced malmsey?"

"No, thank you. Do not put yourself to any trouble. I have one or two questions, that is all."

"And how should I answer you? Truthfully and risk my head? With comedy and set myself on the road to Tyburn? Or should I dissemble and stay alive, sir?"

Shakespeare ignored her barbed remarks. He knew he could match her atrocity for atrocity and more. He could mention the French Catholics' slaughter of thousands of Protestant Huguenots on St. Bartholomew's Day; he could regale her with the horrors of Torquemada's Inquisition burnings. Instead he got straight to the point. "Did you know Lady Blanche Howard?"

Catherine barely hesitated, but it was enough for Shakespeare to notice. "I did, Mr. Shakespeare. I loved her like a sister."

The honesty of the answer caught him off guard. "Why did you not mention this before?"

"Why, sir, I did not know it was pertinent

to your inquiries. And, anyway, you did not ask me."

"Please tell me how you knew her."

Catherine stepped toward the door. "Come, let us go and sit in the library while we talk; we will not be disturbed by children's prattle. Are you sure you will not take refreshment?"

Shakespeare thanked her and said that he would after all take some mulled wine. While he waited for Catherine to return with the drink, he paced the library, examining Woode's extensive collection of books, many of them Italian. From somewhere, in another part of the house, he heard the sounds of hammering. When Catherine reappeared a few minutes later, he thanked her for the wine and asked about the noise.

"This house is not yet finished, Mr. Shakespeare. The carpenters and stonemasons are still working on the area to the west of the court."

"It seems curious to me that such a large house should have so few members of staff."

"That has been the way while the construction work has been continuing. Master Woode did not want to move away and disturb the children any more than necessary, so instead we stayed here and he reduced the household; I confess we have lived in a rather confined space. I have been the only one staying here; it is only recently that we have had so much room. Maids and cooks come in by day, as and when necessary, and I direct them. Happily, I believe we will have more domestic servants when the work is complete."

Shakespeare gathered his thoughts. "Mistress Marvell, you were telling me about Lady Blanche. I confess I am surprised that you knew her. She was a lady of the court; you are governess to a merchant's children."

"I think you are trying to say that I was not of her standing. . . ."

Shakespeare reddened. "I am sorry, I did not mean to imply that."

"Really? I am sure that is *exactly* what you meant to imply. And you are quite right. I am a humble schoolteacher's daughter from York, Mr. Shakespeare. I have no fortune and few prospects. Blanche was a daughter of one of England's great families and might well have been expected to marry an earl or a duke. How could there possibly be any common ground between us?"

"Well, how *could* there?"

Catherine tilted back her head. "I feel sure you have already divined that, Mr. Shakespeare. It was, of course, our religion. Blanche had lately returned to the Roman church and we met at Mass."

"Where, pray, was this Mass held?"

"Mr. Shakespeare, you must know I cannot tell you that. I am only telling you this much because I wish the perpetrator of the terrible crime to be caught. And . . ."

She looked away from him to the window. The sky outside was winter white. Shakespeare waited. She turned back.

"And because I trust you, Mr. Shakespeare."

Her words sent a shiver down his spine. The intelligencer in him, the state agent, feared her trust. The last thing he wanted was to be drawn into secrets that he could not keep. He sipped the wine and savored its warm sweetness. "Mistress Marvell," he said at last, "you must realize that I cannot promise to keep secret anything you tell me. My first duty is to Mr. Secretary and Her Majesty the Queen."

Catherine laughed dryly. "I know that. Don't worry, I do not intend to compromise you in any way. All I mean is that I trust you to use whatever I tell you judiciously."

"Then tell me more about Lady Blanche."

"Well, she could seem very young at times — full of life and laughter. At other times she was serious and devout. She had ideas of going to Italy or France to join a convent, but then she changed her mind. At the time I did not understand what had altered. Now, of course, I know. She fell in love."

"The father of her unborn child?"

Catherine closed her eyes and held her hands to her face, like a girl at the bear-baiting who has to avert her eyes from the sight of blood. "I think so," she answered quietly. "I don't know. I did not know she was expecting a baby until I heard the news of her death. Please do not ask me more. I cannot name him."

"What sort of man was he? Was he a stranger to these shores? Was he a friend of yours, another Papist?"

"Please, Mr. Shakespeare."

"But you want to find her killer. I cannot work in the shadows. Shed some light on this dark affair for me, Mistress Marvell. I must tell you that there could be a great deal more to this tragedy than meets the eye. I have reason to believe that her killer was sent by Spain and is conspiring against the realm. Perhaps she found out more than she should have and became a threat to this killer. You say you are a loyal subject of the Crown; now is the time to prove it. If the man who killed Lady Blanche is the same man who brought her with child, then it is your duty as an Englishwoman to tell me his name. Also — and I have no desire for this to sound like a threat — you must know the danger to yourself and this household if you hold back important evidence."

She shook her head vehemently. "The man Blanche loved would not hurt a mouse. He is a gentle soul. It was a sadness that they could never have married."

"Then you know him?"

She nodded slowly. "Yes, I know him. But I will not reveal his name to you."

"How do you know he did not kill her? Only God can see into the heart."

"Mr. Shakespeare, I am not a gull. I am trusting you as far as I may, so please trust *me* on this: the man she loved did *not* kill her."

"Do you know who did?"

Outside, a bird drifted lazily across the sky; a crow, perhaps, or a kite, looking for carrion. There were jarring sounds out there: the hammering of carpenters driving nails into rafters and joists, the slow beat of funeral drums somewhere to the west. She was silent. She had her suspicions, but no proof. And she could not speak her fears, for that would be a betrayal of those she loved. "No," she said softly. "No, I do not know who killed her."

"But you have an idea, don't you?"

"If I have any suspicions, they are without any evidence and so must be considered unfounded. It would be pointless to tell you."

"Will you let *me* be the judge of that?"

"I cannot."

Shakespeare gritted his teeth. He was beside himself with frustration. With any other witness he would, by now, have brought her into custody for hard questioning. Why was this woman so different from Walstan Glebe, presently languishing in Newgate's dungeon, threatened with mutilation and years of hard labor? Perhaps Topcliffe was right; perhaps he was too soft for this work. He scowled at her. "All right, Mistress Marvell, we will come back to that. But for the present, let us move on to other matters. What of the printing? What connection did Lady Blanche Howard have with the printing of seditious tracts? Are you and Mr. Woode involved in this?"

"Mr. Shakespeare, I know nothing of printing. And I have no knowledge whether Blanche was involved in anything like that either."

"But Mr. Woode knows something. Of that I am sure. I saw his reaction when I questioned him; he recognized the paper or the printing or both."

"That is something you will have to ask Mr. Woode himself. I cannot answer for him."

"What then of the house in Hog Lane, where Lady Blanche's body was found?"

Catherine shook her head vigorously. "Again, nothing. I have never been to a house in Hog Lane. I had not even heard of the place and certainly could not tell you where it is."

"Is there anything you *do* wish to tell me, Mistress Marvell? Any information that may help us find this foul murderer?"

"Mr. Shakespeare, please believe me: if I knew the name of the killer I would tell you his — or her — name without a moment's hesitation. I want the perpetrator of this wicked crime brought to justice so that he will never do such a thing again." Catherine leaned forward and spoke with a firm voice, yet even as she said the words she felt a chill inside. For though she was careful not to lie, she was horribly aware that she was not quite truthful either.

CHAPTER 24

Rose Downie reached up to the cheese cratch in the buttery and brought down the Parmesan and the Cheshire and a small sheep's cheese and a soft pungent cheese of Rouen. She also found a piece of spermyse, a creamy, herby cheese, but it had gone moldy and so she set it aside for feeding to the pig. Tonight, she had been told, was an important dinner, and the countess was expecting a fine spread of food.

She laid out the cheeses on a big wooden trencher, then set to cutting some cold meats to go alongside the cheese. Like the other two maidservants in this huge and rambling old house in the ward of Farringdon, Rose was curious who her mistress, Anne, the Lady Tanahill, might be entertaining this evening. Such an event was a rarity these days; since the Countess's lord, Philip, had been consigned to the Tower two years ago, she and her small child had lived an isolated, sad life. Though tall with fair hair and a skin that glowed like a girl half her thirty years, she was shy and thin. And yet she had a grace that Rose had immediately loved and admired.

The house was pleasant, if old and in need of attention. It had been the town house of bishops and other men of distinction before passing into the hands of the Earls of Tanahill some forty years earlier. It had a long and broad garden leading down to the Thames, where it had its own landing stage. It stood brazenly close to the grand mansion of the Earl of Leicester and to the Queen's palace, Somerset House, which was not a comfortable position for a family that clung to the old faith, when so many of those around were steeped in the new.

Usually the maids, the manservant, and their mistress took to their beds as soon as dusk fell. But tonight there was candlelight throughout Tanahill House. Amy Spynke, the housekeeper, had organized the cooking of two fowls and a rump of beef. There was a broth, too, and winter vegetables and sweetmeats.

At seven, the guests came. First the Vaux family, then the Brownes, followed by the Treshams and Mr. Swithin Wells, gray and stooped. Mr. Wells was the Countess's most regular visitor these days. Rose knew them all well and knew them to be Papists every one, but that had never concerned her. They were all kind to her and treated her with respect. She had no interest in religious mutterings and utterings; she went to the Anglican parish church each Sunday because failure to do so would cost her a fine under the recusancy laws, and that was all.

The last two guests were not known to Rose, but they were introduced to her as Mr. Cotton and Mr. Woode. She curtsied to them, for both men were dressed in the fine clothes of the gentry. As the three maids — Rose, Mistress Spynke, and the girl Beatrice Fallow, who was only eleven years of age — retired from the dining hall back down to the buttery, the baby started to wail from upstairs in Rose's room. Rose froze in mid-step. *Oh please, not again,* she said beneath her breath. She would have to go to him, though she knew that no amount of cradling would bring an end to his unearthly cries. The only thing that might bring relief from the catlike wailing was her milk and, eventually, sleep. But he had slept these past two hours and would not now be likely to go to sleep again this evening until well after midnight.

"I'll have to go to him, Amy. Tonight of all nights."

Amy nodded. "All right, Rose love. Get back when you can. Beatrice and I will manage."

In her small room at the top of the house, Rose stood over the baby's basket. For a minute she just looked at its round face with its low ears. Its curious froglike black eyes, so widely spaced, gazed back at her uncomprehendingly. The child's mouth was fixed wide open in a scream. Rose thought it monstrous, like some animal she had never encountered. With the cushion from her bed, she could snuff out its life like a candle right now. There were times that she wondered whether she had been visited at night by an incubus that had put this thing in her womb, but then she remembered that it was not hers and that it had never been in her belly, that *her* baby was called William Edmund and he was beautiful. Who had taken her son and replaced him with this . . . *thing?*

She loosened her blouse and brought the baby from the cot up to her breast once more. Its screaming mouth, open and demanding like a newborn sparrow in the nest, took her teat and sucked ferociously. It occurred to her that she should give it a name. She couldn't call him Edmund or

William, because they were her own baby's names. Perhaps she might call him Robert after her late father. Had it even been christened?

Rose lay back on the cushion with the child at her breast, letting these thoughts and questions wash over her until she began to get drowsy. She had almost drifted off when there was a soft knocking at her door. "It's me. Amy. M'lady has asked that you bring the baby downstairs."

The child straightway set to wailing once more. "Why would she want me to bring it down when she has guests?" Rose sighed. She owed a huge debt of gratitude to the Countess. Many employers would not have taken back a young widow with a child as she had done.

She arrived downstairs to find the dinner table cleared away and the guests sitting talking quietly and sipping wine. Rose stood in the doorway, cradling the swaddled baby in her arms. It was screaming at the top of its high-pitched voice now, an urgent monotone of noise that pierced her ears. The guests all turned to look at her. The Lady Tanahill stood up from her chair and walked over to her. She gently guided her across to the table. Smiling, she took the baby from Rose's arms and held it out for all to see.

"This is Rose's foundling child," the Countess said, ignoring the incessant wailing. "Her own baby was stolen from her while she was at the market, and this baby was left in its place. I am afraid that the courts and the constable have done nothing to help her get back her own baby, William Edmund. But Rose has cared for this child with fortitude. In this she has shown true Godliness, for this also is one of His creatures, and she is to be commended." She turned and smiled at Rose. "I hope I do not make light of your tribulations. It can be no easy thing to lose a child in this way. Many a woman would not have accepted the burden of feeding and taking care of someone else's baby as you have done." She held the baby's head up for closer inspection by her guests. "As you can see, this child is not as other babies."

The guests peered at the child with interest and sympathy. The women rose from their seats and crowded around to look closely at it and to touch its face. Rose Downie watched them, astonished. She had not thought this grotesque infant could elicit such interest and compassion from others.

"Father Cotton," the Countess said at last, "will you bless this child?"

313

Cotton took the shrieking infant from the Countess's arms. He stroked its face softly with one hand while cradling it in the other arm. Then he murmured some words in Latin and made the sign of the cross over its forehead. The baby ceased crying. Then he handed it back to Rose Downie. "*Pax vobiscum,* my child," he said to her. "Peace be with you. Truly you are blessed among women, for He has chosen you to care for this baby, as once our Holy Mother was chosen."

Rose said nothing. She didn't know what to say. They were all smiling at her and yet she also felt small and insignificant in the presence of these people, especially this holy man with his gift. If she hadn't realized he was a Papist priest, she would have thought him a sorcerer for silencing the baby so. Uneasily, she bowed her head to the Countess, then backed out of the room. Outside she was met by Amy and Beatrice, who had been watching at the door.

"How did he do that then?" asked Beatrice. "That's some trick, that is."

"I confess it did seem almost like conjuring to me," said Amy. "But if it gives you a night's sleep . . ." She moved closer to Rose and whispered in her ear. "The good news is that he'll be staying here, hidden away.

But not a word, not a single word to anyone or we'll all be in trouble. I know you do not share our faith, but I do know you for a good person, love. With a bit of luck, Father Cotton might keep that baby quiet for you when you need a rest."

Rose felt sick inside, sick and ashamed for the terrible thoughts churning her mind. For she knew that this man Cotton, this saintly priest of the Romish church, was the man Richard Topcliffe was so desperate to find. And she believed that Topcliffe in his turn had the power to find William Edmund for her and return him safe to her arms. If it meant allowing him to occupy her body whenever he pleased and if it meant betraying not only Cotton, but her benefactress and this whole household, then so be it. What mother in the world would not do *anything* — at whatever cost to themselves or those around them — for their child?

The baby was still sleeping soundly and she went back upstairs to put it in its cot. Then she gathered her warm woolen cloak and hood about her before slipping silently down the back stairs. Outside, the high crenellated towers of Tanahill House blotted out the light of the moon, but there was enough candlelight through the leaded windows of the great houses along the

Strand for her to make her way as she hurried westward the few hundred yards to Charing Cross, then down through Whitehall Palace toward Westminster.

CHAPTER 25

The iron fist of Topcliffe and his pursuivants came at first light, just as Cotton was saying Mass for the Countess, her two children, and her staff in a second-floor chamber. The manservant, a tall young man named Joe Fletcher, raced down the small flight of stone steps at the back of the hall, but by the time he reached the front door it had already been flattened by a battering log. Joe stopped dead in his tracks, confronted by a wall of dazzling blades, blazing pitch torches, solid leather chest armor bearing the Queen's escutcheon, and heads encased in steel morions.

Topcliffe stood at the forefront of ten dark-clad men, casting a menacing, moving shadow from the light of the torches fanned out behind him. Those with him included London's chief pursuivant, Newall. All but Topcliffe had their swords drawn and there was much shouting and stamping of boots.

Acrid smoke streamed from their torches and from the sotweed pipe stuck hard between Topcliffe's teeth.

Topcliffe took a step toward Fletcher so that their faces were no more than a foot apart. He was half a head shorter than the manservant, but exuded twice the power. "Where are they?" he growled, smoke billowing toward Fletcher. "Bring me straight to them or I will kill you where you stand."

Upstairs, the Lady Tanahill's hands shook with terror as she cleared away the sacred vessels. Cotton gathered up his vestments, ducked through into the stairwell, and climbed two steps at a time to the third floor. His heart pounding, he went through a great chamber into a garderobe tower, and up a few more steps into a cramped privy closet that housed the jakes. There was clearly something wrong with the pipework, for the stench of human waste was atrocious.

He flicked open a concealed hinge and lifted the jakes, revealing a hole in the floor. The Countess had shown him this place after the other dinner guests had gone. The hole was big enough for a man to slip through but no more. Cotton half-turned and sank to his haunches, then dropped into the hole, pulling the jakes back into place above him. Immediately he was enveloped by total darkness. He had no candle with him and even if he'd had one he could not have used it, for the smell of burning wax would give him away. He prayed that the Countess — the only other person in the house to know of this place — would remember to replace the concealed hinge.

Joe Fletcher was backing off from Topcliffe and the pursuivants, fearful for his life but saying nothing. Suddenly Beatrice appeared at the bottom of the stairs. She was not tall and it must have been obvious to all the men that she was merely a child. "Put down your swords," she said in a firm voice that showed remarkable self-possession and courage. "Put them down, I say!"

"Who are you?" Topcliffe bellowed at Beatrice.

"I am Beatrice, maidservant to the Lady Tanahill," she said boldly. "Who are *you*, sir?"

"Never mind who I am, girl. Where is your mistress?" Topcliffe saw the Countess framed in the doorway by the stairs. She looked slight and frail. "Ah, Lady Tanahill, what a pleasure to see you. Now, where is Southwell?"

"Southwell?" she said. Her voice was barely audible.

"Tell me now where he is or I will tear this house apart, board by board, panel by panel, brick by brick, for I *know* that the priest is here. And I will have him, however long it takes."

The Countess could scarcely breathe. She had hidden the sacred vessels in a secret compartment in the paneling in the chamber above. Topcliffe had been to this house before, to taunt her over her husband's imprisonment and to seek evidence against him in his papers. He had found nothing, though he had searched for a day and a half. It was after that visit that she'd had the hiding hole built beneath the jakes by a carpenter introduced to her by her friends in the Church of Rome. It was a construction of breathtaking complexity and ingenuity, so hidden within the fabric of the house as to be undetectable. To find it, a pursuivant would, indeed, have to tear the place apart brick by brick and stone by stone until there was nothing left.

When she didn't reply, Topcliffe confined the servants to the kitchen and Lady Tanahill to her chamber. Outside the house, he had fifteen more men, who surrounded it on all sides, watching over every doorway and window as the sun came up. Systematically, he and his cohort began searching the building, stamping heavy-booted through its multitude of rooms. He looked in and under every coffer, bed, and cupboard. His men hammered or tapped on every panel of the wainscot looking for one that sounded different. In the library he cast down all the books in his quest for a false bookcase that hid a doorway. He took each of the servants aside one by one and threatened them with torture and execution. "If you tell me now where he is, you will be spared. If we find him and you have not divulged his whereabouts, then you will be racked and executed for treason with all that entails." These words he even used on Beatrice. When it was Rose Downie's turn to be taken into another room for questioning, he handled her even more roughly than the others until they were alone. Then he told her to sit down and poured her some wine.

"You're a pretty girl, Rose," he said.

"Thank you, Mr. Topcliffe." Rose took a seat, the baby in her arms.

"Is it difficult for you working among these base and filthy Papists?"

"It is easy enough, sir. They are good people. They do me no harm."

"But they harbor traitors, Rose. Jesuits. These are men who would kill our beloved Queen Elizabeth."

Rose hung her head.

"And they won't help you find your baby . . ."

She looked up at him, expectantly, eyes brimming with sudden hope.

"Now, Rose, where is this priest?"

"My baby, sir . . . ?"

"All in good time. First, Southwell."

Rose clutched the foundling baby to her breast. She had noticed strange looks from the other servants. She could not meet their eyes.

"I promise you, Mr. Topcliffe, I do not know where he is hid. I only know he is here. They told me he was staying. I beg of you, believe me . . ."

"God's teeth, Rose, that is not good enough. Talk to the others. Find out what they know." Without warning, he raised his fist and hit her full in the mouth. The blow knocked her down and the baby sprawled from her arms and slid across the floor. It began screaming. Rose scrabbled around, dazed, until her hands located the baby and she picked it up. Blood was dripping from her mouth and she could feel that a front tooth was loose. Her fingers were bloody, and the blood stained the baby's swaddling wraps. "That was to prove to the others that you have not betrayed them, Rose. Now get back out there and discover where this priest is."

In the black hole, the stink was overpowering and, at first, Cotton gagged, bile rising in his throat. The hole was five foot square and seven feet high. There was a cold brick seat and nothing else, nothing of comfort. All there was by way of sustenance was a pail of water and a beaker with which to drink it. It seemed to Cotton that the air was stale and there wasn't enough of it circulating in here. How would he breathe if he was forced to stay here any length of time? He had never known such darkness. This was darker than the blackest night; it made no difference whether his eyes were open or closed. *This is what the tomb is like,* he thought; *this is what it was like for Christ when first* He *rose in the grave.* He felt ashamed of the thought and put it aside; how dare he compare his own plight to the suffering of the Messiah?

He tried to still himself, to quieten his breathing and his heart so that the air might last longer. He drank some water and counted the seconds, then the minutes. The minutes stretched to an hour and then more and more hours. From all around he heard hammering and cracking, the splintering of wood as paneling and floorboards were jimmied and smashed. He knew that he must not make a sound. At one point they were close to him, laughing and joking, swearing and threatening. How could they not hear his racing heart? "Come on out, you Popish dog," one of them called. "You smell like a dungheap!" Then they all laughed, and one of the pursuivants, barely two feet from him, used the jakes to defecate, jeered on by the others as he strained. It seemed to Cotton that the foul smell redoubled. The same words kept turning and churning in his mouth, though he never uttered them out loud: *"Fiat voluntas dei, fiat voluntas dei, fiat voluntas dei . . ."* God's will be done.

After sixteen hours, Topcliffe brought in a new squadron of men and sent his first troop home to their beds. Yet Topcliffe stayed. He would remain throughout the night. The hammering and the breaking, the shredding of great tapestries and smashing of glass continued all through the dark hours. In the morning, Topcliffe sent for two builders and told them to bring their measuring equipment. When they arrived at the devastated house, he ordered them to take measurements of every wall and every floor in the building to find a hidden cavity. For many hours they took measurements, arguing and scratching their heads. At one point they were certain they had discovered a space that was not accounted for. When Topcliffe's men were breaking through the wall, it began to move perilously and they had to run for props to shore it up. Finally they broke through, only to find themselves in the larder. Angrily, Topcliffe sent them away without pay. When they protested, he told them to send their reckoning to the Lady Tanahill.

On the second night, Topcliffe called his men off but left several guards outside, and one in the great hall. "I will be back at dawn," he told the Countess. "Do not even think of trying to get him out of the house."

In his hole, Cotton slept fitfully from time to time. The hours passed and he lost track of whether it was day or night. To sleep, he leaned on the bench against the wall, fearful that he would snore or talk in his sleep. He shivered with cold, but that did not concern him much for he had learned about harsh living and deprivation at the Jesuit colleges. The hunger gnawed at his belly, but neither was that new, for he had fasted often. He spent much of his time in prayer and he thought at length of what would happen to him if — when — he was caught. Would he be able to endure a martyr's death? Many failed, even to the extent of yielding up the names of their fellows. Some men could take the rack without begging for mercy and telling their tormentors all they wanted to know, but most could not. Which category of man would he fall into? It was well and good to long for a martyr's death when one was not suffering, quite another to hold firm when it was so close.

In the absence of light, his sense of hearing and of touch became more acute. He seemed to hear every sound in the old house, and he could soon move with absolute silence in his cramped hole, feeling his way around brick by brick. Yet his sense of smell dulled, mercifully, so that he longer noticed the stench of the ordure that permeated from the jakes, nor of his own, dumped as carefully as possible in one small corner of the hole.

Most of all, in the endless hours, he longed for light and reading material. He comforted himself by reciting poems and tracts from the Bible in his head.

And then, in his mind, he began to compose a letter. It was an uncompromising letter to an imaginary prisoner: perhaps to Philip, the Earl of Tanahill, whom he had never met, now languishing in the Tower, sentenced to a traitor's death; perhaps to those other sacred brothers from the Society of Jesus, such as Campion, who had come here before him and had suffered grievously for it, or to those who were yet to come; perhaps to his friend and companion on this journey, Henry Garnet, now at large somewhere outside London; perhaps to himself, to convince himself yet again that this was God's will and that He would enable him to endure.

"Let neither fury nor fiction nor the sword, nor glory of splendid attire, nor bribes, nor entreaties, nor any other violence seduce you from the charity of Christ. You were born to be God's; by Him you live, and for Him you are to die. It is a death that will confirm the wavering and make the strong yet stronger. The cause is God's, the conflict short, the reward eternal. The contrition of a humble heart, expressed by your bloodshed in this cause, will remit all sins as fully as in baptism, so great is the prerogative of martyrdom." Martyrdom. The very word made him shudder. The extreme mortification of the flesh that would bring him as close to the love of God as it was possible to be. How often had he dreamed of martyrdom in the long nights of his college years?

After nearly two days in the hole, he heard a whispered voice and wondered whether it was the voice of God or an angel come for him. It was a woman's voice, as sweet as the sound of church bells on a summer's day. And then, above him, he saw a chink of light — a light more blinding than he had ever seen — and he closed his eyes as tight as they would shut and covered his face with his hands.

"Father Cotton, it is me. Anne." The Countess's voice was very quiet.

"Is it safe?"

"No, they are still here. But it is late and they are playing cards down in the great hall while Topcliffe is away. I have brought you food, Father."

"I cannot look at the light. It is too bright."

The Countess recoiled from the smell. "Father, I am so sorry you have been brought to this."

"*Fiat voluntas dei,* my dear Anne."

She had a cloth with some food — bread, cheese, pieces of cold meat, some wine — very little because Topcliffe's men were keeping a close watch on the food in the larder. She and Amy had gathered it together hastily in the remains of the kitchen while Rose Downie was up in her room with the baby. They would not have believed that Rose could betray them, yet she would not meet their eyes.

"Thank you for this food. It is most welcome. And please, do not fret for me. If it is God's will, then I will be safe. If you feel that any here in this house are in danger because of my presence, then you must tell the pursuivants. You must save them ahead of me."

"I cannot do that, Reverend Father. Nothing we could do would save us from the wrath of Topcliffe now."

"Topcliffe? I have heard of him."

"He is a cruel man, Father Cotton. He will not desist in his search for you until this house is rubble, for he knows that you are here. We are fortunate that this hole is so secure, but it was difficult for me to get here to fasten and conceal the hinges before it was found. I think you would have been discovered if I had not done so."

Her voice was choked and feeble. He feared she was in a worse state than him. "I beseech you, Anne, endure. For this *will* end." He tried to open an eye, yet it merely watered and he closed it once more. Eyes closed, he made the Sign of the Cross and blessed her before she closed the trapdoor once again and secured the hinges.

In the blackness of the hole, the fresh air and food brought Cotton new hope. With the wine and bread, he spoke Mass, then said Grace over the food and began, slowly, to eat and drink.

Topcliffe summoned Rose Downie again.

"Tell me more about this gathering. Did this Jesuit priest come alone?"

Rose's mouth was bruised and swollen. Her face was streaked with dirt and tears.

"He arrived with another man, Mr. Topcliffe, called Thomas Woode. I had never met him before but we were introduced to him."

Thomas Woode? The name was familiar. "What more can you tell me? What did he look like? What did he say?" Topcliffe pressed her.

Rose described him as best she could but insisted that he had spoken very little. Then, tentatively, she said, "What of my baby, Mr. Topcliffe, sir?"

"Your baby is safe and well, Rose. That is all I am prepared to tell you for now. When Southwell is delivered into my hands, alive or dead, then I will reunite you with William Edmund. Do you understand me, Rose?"

"But I have done all you asked! I know he is here. I know they were having their Mass when you and your men arrived. He must be here in this house unless . . ." She stopped, seeing the blood rise in Topcliffe's face.

"Unless?"

She had been about to say "unless you let him slip away" but thought better of it. "Unless he has somehow managed to get away, Mr. Topcliffe. Perhaps there are tunnels from the cellars. I have completed my side of the bargain, sir. Please, let me have my baby back."

"All in good time, Rose. All in good time."

CHAPTER 26

Lord Howard of Effingham, the Lord Admiral of the Navy and adoptive father to Lady Blanche Howard, was not at home.

His steward, Robin Johnson, welcomed John Shakespeare into the grand entrance hall of the imposing house that Howard often used in these days. Standing tall on the edge of Deptford Green, close to the scene of the attempt on Drake's life little more than thirty hours earlier, it was a house perfectly located for Howard's work preparing the Navy in case the Spanish ever launched their infernal war fleet, and also for his frequent visits to court at Greenwich Palace, less than a mile to the east. Howard's steward was a man of charm and ease. He offered to take Shakespeare to meet his lordship at the Royal Dock, where he was overseeing provisioning. Together the two men set out across the green.

"These are difficult days for your master,

Johnson."

"Indeed, sir. The whole household is in mourning for the Lady Blanche."

A fresh breeze blew up the Thames from the east. Gulls played in the wind, holding themselves against its force by slight movements of their wings so that it seemed they were stationary in the air.

"Do you have any theories about who might have done this terrible thing to her?"

"I fear not, sir. I only wish that whoever did it might be brought to justice as soon as possible." Johnson stopped. "Ah, here we are. I think I see his lordship now." He pointed to a bark where a group of men were clustered on the quarterdeck. In their center was the tall figure of Howard of Effingham, his shock of snow white hair unmistakable.

Shakespeare strode to the ship. Howard was standing with Diego, Captain Stanley, and three other men, while Drake was kneeling on the deck scratching plans of attack on parchment. Shakespeare wished the Vice Admiral would think to do such work belowdecks, where he was out of musket range. A little way off stood Boltfoot Cooper, watching them and surveying the crowded quayside. He spotted Shakespeare immediately and raised his head in recognition. At least *he* was suitably alert. But it was obvious that Drake was as exposed, nonchalant, and vulnerable as ever. The attempt on his life had bothered him not a whit.

Drake looked up from his sketchings. "Well, Mr. Shakespeare, how do you do?" he boomed. "Come to check that I'm still alive, have you? Well, damn it, I am. And so, unfortunately, is the accursed Boltfoot Cooper."

"Sir Francis, it is indeed good to see you alive and well. How is your coxswain?"

"Not well, I'm afraid, but the surgeon says he might survive. As with all things, God will decide. Anyway, what do you want here?"

"To ask you a question, Sir Francis. How did your would-be murderer know when and where you were to disembark and land?"

Drake tossed the question aside. "I imagine the cur just watched and waited. I am always coming here. I am a sea captain; this is where my ships are."

Shakespeare was not impressed by this explanation but let it pass. He knew from experience that there was no point in gainsaying Sir Francis Drake. He thanked him and turned his attention to Lord Howard of

Effingham. Their previous meeting had been unsatisfactory; this time he would not be brushed off. Howard must have more information to give about his adopted daughter. "Might I have a word with you alone, my Lord?"

Howard led Shakespeare down below-decks to the great cabin of the bark and closed the door. A flask of brandy stood on the captain's table, and Howard poured two goblets. "How do your investigations proceed?"

"We have made progress, my lord."

"But you have not yet apprehended the murderer?"

"No, my lord." Shakespeare hesitated. How much could Howard bear to hear?

As if reading his thoughts, Howard smiled faintly. "Please, Mr. Shakespeare, do not try to spare my feelings. It is enough that she is dead."

Shakespeare bowed. "I fear I must tell you there is possibly more to the killing of the Lady Blanche than we had first thought. I have discovered that she had recently taken up with a group of Roman Catholics. She was following the old faith, my lord."

Howard laughed humorlessly, a short yap of a laugh like a small dog. "Mr. Shakespeare, that is *no* surprise to me. It is a family failing of the Howards, I am afraid. I told you before that she had been associating with people of whom I disapproved."

"But there is more. She had certain injuries . . ."

"Yes?"

"A crucifix cut into her back . . . after death. I had not noticed it at first. And she had been tied up, too, for there were rope marks around her wrists."

Howard looked aghast. "Good God, this is horrible."

"I am sorry. I mention it only because I suspect there to be a religious significance and wanted to know whether you have any ideas on the matter. My lord, I fear that the assailant may be the same assassin who has been sent by Spain to kill Sir Francis."

"What possible connection could there be between Blanche and a plot against Drake? Have you taken leave of your senses, Mr. Shakespeare?" Howard was incredulous.

"There are certain curious connections that lead me to this belief." Shakespeare outlined his theory, including the conspirator's viciousness toward prostitutes in Delft and Rotterdam.

For a moment, Howard simply glared at Shakespeare, as if trying to decide whether he had heard him correctly. "Did you say *prostitutes,* Mr. Shakespeare?" he said at last. And then he exploded. "Are you suggesting that my daughter was a *whore?*"

"My lord, certainly not."

"How dare you come to me with such scandalous imaginings?"

"My lord, you misconstrue me. Lady Blanche was a devout young woman. Of that I have no doubt. There is not the slightest suggestion that she was a whore. But I do believe she may have known this man. And if this man *is* in London, as I believe, then there is no reason to suspect he has changed his brutal treatment of women. *All* women, not just whores. The nature of Lady Blanche's injuries . . . the fact that she was moving in Catholic circles where the assassin might have sought sanctuary . . . these lead me to the possibility of a link. It is tenuous but I cannot ignore it. Perhaps she had discovered something and he killed her to silence her."

Howard's face was still set in fury, but his rage subsided. "So you believe the man who killed Blanche may be the same man that shot at Drake and wounded his coxswain?"

"It is possible. I can put it no stronger than that." Shakespeare downed the remainder of his brandy in one. "Now I must ask you, my lord, whether you know the name of the man with whom the Lady Blanche was consorting and by whom she came to be with child?"

"I really do not like this line of questioning, Shakespeare. It is . . . *indecent*. Poor Blanche is not yet interred and yet you spread tittle-tattle about her."

"No, my lord. That is not the way it is. I have spread no word about her."

"But someone has. The broadsheets have been brought to my attention with their scurrilous stories."

"I am investigating that, sir. I already have the most notorious of these people, one Walstan Glebe, in Newgate, awaiting trial on a number of charges. He is likely to lose his ears, his liberty, and his right hand."

"Good. That is the sort of thing I wish to hear. Let us leave it at that. Find my daughter's murderer, Mr. Shakespeare, and when he hangs at Tyburn, you shall have my gratitude. Good day to you."

Shakespeare wanted to press for more information, for any clues in the background of Lady Blanche, any word of her friends and acquaintances, but it was clear that Howard considered the interview over. Shakespeare knew only too well that there was no profit in pushing matters with such men of power. And so he bowed, thanked

Howard, and together they left the cabin.

On deck, Drake was standing up now, jabbing his finger at the parchment and muttering something about the weather gauge. Shakespeare left Lord Howard with his naval consorts and wandered over to Boltfoot Cooper.

"I trust you are well, Boltfoot."

Boltfoot made an indeterminate noise from the back of his throat.

"It sounds as if we nearly lost our Vice Admiral. The Royal Armory has looked at that weapon you found. They tell me they had never seen anything like it. Accurate to an extreme degree. Made to order by a Bavarian named Opel for Gilbert Cogg. It was clearly made with only one purpose in mind and should have been brought to our attention. Mr. Opel has one of two choices: expulsion from these shores or he can work for the Armory."

Boltfoot lifted his head in the direction of Deptford Strand. "You need to talk to them in Roberts Chandlery over there, Mr. Shakespeare. Bob Roberts. And the ostler, Perkins, of the livery stables at the Eagle Tavern by Sayers Court. They'll tell you more about the man who fired the shot. They both saw him and spoke with him."

"I spoke to them both on the way here.

They gave me good descriptions of our man, but no clue as to where he has gone. The horse he rode has not been seen again. I believe you hit him?"

Boltfoot shook his head. "Nothing more than a small hole in his side, I think. He was too far away. Should have got him straight through the back but I was losing ground against him."

"I am sure you did well to hit him at all. Did you get a good look at him?"

"No. But I might recognize him running. All I know is that he didn't have a beard and he was tall, slender, and could move quick."

"All right, Boltfoot. Stay vigilant. I have put out word to the surgeons, physicians, and apothecaries in case he should seek treatment."

Shakespeare left the teeming Royal Dock and headed through the crowds toward Deptford Strand for the tiltboat back to London. Then he changed his mind, turning instead toward Howard of Effingham's house by the Green.

Robin Johnson, the steward, answered the door to his knock. He did not seem surprised to see Shakespeare again. "I trust the Lord Admiral was not too harsh on you, Mr. Shakespeare."

"No, no."

"I am sure that he wishes this matter to be resolved as much as any man, but he worries about the effect on his family's reputation. These have not been easy times for the Howards, as I am sure you understand."

Shakespeare understood. Too many Howard heads on pikes had decorated the gatehouse to London Bridge in the past half a century.

"Quite. But it is *you* I wish to speak with now, Johnson. Do you have somewhere quiet where we could talk awhile?"

Johnson led the way through the hall into some side corridors down to his own room in the servants' quarters. It was bare by comparison with his master's sumptuous hall, but it was warmed by a fire and had chairs and a small oak table. "This is my sanctuary," Johnson told him, "where I escape from the trials of the day and plan the work of the other staff."

He wore the livery of his station as steward to one of the most important men in England: a white satin doublet with gold trimming and black hose. He was a handsome man in his late twenties or early thirties, of medium height with dark hair and a trimmed beard. It was his good looks and easy charm that had made Shakespeare think twice. And he had recalled, also, something that Catherine Marvell had said almost in passing — that Lady Blanche and her lover could never have married. A woman of noble blood could never wed a servant, that was certain.

"So, Mr. Shakespeare, how can I help you?"

"I would like to know more about the Lady Blanche."

"As I said, sir, her loss was felt by all of us."

"Tell me, Johnson, how long have you been in the service of Lord Howard?"

Johnson was as stiff as an oak stave. "Since I was a boy, Mr. Shakespeare. My mother worked in his lordship's kitchens and I was brought up in the household. I have worked my way up to steward."

"I am sure you have been very diligent. You are a good-humored man, Johnson. I am sure the household likes you well."

"I hope so, sir."

"I imagine the Lady Blanche was fond of you, too?"

"What are you implying, Mr. Shakespeare?"

"You were her lover, were you not?"

Johnson was shocked into silence. Then

he said, "I wonder, sir, if I were to talk openly, whether I might forbear on you not to reveal to his lordship what I say."

Shakespeare studied his eyes and saw some kind of honesty, but that was not enough. "I can promise no such thing, Johnson, as you know. But I *would* have you speak your heart to me. I promise it will be better for you to proceed that way. I respect openness. The alternative would be questioning under duress, which I am loath to do."

Johnson nodded slowly. The ghost of a smile crossed his lips. "I understand, I hope. And yes, Mr. Shakespeare, I was Blanche's lover. But more than that, we were *in* love. Her death has torn out my heart, sir."

"You would have become the father of her child had she lived?"

The steward seemed close to tears, but he held them back. "Yes. But, as you can imagine, things would have been very difficult for us. His lordship would never have countenanced her union with a commoner. We had talked of running away, perhaps across the sea to France, but I fear that would have been impossible. How would we have lived?"

"Did you bring her to the Church of Rome?"

Johnson looked away so that Shakespeare might not witness his distress. "It was not quite like that. She was quite a lonely girl for a long time, not really accepted by many in the family, apart from his lordship. She used to seek me out in this my sanctuary, where we would spend hours together, talking about everything: religion, music, exploration. Serious subjects, I suppose, for young people. But we were both intensely interested in the world around us. We had a lot in common; we were both outsiders in the household. One day she asked whether I was a Papist, because I suppose it must have been obvious from the way I spoke on certain matters. I admitted that I was, indeed, a Roman Catholic. She then expressed an interest and I agreed to take her to Mass. That was how she met Catherine Marvell, whom I understand is known to you, and various others."

"But you still were not lovers at this time?"

"No. That happened at the end of last summer. For a while Blanche had been talking of entering the novitiate in an Italian convent. But then she changed her mind. I could tell then that her feelings for me were the same as mine for her. We became lovers soon after that." He paused and said more quietly, "I beg you not to judge us too harshly."

"That depends on how much help you give me, Johnson. Tell me about these secret Masses. Who was there? Was there a Fleming among their number? Which priests said the Mass?"

"I cannot tell you any of that, Mr. Shakespeare."

"I need this information. It is imperative that you tell me."

"Mr. Shakespeare, I cannot. Would you have me betray those who have laid their trust in me?"

"Yes, Johnson, I would. This is a matter of state. I believe there is a Fleming at large who is an extreme danger to the realm. I would know his name and whereabouts. I believe you can help me."

"I am sorry, I can say no more."

"Then, Mr. Johnson, I must consider you my main suspect in the murder of Lady Blanche Howard. You had the motive. The next you see of me will be in Newgate, where I will interrogate you with all the powers invested in me by Her Majesty the Queen. I do not have time for niceties."

"Mr. Shakespeare, please . . ."

"A warrant will be issued by day's end and the sheriff or his constables will come for you. In the meantime, do not leave this house or I promise you that you will suffer the worse for it when you are taken." Shakespeare walked for the door.

"Mr. Shakespeare, wait . . ."

He stopped and turned. "Yes?"

Johnson opened his mouth as if to say something, but then closed it again and shook his head in despair.

Shakespeare turned like an enraged bull and barged his way out. He was angry — angry with Johnson for putting him in this position, angry with himself for using the threat of violence against a man who deserved better. But this assassin had already made one serious attempt on Drake's life. How long before he made his next?

CHAPTER 27

Thomas Woode awoke in such terror that he thought he would never draw breath again. A hand was at his throat and two other powerful hands pinned his arms to the bed. He twisted his body with all his strength to free himself, but could not move.

It was dead of night. Midnight. Somewhere in the distance he could hear the watchman calling the hour. One minute a comforting dream of lust, as every man has, the next a waking nightmare. He fought for breath. The hand at his throat was crushing his windpipe.

"Woode? Thomas Woode?" The voice was coarse and blunt and smelled of pain. The hand clasped Woode's throat and pulled him from the pillow, then his arms were wrenched behind his back and fastened with rough ropes by a second intruder. At last the hand moved away from his throat and he gasped, his mouth opening and closing like a tench pulled by hook from the water.

Woode was sitting up in the middle of his sumptuous four-post bed, with rich damask drapes on all sides and bedding of gold and crimson. His chamber was large and entirely paneled in fine wood. He was dressed in a white lawn nightgown and cap. But now this fine room was lit by the flickering tar torches of six brutal men. The one closest to him, the one who had spoken, eyed him up and down with disdain. Woode tried to say something, to protest, but nothing but a broken hiss emanated from his throat.

"Thomas Woode?"

Woode nodded.

"Thomas Woode, you have committed a felony and you are under arrest. You will be taken from here to be questioned, then brought to trial by jury of your peers, where you will be found guilty and hanged."

"What? What felony?" Woode rasped.

"Larceny, Woode, larceny of timbers destined for Her Majesty's ships. Don't think we don't know how you've built this pretty pile."

"What are you saying?"

The man stood back. He was wearing a dark cape of black fur. "You know well what I am saying, Woode. You have used Navy timbers in the building of this house. They have been identified as such and there is no doubt. You build a fine home and the Spaniard sends his ships of invasion in safety."

"It is a lie!"

"So, you have found your voice."

"I tell you these timbers are brought here by my carpenters, who are reputable masters of their craft. I have stolen nothing, Mr. . . . who are you?"

"Topcliffe. The name is Topcliffe. And the jury will decide who tells the truth, Woode. You're coming with us." He turned to his men. "Take him away."

After three days in the fetid hole, Father Cotton began to see in the dark. He saw strange things: angels with blue spider-thread wings, demons with seven-clawed talon feet, and red raw cocks that caught the light like blades. He saw women, naked and pink and sprawled on sheets of white linen. He saw feasts of forbidden fruits and meats that stank of morbidity like autumn apples hung too long.

When he saw them, he closed his eyes and prayed. But closing his eyes did not remove his sight. He still saw these things. After a while he could not tell whether his eyes were open or shut.

At times he put his hands beneath his

vestments to see if his body was still there. It occurred to him that he was dead. More than that, at times he was *certain* he was dead. When the senses are denied, how can a man tell on which side of the line he stands between life and death?

The food had not lasted long, though he still kept a moldy piece of cheese, which he cut in half every time he had to eat. It gave him comfort to feel his body working, digesting. He wondered how many times you could cut a piece of cheese in half before it disappeared. Hunger was not the most insistent of his needs. He knew he had to drink to survive, so he drank constantly and pissed frequently in the corner.

The noises from outside this stinking hole were becoming fainter and less frequent. He knew now that he would *not* die from lack of air. He longed for the freshness of the air in the outdoors, but it was clear that whoever had designed and built this hiding place was no fool and had factored ventilation into his plans.

At times he wondered whether anyone was still in the house. Were Topcliffe's guards still there? If not, why had the Countess not come to release him? Perhaps she herself had been taken. When this thought entered his head, he began breathing in short, sharp gasps of fear. Perchance this would be his tomb. Without the Countess to free him, he could die here and no one would be the wiser. He prayed often, most commonly "O Lord, my work here is not yet done. Release Your humble servant that I might go out into the world like a shepherd among wolves and bring Your flock home."

He tried composing poetry, as he had done during his eight years in Rome. As in a dream, he thought at times of his days there and of his idyllic Norfolk childhood, paddling in the crystal clear Hor, a stream that meandered through the villages north of Norwich. He had always been a quiet, thoughtful child, not given to some of the rougher games of his fellows. So somber a child was he that he recalled his own father calling him "Father Robert" from a young age. And yes, he *had* been solemn, perhaps thinking too much on the cares of God and the world when he should have been kicking a pig's bladder through the fields or hawking for rabbits like his big brothers.

The gaunt ruins of St. Faith's Priory entered his mind's eye. He had lived in their shadow half his life. The old Benedictine monastery had been torn down by his own grandfather, Sir Richard, on the orders of Great Henry, and the family had prospered as a result with the reward of church lands and property. Sir Richard had built a fine manor for the family, yet the stones of the old priory remained as a constant reminder of where the riches had come from. Wealth garnered in such a way, at cost to the true faith, could never go unpunished. For as long as he could remember, he had known that one day *he* would have to accept the burden, to seek redemption in order to remit the sins of his family.

His back and shoulders were wracked with pain and his legs felt shaky and unsteady. He was perpetually cold and could never find comfort. How long had he been here? He had no way of knowing. Night and day melded into one long night. He would go mad before he died.

He fell once more to his knees, clasped his hands together in supplication, and prayed.

By early afternoon, word reached Shakespeare from the Deptford constable that Robin Johnson was no longer at Howard of Effingham's house. Shakespeare shook his head in dismay and cursed Johnson for a cogging fool. He sent the messenger back to Deptford with orders to raise a hue and cry and bring the steward to Newgate in chains.

After the messenger had left, Shakespeare sat on the settle in his solar room enjoying the last wispy hour of daylight. He had much to consider.

The main question was whether there was really a link between the killing of Blanche Howard and the attempt on the life of Sir Francis Drake, or whether fancy had taken flight in Shakespeare's overwrought imaginings. Beyond that, he needed to know the meaning of the papers he had found at the burnt-out house in Hog Lane. Was it something to do with an illegal printworks — and, if so, how was Thomas Woode involved? He knew that Woode's governess, Catherine Marvell, was acquainted with Lady Blanche and with Howard of Effingham's steward, Robin Johnson, who was now revealed as her lover. What was unclear was whether any of them were in any way involved in Blanche's murder. Could Johnson have been her killer? Shakespeare's instinct told him no. So who then? There was a sickening similarity between Blanche's injuries and those inflicted on the whores in Holland. So, was the Spanish King's mercenary, the man he now knew had stayed in Deptford under the name of van Leiden, responsible? If so, why kill the girl? Why draw attention to himself?

As he was pondering all this, there was a knock at the solar door and Jane entered. "A Mistress Catherine Marvell is here, sir. I told her you were busy, but she insisted it was urgent and that you would see her." She gave him a long look and Shakespeare found himself reddening.

"Yes, yes, Jane. Please show her in."

He could see instantly that Catherine was out of sorts. She was breathless as if she had run here from Dowgate. Her hair was tousled and her eyes were wild.

"Mistress Marvell . . ."

"I cannot believe you have done this to us!"

Shakespeare was taken aback. "Done what?"

"I trusted you!"

"Mistress Marvell, what is this? I do not know what you are saying. What do you think I have done to you?"

She stepped forward, close to him, her bright eyes staring angrily into his, and raised her hands, beating him on the chest with surprising strength. He reeled back but did not respond. In the background, framed in the doorway, he caught sight of Jane, smiling the knowing smile of a woman who sees things that men don't. At last Shakespeare took Catherine by her wrists, firmly, and ceased her beating. Then he led her to the settle, where he sat her down forcibly. She slumped, head in her hands.

"Mistress Marvell, start from the beginning. I am sure I have done nothing to offend you." He nodded to his maid. "Jane, please fetch some strong wine or brandy for us."

Catherine looked up. "Are you saying you know nothing about the pursuivants who came for Master Woode? They have taken him away in brutal fashion, accused of God knows what."

Shakespeare's mouth set hard. "Was it Topcliffe?"

"Of course it was the foul Topcliffe. And his henchmen Young and Newall. You must know all this — for you must have sent them."

"No. Not me. Topcliffe is no friend of mine."

"Then you told Walsingham about us — and *he* sent them."

"No."

"They came at midnight like thieves and housebreakers and took him from his bedchamber. They woke the children so that they could see their father marched away in ropes by men with swords and daggers. This is the state you work for, Mr. Shakespeare. These are *your* bedfellows."

"Did they say where they were taking him?"

"No."

"Did they say anything to you?"

"They cursed me and jeered at me. Topcliffe tried touching me, but I pushed him away. He called me a Popish whore and damned me to hell. He said he would have the children taken to Bridewell, where they might be put to useful employment."

"But he didn't do that?"

"No."

"Have you spoken to anyone about this?"

"I have been at Lincoln's Inn with a lawyer all day. Cornelius Bligh. He is an old friend of Mr. Woode's. He has tried to secure a writ of habeas corpus and discover where Thomas — Mr. Woode — is being held, but without success."

"And where are the children?"

"They are here. I have left them in your anteroom. I wanted to keep them with me."

"I will ask Jane to bring them in. They must be most distraught. I will get her to fetch them some cake, too, and something to drink."

"I think she is already doing that."

Shakespeare walked back to his table to create some distance between himself and Catherine. He had to tread very carefully. Any intervention he attempted could make matters worse for everyone, especially where Topcliffe was concerned. Topcliffe had clearly become a law unto himself, answerable only to the Queen, and neither Walsingham nor the Lord Treasurer, Burghley, seemed able to exert much control over him. Nor did the courts.

"Let us try to think about this clearly, Mistress Marvell. Had Mr. Woode crossed Topcliffe before?"

"Not that I know of. I thought straightway it must have been your doing. But if not, then all I can think is that it must have something to do with my master's association with Lady Tanahill. They are friends of old. He went to sup there the night before the raid."

"Ah yes, I know of that. All London is talking of it. So Woode was there?"

Catherine shook her head. "Not at the time of the raid, but earlier. I think Topcliffe is looking for a priest. Tearing the house down bit by bit from what I have heard."

"Yes. He is looking for the Jesuit Robert Southwell, as am I. But I think the Queen is like to intervene. Even she cannot stomach the destruction of one of the great houses to no end."

"I suppose someone must have told Topcliffe that Master Woode had been there."

"That certainly seems the most likely cause. And I fear he will be questioned under great duress as to the whereabouts of Southwell. It is Topcliffe's way . . ."

"It is too awful to imagine."

"Mistress Marvell, if you have any information on the whereabouts of Jesuit priests in England, you would do well to tell me now. The sooner we find them, the sooner may end the torment of Mr. Woode and the tribulations of Lady Tanahill. Yes, I am looking for this Southwell, but I am also looking for another Jesuit or one associated with the Society of Jesus. I do not know his name for certain, though he has used the name van Leiden. He is a Fleming and he is not what he seems. The chances are, however, that he is known by Southwell, for these people arrive in pairs and support each other." As he spoke he studied her closely for reaction, but just then Jane arrived with fortified wine and Shakespeare asked her to bring the children through with cakes.

"Well, mistress," Shakespeare said after Jane had gone. "Do you know any Jesuit?"

"I do not." They were the most difficult

three words Catherine had ever spoken. They were a lie, and no amount of equivocation could disguise the fact in her mind. Her parents would be horrified that she had to stoop to this. And yet the alternative would be betrayal of all those she knew in the Church of Rome. Her friends.

Shakespeare did not believe her, but all he did was nod. "Good. Well, the first thing to be done is to find out where Woode is being held. I will make inquiries. In the meantime, what will you do, Mistress Marvell?"

"I will return to the house in Dowgate with the children."

"Will you be safe there?"

"I can only pray — if I am still allowed to — that I will be, Mr. Shakespeare."

CHAPTER 28

Topcliffe cracked the silver-weighted end of his blackthorn stick into one of the few remaining glass windowpanes at Tanahill House. The glass shattered, sending shards crashing into the entrance hall. On the orders of the Queen, he was leaving. Reluctantly. After four days he was still convinced Robert Southwell was hidden in the house, but Elizabeth had commanded him to call off his hounds.

He stood directly in front of Lady Tanahill and scowled at her. "I will be back," he said. "And I will have this house as my own. Listen carefully to my words, you Popish whore bitch. This will be mine and you and yours will be broken."

"And I will pray to God for you, Mr. Topcliffe. That He may teach you the error of your ways."

He spat at her and stormed off. Anne Tanahill wiped his spit from her soft ruff, where it had landed, then turned back into the house. She felt that nothing could hurt her anymore. As she surveyed the remains of her house, she could hardly believe that this had once been a beautiful family home. In the quieter days, before her husband was taken away to the Tower, they had spent long hours of joy within these walls; now, as she walked from room to room and from floor to floor, she saw only rubble and broken woodwork. Every panel had been torn out and thrown aside, every floorboard jimmied up. The backs of every fireplace had been hammered into with heavy mallets, shattering the brickwork, as had the backs of cupboards and spaces under the eaves. Even plastered ceilings, exquisitely crafted, had been destroyed.

"How can they be allowed to do this, m'lady?" her housekeeper, Amy Spynke, asked when they had finished their tour and returned to the kitchens, where they all spent most of their time now. "Surely they must make reparations to you."

The Countess laughed without humor. "I think that is about as likely as peace on earth, Amy. Topcliffe has made it plain he will not rest until this house is his. The people who make the accusations end up with the property of the accused. It is all vanity."

Rose Downie sat huddled in a far corner, by the fire, cradling the baby that was not hers. She could not meet their eyes.

Amy and Joe Fletcher, the manservant, had already interrogated Rose, but she had refused to say a word, either of denial or confession. Every day, they had demanded whether *she* had brought Topcliffe, and every day, when she refused to answer, they knew that she had. And yet they also knew that Topcliffe had struck her in the face with great savagery, so there was still sympathy for her and the slightest sliver of doubt in their hearts.

"She must answer to God, not us," said Lady Tanahill to Amy in a low voice, looking over at Rose. "But we must *never* trust her again. She must be kept away from all aspects of our faith — and in particular she must never catch sight of any priests who might come here. Topcliffe will keep a constant watch on this house."

A little later, when the household sat down to eat, exhausted by the start of the clearing up, the Countess left them all in the kitchen and went up to take Father Cotton fresh food and water. She feared the priest was in desperate straits, but felt that the Jesuit should stay in the hole a few days more and then escape at night to a safer house. The Bellamies and the Vaux family would, she knew, take him in. But she knew, too, that he had other sanctuaries of his own.

She raised the jakes and prized up the trapdoor and peered in. By the light of her candle she could see Cotton sitting on the brick bench, legs hunched up with his arms around them, head into his chest. He was shivering and she could hear his teeth rattling.

"Father Cotton, we believe it is safe now. They have gone."

He made no move, nor signaled in any way that he had heard her. "Father Cotton?"

She knew he was alive by the violent shaking of his body, but apart from that there was no movement. The smell in the place was repulsive, but she slid down into the hole with him, leaving the candle standing above her on the lip of the trapway. She sat beside him on the brick bench and put her arm around his shoulders. His body was as cold as stone yet he trembled as if he had a fever. She stroked his forehead like a mother with a child, combing his lank hair with her fingers.

She thought she heard him say something

but it was so soft she could not make it out. She talked to him with gentle, reassuring words. Once more he seemed to say something, so faint she could scarcely hear him, but she thought it was "I have seen God." She felt her skin prickle and held him closer, and she knew that she could not leave him in this hole a moment longer.

Harry Slide swept into John Shakespeare's house in Seething Lane with his usual flourish. All he needed to complete the regal touch was a herald to announce his coming. "I have juicy tidbits for you today, Mr. Shakespeare," he announced with no preamble. "Firstly, it seems our friend Walstan Glebe, publisher of *The London Informer,* is willing to talk — in return for his freedom."

"Well, that's what we wanted." Shakespeare rose from the table where he had been writing a report on his investigation for Walsingham and shook Harry's hand. "But I'm not letting him out of prison until I hear the quality of what he has to say, Harry. We'll go to see him at Newgate. What other news?"

"Two of the 'Winchester geese' from Cogg's bawdy house have flown the nest — and a third is dead."

"Now that *is* interesting. Tell me more."

"The dead one is called Alice Hammond. There is nothing sinister about her death. She drank herself into oblivion and then choked on her own vomit. However, it is curious to note that her cousin, Starling Day, and the procuror of the bawdy house, Parsimony Field, are missing. Girls like this go missing all the time, of course. But I am told that Parsimony and Cogg were as close as two stoats in a hole. If anyone might have known his secrets, it is her."

"Do we know where these women have gone?"

"I fear not. The trail is cold. But I have word out that we are looking and that any information will be well rewarded. Unfortunately, we are not alone in our search. Topcliffe is looking for them, too."

Shakespeare groaned inwardly. He wasn't surprised, of course; he already knew of Topcliffe's interest in the murder of Cogg. But why would Topcliffe be concerned with preserving the health of Sir Francis Drake? His only interests were the evisceration and butchery of Papist priests and the accumulation of riches. "Well, let's find out what has happened to these two young ladies. Perhaps they murdered Cogg. Let us not lose sight of our targets, Harry. We are to find the murderer of Lady Blanche and to discover and dispose of the would-be killer of Sir Francis Drake. Nothing more, nothing less. There is, however, one other matter of interest to me: have you heard anything of the whereabouts of Thomas Woode?"

Slide was in an ebullient mood. "I may well have intelligence about Mr. Woode. What might it be worth to you, Mr. Shakespeare?"

Shakespeare winced. "How much do you *think* it's worth, Harry?"

"Four marks, Mr. Shakespeare. Plus two for the news about Walstan Glebe and Cogg. And I have expenses. The whores had to be paid to talk."

"And for what else, Harry? Three marks, for *all* your pieces of intelligence. I would have found out about Glebe's change of heart anyway. And half a crown for garnishing the whores."

"You are a hard man, but I will accept your offer with grace. Talking of grace, did I tell you what I heard about His Grace, the Archbishop of Canterbury?"

"Yes, Harry, you said he was caught swiving a member of his flock, then had her for lunch with mint the next day. A good tale . . . but an old one."

"No, Mr. Shakespeare, this is even better.

It seems he didn't eat her after all. Instead, he has set her up as his mistress in the gardens at Lambeth Palace. All the swiving he wants is right there on tap, she doesn't answer back, and he gets the grass kept nice and short, too. Oh, and he'll have some warm woolen nether-stocks when shearing time comes round — so long as he can teach her to weave. Seems he's promised to marry her to make it all honest, but I expect he says that to all the girls."

"Harry Slide, you will find yourself carried westward to Paddington Fair if you continue with these slanderous jibes. Just be sure you don't tell your stories to the wrong person. Now, *where* has Topcliffe taken Thomas Woode?"

"Home, Mr. Shakespeare. He's taken him home."

"Back to Dowgate? I had not heard —"

"No, no, to *his* home. In Westminster."

"I don't have time for this, Harry."

"I speak the truth. He has taken him to his home. The Council has licensed it as a holding prison for questioning. Topcliffe has a strong chamber there, with his own rack and wall."

Shakespeare was aghast. "Do you believe the Queen knows of it?"

Slide smiled strangely. "It is said Topcliffe

is the Queen's dog, Mr. Shakespeare. Beyond that I cannot say . . ."

"But that should not mean he is beyond the law. The question I would ask is: How can habeas corpus be effected if a prisoner is held there? Who has jurisdiction over such a place?"

"I am not a lawyer, Mr. Shakespeare. I know little of such things."

Shakespeare was horrified. Walsingham must know if the Council had agreed to it — but why would they do such a thing? "Whatever's necessary," Walsingham had said to him. "Whatever's necessary in these days of threatened war and invasion." Did that mean anything was permissible in the struggle against Rome and the Escorial?

"God's body, Harry. These are difficult days. Come, let us ride to Newgate together."

Besides the Tower, Newgate was London's most feared prison. This was where condemned men found themselves in a foul hole called Limbo, awaiting their last journey to the scaffold, usually at Tyburn by the village of Paddington, but also in London itself at Smith Field, Holborn, and Fleet Street.

Walstan Glebe was not with the condemned, but in a hole with those awaiting trial, about forty or fifty of them in all, mostly men but a few women, too. All were fettered to the floor or walls, languishing in stinking, dung-clogged straw. Glebe was in a bad way. The printer's head was bandaged with a dirty rag and one eye was swollen shut. His clothes were alive with fleas and other insects. Rats scurried among the prisoners at will, though occasionally one would be caught and dashed to death for a tasty addition to lunch.

"You seem to have done yourself an injury, Glebe," Shakespeare said by way of greeting.

"The tipstaff decided to play tennis with my head, using his cudgel as a racquet, Mr. Shakespeare."

"And I trust they are feeding you well."

"Most certainly. I have developed quite a taste for raw cat, sir. As for the gruel, it passes in one hole and out the other without noticeable change of smell or texture."

Shakespeare turned to Slide. "I think Mr. Glebe has things too easy here, Harry. He retains his humor. Perchance we should move him to Little Ease in the Tower . . ."

Slide chuckled. "I hear the hole in Wood Street Counter is particularly unpleasant at this time of year."

Shakespeare turned back to the prisoner.

"So then, Glebe. I am told you have information which you now wish to pass on to me. I trust you have not wasted my time in bringing me here, for if you have it will be the worse for you."

Glebe scratched his lice-ridden hair and a couple of plump grubs fell out. He picked one up and ate it. When Shakespeare raised an eyebrow, he smiled sheepishly. "It is all nourishment, Mr. Shakespeare. The stuff they feed you would not keep a mouse alive."

"Well? What do you have to tell me? I do not have all day."

"Do I have your word that I will be freed after you have what you want?"

"Only when I have checked it thoroughly."

"And will I have my press back?"

"No, Glebe. By now it should be firewood. But if I like what you say, I will leave a little silver so you will be fed."

Glebe shrugged helplessly. "Then I have no option but to accept your terms. You wanted to know how I heard about Lady Blanche Howard's death. I'll tell you: it was the famous Mother Davis herself that did give me that information about the piece of bone and the silver crucifix said to have been found within her person. I take it this is what you wished to know."

"Mother Davis? Which Mother Davis would this be, Glebe?"

"*The* Mother Davis. Is there more than one? The very same sorceress said to have made lusty potions for the Earl of Leicester."

"Are you saying this woman really exists?" Shakespeare wanted information, not superstitious rumor.

"Of course she exists, Mr. Shakespeare. I depend on her for much of my gossip."

"I had thought she was plucked from some Papist's fevered imagination."

"No, indeed, sir. She is real enough and larger than life. A very notorious witch who can hex you wealth or depravity, love or murder, whichever it is you require. But you will always pay her a heavy price, as I am doing now."

"Are you suggesting, Glebe, that your present predicament is something to do with this Mother Davis?"

"Of course. I failed to pay her the full sum that she asked. Not an error I will make again, Mr. Shakespeare. . . ."

"And where might I find this witch?"

Glebe laughed bleakly. "You will not find her, sir. She will find you."

"And how, pray, will she know that I am looking for her?"

"Because she is a witch, sir. She knows things that others do not."

Shakespeare turned to Harry Slide. "Have you heard of this woman?"

Slide nodded his head gravely. "I think I would not like to get on the wrong side of her, Mr. Shakespeare."

Shakespeare's instinct was to disbelieve such tales. Yet even if she were no witch, she certainly knew something of the murder of Lady Blanche. "Will she contact me soon, Glebe?"

"Very soon."

"And where does she live?"

"In the air, Mr. Shakespeare."

"What scurrilous nonsense you talk! What does this witch look like?"

"Whatever she likes, sir. One day she might be a foul hag who would not be out of place here in Newgate, another day she might be a beautiful, nubile wench."

"And which of these forms did she take when you met her?"

"Well, to tell truth, sir, she looked rather homely, like my mother. But I know that sometimes she does take the shape of a cat, which is her familiar."

At that, Shakespeare laughed out so loud that the other prisoners turned his way to see who could find anything of amusement in this dungeon. "A cat! Then perchance you have *eaten* her, Glebe. You are staying here, man. Your only hope of release is if this Mother Davis — of whom I have grave doubts — contacts me and if she then makes any sort of sense. Good day to you. I will leave a shilling with the turnkey for some food, which is more than you deserve."

CHAPTER 29

Jane was at the door when Shakespeare arrived home at Seething Lane.

"Mr. Shakespeare, Mistress Marvell called on you again. She said she wished to speak with you on a matter of urgency."

"Anything else?"

"Yes, sir, this." Jane handed him a sealed letter. "A messenger brought it to you an hour since."

Shakespeare broke the seal. Inside was a short missive. *If you desire to know the truth of certain matters, come at three of the clock. You will be met in the Bear Garden, at the main entrance to the Baiting Pit. MD.*

MD. Mother Davis. He felt the prickles rise on his neck. He would have to go, of course, though his instinct was to go straight for Dowgate to see Catherine Marvell. But that would have to wait. If this witch Mother Davis really knew something, then she was the key to the murder of Lady Blanche and, perhaps — if his surmise was correct — the attempt on Drake's life. Only the killer or someone close to him could have known about the objects found inside Lady Blanche's body.

"There was one more thing, Mr. Shakespeare. Your brother William was here."

Shakespeare frowned. "William?"

"He is with a players' company. The Queen's Men. They have come to London."

"Ah. Well, I shall seek him out. In due course." The arrival of his younger brother was a distraction Shakespeare did not need.

Shakespeare took horse and rode across the bridge, turning after the Great Stone Gate, along through the mass of narrow streets and poor housing that crowded the Stews Bank area of Southwark. A modest wedding party was just stepping out joyously from the porch of St. Saviour's as he trotted past, and he raised his hat to the plump bride. It was good to see some normality in these terrifying times; it reminded him of all that he was fighting for in Walsingham's war of secrets. For a moment a picture came into his mind, an image of Catherine Marvell in a silken gown of ivory and damson, trimmed with gold and sable, her dark hair cascading across her shoulders. But he shook the vision from his head and trotted on. Such thoughts had no place in this day's work.

The Bear-Baiting Pit was closed and the gardens looked skeletal and out of sorts, but in a few weeks' time, when spring arrived, the dreariness would disappear and jollity would begin afresh as the much-loved bears — Harry Hunks, Bold Tarquin, and the others — came out again every Wednesday and Sunday to perform. Then the people would throng this park and, on a baiting day, all sorts of hawkers selling nuts and fruits and saffron cakes would shout their wares while minstrels sang and played for tossed farthings.

A woman stood waiting at the gate as promised in the letter. Though wrapped in a cloak from head to foot, she was striking to look at. He leaned over from the saddle. "I take it, mistress, that you are *not* Mother Davis?"

She smiled a beautiful smile. Shakespeare took her to be of African blood, for she was dark-skinned. "*Mais non.* My name is Isabella Clermont, but I am here on behalf of Mother Davis. Won't you please accompany me to meet her?" The accent was husky and richly French. Shakespeare bowed slightly in acknowledgment, then dismounted and took his horse by the reins as he followed

her back to Long Southwark, then along
Bermondsey Street, turning northward into
the maze of back streets that crowded near
the water downstream of the bridge.

As they walked, he wondered about
Mother Davis. He tried to recall all he had
read in the seditious tract known as "Leicester's Commonwealth," published illegally
two years earlier. It was a vicious attack on
Leicester — Robert Dudley — renowned as
the Queen's favorite courtier and, it was alleged by many, her secret lover.

The tract had been banned, but everyone
in London seemed to know its content. It
alleged that Leicester used the services of
Mother Davis to fashion a love potion for
him so that he might seduce a married
woman, commonly believed to be the beautiful Lady Douglass Sheffield. The ingredi-
ents of the potion were young martins —
which Leicester had been required to steal
from their nest — and his own seed, which
he spilled at Mother Davis's behest.

Mother Davis then distilled the birds with
his essence and some herbs into a powerful
potion that Leicester gave to Lady Douglass
in a glass of wine. When the potion had
taken effect, the young wife succumbed to
him willingly. One rumor even said that
Douglass's then husband, John Sheffield,

had caught the lovers in a frenzy of lust in the marital bed. It was also put about that Leicester later poisoned Lord Sheffield. But then, who *hadn't* Leicester been accused of poisoning? Some said, too, that Leicester and Douglass went on to wed in secret to avoid fomenting the Queen into a jealous rage. Naturally, Elizabeth discovered the truth eventually and exploded into a towering fury. Then, as the fall of the leaf follows summer, Leicester tired of Douglass and cast her aside with cruel indifference. She was said to hate him now, seething in her Paris exile with her new husband, England's ambassador Sir Edward Stafford, who loathed Leicester with a fervor equal to his wife's. For the common people, though, the story was the stuff of great mirth. Whenever Leicester passed in a procession through the City, the apprentices would call out, "Fresh martins for sale! Get your fresh martins here, Your Lordship!" and would fall about laughing. Leicester could ignore such jibes, yet when he saw his peers sniggering into their ermine collars he noted their names and vowed vengeance one day. Exacting retribution on all who mocked him was likely to take several lifetimes.

As to Mother Davis, the tract gave no more information except to say that she was a famous and notable sorceress and that she lived across the River from St. Paul's. Shakespeare had taken little note of the scurrilous pamphlet; he had never believed Mother Davis really existed or that the event with the martins ever took place. Even now, he was far from certain. He found it laughable that the seed of a man's loins mixed with the essence of some fledglings could make a woman fall for a man; if there were any truth in such dark things, it would make a mockery of all that was Christian and good.

Within fifteen minutes Shakespeare and the Frenchwoman were outside a large, old, galleried building that gave the impression that it had, at one time, served as a warehouse. Still following Isabella, who said not a word on the journey, he trotted his horse into the cobbled courtyard, where an ostler took the reins and tethered the horse by a trough.

His guide signaled with her elegant hand. "Come with me, please, Monsieur Shakespeare."

She led the way through a postern door. From farther inside the building he heard the sound of music and laughter. They went up a narrow staircase to the second floor. Isabella pushed open a door and they entered a small room with a blazing open fire and a dozen or more flickering candles. "Please, Monsieur Shakespeare, would you wait here a short while? Madame Davis is a little delayed. Would you like something to drink in the meantime?"

Shakespeare was irritated. He wished himself elsewhere — Dowgate with Catherine Marvell, to be precise. He certainly did not want to be kept waiting by the ludicrous Mother Davis and her heathen trickery "Yes, I'll wait," he said curtly. "And you can bring me some brandy, Mistress Clermont."

She nodded and went out and he sat himself close to the crackling flames and looked around at his surroundings. The walls were hung with opulent, inviting tapestries. Over the fireplace, he noticed a series of small, framed pictures, ranged in two rows of eight. He rose to get a closer look and was taken aback to see their content. He gazed at them, fascinated. It was not the first time he had seen images of men and women fornicating, but these were of a different order to the laughable stuff that could be bought for a crown or so from the sellers around St. Paul's. They were originals drawn in ink, rather than poor woodcut prints, and the drawing was exquisite, which only served to heighten the erotic content of the pictures. It would be difficult not to be aroused by such highly charged images. Feeling self-conscious, he sat down again.

The door opened and a woman entered carrying a tray with a glass of warm spirit. Shakespeare stared, astonished. She was slender and fair and naked. He could not take his eyes from her breasts. She brought the drink over and handed it to him. He took it, as if in a trance, and drank.

"Would you like anything else, master?" she asked. Her hand touched his as she spoke.

"No, no," he said. "That will be all."

"Are you certain, master?" She guided his hand to the softness of her inner thigh. The effect on Shakespeare was dramatic and he pulled away. Yet all the pent-up frustration of these past days welled within him and his hand moved back, guiltily, to touch her there again. She pushed herself toward his touch. He wanted to caress her over every inch of her smooth skin.

He closed his eyes, drinking in the sensation. And then he pulled away again, though he could hardly bear to do so. "No. Go now."

She hesitated a moment and reached once more for his hand, but this time he did not react to her touch and so she bowed and turned to leave the room. He downed the remains of the brandy in one gulp and gasped at its potency. What *was* this all about? He had made a wrong decision in coming here, especially alone. He should have brought Harry Slide with him.

What to do now? He couldn't just sit here waiting for Mother Davis to deign to appear. Would she be five minutes, five hours? He put the glass down by the fire, which seemed to be burning more ferociously. The room was too hot. He felt a bead of sweat dripping from his forehead, down his cheek and neck into his ruff.

He went to the door and lifted the latch, opening it a fraction, then fully. It gave onto a hallway, lit all along its length by sconces with broad, expensive candles. He stepped out into the corridor and walked along it. At the other end was another closed door. Behind the door was music and strange sounds — laughter and moans.

The door opened easily. He stood in the doorway looking onto a scene that might, he thought, have come from someone's sordid imagination of hell. Eight years ago, at the age of twenty, when he was a young lawyer, he had traveled to Venice and Verona and he had encountered many engravings and paintings based on the infernal visions of the great poet Dante Alighieri. He had also seen paintings of orgies during his travels and, indeed, here in London, and he was no virgin; yet he had never seen such a scene of debauchery in the flesh. Here were a dozen women of every hue of hair and skin, each one naked, entwined with each other on a bed large enough for a monarch. The bed was all hung in red draperies and bedding that glowed like blood in the firelight. Frankincense infused the air with its luscious scent. The girls were writhing like overheated snakes in May, employing tongues, fingers, limbs, and implements made to represent the male pizzle, in all manner of positions. They moaned and mouthed obscenities, seemingly oblivious to his presence. In a corner, two of the naked women played music on a lyre and a harp. No man could watch this unaffected. As Shakespeare stood there transfixed, he suddenly realized that this was all for *his* benefit.

With a mighty effort, he slammed the door shut. He was shaking. He closed his eyes but could not dismiss the vision of that bed of flesh from his sight. He turned quickly and came face to face with the seductive smile of Isabella Clermont.

"That was most pleasurable, no?"

"You presume too much upon my forbearance, Mistress Clermont."

She feigned surprise. "I am sorry, Monsieur Shakespeare."

"I tell you what would be pleasurable: this place closed down and everyone in it thrown into Bridewell, yourself and the famed Mother Davis included. And I will ensure you tread the wheel day after day until you are fully cleansed of this wanton depravity."

"Forgive me, sir. I am sorry. Most men enjoy this. They like to see beautiful women taking pleasure from their bodies. Perhaps you prefer boys. We could arrange that for you —"

"I am going now. And I will be back with the Sheriff and constables."

"But monsieur, Mother Davis has arrived and would speak with you. Do you not wish it?"

"And how long will you keep me waiting this time?"

"No, please, come with me now." She took his hand, but he tugged it away. He did, however, follow her farther along the corridor, away from the anteroom and the chamber of naked women. Shortly they came to another room, where a small, well-rounded woman with gray hair sat by the fire, alone. She was dressed modestly and sat quietly, her hands demurely in her lap. If this was Mother Davis, she was, indeed, as Walstan Glebe had suggested, rather like any man's mother.

"Monsieur Shakespeare, may I introduce you to Mother Davis." Isabella extended her palm by way of introduction.

"Mr. Shakespeare, I have so wanted to meet you," said Mother Davis. "I have heard so much about you and your good work for the safety of our beloved Queen and this England which we all love so dearly. Please, won't you come and sit here beside me?" She patted the cushioned daybed at her side.

Shakespeare moved closer to her, but did not sit. "Mistress Davis, I have no idea what sort of a house you run here, but I will do my utmost to close it down. In the meantime, I am led to believe you have some information for me concerning a heinous crime. I demand that you pass this on to me forthwith or face the full force of the law."

Her voice was warm and cooing. "I will do everything I can to help you, but I am just a poor old woman, so I am not at all sure how much assistance I can be. Please, do sit down, Mr. Shakespeare. You look so uncomfortable standing there."

"I will continue to stand." He knew he sounded brittle, but he wished it to be that way. This woman was a succubus and he would not be drawn in. "Will you tell me about the information you gave to Walstan Glebe about the murder of the Lady Blanche Howard? How did you come across this intelligence?"

"All in good time, sir. All in good time. I am sure we have much to talk about."

"We have nothing to talk about. You have information; I want it."

The old woman shook her head. "I fear I have upset you in some way. Forgive me. Something is building within you, Mr. Shakespeare, and I worry that if you do not release it you will explode like a cannon. I was sorry you did not want any of my girls. They are such lovely, kind girls and I do think one of them would have done you a great deal of good. But anyway, at least take some refreshment with me. Isabella, some malmsey, please."

Shakespeare paced the room, conscious of the old woman's eyes following his every move. "Will you tell me or no?" he demanded. "Do I have to fetch the pursuivants?"

The old woman was silent.

Isabella reappeared with the malmsey and

a platter of small things to eat: pastries and cakes. She offered them to Shakespeare but he waved them away.

"Mother Davis, it is *you* who have brought me here to this place. If you have aught to say, then say it now."

"I will tell you this, Mr. Shakespeare: there is plot and counterplot. Who plots with one, plots with another against the first. And the first plots with the third against the second. The man you want has ill-used my Isabella, who led you here. The Devil and his demons are welcome to him and you shall know his name."

"Then tell me it. I do not need your riddles and potions and foul practices. Just the name."

Mother Davis signaled with her hand to Isabella. She clapped her hands and two maids appeared and immediately started to undress the young Frenchwoman from her rich blue dress of silk and satin.

"I hope this does not disturb you, Mr. Shakespeare," Mother Davis said, her old eyes sharp. "But I vouchsafe it is necessary in this instance."

When Isabella was naked, her dark skin glowing a rich golden brown in the light of the fire and candles, she stretched out her arms in the form of a cross.

Shakespeare watched, unwillingly beguiled. His gaze went to her wrists. Though her skin was dark, he could see that there was a purple raised weal around each wrist, like those on Blanche Howard. Shakespeare's eyes turned to Mother Davis. She smiled comfortingly. She nodded to Isabella, who then turned around. The wound cut into her back did not seem a bad one, difficult to say how deep it had been, but there was no doubting its form: it looked very like the crucifix carved into Blanche's dead body.

"Enough!" Shakespeare said to Isabella. "Get dressed."

Mother Davis signaled to the maids, who began to dress the girl.

"Well, Mr. Shakespeare, does this give you pause for thought?"

"You are not telling me what I need to know, mistress. You passed on information to Walstan Glebe. Where did you get that information? And what was the name of the man who did these things to Isabella?"

"It was Isabella herself that gave me this information. Isabella, show Mr. Shakespeare the items."

From the mantel, Isabella took a silver crucifix and a piece of bone. She handed both to Shakespeare. He turned them over and over in his hands, but the objects alone meant nothing. "And whence came these objects?"

Mother Davis did not smile. Nor did her eyes leave John Shakespeare's. "They came from within her, sir. They were placed there, most savagely, by a man who gave his name as Southwell."

"The Jesuit priest?"

"We believe so, Mr. Shakespeare. At the time, we did not know of him, but we have since heard tell that this priest is sought by Mr. Secretary, among others; that is why we are talking with you. We thought this intelligence might be important to the safety of the realm."

"But where is the connection to the murder of Lady Blanche? You gave Glebe the information about the crucifix and bone in relation to the murder of Lady Blanche Howard."

Now Mother Davis did smile. "For a very good reason, Mr. Shakespeare, but one that I cannot yet divulge. But before you delve too deep, let Isabella tell you her story. Isabella, please . . ."

Isabella Clermont was almost dressed now. The maids fussed over her stays and hooks. "He came to me two days ago, Monsieur Shakespeare. At first he asked me to beat him. This is not unusual. There are many men in the world — particularly those of a religious nature — who ask this." She shrugged. "But if they pay, then it is none of my business and I am more than willing to comply for the right price. This Southwell asked me to tie him down and then I whipped him. I do not do it hard because I do not wish to cause any real harm. He seemed to enjoy it well enough — at least, I thought that he was satisfied. But then, when I loosed him, he seized me and tied me down in his place, my wrists bound tight in the ropes. That is when he did his evil work, thrusting those things into me and cutting my back with his poniard. I thought he was going to kill me."

"But he didn't kill you. Now, why would that be if he killed the Lady Blanche? Why would he free you?"

"Because of me," Mother Davis answered. "I look after my girls, Mr. Shakespeare. I heard Isabella's screams and came in while the foul brute was about this Popish business. When I called for help, he ran and that was the last we saw of him."

Shakespeare laughed, a strange, high-pitched giggle that came unbidden, and wondered why he was laughing, *A woman is nearly murdered and I am laughing,* he thought. But the thought made him laugh all the more. He put a hand to his mouth, trying to focus. "Can you describe this Southwell?"

"We both saw him. He was a pretty boy," Mother Davis said. "Half man, half girl, with golden hair, scarce bearded. Not tall, not short. He spoke precisely, perhaps too precisely. I am sure we would both recognize him again. Catch him and we will identify him for you and bear witness against him in a court of law."

"And you, Mistress Clermont, how would you describe this man?" His words came out strangely, twittering and light. His legs were wobbly, as if he had drunk too much strong ale. He was swaying.

"Much like Mother Davis. I would also say that his eyes were green. Though it is never easy to be certain of such things. It could have been a trick of the light. For a *religieux,* it seemed to me he was strong in the arm. I could not have fought him off."

Shakespeare giggled as he sat down on the settle beside Mother Davis. He slumped forward, head in his hands, and closed his eyes. She stroked his head. "Mr. Shakespeare, what *is* the matter?"

"I . . . I feel out of sorts. I think I need to lie down for a few minutes."

"Of course. Isabella, go and fetch help. Have a bed prepared immediately."

The room seemed to be expanding. He began to feel smaller, as if he were shrinking to the size of a cat. He was vaguely aware that his mind was no longer functioning as it should. Where was he? Who were these people? And after that, darkness fell and he remembered nothing.

CHAPTER 30

He awoke in a crimson bed with blood-red sheets. His body was weak. He was too tired to move. Hazily, he realized it was the bed in which Mother Davis's women had performed their squalid tableau of an orgy for him. Now he was alone. It occurred to him that he should get up and get out of this place, but he could not move. He raised his head from the cushions, just long enough to see that he was not alone after all. Isabella Clermont was sitting quietly on a wooden chair in a corner of the room. His head fell back onto the bed, overcome by the exertion of raising it.

"Monsieur Shakespeare, you are awake."

He tried to reply but could not. His mouth moved like a fish's but no sound came forth. He felt blissful; there was nothing to concern him in the world. He could hear his breathing and it was like listening to the calm lapping of the sea on the shore.

All he had to do was close his eyes again and drift away.

"I shall fetch Mother Davis."

Yes, he thought. *Fetch Mother.* A picture of his own mother floated across his closed eyes. She was smiling at him beatifically and he was a little boy again, back in their lovely house on a summer's day, with flowers growing in abundance all around the doors and windows.

When next he opened his eyes, Mother Davis stood at the side of the bed with Isabella.

"How are you feeling now, Mr. Shakespeare? That was quite a funny turn you had there."

He looked up into her eyes and noticed that they didn't smile. It was her mouth that smiled like a mother, not her eyes. Her eyes held secrets and dark things, things he didn't wish to know.

She held up a small glass vial between the thumb and forefinger of her left hand. "I have your essence here, Mr. Shakespeare. Isabella procured it from you. I think its release has been good for you. Something *was* building within you and it did, indeed, explode like a cannon. You will feel much the better for it, I am sure. These things are better expended than held in."

Through the haze, it registered with Shakespeare that she held a vial containing his seed. Why? As if reading his mind, she said, "It is by way of payment, Mr. Shakespeare. There is always a price to pay. Hear this and remember it."

As he watched, unable to speak or communicate, Mother Davis closed her eyes and her voice became high and ethereal:

"The Fathers plot and the vain ones play, yet a man called Death is on his way. Heed what I say, John Shakespeare, or pay. For a price there is, though you say nay. And the price you will pay, in love, is named Decay."

She patted his hand. "There. Be clever. I have your seed. I still have Leicester's seed and he is forever mine. Always remember the price. Walstan Glebe forgot it and now he shivers and thirsts in Newgate. In return you have the name of your killer. Now all you need do is find him. The key is with you. You can unlock the doors if you desire. But never betray the messenger, Mr. Shakespeare. Never do anything to harm Mother Davis."

He slept. When he woke again, the room was cold and lit by a single candle that had burned down to less than an inch. This time he was alone. He found he could now rise from the bed, though he was still woozy and his head ached. The paralyzing torpor had gone.

He was naked. His clothes were on the chair where Isabella had been sitting watching him. As he dressed himself, he realized they had taken his seed. He listened for sounds, but none were forthcoming. He picked up the candle and walked to the door. A looking glass hung from the wall and he caught his reflection in it. He looked closer and gasped in surprise; his right eyebrow was missing, shaved clean off. What spells was the witch Davis weaving? The corridor outside was dark, but for his rapidly diminishing candle. It was just enough to get him to the antechamber where he had first waited and had seen the pictures of fornication on the wall, before the flame guttered and died. In the antechamber, the fire was reduced to glowing embers, but that gave him some light, enough to find another, half-burnt candle, which he lit from the embers. He walked back down the corridor to the room where he had met Mother Davis. All was emptiness and darkness. What time was it? From the embers, assuming no more wood had been thrown on the fire, he guessed it must be early evening. Suddenly he remembered Catherine Marvell. She had been desperate to see him about something. He had to get home, then go to her. A wave of guilt crashed over him as if from nowhere as a flickering image came into his head of Isabella Clermont kneeling astride him, toying with his tumescent member, harvesting his seed.

And still he did not know how Walstan Glebe had come by the information he wrote concerning Lady Blanche Howard's fatal injuries.

As he arrived back at Seething Lane, he was still groggy. He had ridden across the bridge slowly, fearing he might fall. Once home, he walked his mount around to the mews, where a groom took the reins. Shakespeare then ambled unsteadily back toward his front door.

A cowled figure emerged from the shadows and his hand went to the hilt of his sword. He breathed a sigh of relief and slid the weapon back into its scabbard when he saw it was Catherine.

"Mistress Marvell. I was about to come to Dowgate to see you."

"I couldn't wait. I have heard nothing from you about Master Woode. I am desperate with worry."

"All right. Come in."

Indoors, Jane took their cloaks and offered them food and drink. "What happened to your eyebrow, master?"

Shakespeare scowled at her. "Don't ask."

"I'm sorry, Mistress Marvell," Shakespeare said, when Jane had left. "I have not been able to come to Dowgate. But, please, you are welcome here." Seeing her, Shakespeare's thoughts returned to the events in Southwark. He felt shabby and unclean, wanted nothing more than a bowl of water and a cloth to wash his body from head to toe. He felt mighty tired, his head was throbbing, and he longed for his own bed.

He took Catherine through to his small library. It was his place and his alone, a place to think and pray, when the humor took him. He was waking up fast and it was becoming clear that Catherine was deeply distressed. Her hair had not been combed and her eyes were lined with dark shadows. Yet she contrived still to be beautiful.

"We have to save Master Woode from the clutches of that monster," she said. "Where has Topcliffe taken him? Is he alive or dead?"

Shakespeare had never imagined her like this. Her character was all fire and defiance and here she was almost begging, though not for herself.

"Mistress Marvell," he said gently, "I have

discovered the whereabouts of Mr. Woode and it is not news that will comfort you. He is being held in Topcliffe's own home in Westminster. I am told he has there a strong chamber with a rack. There is no way to remove your master from that place. We can only wait until he is brought to trial on whatever charges Topcliffe can muster, and then ask Mr. Woode's lawyer to do his best. This is bad, but I must speak plain with you."

He half expected Catherine to erupt in tears or to collapse swooning in a heap, but instead she looked at him steadily. "Mr. Shakespeare, I refuse to believe that all is lost. We must bring my master out of that place. I have a proposition for you. And a confession. I will tell you things trusting in your Christian goodness and in my belief, which I pray will not prove misguided, that a human heart beats within your chest."

He held her eye for a few seconds, then nodded. "Go ahead. Sit down and talk. I will listen."

She lowered herself onto the cushioned window seat where he often sat to read. Her hands were tight balls of tension, but she spoke firmly and directly. "I have not been honest with you, Mr. Shakespeare. I told you I did not know anything of Jesuit priests, but that was a lie. The truth is I know two such priests, one of whom concerns me greatly. It pains me to say such a thing, for I am betraying a trust placed in me, but I now believe it would be better for people of all religions if he were apprehended. I am afraid he may be capable of terrible crimes, which will sow discord rather than harmony. I fear, too, that it is possible he may have been responsible for the murder of Blanche."

"Do you have evidence that this is so?"

"Only circumstantial. And my instincts, which are powerful. I am proposing a trade if you like. I will take you to meet the other priest, of whose character I have no doubts. He has agreed to talk with you and will, I believe, provide you with intelligence that might bring a conclusion to these unhappy events. For me to do this thing, you must vouchsafe not to arrest him. But first you must do everything within your power — which I know to be considerable — to effect the release of Master Woode. If that involves prostrating yourself before Mr. Secretary or petitioning the Queen, then you must do it. My master is a good and innocent man and does not deserve this. His life and the future of two small children are at stake here."

Shakespeare's head was clearing fast. He was angry with Catherine for her lies, yet he had suspected all along that she knew the whereabouts of the hunted Jesuits, had even helped to harbor them. For her now to offer up one of them in return for the life of her master, she must indeed have severe doubts about the priest. She must also, he realized with dismay, have a deep affection for Thomas Woode. What exactly did their relationship amount to? Were they lovers? If not, did she wish it so? For one brief, unworthy moment it occurred to Shakespeare that it would serve his purposes to let Woode die, leaving the way clear for him to woo Catherine. And then, discomfited by his feelings, he recalled the Old Testament tale of David and Bathsheba. Was he, like David, willing to allow another to die for his own happiness? The words of Mother Davis came back to him: *"The price you will pay, in love, is named Decay."* He shuddered.

"Yes," he told Catherine Marvell. "I will do all within my power to save your master from Topcliffe. Yet if there are charges against him, I cannot protect him from the law. If he has harbored traitors, he must pay the price."

"I understand that."

"But first tell me this: what is Thomas

Woode's connection with the tract we found close to the body of the Lady Blanche? There was something in the printing of the lettering that he recognized."

"When you get to him, Mr. Shakespeare, you can ask him yourself. I am sure he will tell you what you want, for he loves me and *will* be influenced by me. Just say the words 'I bring you solace, Mr. Woode.' "

CHAPTER 31

In the morning as he walked down Seething Lane, Shakespeare still felt the after-effects of Mother Davis's potions. Walsingham was reluctant to provide him with the warrant he required. The old man looked at his chief intelligencer curiously, but did not see fit to comment on the missing eyebrow; he had weightier matters on his mind. "I do not like to cross Mr. Topcliffe, John. These are not days for such politicking between ourselves. Fight the enemy, not each other. If Woode has information, Topcliffe will discover it."

Shakespeare had to argue his case forcibly. It was, he said, critical that *he* see Woode, for, unwittingly, he might have the key to finding the killer of Lady Blanche and the assassin sent after Drake. He did not elaborate on the source of his intelligence, nor that it involved the Jesuit priest Southwell; he did not want to give any information that might serve to incriminate Catherine Marvell. But he did explain his theories concerning the link between the two crimes and his belief that Woode might reveal things to him that he would never reveal to Topcliffe.

Walsingham was not convinced, yet he saw Shakespeare's conviction and reluctantly relented. "But this warrant will only allow you to *talk* to this Woode; it will not enable you to carry him away from Topcliffe. Go today and I will ensure Topcliffe expects you and obeys the warrant. And try to be civil, John."

"And do you think Topcliffe will be civil to me?"

Walsingham did not reply.

Shakespeare rode through the chill streets clutching his warrant in his doublet. He was not expecting Topcliffe to grant him admission to his house but knew he must try.

Topcliffe was waiting for him and seemed uncharacteristically good-humored. "Welcome, Mr. Shakespeare. Welcome to my humble abode." He held back the great oaken door to give Shakespeare admittance. "Can I provide you with aught to take away the cold of the day? A tot of brandy perchance?"

Shakespeare thought that he would rather sup with the Devil than with Topcliffe and declined. "I am here to see Mr. Thomas Woode."

"And I am more than pleased to show him to you. Perhaps you would like to see inside my strong chamber. It is a remarkable piece of work. The Tower has nothing to compare, I believe."

"Is Woode there? Have you tormented him?"

"Come."

Topcliffe led the way along a short passage to a door with heavy iron ties and straps that gave it a look of impregnability. He threw the door open to reveal a room of darkness relieved only by the guttering light of a few pitch sconces and a small, grubby skylight. The windows to the street were all boarded up and blacked out.

"Step inside, Mr. Shakespeare, do not be afraid. I will not eat you."

"I promise you this, Topcliffe. Whatever things I feel about you, fear is not one of them."

Topcliffe barked his mongrel laugh. Shakespeare stepped inside and looked around the gloom. The room was dominated by the rack, a grotesque bedlike structure constructed of bright new timber and measuring ten foot by four. At each end was a roller, with thick ropes for attaching to the wrists and ankles.

"Brand new, Mr. Shakespeare. Do you like it? I paid for it from my own purse. Twenty-one pounds, fifteen shillings. How much have you paid of *your* money in defense of the realm?"

In a corner was a brazier with cold dead coals and ash from another day. On the wall was a bar attached to two iron rings, bolted firmly into place just below ceiling height. Topcliffe saw Shakespeare's eyes move there. "Now *that,* Mr. Shakespeare, is my pride and joy. All you must do is put a pair of fetters to their wrists with a nice metal point pressing into the flesh, then hang them by the hands from that bar up there. If I'm in a hurry, I'll hang them loose; but usually I like to take my time, so I'll let them touch their back to the wall or have their toes touching the ground. That way they don't die so quick. The pain that such a simple device can provide is a mighty thing to behold. They go mad with it, Shakespeare, mad as Bedlam fools. It does grip their torso most, their belly and chest, a crushing pain worse than any that a man can endure. They believe blood is leaking like sweat from their hands and fingers, though it is not. My one problem with it is that they can scarcely say a word while they're up there, so I can't tell when they want to provide the information I require. But I let them down every once in a while to see whether they wish to talk. Usually they do."

"I am here to see Mr. Woode, not to discuss the merits or otherwise of your foul, un-Christian instruments."

Topcliffe looked satisfied with the impression his chamber had made. "Ah, yes, Woode. Now there is a gentleman most fearful. He certainly is a talker, told me everything I wanted to know and more. I think I now know the name of his aunt Agnes's best milk-producing cow. And, of course, the truth of the priests he has had at his house. He's admitted everything: names, dates, descriptions, present whereabouts. He tells me Robert Southwell was one of them and that the traitor was at Tanahill House all the time while I was searching — proof enough that I was right not to stop looking and proof that Her Ladyship is in league with the Romish Antichrist and all his devilish works. I hope Southwell starved to death in his dismal hole and that his rotting flesh stinks the place out."

"I have a warrant allowing me to talk with

Mr. Woode."

Topcliffe took a cold branding iron from the brazier. He idly slapped it down on his hand before replying. "Not necessary, Shakespeare. He's told me all, as if I was his priest in the confession box and he was revealing all his dirty little secrets. Why, he even admitted stealing timbers from the Royal Docks. Now, if that isn't a treasonable offense, then I'm a Dutchman's donkey."

"A man will testify that black is white under torture, Topcliffe. Now take me to Woode or answer to Mr. Secretary."

Topcliffe bared his teeth with contempt. He threw the iron back into the brazier. "Woode it is then. Come on, boy. Through here."

There was a door in the side of the strong chamber, set into a brick wall. Topcliffe unlatched the bolt then kicked it open. There was no light in this room except the flickering of the torches. Shakespeare could see nothing at first, but then as his sight adjusted he thought he could see a mound, like a sack of beets, in the far corner. Shakespeare strove to avoid recoiling from the habitual prison stench of ordure, then stepped forward into the room.

"Mr. Woode?"

There was no reply. He could hear breathing, coming in short, painful gasps.

"Mr. Woode, it is John Shakespeare. I am here to talk with you." Shakespeare turned to Topcliffe. "Do you have drink for this man?"

"He has water. If he doesn't like it, he can drink his own piss."

"I would talk with him."

"Then talk."

"Alone."

"As you like." Topcliffe stepped away and was about to slam shut the door. Shakespeare intervened with his foot.

"I want light in here. And get this man good food and some small ale or I will write to the Queen giving detail of how you care for those you question in her name."

"Your threats mean nothing to me. The Queen knows what I do for her and she revels in it."

"What febrile nonsense you talk."

"Oh, but she does, Shakespeare, she does. I tell her all about it when I'm on top of her thrusting in and out. How that do work her up into a frenzy, until she cries out in pleasure." Topcliffe laughed, but Shakespeare wasn't deceived. He knew he had touched a raw nerve, that Topcliffe's relationship with the Queen was the one area he could be vulnerable. Elizabeth would never allow herself to be embarrassed or shamed by one of her hirelings.

"Would you like me to tell her you said that?"

"Would you like your head broke with an iron bar? Would you like me to bruit it abroad to Mr. Secretary about your strange bedtime cavortings most recently? Tell me, Shakespeare, what *did* become of your right eyebrow? Hah! I know everything about you, Shakespeare. You're as bad as one of those Popish girl-boys. God's blood, have your damned candle and food. Perhaps the prisoner would care for a baked pie of elvers and thrushes, with some dainty marzipan sweetmeats to follow . . ."

Shakespeare's color rose. How did Topcliffe know about Mother Davis and Isabella Clermont? Had he followed him? Had the witch told him? And if so, why?

As Topcliffe went off to order some scraps of food from one of his servants, Shakespeare took a deep breath and went to the huddled figure in the corner. His clothes were still those of a gentleman, but covered in the dust and filth of this hellish cell. Shakespeare put an arm around him.

"Mr. Woode, can you talk, sir?"

Woode's eyes shone in the gloom. "Yes,

Mr. Shakespeare, I can talk. But I will not."
The voice rattled like a bag of beans, but it
was strong enough and more than a whisper.

"I am here to help you."

"Another Walsingham trick, I presume."

"Catherine — Mistress Marvell — has
told me things. She says you are an innocent
man."

"And what difference does that make? My
body is already broken. That is what the law
of England does: breaks innocent men until
they confess to things they did not do. Well,
sir, I will not talk with you. And nor will I
talk with that wild animal Topcliffe. Despite
what he says, I have told him nothing."

The effort of talking took its toll and he
slumped back against the wall.

"Trust me, Mr. Woode. In Christ's name
— your Christ and mine — I swear that I
am here to bring you succor, not harm you.
Please trust me. It is our only hope. . . ."

Topcliffe's servant, a thickset boy with
slicked hair and the beginnings of a wispy
beard, arrived with a jug of ale, some bread,
and a lit candle in a candle-holder. He slid
the candle to Shakespeare, ceremoniously
spat into the ale, then put it on the floor,
slopping out a fair part of it in the process.
He dropped the bread and kicked it as it
landed.

"Hope it kills you," the boy said with studied sullenness.

"Thank you, boy. Now go."

"Don't worry, I'm going from this dung heap. And the name's Jones. Nicholas Jones. I ain't no one's boy."

Shakespeare closed the door and gave Woode a long draft of ale. In the candlelight, he examined the prisoner, who yelped when touched but otherwise put up no resistance. He could scarcely move. His arms hung limp at his sides. There were marks from the manacles, red rings of broken skin around his wrists, but those were the only outward sign of torture. His eyes remained open, alert, and bright.

"How long did he hang you on the wall?"

"It felt like hours. Maybe just minutes. I have no idea. There is more torment against that wall than I had ever thought possible. I do not think I can suffer it again without dying."

Shakespeare drew closer and spoke quietly in the prisoner's ear. "I bring you solace, Mr. Woode." He then moved away. "Catherine has been talking with your lawyer, Cornelius Bligh. He is trying to get a writ of habeas corpus, but Topcliffe has been doing his utmost to block it."

Woode sighed heavily. Those words — *I*

bring you solace, Mr. Woode — were the very words Father Cotton used when first they met. Only one other person would have known that: Catherine. "It will be too late," he told Shakespeare. "I will be dead before I leave this black hole."

"Don't say that. Try to stay strong."

"He won't give up on me. Nor will he let me come to trial, for he has no evidence. He will never let me out of here alive. My only hope is a quick death. Will *you* grant me that boon?"

"I will not kill you, Mr. Woode. Nor is it in my gift to set you free. I had to obtain a warrant to see you here. You belong to Top-cliffe."

"But you and he are the same creature. Between you, and with the patronage of Walsingham, Leicester, and Burghley, you will squeeze and choke all those who cling to the old religion until they are no more. Only then will you be content."

Shakespeare held the jug to the injured man's lips once more and he drank deeply.

"Well, Mr. Shakespeare, you do not deny it. You come to me as a friend, but it is false. Whose side are you on?"

"The side of truth, Mr. Woode. If you are guilty of treason, then I will do nothing for you and you must suffer a traitor's death."

413

"I am no traitor."

"But you sail precious close to the wind. I discount these tales of stolen timbers, but you do yourself no favors consorting with Jesuits. They are seditious liars. They sow discord and many do not balk at regicide. But let us cease this talk. We do not have long. Mistress Marvell asked me to tell you that your children are well, as is she. She said you were not to worry about them. She hoped you would help me. . . ."

"My children. Who will look out for them? Will *you* care for Catherine and my children, Mr. Shakespeare?" Woode looked ten years older than when Shakespeare last saw him. His eyes shone, but there was resignation there.

"Do you have relatives? Some brother or sister to care for them while you are here?"

He shook his head slowly but said nothing.

"They will be looked after."

"Swear this in Christ."

"In God's name, I do swear it."

"Then I must help you and trust in God that you will not betray my trust." His weak voice became even quieter. "You showed me paper with some print on it . . ."

"Indeed. And you recognized it."

Woode winced from the pain that invaded

every portion of his body when he tried to move. "Yes, I recognized it. I fear I am a poor liar. I know the press on which it was printed, for it was once mine. I no longer needed it, so I gave it to certain priests who wished to publish religious tracts. There was to be nothing seditious or libelous, I promise you. Things more innocent and pure than you would find in any Paul's bookseller."

"That was *not* the paper I found. There was nothing innocent or pure or even religious about that. It was a seditious libel against Her Majesty and others. It has been burned as it deserved."

"Then I am at a loss. That is not the work of my friend Ptolomeus."

"Ptolomeus?"

"An old Marian priest. He lives the life of a beggar in an old mill in the village of Rymesford, by the Thames upstream of Windsor. He makes his own paper, which is why it was such poor quality, and does some printing for the Fathers who come to England from France and Rome. He is a harmless, spiritual soul, Mr. Shakespeare. He would never allow anything seditious to be published. But I must plead with you: do not harm him . . ."

Woode's rattling gasps were becoming weaker and Shakespeare realized that any further questioning would be pointless. He touched Woode's face, one human to another. Holding up the candle, he saw that the prisoner's eyes were closed now and his lips were fixed in a rictus of pain. Shakespeare rose to go, away from this wicked place. Before he opened the door, however, he looked at the huddled heap of a once-strong man. "I pledge that whatever happens, Mr. Woode, Mistress Marvell and your children will be under my protection."

The words from the slumped figure were lower than a whisper, but Shakespeare heard them well enough as he went out.

"I know you will. You love her."

Richard Topcliffe moved away from the thin section of wall where he had listened to every word of the conversation between Woode and Shakespeare. He lit a pipe of sotweed and sucked it enthusiastically, churning out plumes of rich, aromatic smoke. He laughed to himself. Where the rack and manacles failed to produce results, man's green stupidity always filled in the gaps.

CHAPTER 32

Catherine Marvell brought the children to his home that evening. When Shakespeare told her it was Woode's wish, she happily agreed to it. The house in Seething Lane was not large, with just one spare room, which she was to share with Andrew and Grace. Jane was pleased to have extra mouths to feed, and the children took to her immediately. That evening Catherine and Shakespeare talked until nine and took wine together. Shakespeare told Catherine of his meeting with Woode, sparing her the worst of the details. Yet he knew that she was well aware of the severity of the position her master was in.

"He fears his children will be orphans?"

There was nothing to say to that. "We will do what we can, that is all."

"In the morning I will keep my side of the bargain."

Shakespeare barely slept. He lay awake

thinking of the dark-haired woman who slept so near, in a room not ten yards from his. He thought of her warm body, naked beneath her nightgown. He could not know that she hardly slept either.

They breakfasted at dawn, the children racing around the table, then set off on foot, leaving Andrew and Grace playing with Jane.

"Where are we going, Mistress Marvell?"

"You will discover soon enough. One thing I ask: look about you as we go. We must not be followed."

It was a cold, misty morning. Eddies of fog blew up from the river and at times it was like walking in cloud as they set off northward, through the city.

"Where are you from, Mr. Shakespeare? Your voice is not that of a Londoner."

"Warwickshire. A town named Stratford. I left to follow the law but was waylaid by Mr. Secretary and pressed into his service." Shakespeare laughed. "I think the law might have been a more comfortable life."

"And a more honorable one?"

Shakespeare bridled. "I believe the defense of the realm is an honorable calling, mistress. In fact I can think of none *more* honorable."

"And yet you find yourself a bedfellow to

Topcliffe."

"Topcliffe is a man apart. He is a stain. We share some aims but we do *not* work together. He is beyond the law. I work for Mr. Secretary, who is answerable to the Queen and the Council and operates *within* the law. No system of human governance is perfect: look at Rome and Madrid. How many Topcliffes do they employ in their foul Inquisition? How many rackmasters do they have? Topcliffe learned his art from the Spanish. And the fact that a dog such as Topcliffe is employed in the struggle against these forces does not make England any the less worth fighting for."

They turned left from Seething Lane into Hart Street. There was silence between them for a few moments, and then Catherine spoke, and it was as if the floodgates had opened. "No, Mr. Shakespeare, *you* are the Queen's dog. It is you who gives her an aura of honor and decency. It is you who cleans the filth of Burghley, Walsingham, Leicester, and Topcliffe. They conduct themselves like feral beasts, tearing men's limbs from their bodies and tossing their severed parts into cauldrons like the bones of chickens, for daring to worship God in the way their conscience dictates. And you, you in your reasonableness and innocence, wash the blood from the hands of those who do these monstrous things."

Shakespeare stopped in his tracks. "Do you think it wise to speak to me like this, mistress, when you have called on me for assistance?"

Catherine stopped, too. Her blood was up. "I am sorry if I have offended you, sir, but I cannot contain my anger. Even now, that wild animal is destroying the body and mind of a good man. For all we know, he might have killed him already. How many of his prisoners never make it to the scaffold? One racking can kill a man or break his health forever. I have to say these things because they are true. This is how I feel. I know you are a good man. It is why I have come to you. Yet I hate to see your goodness used and abused by others less worthy —"

Shakespeare held up his hand, to silence her. "I will not listen to this, Mistress Marvell. I am no one's dog. I serve my Queen and country in the face of an implacable enemy. And I will defend the honor of my sovereign lady. She has made it plain that she does not wish to make a window to men's souls. Yet we know that these Jesuits come here to subvert the state, not just to bring comfort to their flock. You know it yourself, for you have told me so."

For a moment it seemed they could go no further. The air between them was a wall of ice and fire; there was no way through. And then Catherine Marvell nodded. "I have spoken out of turn, Mr. Shakespeare. It was unpardonable. I had meant to say how highly I esteemed you for your honesty and decency and for going to see Master Woode, but it did not come out like that. Forgive me."

Shakespeare still stood on his dignity. Yet how could he not forgive her? "I am sorry, too, Mistress Marvell. Not for anything I have done, but because you and those you love are suffering in this way."

"Will you not call me by my given name?"

"If you ask it, I would be honored. And I would be pleased if you would call me John."

They walked on through the mist. Catherine touched his arm. "Let us stay a while to see that we are not followed," she said softly. They stood under the eaves of a tailor's shop, watching the street around them. When they were certain they were not followed, they moved on once more, walking faster now up to East Cheap. Despite the earliness of the hour, the streets around the butcher's market were abuzz with life and movement. Here was the bloody stench of the slaughterhouses, the lowing of the great beasts come for their throats to be cut to provide fresh meat for the city, the roads thick with new sawdust to soak up the gore. "Keep close to me," she said. "We must move quickly now."

She slipped into a side alley, barely wide enough for a man to pass without turning his shoulders sideways, and Shakespeare followed her. They ran down the alley, then turned into another lane beside some cattle stalls and waited. When no one followed, they moved on into the labyrinth of lanes, with overhanging jetties from the houses. Finally, at the end of a woodframe, they came to a brick wall with a wooden gate set into it. Looking both ways to see there was no one else about, she knocked on the gate and it was quickly opened from the inside. She and Shakespeare ducked through and found themselves in a small knot garden, divided by beds of box into geometric patterns where herbs would bloom in summer, filling the air with heady scents of lavender and thyme. To Shakespeare, it looked like a little maze in which a hedgepig might lose itself.

The door to the garden closed and there stood a man, within arm's length of Shakespeare. He was shorter, perhaps five foot six inches, a slight figure who looked in want of a good meal. His golden beard was straggly, as if it had not been trimmed for weeks. His eyes were blue-gray and shone. Shakespeare knew instantly that this was Southwell. He judged, too, that this man was no killer of women, no assassin sent against Drake.

"Mr. Shakespeare," said Catherine, "this is the person of whom I told you. I will not give you his name for fear of compromising you."

The men shook hands. "Good day to you," Shakespeare said to the Jesuit.

"And to you, Mr. Shakespeare. I am sure you have a good idea as to my identity, but please, let it not be a matter of concern between us. We have a common purpose here: the release of Mr. Woode in exchange for the imprisonment of a man who I believe should not be at large. Come, sit with me a while." The priest indicated a bench at the side of the garden.

It was important to Shakespeare that the standing between the two men should be clear from the start. "Father, I will talk with you here today and I will leave you unmolested. But I must tell you that the hunt for you will continue after this, and if you are caught, the full process of the law will descend upon you. And I will not intervene on your behalf or shy away from doing my duty."

"I understand that, Mr. Shakespeare, and I thank you for your forbearance in meeting me under these circumstances. But my life is not important. As in all things, God's will be done."

Catherine stood away from them, her back against the arched wooden door that had given them access to this garden. She watched them, but this was no longer her business; this was between the two men.

"I will give you no more information than is necessary, Mr. Shakespeare, for I do not want to bring down misery on those who have helped me. I will tell you only that there is a supposed member of the Society of Jesus here in London whose motives I distrust. Every tree has its rotten fruit; at first I tried to ignore the possibility that this man was that worm-eaten apple. But now I have to speak plain. I knew and loved Lady Blanche Howard. She had come into the fold and was a much-loved daughter of the Church . . . my Church. This other priest, though I am reluctant to honor him with the title 'priest,' seemed to want to get close to her. At times, I would say, he took *too great* an interest in her. She was a lovely young woman, physically as well as spiritually. I saw the way he looked at her and touched her and I did not like it. She seemed unaware of any impropriety. She was talking, at that time, of traveling abroad to join a convent. But then she began to realize she was in love with another man . . ."

"Robin Johnson, the Lord Admiral's steward?"

The priest nodded. "I would not admit his name to you if I had not heard that he has said as much to you himself. He is safely out of the country now. Lady Blanche spent more and more time with Robin and pushed the priest away. It was as if she found him repellent. Something had happened, something she did not like. And my feelings were the same. It seemed to me he was sent here for another purpose than to save souls. This man could be charming, but he could be intimidating, too." He looked over at Catherine. "Lady Blanche was not alone in growing afraid of him; other women in our flock shied away. But what could I do? In the Society of Jesus, one learns obedience; it was my duty to help him."

"What made you change your mind? Why are you now willing to tell me these things?"

"The murder of Lady Blanche. This man had the opportunity. He would disappear for nights and never thought fit to explain his movements to me. The house in which Lady Blanche's body was found in Hog Lane was a safe house for us, which this man used a great deal for various purposes, though I was never sure what. We rented the house under an alias so that none should molest us there. I had never thought it to be used for such infamy."

"Why do you think he did this thing?"

"I believe he feared she knew too much. I think he had taken her into his confidence, and when she moved apart from him, he felt it was no longer safe to leave her alive."

"And the printing?"

"I know nothing of that. But I do read the broadsheets, Mr. Shakespeare, and I saw that a man called Gilbert Cogg had been murdered at his property in Cow Lane. I was given the name of this Cogg by a contact and, under orders from my superiors, I passed the name on to this other priest. I confess I had my doubts about doing it, grave doubts. And now I believe my doubts have been confirmed, for I think he killed Cogg, though I have no idea why."

"And do you have a name or description for this priest?"

He laughed. "I am not sure a name would be of much use to you. We do not use our real names, Mr. Shakespeare. However, while he was with me he used the name Herrick."

"Did he ever use the name van Leiden?"

"Not to my knowledge, but that means nothing."

"So describe his likeness."

"He is a Fleming, a tall man, perhaps six foot or more, clean-shaven, short hair. He always dressed modestly, like a Presbyterian almost. And though he spoke perfect English, he had a Low Countries accent."

"Thank you. That sounds very much like the man I seek. Where can I find him?"

"We have another safe house. I have reason to believe he may have gone there. It is a small tenement over the river, on the west side of Horsley Down. The house is old, from the time of John of Gaunt, I believe. It is not in good condition and should probably be razed to the ground, but it serves our purposes. At least it has done until now. It is apart from other buildings, within a copse on the edge of the common land. It will not be difficult for you to find."

"Will anyone else be there?"

"No. And that is the last question I will answer, Mr. Shakespeare. I will, however, tell you one more thing. On the day I last saw this Herrick, as I then called him, he said something that made my blood turn to ice."

"Yes?"

"He said, 'Your weakness, Father, is that you are merely willing to die for God. You are not willing to kill for Him.' "

CHAPTER 33

The man stared at his reflection in the small looking glass. He liked what he saw. With practiced ease, he cupped his hand around his beard and brushed it down repeatedly until its point was sharp. If he had doubts about the course of action upon which he was set, his reflection did not reveal them. He looked as confident and potent as ever.

Adjusting his ruff, he turned the glass's face to the wall — an old superstition of his — then picked up his belt with attached sword scabbard off the bed, fitted it around his waist, and stepped from his chamber.

He wrapped himself in a fur cloak, donned his favorite beaver hat, and walked out into the street. He had a meeting with Herrick and the prospect set his nerves on edge. Until now he had avoided all contact with the man, dealing always through intermediaries at the French embassy, but now that the attempt on Drake's life had failed, he had no choice. Until now, he had been firmly in control of events; it was he who had organized the required weapon through Cogg and he who had sent messages to Herrick informing him where Drake would disembark and from which ship. They were unlikely to get such a chance again before the Vice Admiral sailed.

Drake had received orders from the Queen, and the English fleet was due to weigh anchor any day. The plan was for Drake and his young wife, Elizabeth Sydenham, to ride for Dover and then take the wind along the Channel to Plymouth. The ships now in the Thames — four royal galleons and a group of fighting merchantmen — would be taken westward by others. After that, who could tell? The best guess was that they would head west for Panama to plunder Spanish shipping. But whatever the plan, the Spanish King and his ministers wanted Drake stopped. They wanted him dead.

They must act, and soon. Both he and Herrick were equally set on their course of action, but their motives were very different. For him, it all came down to the filthy stink of tallow candles. His family had suffered intolerable insult and financial hardship through their disagreements with the Crown. At the lowest point, when his father had lost his head to the axe, they had been reduced to lighting their poor cottage with tallow made from sheep fat. He could recall the bitter tears of his mother as the tallow belched out its acrid smoke, where once she had lit her great hall with beeswax. If Drake died, he would get the seventy thousand ducats promised by King Philip, enough to restore his family's fortune and standing.

He did not use his real name. He was a Percy, a younger forgotten cousin of the proud Catholic Percy family from the borders. The family that had once sired the great warrior Hotspur had suffered grievous hardship through the putting down of their abortive uprising in 1569: many had died by rope or axe, among them the head of the clan, Thomas Percy, who was attainted and executed. The loss of lands and wealth and reputation had been devastating. And it had not ended there; the family had been persecuted without mercy ever since. Henry, the eighth earl, had died in the Tower not two years since, accused of complicity in the Throckmorton plot to place Mary Queen of Scots on the throne of England. How could the family *not* harbor a grudge? And yet this Percy was not made of martyr stock. Enough Percys had died for the cause of Rome; he wanted others — their enemies

431

— to die instead.

It had been hard keeping up this pretense all these years. The early years were the worst, learning to dissemble, to become a loyal servant of the Crown fighting the Spaniard, but the deception had been vital to his long-term goal. Eventually, through the offices of Mendoza — Spain's former Spanish ambassador in London and now in Paris — he had persuaded King Philip that he could perform this task for the right price. Seventy thousand ducats was that price. All he needed was a professional killer to be sent and he, the forgotten Percy, would organize the wherewithal and the opportunity to put an end to Drake. His own hands had to be clean of blood, at least until the armada landed. That was where Herrick came in. Herrick was his weapon; the priest was the stuff of martyrdom and did not fear death. The first attempt had been a miserable failure thanks to that accursed coxswain putting his body between Drake and the musketball, but there would be other chances.

Now Percy and Herrick were meeting. It was high risk, for to be seen with such a man would be tantamount to treason, and Percy did not relish a traitor's death.

As arranged, Herrick was waiting in a

corner booth of The Bull, sitting alone, eating a platter of beef and pork with gusto, as though he had not supped for a week. Percy watched him for a time, to be sure he had the right man. When he was certain it was not a trap, he approached. Herrick was just raising a tankard to his lips, quaffing fresh water. The Jesuit never touched wine or any other alcoholic beverage except at Mass. But that was the Blood of Christ, not wine; just as the wafer became Christ's body on entering the mouth of a communicant, so the wine became His blood; every Roman Catholic knew that to be true and every Protestant declared it false.

"You take your life into your hands drinking that stuff," Percy said by way of greeting. "Get some beer down your gullet."

Herrick looked at him sourly. "This is good spring water. Your countrymen take too much strong liquor. There is nothing wrong with the pure water which God provides."

"Well, if you die before your day is run, blame no one but yourself, Herrick. Or whatever name you are using today . . ."

"Herrick will do."

Percy raised his head in signal to a serving wench to come over. "How did you miss?" he asked Herrick.

"I think you know what happened."

Percy shook his head in practiced dismay. "I do indeed. You have bungled, Herrick. And it must be put right."

"I need more information. Where can I find Drake next? How can I get close to him? I no longer have the long-range weapon. I believed I had no further use for it."

"Things will be more difficult from now on. The admiral has his commission. He will be heading west, to Plymouth, to gather his fleet within a day, no more. He will have four royal ships of war along with ten more at the least. With surprise on their side, they can do much harm."

Suddenly Herrick became angry. He beat his hands on the oak table so that the trencher of food jumped in the air. The movement caused a sharp pain in his side where the ball had scored him, and he winced. At least the wound had not turned to gangrene, but it slowed him. "Then you must play *your* part. You will surely be with him. You must do that which you have avoided for so long."

The wench had returned. She looked startled by their angry words, though she had no idea what concerned them. She was a comely girl, big breasts spilling out of the front of her dress in most generous measure. Percy smiled at her and preened his whiskers. "Ah, girl, I will have a pint of your strongest beer and a large trencher of meats. Spare no expense, for my friend here is paying."

As she left, Herrick reached out and grasped Percy's wrist. "Do you hear me?" he said in an urgent whisper. "You are in deep, sir, deeper than the raging western sea. I know how you have tried to work this. But that will no longer suffice. Will *you* be aboard ship with Drake on his way to Plymouth?"

Percy tried to wrench his wrist free, but he could not dislodge himself from Herrick's iron grip. "Take your hand off me!"

"Do you hear me?"

"Yes! I hear you. And yes, I will be with Drake. But I am the whetstone, Herrick. I do not cut the barley: I sharpen the blade to do it."

"God's blood, that is not enough! You will be there. Throw him overboard. Or whatever it is you pirates do by way of expedient killings."

"I will try, of course. I will look for opportunities. But he is more heavily protected than ever now. He has his blackamoor Diego, and an agent of Walsingham constantly at his side. I can see no way of approaching him to do the deed."

"Find a way." Herrick's grip tightened, then, of a sudden, broke loose as if his hand had been bitten by a snake. Herrick's hand flew back theatrically and hung for a few moments in the air.

Percy sighed. "If there is a way, I will find it. I want this as much as — more than — you, Herrick. My family, my life, depends on it."

Herrick sneered. "I despise your cowardice. You and those like you — Southwell or Cotton — say the words but do not do the deeds. Do you think God will thank you for your craven dealings on the Day of Judgment?"

"I am not a cleric, Mr. Herrick. I do not wish to take Holy Orders, so do not berate me for not being a martyr. That is *your* business, sir, not mine. And I scorn your airs. I noted the way you looked at that serving wench and I would wager ten marks to your one that you would unfrock her and fuck her without hesitation. Would you have me cheapen a price on your behalf, Mr. Herrick?"

Herrick swept his platter away. It clattered across the table and onto the floor. "So that is it. You think we have missed our chance and you are giving up. Well, I tell you, Percy, I will not give up. If Drake is going to Plymouth, then so must I. But if you have any thought for your mortal flesh and immortal soul, then I suggest you make sure that my journey is in vain. If Drake survives to wreak havoc on the King of Spain's war fleet, I will kill you myself, first plucking off your stones, then forcing them down your throat. And that will be just a beginning. After that, I promise you, things will become most unpleasant."

Shakespeare gathered together a force of twenty pursuivants and rode for Horsley Down.

It was dark when they arrived a quarter of a mile from the house. Shakespeare reined in his gray mare and raised his hand to halt, then signaled them all to dismount. The men tethered their horses within a clump of trees. There was no moon, but they had pitch torches. He ordered all but two to be snuffed.

He had Newall there, sneering as ever. It had been unavoidable; Shakespeare did not have his own squadron of men and Walsingham had insisted he go along. At a short meeting not two hours since in Seething Lane, the old man had given the go-ahead for this raid and had also informed Shakespeare that Drake had his commission. "Soon he will be safe at sea. Then the Spaniard shall feel the heat of his fire. But keep him alive until then, John. Keep him alive until his fleet is afloat."

Shakespeare looked with cold eyes at Newall. He would take no insubordination from him. Even though Newall had the title Chief Pursuivant, Shakespeare was in charge here. "Mr. Newall, you will take four men to the back of the house. And be wary; Herrick is a hired killer and will not hesitate to attack with whatever is to hand. And he is wounded. Like an injured animal, he may feel he has nothing to lose in attempting to fight his way out."

Newall grunted. He knew he had to take orders from this squeamish, book-hugging official, however much he despised him and his soft manners. If it were up to him, he would simply torch the house and all in it and thus save the state the cost of a trial and execution.

Shakespeare waited sixty seconds while Newall and his men moved through thickets to the back of the house. There were no lights from inside. Shakespeare ordered the other group forward to the front door with the battering tree, and when they were positioned, he brought his sword down as the signal. With a mighty swing, they wielded the heavy oak log at the door, splintering it on impact. The front men charged in shouting while those at the rear quickly lit their torches and surged forward to block all exits through windows or roof lights. Shakespeare followed the vanguard, ducking into the low-ceilinged hallway. It had the feel of a neglected old farmhouse, with dirt floors and ragged walls where the lime plaster had broken away to reveal the wattles.

"Upstairs straightway. Do not give him time to hide!"

The men at the front raced up the rickety, half-broken steps, shouting and banging as they charged. Within moments they had scoured every room of the house. It was empty.

"Keep moving," Shakespeare ordered the sergeant. "Spread out. Take the ground-floor rooms first. Search every cupboard, every cranny, break open wainscoting, turn over beds. If he is here, find him."

Within three hours it became clear they were not going to find Herrick. But in the main bedchamber they did find a blood-stained rag, which, it seemed to Shakespeare, was probably used to staunch Herrick's wound from Boltfoot's shot. More importantly, Shakespeare spotted a small piece of rolled linen, discarded casually beneath the bed. He picked it up and unfurled it. There, poorly painted but easily recognizable, was a portrait of Sir Francis Drake, one of the many such pictures sold throughout England and the rest of Europe since the Vice Admiral's daring circumnavigation of the globe. "So Herrick has been here," he said under his breath. "And we have missed him. God in heaven, we have missed him."

Shakespeare left late in the evening, cursing his fortune and leaving a guard of three men.

Across the road, in the shadows, Herrick stood and watched the activity for a short while. He had arrived back at the house barely a minute after the onset of the raid. Shakespeare could not have known how close he had come to trapping his quarry.

Quietly, Herrick slipped away down the alleys to Southwark. He would have to find an inn tonight, then take horse on the morrow. The question that would not go away was how the pursuivants had found this house. Had the locals become suspicious — or had someone informed on him? His only hope now was to follow Drake before he gathered his fleet and set sail from Plymouth. It was time to kill . . . and time was running out.

Starling Day was enjoying life. She had everything she needed. Treasure, a beautiful new house and business in the heart of Southwark, the best food that money could buy, and clothes that would not have looked out of place on a court lady. But behind the happiness, there was a worry. It was a worry shared by Parsimony Field: they had heard from a girl they brought over from the Bel Savage that Richard Topcliffe was looking for them and they feared it was only a matter of time before he found them.

They had changed their names. Starling was now known as Little Bird and Parsimony was Queenie. Their establishment was called Queens and it had one of the best positions of all the Southwark stews. Prices were high, as befitted a bawdy house with good-looking young girls and comfortable rooms, but it was well frequented. Men of money from across the river came here, as did foreigners whose wives were left far behind in France and beyond, ships' officers and seamen happy to blow a year's wages and plunder in a night or two of bliss.

Parsimony was in her element. She was able to indulge her passion for the arts of love with whomsoever she pleased. Starling, meanwhile, decided she had had enough of such things and had retired from the game, restricting her role to greeting the customers.

They even had their own strong-armed guard, Jack Butler, to look after them, and kitchen staff to provide sweetmeats and fair drinks for the guests. The worry, of course, was that they were flying too high. Someone would be sure to recognize them and go to Topcliffe with the information.

"Maybe we should go to Bristol or Norwich," Starling said. They talked about it, but kept putting off a decision. And the longer they did so, the more business boomed and the more settled they became.

Tonight, Starling was dealing cards for some gentlemen in the grand withdrawing room. The house, as always, was winning handsomely, but none of the men seemed to care.

"I'll be in the Clink before you're done with me, Little Bird. Up to my ears in debt!" the eldest son of a northern bishop, who seemed intent on disposing of his inheritance before he had inherited it, said with a laugh.

"Never mind, Eddie, I'll get one of my wenches to bring you broth and a kindly hand every now and then."

"The devil with it. Deal on, Little Bird, deal on."

Parsimony was upstairs and unhappy. She liked swiving as much as the next girl. A lot more than the next girl, if truth be told. But she didn't like this sort of thing. Not one bit.

She stood with her back to the wall, dressed only in a light kirtle, lash in her right hand, and looked down at the man on the bed. He was a strange one all right. He'd come in to Queens pissing money like a conduit of gold and demanded a room and a girl for the night. He took one look at Parsimony and said, "You will do, mistress. I like the look of you." Parsimony was in the mood and the man seemed presentable, so she readily agreed. But then he started asking for little extras like this: he wanted her to scourge him. And do it proper, so it hurt. Funny thing was, he was already injured, a nasty oozing wound on his side. She had offered to bandage it for him but he didn't seem interested; just wanted his lashing. So here they were.

"Do it, mistress, do it."

"Look, I don't mind a bit of messing

about, a few light strokes before a good fuck, but I'm not doing it any harder than I've already given you."

"How much do you want?"

"I don't need your money, sir. I run a respectable business here and I don't want no dead bodies on my hands."

"Then get another girl, who *will* do it."

Parsimony shrugged her shoulders. This was a difficult one. She needed to have a word with Starling. "All right. Wait here, sweeting."

She left him on the bed and traipsed downstairs. Starling would know what to do. In some ways she was the cleverer of the two.

Parsimony touched her arm at the card table. "A word if I might, Little Bird."

"Of course, Queenie."

They went off to a private room. "Got a cove upstairs wants me to beat him raw like a Bridewell penitent. Thing is, he's got good money. Shame to turn him away."

"Then give him what he wants."

"Don't like to, Starling. It's not me."

"Well, I'd happily give any man a thrashing. All I'd have to do is close my eyes and think of my husband."

"Would you do this one for me? I'll owe you."

"Of course, ducks. You take over the dealing. And give the bishop's son a break. It's not good for business to skin customers into the gutter."

CHAPTER 34

Every muscle was taut like a drawn-back long-bow string. How close had he come to Herrick? The assassin had been there. He had definitely been there at the house by Horsley Down — and recently. Now he was gone, lost in the sea of people of all shades that inhabited this infernal town.

Shakespeare sipped his wine by the fire. On the morrow, he would ride to Windsor and find this Ptolomeus. But he lacked enthusiasm for the task. What purpose could such an outing serve? How could an old, decrepit priest help him find the murderer of Lady Blanche Howard or prevent the murder of Sir Francis Drake?

The good news was that Drake would soon be traveling to Plymouth by sea. Reason told Shakespeare that Drake would be out of harm's way, yet there was a gnawing pit of worry in his stomach that suggested otherwise. There was something terribly wrong here. For the first time, Shakespeare had a sense of dread; he began to fear he was going to lose this battle.

And then it struck him. He knew, for certain, the identity of the man sent to kill Drake, though he did not know his present name, but this killer had not worked alone in Delft, so why would it follow that he was working alone now? Who was the other man in this conspiracy? A cold foreboding descended. He recalled the story of Balthasar Gérard, the man who fired the shots that killed William the Silent. Gérard had spent weeks, months even, inveigling himself into a position of trust inside Prince William's household. Could Herrick's accomplice be doing the same here in England? The sense of dread crept like tentacles of ice through his soul. *A man called Death is on his way . . .*

"You are lost in thought, John."

He looked up. Catherine was watching him with concern in her eyes. Like him, she held a goblet of claret. She was sitting on the settle close to his wooden chair. The children were in bed asleep, as was Jane. Without thinking, he reached out and touched her dark hair.

She had stayed awake until he returned from the Horsley Down raid and had welcomed him in. There had been something natural about the way she opened the door to him, almost as if she were more to him than a house guest under his protection. A disturbing vision of Mother Davis and her whore Isabella Clermont came to mind; the elder woman's head was half flesh, half bone, and she was urging on Isabella, naked astride him and riding him like a horse of the apocalypse. He thrust the vision aside. He would have *naught* to do with hexes and spells. Such things were not for Christians of any denomination.

Catherine did not shy away from his touch. Instead, her hand went to his hand and held it to her face, warmed by the fire. His fingers curled through hers and tangled in her hair. Without premeditation, their lips moved toward each other and they kissed. Shakespeare sank onto the settle beside her. His right hand caressed her hair and face, his left moved down the slender length of her body and she did not resist, though she had never been touched like this before.

Their kissing became urgent. Of a sudden he had her in his arms, pulling her down on the settle, devouring her. She pushed him away.

She said, "We can't stay here. The children might wake. Jane might come down."

"Will you come to my room?"

She smiled and kissed his lips quickly. "I will."

As they stood he held her in his arms again and kissed her with ferocity, at once hard and gentle. They stood like that for a minute, fused together, scarce able to consider the possibility of not touching for a few seconds.

They broke apart and went silently to their rooms. Shakespeare lit candles and stood beside the dresser in his shirt and breeches, not knowing what to do next. Would she really come to him? Or was he to be left here like a dying man offered water only to have it snatched away?

The door opened and she stood before him, her skin golden in the candlelight, her hair as lustrous as fine black satin. He went to her and, with unpracticed fingers, tried to negotiate the ties and stays that held her clothes in place. She laughed lightly and helped him until her underskirts fell away and she stood before him naked and unashamed.

His hunger for her was almost unbearable. She moved toward him, to help him disrobe, and the closeness of her bare skin brought him to the hardness of oak. She whispered in his ear, "You seem quite lost for words, sir."

He kissed her, long and deep, then ripped the clothes from his body and pulled her to the bed, entering her in a hurry born of longing. She cried out from the sharp pain of her torn maidenhead and he froze momentarily. "Don't stop," she murmured. "Please, John, don't stop."

The joints of the old wooden bed creaked with their movements. He had not used the bed for this purpose before. She kissed the palm of his hand. He kissed the bud of her breast. He moved between her legs as in his dreams. The light of candles flickered their shadows on the ceiling and walls of his plain room. The only sounds were of wood on wood and their breathing.

He arched away from her so that he could see her. Her eyes were closed, her long lashes sweeping like crescent moons beneath. His hands reached down to the inside of her thighs, that tender flesh that draws men in. He caressed and traced patterns across her soft, dark down and up to her belly, holding her pinioned with the whole palm of his hand, pushing himself in, withdrawing, pushing in.

She felt no guilt, just abandonment to her senses. If this made her a sinner, she would face up to it at another time. Not now. Now she was lost in the moment and she *would* reach that ecstasy of which she had heard from friends when she was a girl and which she had practiced on herself in the long nights alone.

He became more urgent. She pushed up immodestly to meet the quickening pulse of his movements. They were so lost in each other now, so frantic in their passion, that pleasure and pain dissolved into one entity. She would part her legs wider and wider still, until they engulfed him and took him into her the more. He would go deeper into her, deeper.

She cried out and he gasped and shuddered and collapsed upon her breasts.

They lay like this, not wishing to move, saying nothing, nowhere near sleep until, soon, their desire awoke again simultaneously and they began once more. This time it was slower, more gentle, and they instinctively found new positions on the small bed. In the candlelight he spotted blood on the white sheets and he wondered vaguely what Jane would make of it when she took the sheets for laundering. She would know, of course. How could she not? But he did not care. Not now, anyway.

■ ■ ■ ■

Starling Day and Parsimony Field talked a long while about the man upstairs. When Starling first saw him on the bed, she did not recognize him. He was lying facedown, waiting for her, for anyone, to come and flagellate him as he required. And so she beat him, harder and harder, imagining all the time that he was her husband, Edward, getting what he deserved for all the pain he had administered to her. When she had finished, when he called enough, he turned painfully on the bed, sitting on the edge. Even then she could see only the back of his head.

Slowly he turned to face her and bowed his head graciously. Starling fell back two steps, shocked by the face. It was a face carved into her memory like an epitaph on stone, the face of the man who had plunged a thin poniard dagger into the eyes of Gilbert Cogg, one by one, straight through into his brain. The sound of the fat man's scream and the sight of the spurting gore haunted her still.

"I must have gone as red as a smacked arse when I saw who it was, Parsey. But of course, he had no idea why. He never knew that anyone saw him doing for Cogg."

"So what are we going to do?"

"How about nothing? I didn't let on that I recognized him and he gave me two pounds in gold, then and there, like money meant nothing to him. I say we give him a nice sleep, feed him breakfast, and send him on his way as if nothing has happened."

"We must be able to get something out of this. Cogg's murder was big. And I liked Cogg. He looked after me."

"Yeah, but the problem is Topcliffe. He's after us. Cogg and him were close and he reckons we did for him and took the treasure. Don't stir up a hornet's nest, Parsey."

Parsimony finished her brandy and spread rich butter on some two-day-old bread. She was hungry. It was late at night, but the night would go on a lot longer yet. Cogg deserved some sort of justice. But more to the point, this knowledge could help them protect themselves against Topcliffe. They would have to act fast, though; the killer would be gone within a few hours. It was an opportunity not to be missed. "I've got an idea, Little Bird," she said, her mouth full of bread and butter. "An old friend of mine called Harry. Harry Slide. He works for Walsingham now and then. He'll know what to do, how to make the best of it. I'm going to send for him."

"I don't know, Parsey —"

"I'm going to send for him now. It's got to be tonight because our man says he's going in the morning. I know where Harry lodges. I'll send Jack Butler up there on the mare. Trust me, Little Bird. Trust me. Harry'll know what to do. He'll see us right."

Shakespeare was asleep when Catherine left his room soon before dawn and returned silently to the chamber she was sharing with Woode's children.

When they were sated from lovemaking, they had talked. Shakespeare's childhood in Warwickshire, blue-sky days and dreams, friends and relatives with all their peculiarities and eccentricities, Catherine's strange accent, so different from anything he had heard before. He teased her gently about it, mimicking her short vowels, and she jabbed him with her elbow, a little harder than she intended. He retaliated by tickling her, which made her squirm and ended in them making love yet again, though they scarcely had energy left for it.

Catherine Marvell told him she had come to London from Yorkshire, where her father James was a schoolteacher. "Thomas

Woode's eldest sister, Agnes, was married to a York squire. She died in November last. Her husband knew my family because Father taught her three sons at the grammar school. Three years ago, when Master Woode's wife died of consumption, Agnes asked me whether I might consider going to London to become governess to Andrew and Grace. She knew me to be a Roman Catholic. And so, aged eighteen, I made the long journey south by palfrey, accompanied by one of Agnes's retainers. In truth it was a welcome relief to me. I had grown to hate the smallness of my hometown. London offered a wide world and excitement."

"And how does it measure up now you are here? Exciting enough for you?"

She laughed. "It has its good points, sir." She recalled that first meeting with Thomas Woode and the children. It was a household of impenetrable gloom. Grace was being looked after by a wet nurse, who was most unsatisfactory. "She smiled ingratiatingly whenever the master was about, but I did not trust her. One day I caught the woman beating the little girl, even though she was but an infant; when I told Master Woode about it, the slattern was immediately dismissed. But the boy, Andrew, was also unhappy. The poor lad sat in a corner the day long, missing his mother. Master Woode himself was lost in melancholy and would spend days alone in his study, planning the building of his house. His plans seemed to remain always as ink drawings on parchment. I encouraged him to start the building. Finally, work began. It is a wondrous modern construction, John, of finest timbers and brickwork. By day there are views across the steelyard and the river, to the bridge."

She was silent a while, thinking of Master Woode and the torments he was now enduring. She did not tell Shakespeare more; not her feelings for Thomas Woode, which had grown fonder day by day while she had lived with him, for she had no wish to engender jealousy in his breast. Nor did she mention the decision to allow Jesuit priests to lodge in their home.

Such things had no place in this bed. Not once did they talk of Woode's plight, the threat from Topcliffe, the death of Lady Blanche, the looming Spanish invasion, or the severing of Mary Stuart's head; they took care to avoid all the subjects that divided them. Instead, they concentrated on what they shared.

It was well after dawn when Shakespeare awoke. He was alone and panicked when he found she was not there on the pillow beside him. He could still smell her earthy scent on the sheets and see the telltale sign of her lost virginity.

Jane was already downstairs making breakfast. The children were running around but there was no sign of Catherine. If Jane suspected anything of the night's events, she did not signify it by look or word. But she had news for him. "Harry Slide called in, about four of the clock. I could have murdered him. He woke me up with his hammering on the door, and he was so insistent that I had to go down and see who it was."

"What did he want?"

"To leave a message for you. Said he had found Starling and Parsimony, whatever that means. Gave an address in Southwark. He was going there and might have some important news for you later."

CHAPTER 35

Shakespeare did not wait for breakfast. He threw his bear cloak over his shoulders and rode for Southwark. The wind was howling off the river, billowing his cloak like demonic wings. He reined in his mare beneath a sign that swung vigorously in the gale tunneling through the narrow street. The sign was fresh-painted in black and white, with a picture of two women in coronets and the word *Queens.* A bawdy house, and a very pleasantly appointed one at that. He dismounted and knocked at the great door. Almost immediately, it was opened by a strong-armed man of forty or so years who towered over Shakespeare by at least six inches. He looked most discontented, and a mite intimidating, too.

Shakespeare got straight to the point. "I am here on royal business. Where is your master?"

"I have no master."

"Then this is *your* stew? Who are you?"

"I am Jack Butler, sir. This house is not mine. I have no master, but for a while, anyway, I do have two mistresses."

"Take me to them."

Parsimony and Starling had not slept. They had been chasing around the house gathering their things together in any bags or boxes they could find. The treasure had mostly gone days ago, sold off cheap to a fence to raise money to pay off the lease on this brothel and the furnishings inside. Now, Starling and Parsimony were in the parlor arguing feverishly. They had drunk too much and were befuddled. What seemed clear to them, though, was that they must say nothing and leave immediately for one of the great cities such as Bristol or Norwich with the remnants of their treasure.

The door to the parlor was thrown open. Butler stood back to let Shakespeare through and followed him in. The two women turned sharply and glared at him.

Parsimony looked with venom at Shakespeare, then at Butler. "Who's this, Jack? We don't want any visitors. Get rid of him."

Butler looked straight back at Parsimony and raised an eyebrow insolently. "He can speak for himself. You deal with him."

"You're going to be out of a job if you

don't watch yourself, Jack Butler."

"Don't worry. You can stuff your job up your pox-rotten cunnies. I don't want no more of you. Think you can just walk away on this, don't you? I heard you and your plans. Bristol! Norwich! Filthy, cautelous whores. You are drawn foxes and will hang for it."

Shakespeare stepped forward. "I am John Shakespeare and I am here on behalf of Sir Francis Walsingham. Royal business, madam. And I will *not* be got rid of."

"We got nothing to say to you," Parsimony spat.

"Ask them what happened upstairs, Mr. Shakespeare," said Butler. "That's why they're in a hurry. That's why they got plans to fetch off from Southwark."

Shakespeare had no idea what he was talking about. These two women must be Starling Day and Parsimony Field, but where was Harry? "You two are not going anywhere. One of my men, Harry Slide, came here. Where is he?"

Parsimony and Starling looked at each other with something akin to panic. They rose at the same time and tried to get to the door. They didn't stand a hope. Awash with strong drink, they stumbled. Shakespeare and Butler stopped them and restrained them easily in a couple of steps.

"I was sent to bring Mr. Slide here, sir," Butler said. "And these two purveyors of the French pox have stabbed him through the gulf, by the look of him, poor sod. Blood all over the place. I was just going to fetch the constable when you turned up. Fine gentleman he was, Mr. Slide, sir."

"Harry dead?" Shakespeare said. "Harry Slide?"

"We didn't kill him!" Parsimony shouted. "He was a friend of mine. That's why I called him here. My lovely, fine-dressed Harry. I can't bear to think of him dead. The flagellant done for him, not us."

"Flagellant? What flagellant? Where's Harry?"

"The one that murdered Gilbert Cogg. Now he's knifed Harry in the neck and run."

"Where is Harry? Take me to him."

"He's up in one of the whores' chambers. I'll show you." Butler pushed Parsimony and Starling toward the staircase, with Shakespeare following.

The scene in the bedroom was horrible to behold. Shakespeare immediately went down on one knee beside Harry's body. It was obvious he was dead, an hour or two maybe; his body was cold.

A gash, no wider than an inch, had opened up the right side of Harry's throat. Blood had poured out in a flood, spraying across a wide area of the floor at the foot of the bed. Shakespeare touched Harry's cheek and pulled back from the coolness of his skin. His eyes were wide open in horror; his beautiful clothes splattered red.

How had poor Harry come to this? Shakespeare put his hands together to pray for Harry's soul, but it did nothing to ease the pain and anger. He turned furiously to the women. "Tell me again, who did this to him?"

Parsimony looked at Starling. This man seemed to be a friend of Harry Slide, so perhaps he was all right. "We had better tell him everything, Starling."

Starling nodded and Parsimony turned back to Shakespeare. "But you got to protect us from Topcliffe. He won't listen to reason. We'll be gibbeted at Tyburn tree before he gives us a hearing."

"I promise nothing, but if you do *not* tell me the truth it will be the worse for you. In the meantime, you," he nodded to Butler, "consider yourself my deputy. Go now and fetch the constable, then arrange for Mr. Slide's body to be consigned to the coroner." Shakespeare turned back to the women. "Who else is in this house?"

"Some whores, that's all," replied Butler. "They'll all be swiving or sleeping."

"They're good girls," Starling put in. "They don't know anything about any of this."

"Right then. *You* tell me everything."

They went downstairs, out of sight of the body. Jack Butler went off to fetch in the constable, while Starling told Shakespeare her story.

"The killer. Tell me about the killer." Shakespeare was insistent.

She described Herrick in great detail. She told Shakespeare that he took a bag with an implement from Cogg after bundling his body into the barrel. She told, too, of the nature of his wound — as well as the new weals received from her beating. "His back was red with scars. I reckon he must have been one of them religious madpikes. His hair was short and he didn't have a beard. I think he *couldn't* grow a beard. No sign of stubble. And he was scornful," she went on. "He paid good money, but he looked at me like I was dog turd. He was tall and well muscled, too. Didn't laugh or smile. Didn't say nothing good, but then again, he didn't say nothing bad neither."

"Did he say anything religious? Did he have any religious symbols? Crosses, beads, that kind of thing?"

"If he did, I didn't see them."

"And what did he talk about?"

Starling was getting bored. She was also sobering up. "This and that. He asked me questions."

"Like what?"

"Like where I came from. I told him Strelley. A pit village full of men like my husband. Mr. Flagellant asked me if I knew Devonshire and Plymouth. Now, why would I know fucking Plymouth?"

"Did you get the idea he was going there?"

"Well, what do you think? You're supposed to be the cunning man around here. I tell you this, though: he kept asking about post horses and suchlike."

"And what did you tell him?"

"Nothing. What could I tell him? I don't know nothing about post horses. Why should I? I've never been on a nag in my life. Shank's mare does for me. I *walked* to London."

So Herrick was making for Plymouth. And sooner rather than later. But would he get there by horse or try Drake's own route: by horse to Dover and take ship from there? The Dover route might be quicker, but that would depend on the winds. If the weather was inclement, he could be holed up in Dover for days. Shakespeare reckoned he would have gone the more certain overland route. Whichever way he went, the highways were likely to be bogs of mud at this time of year, but Shakespeare decided he would have to follow him, riding fast across country. He had to leave immediately; there was not even time to go home. Herrick probably had two or three hours start on him, but with good fortune, he could be caught.

Jack Butler arrived back with the constable, a lumbering oaf with the dead eyes of a cod.

"I want this place closed down with immediate effect," Shakespeare told the constable. "These two women will be held in custody while I decide what to do with them. Keep them in the Clink, but tell no one they are there. And I mean no one. I promise that you will answer to Mr. Secretary Walsingham himself and suffer for it if a single word of this gets out. And when you remove Mr. Slide's body to the coroner, you will treat it with honor. Do you understand? You, Mr. Butler, find me a quill, ink, and some pieces of paper, for I must write urgent messages which you will deliver, in person. The one to Mr. Secretary at his home in Seething Lane, the other to my own home in the same street. There is to be no delay."

CHAPTER 36

Drake was in an ebullient mood as his small party took the barge from Greenwich Palace to Gravesend early in the morning. The Queen had wished him God speed during a short private meeting in the presence chamber. Now, with a salty cry as if he were weighing anchor and setting sail for the Indies, he waved his hat and urged the rowers forward like a knight spurring his destrier at the tilt.

At Gravesend they took horse and settled into a goodly trot on the well-trodden road that would take them south and east through Kent toward the Channel port of Dover. Diego took the lead on his bay, followed by a band comprising Drake; his wife, Elizabeth — sidesaddle on a beautiful gray palfrey — her maidservant May Willow; Captain Harper Stanley — his mustaches bristling — two servants of Drake; and the deputy lieutenant of Devon, Sir William

Courtenay, returning home to Powderham Castle. The group was accompanied by two of Drake's most trusted mariners, men known to be handy with wheel-lock and sword. The rear guard was taken by Boltfoot Cooper, his caliver primed and his hand ever close to the hilt of his cutlass.

Drake settled in the middle of the group, between his wife on the right and Courtenay, whom he knew to be a Roman Catholic, on his left. "Well, sir," Drake said, "have you said confession today for all your manifold sins?"

Courtenay laughed wearily. He was used to jibes at the expense of his religion. "I am afraid, Sir Francis, they are too many for the priest to reckon with at one sitting. I have a seven-week rotation: lust one week, gluttony the next, then greed, sloth, wrath, envy, and pride, in that order."

"And which is it this week? Lust?"

"Of course, Sir Francis. I could not possibly travel without a goodly helping of lust to boost my spirits." Courtenay was a dark-haired man in his mid-thirties, of exceptional good looks, fit and strong. While he made mockery of his sins, he had a reputation as one of the court's most ardent ladies' men. He was said to have brought two serving girls with child before he was fourteen years old and had scattered several other children around Devon since then.

"Hah! What do you make of it, Lady Elizabeth? Will Sir William go to heaven? Or hell?"

Elizabeth looked across at Courtenay and smiled at him. She looked sweet and demure, her face glowing beneath a fashionable French hood of black velvet that controlled her hair in the mighty wind that assailed them. "Possibly hell, and most certainly Devon. I would not hazard gold on heaven, though."

"By God's faith, Sir William, I think I shall have to look out for my wife in your company! I fear she does hold a little piece of her heart in store for you."

"Indeed, Sir Francis. But how will you keep me from her when you are at sea? And tell me this, as a land-shanks, how do you sailor men care for your requirements in the middle of the ocean, sans ladies, sans whores, sans pleasure itself?"

Drake scowled. He glanced at his wife irritably, then at Courtenay. "There are other pleasures, sir. Putting Catholics to the sword foremost among them. And oft they deserve it for their base cruelty. Your list of sins, Sir William — where does cruelty fit into that? Or does your church not require you to

469

confess it? Perhaps cruelty is considered a virtue by the apostolic Antichrist. For certain, you do belong to the cruelest religion in the world."

The banter, half in jest, half meant with severe intent, continued along the miles down into Kent. At times Drake fell back to talk with Captain Stanley about provisioning and naval strategies; at those times he watched in silence as his wife moved closer to Courtenay and engaged him in conversation.

Boltfoot's eyes were constantly moving, watching Drake one second, scouring the countryside for dangers the next. This road was known for its banditry, though he could not imagine anyone would dare attack a group this well armed. Hunger, however, could make men do desperate things. And there was much poverty in England.

They had taken an early lunch at Gravesend and did not stop again until they came to a halt soon before six of the clock at a post inn close to Rochester. Boltfoot stayed with Sir Francis and Elizabeth while the servants organized the horses and Harper Stanley and Diego ordered some supper and wine for them all in a private room.

They ate well and Drake regaled the company with tales of his adventures when he lived within two or three miles of this inn as a child. The family had come here from Devon, he said, because his father, a Protestant preacher, had been persecuted during the burnings of Queen Mary's reign. The Drakes had ended up living poverty-stricken in a rotting hulk stranded on a Medway mudbank. "Back then, I foraged for oysters and blackberries to stay alive. And look at me now, as rich as a Mussel-man potentate, with the world and all its seas at my feet! And all thanks to gold supplied by that same King Philip who shared the bed of murdering Mary."

Boltfoot Cooper snorted loudly. He didn't believe a word of the story of religious persecution of Drake's father any more than had anyone else around their hometown of Tavistock. The word there was that Drake's father, Edmund, had left in a hurry having been convicted of horse theft and assault and robbery on the highway.

"Something wrong with your nose, Mr. Cooper? Can someone lend him a kerchief?" Drake clapped his hands, then smacked them down with a thud on the table. "And now, let us drink our fill that God give health and long life to our sovereign majesty Elizabeth. Long live the Queen!"

They ate and drank too much, as travelers

will. As the serving wenches cleared away the last of the dishes and brought more flagons of wine, Drake picked up a book that was on the table at his side. "Charge your cups, for I shall now read to you, as I have read to my officers and gentlemen aboard ship on many a long night in the great Pacific Ocean, which, I must tell you, is the worst-named sea that ever mariner sailed; there was nothing pacific or tranquil about her or her depths when we did enter her. We were wracked by tempests for weeks without end. But all waters are stormy and I would have it no other way. Soon we shall be at sea again. Soon I shall have the salt spray in my face and, beneath my feet, six hundred tons of English oak and blazing cannon."

He tapped the book and continued. "With that thought, it seems apt that I should read 'The Shipman's Tale' of Geoffrey Chaucer, for we do go the pilgrim's way through Canterbury, then down to the sea. And in the instance that any of you do not understand, I shall first explain it to you, for the well-loved Mr. Chaucer did not write English as now we know it. It is right that I do commend this tale to my good lady wife, Elizabeth, for her pleasure and nothing more. For I know her to be nothing in the way of

472

the faithless goodwife of Mr. Chaucer's tale. And I trust that none here present shall think her otherwise than a chaste companion to me."

Drake raised his golden-pointed chin to his wife.

She smiled back at him guilelessly. "Why, my lord, I cannot think you even need to defend me so. For certain, none here could think me other than a loyal and loving bride."

"Quite so, by God's faith! But perhaps Sir William Courtenay might look out for himself in this sorry tale. It is the tale of an adulterous wife and of a cunning monk who pretends friendship of her husband — and then beds his lady. Do you see anyone you know in there, Sir William?"

Boltfoot Cooper was not listening. His eyes were fastened on the face of Sir William Courtenay, which was a mask of rage.

"But enough!" Drake continued. "It is naught but a story. I cannot believe any man would betray another like that, for they would surely be gelded and run through the heart for such foul dealing. That is nothing less than any husband would do, would you not agree, Sir William? You are a married man, I believe?"

Courtenay hesitated. His eyes strayed to

Elizabeth's, then back to Drake. "You must know it, Sir Francis." He had not an ounce of humor in his voice.

"You would not allow any man to make a monkey of you, would you, sir?"

Suddenly Courtenay rose from the table, his sword already half-drawn. "Of what do you accuse me?" He lunged forward, scattering goblets and flagons and knocking the large table to one side. "You insult my religion, sir, and now you insult me."

The room was immediately in an uproar. The armed mariners leapt forward but were slow off the mark. Both Boltfoot, from one side, and Diego, from the other, were on Courtenay in an instant. Boltfoot had his cutlass at Courtenay's neck. Diego had the point of his dagger beneath the young courtier's rib cage, ready to thrust upward into the heart. Courtenay looked wildly around those present in the room.

"Will no one take my part? I have suffered calumny here." He looked again at Elizabeth Drake. "Madam, will you not call your husband to order, for I think he does accuse us of some liaison, of which I know nothing."

Elizabeth laughed lightly. "Oh, Sir William, it is just my master's way. Pay him no heed. I think he likes to make merry with men's sensibilities. It helps to pass the long days and nights at sea when the breeze has dropped and the sails will not billow."

Diego and Boltfoot took Courtenay by the arms and pushed him back down into his chair.

"More drink for Sir William Courtenay!" Drake roared. He had not retreated an inch in the face of the onslaught, and his broad chest was puffed up like a fighting cock's. "God's faith, make the man mellow before he slaughters us all." And then he reached into his doublet pocket and took out a piece of blue velvet, all wrapped like a present. "Here, madam," he said, offering it to his wife with a flourish. "A necklace of gold, pearl, and ruby, each one harvested from the great continents and oceans of the world. Please do me the honor of accepting this humble offering as a mark of my respect for your fidelity and loving goodness."

Elizabeth put her hand to her mouth in mock surprise, as if she had not already received a hundred such rich trinkets from her besotted husband.

"Well, that's one way to keep her from going off with any carnal monks," Diego muttered into Boltfoot's ear.

Boltfoot smiled grimly. There was something that interested him rather more: for

475

he had noted just which men among the assembled company had leapt to the defense of Drake, and which had not.

Shakespeare's ride west was dogged by ill chance from the outset. Riding along a highway rutted with holes that a man could fall into and mud deep enough to drown in, his gray mare went lame ten miles into the county of Surrey. He left the animal with a peasant farmhand, with the promise of sixpence if he took good care of it, then walked on toward the nearest village to find another mount. He had come in the clothes he wore that morning: bearskin cloak, doublet, breeches, hose, and a fur hat. He had no baggage or panniers to carry, just a purse with more than enough coinage for the journey. Trudging alone, he knew he was vulnerable to attack by highway thieves. Even spattered with mud, his clothes were clearly of a fine cut. With so much hunger in the land, there were bands of vagabonds and robbers roaming everywhere.

The walk to the village took two hours. His boots became clogged and the dampness soaked through to his skin. Wind howled around him and every now and then he was forced to clamber over fallen trees that had come down in places across the road. By the time he arrived at a ford across a river, just to the east of the village, he was hungry, weary, short-tempered, and keenly aware that he was losing time in the pursuit of his elusive quarry.

The ferryman was in his riverside hut eating lunch and did not bother to look up as Shakespeare approached. Without any preliminaries, Shakespeare snapped, "God's blood, ferryman, I am on Queen's business and must cross this river straightway and find a horse."

The ferryman looked up languidly from his meal, then raised a tankard of ale to his mouth and drank slowly, sieving the ale through a hedge of whiskers.

"Well, sir, get a move on!"

Putting down his ale, the ferryman looked around as if Shakespeare were not there. "Did someone say something? Or did my old dog just fart?"

"This is Queen's business!"

The ferryman at last met his eyes. "And I am on the business of my luncheon, which I consider of much greater import than your business or that of the Queen or anyone else you may wish to mention. You can either wait until I have finished or you can swim."

Fuming, Shakespeare settled down to wait. The ferryman, a curly-haired man of forty with as many chins as he had years, balanced his platter on his fair belly, lingering long over his mutton stew. Finally he belched, put his arms behind his head, lay back on a straw palliasse, and closed his eyes to sleep. Shakespeare drew his sword and thrust it down until it touched his throat. "You will take me *now,* ferryman, or I will see you lose your license. Or worse."

The ferryman betrayed no concern. "I do not like your manner, sir, and so I have made a decision. I will not take you today. The wind is up too much and I fear it would not be safe, so tomorrow it is. If you're lucky. And I must tell you that my brother has the livery stable, and I believe he may not be able to supply you with a horse once you do cross to the village. But there is another ford twelve miles upriver if you prefer to walk there."

Shakespeare realized his threats were doing no good at all. Ignoring the sword, the ferryman turned over on to his side as if to go to sleep. Gritting his teeth and sighing, Shakespeare pulled the sword back from his throat and re-sheathed it. This called for a change of tack. He looked at the man for a minute. It was hard to admit it, but he had not approached the situation well; his anger at losing the horse to lameness had clouded his judgment. He took a deep breath. "Mr. Ferryman," he said painfully, "if perchance I have offended you, it was not my intent and I must apologize. Let me throw myself on your mercy, because the life of one of England's greatest heroes is at stake. If I do not get across this river and take horse in short order, I will not be able to save him."

The ferryman turned back and raised himself from the straw on his elbows. He cupped an ear with his hand. "Did I hear you say *sorry* just then?"

"Yes, if you so wish it, you may believe that I said sorry."

"Was that *exceeding* sorry?"

"It was indeed."

"I suppose that *could* change things. Tell me more: who is this hero you would save?"

"Sir Francis Drake himself. His life is in grave danger and I must ride to Plymouth to warn him. I am Mr. Secretary Walsingham's man."

"Drake?"

"Yes, Drake."

"Sir Francis Drake, the greatest Englishman that ever drew breath?"

"The very same, ferryman. Even now, he is heading for Plymouth by sea, unaware that a Spanish murderer is sent to kill him."

"Well, why didn't you say so? Come on,

let's get you across. And my brother will give you his finest horse."

"Thank you, ferryman, you will be well rewarded with gold."

"No, sir, I will not take your money. You can pay me by killing the Spaniard with your fine sword. Make it slow and painful, sir, slow and painful. Relieve him of his hazelnuts first, if at all possible. And I shall play my part by serving you some of my wife's mutton stew as we cross, sir. It is goodly fare."

The ferry was little more than a sturdy raft of aged oak, pulled across the river by means of thick hemp cables attached to deeply embedded posts on both sides. It had room for a heavy dray, half a dozen farm horses, and some cattle. Now there was just Shakespeare and the ferryman, who gave him a portion of his mutton stew. As they made the brief crossing, Shakespeare tucked into the food with relish. He had had nothing to eat all day. The food was good. When he finished, he thanked the ferryman and asked whether any single horsemen had crossed the river in the past few hours.

"Indeed, sir. A rider crossed here five hours since. He rode tall in the saddle and I noted he was unbearded. He did not utter above three words to me, though, so I learned nothing of him. I believe he had a change of horse at my brother Ben's livery, so perchance he said something to him. Ask Ben, sir."

"I will. I will. I think, Mr. Ferryman, that you have met the man who means to kill Sir Francis Drake. I have not a moment to lose."

CHAPTER 37

By the time Drake and his band reached Dover, the wind was just beginning to ease. The quay was solid with ships come in for shelter from the Channel storms, their masts and rigging a tangle of sticks that would make a fine autumn bonfire for any Spaniard with a tinderbox.

The group came to a halt on the cobbled quayside. Waves crashed into the shingle beach below them. In the distance, the Channel across to France was white-flecked. No packet boats could make the crossing in such a turbulent sea. If Boltfoot was tired from the long ride, he did not show it. His eyes were ever vigilant; a seasoned mariner never allowed fatigue to interfere with his watch.

Captain Harper Stanley slapped the steaming flank of his mount and leaned over toward Drake. "Shall I find an inn, Vice Admiral?" he asked, fishing for a feather bed for the night.

Drake gazed at him as if he were a madman or worse. "No, Stanley, by God! Are you gone soft that you seek a bed in a tavern when there are ship's cabins and hammocks to be inhabited? Get yourself aboard ship, sir, and clear the captain's cabin for the Lady Elizabeth. You will arrange garlands and see to it that she is served dainties on fine dishes. There will be music as we dine tonight. Viols will suit us well." He glanced toward Sir William Courtenay, who had ridden twenty yards behind him in a sulk and had not looked on Drake except with hatred all day. "Are you a music man, Sir William? Or is that, too, a venal sin in your religion? Come, sir, sup with us this evening and you may confess your wickedness to the Cardinal Bishop afterwards."

"I would rather starve than sup with you, Drake. I will be staying at an inn tonight as Captain Stanley suggests."

Drake bristled. "Aboard my ship, Courtenay, I am king, emperor, and answerable only to God. If you wish to travel with me and if you are a gentleman, then you will sup with me. Otherwise, you may stay here in Dover and await your chances with a tin carrier or some such returning westward to the Stannaries. Do you understand me?"

Courtenay was trapped. "You know I cannot wait. If those are your terms, then I will have to accept them. But I will repay you in kind one day, Drake. One day, what is yours will be mine."

Drake laughed easily. "If I were buttermilk-hued and listened to Papist threats, Sir William, I would never have stirred from my bed."

Suddenly Courtenay pulled the head of his horse sharp sideways and barged into Drake's mount. "I am a patriot, sir, loyal to the Crown. My religion does not preclude my love of England and the Queen!" he roared, his face close to Drake's.

Boltfoot and Diego moved instantly alongside, but Drake was laughing. "So whose side will you be on when the invasion begins, Sir William? Whose side will you be on when the Pope orders you to rise up against our Queen? Has he not excommunicated her and declared it no sin — indeed, God's work — to murder her? Whose command will you obey: your Pope's or your sovereign's?"

"Damn you, Drake. Damn you to hell! Now I know why so many mutiny against you or refuse berths upon your ships."

Richard Topcliffe rinsed his hands in a horse

trough at the side of the road. Newall, the Chief Pursuivant, watched him respectfully. The magistrate Richard Young lolled nonchalantly nearby, his elbow on the wooden post of a picket built to keep the crowds at bay. The large, noisy throng of people was beginning to disperse to go about their daily tasks, for the dance of death they had come to watch had now finished. The body of the condemned man hung limp from the St. Giles gibbet, swaying and twisting gently in the wind.

"A good morning's work," Topcliffe remarked, drying his hands on the butcher's apron as he untied it from about his waist. He never covered his face at executions but he liked to wear an apron to protect his good clothes from the vomit, blood, and excrement of the condemned. The hangman had had very little to do, for Topcliffe had orchestrated the proceedings himself, as a player-manager directs his drama. He had harangued the condemned man, demanding he recant his Papist heresy and treachery. When the man who was about to die asked for a priest, Topcliffe called to the crowd, "Is there a priest out there? Come forward so that I may hang you, too!" And then he laughed and kicked away the ladder from under the condemned man's feet and left him swinging in the air, kicking his legs like a puppet as the rope slowly choked the life out of him. The crowd roared with laughter and Topcliffe took a bow.

"One Popish priest less to concern us," Topcliffe said now to Young. "Ugly brute, wasn't he? His pestilent soul burst through into his poxed face. The world is well rid of him." He grunted with satisfaction. "There is yet more work, Dick. The monstrous Papists never cease their foul, wormish burrowing into the body of England, so we can never afford to sleep. There is one we must take today, late of Dowgate, now lodged in John Shakespeare's den of corruption in Seething Lane. A young she-devil by the name of Catherine Marvell. She has the face of an angel, but do not be deceived. The harlot is diseased with wickedness and the putrefaction of sin. For certain she is occupied by demons. An incubus has taken up residence within her and nightly fills her with the cold slurry of his loins. We must take her, Dick, for fair England's sake."

"Seething Lane, Richard? Shakespeare's home? Bit close to Mr. Secretary's house for comfort that, do you not think?"

Topcliffe called to the hangman, who was about to cut the dead man down. "Leave him up there a week, Mr. Picket. Pin a sign to his front." He turned back to Young. "What should it say, do you think, Dick? Something to warn them, eh?"

"For treason and aiding foreign enemies?" suggested Young.

"That's it. For treason and aiding foreign enemies. Have you got that, Mr. Picket?"

"Yes, Mr. Topcliffe. I'll see to it straightway."

"Now back to this she-devil. I take your point about Seething Lane, Dick. We can't go there in force with a squadron of pursuivants. Mr. Secretary would not like to be embarrassed so close to home. We need to take her *quietly*."

"How will you do that? If this woman is under Shakespeare's protection, he will raise such an uproar that you will never have her."

Topcliffe's mouth turned down in distaste. He put a hand into his breeches and adjusted himself. "Shakespeare's gone off after a Fleming to try to save Drake. She's there all alone with a traitor's spawn. We'll bring her to my Westminster hostelry and the children can do their schooling in Bridewell. I shall show her laid out on my rack to Mr. Woode; that will loosen his tongue. And you're the man to bring her in, Dick Young. As London magistrate you have the full force of Her Majesty's law behind you.

You've got the authority, Dick. You're the man to do it."

As they spoke, a well-dressed man watched them from the crowd. Without drawing attention to himself, he had tried to get close enough to hear what Topcliffe and Young were saying. He had come to say goodbye to the condemned priest, Piggott, not because he liked him or loved him, but because he professed the same faith and had done nothing to warrant hanging. From the cheering crowd, Cotton had spoken the Last Rites, mouthing them so Piggott could see, and had made the Sign of the Cross beneath his cloak. And then the ladder had been kicked away.

Despite drawing near to the picket fence that held back the crowd, Cotton still could not hear what Topcliffe and Young were saying. He cursed his luck and melted away into the throng. Yet he was strengthened in his faith by the day's events rather than weakened by them. The execution of a fellow priest made his desire for martydom burn ever brighter in his heart. He knew with utter certainty that one day he would be the man on the scaffold.

Shakespeare could go no further this day. The sun was long vanished over the horizon and a dense winter fog had settled over the bleak landscape of plowed fields and thick woodland. The road was so poor, he was no longer even sure that he was on the highway that was supposed to lead west to Devonshire.

His spirits rose when he chanced upon an inn, though it did not seem to amount to much. Barely more than a farmer's house with a sign of a white dog swinging outside, it was a low building of thatch and daub. There was, however, a cheery light from within: the light of a warm fire and tallow. A bank of sharpened scythes and plow implements leaning against an outhouse door showed as well as anything that the usual customers here were men that worked the fields.

Shakespeare was cold through to the marrow of his bones. Cold, hungry, and thirsty. His body cried out for a pint of good English ale. He dismounted from the strong black mare the ferryman's brother had provided him and tethered her to an iron ring set into the wall.

Seven or eight drinkers stopped talking as he entered the low-ceilinged taproom. He nodded to them in greeting and strode to the long bar under their watchful gaze. Shakespeare did not care that the locals stiffened at his entry; it was only to be expected. He may have been filthy, but it was still plain that his clothes were such stuff as these farmhands would never have seen in all their lives. For this was not a wayside inn, merely a village drinking house.

The heat of the fire was welcoming. It crackled and gave off a delicious aroma of wood smoke. The landlady was welcoming, too. Shakespeare said he would have some beef and bread, and asked for some small beer. He did not want anything stronger because he would need to be up early. The landlady drew him a pint of ale from the cask that stood at his side. Shakespeare took the beaker and downed it in a matter of seconds, then let out a gasp of satisfaction.

"Have you traveled far, sir?"

"From London." Shakespeare held out his beaker for it to be filled again. "Have you a room for the night and some stabling and feed for my mount tethered outside?"

"I will get my son to see to the horse immediately, sir. We do not have a room as such, sir, no, but I will prepare a bed for you in the parlor."

"Thank you. Before you see to that, let me ask you: Has another traveler passed this way today? A tall, beardless man?"

The landlady swept sawdust from the

great oak bar with her countrywoman's stubby, pink-palmed hands. "Yes — I have most certainly seen such a one. He supped here but then rode off maybe three hours since. I warned him there would be a thick mist tonight, but he said that God would look after him, for he was about God's work. Why, do you know him, sir?"

"Indeed, mistress, I do, and I would speak with him."

"Well, I am afraid you will never catch up with him tonight. Now if you will excuse me, sir, I will fetch your food."

The ride had been hard and Shakespeare was saddlesore and aching in the lower back. Yet he began to wonder whether he should go on: if Herrick could risk the fog and dark, why couldn't he, too? No, it must be better to rest up and refresh himself. Herrick could well get lost in this mist. With luck, perchance, the killer might drown in a bog or be killed by roving bands and never be heard of again. Whatever happened tonight, this journey could not be done in under two days in such poor conditions, so there would still be time to catch his quarry. Herrick would have to sleep sooner or later. Better for Shakespeare that *he* sleep now and get an early start.

He ate heartily. The beef was sliced thin

and served with a well-seasoned gravy, roasted parsnips, peas, and a thick wedge of black bread. When he had finished, he asked for his room. As he stepped out from the taproom with the landlady, he was aware of several pairs of eyes focused on the back of his head, but he cared not a jot. He was so weary he could have fallen to the ground and slept in the sawdust. The room was, as the landlady had said, nothing more than the parlor, but a straw mattress and coarse blankets had been laid out for him on the floor. He asked to be woken before first light, and climbed, fully dressed, beneath the blankets. Within a minute or two he was asleep. A sleep so profound that when the latch to his door was lifted half an hour later, he heard not a thing and slept on contented, dreaming of the one he had left at home.

CHAPTER 38

Drake's ship sailed with the tide at four in the morning. The wind would carry them quickly westward along the widening strait.

When dawn arrived, Boltfoot peered through the small portage outside Drake's cabin in the stern of the vessel. He had been awake all night, with only the light of a candle and years of wakeful watching to support him. The Sussex shoreline, misty and blue-gray, raced past on the starboard side. A fresh and bracing breeze whitened the tops of the coal-gray Channel waves. The great ship lay over sharply and, pushed along by the blustering weight of full sail, fair flew along. They would be at Plymouth, he reckoned, in a day or a little more.

He looked down at Diego, asleep on the wood decking close by. They had braved many adventures together and here they were again, aboard ship, where Boltfoot had vowed never to set foot again. He laughed to himself. The truth was, he was enjoying it. One could never totally escape the sea, and certainly one could never be free of Sir Francis Drake. Once under his spell, a sailor was the Vice Admiral's man forever. And Diego was a good man to share time with. He had a ready laugh at all the vicissitudes the world could throw at him, and there had been many. He had lost so much: his home somewhere in Africa, his family and friends, his freedom. Yet he had adjusted to this extraordinary new life in the manner of one born to it, for he told these stories of his past without a hint of rancor.

Captain Stanley appeared, fully dressed and ready for the day. "Mr. Cooper, get yourself along to the galley for some breakfast. I will sit out the rest of your watch here."

"That won't be necessary, Captain Stanley. I will eat when Diego awakes."

"Come, come, Mr. Cooper. You have been diligent enough. We are safely at sea now. What possible threat could there be to the Vice Admiral out here?"

"My orders are clear, sir. I am to guard Sir Francis at all times."

"As you wish, Mr. Cooper, but Sir Francis will not thank you for your nursery-maid care. He will do nothing but damn you for it and call you a poltroon."

"He has called me worse many times, Captain. It is like water off the shrouds."

Stanley nodded briskly. "Good day then, Mr. Cooper." He turned on his heel and was gone along a gangway and up the companion ladder to the quarterdeck.

Diego stirred. "Did I hear someone say 'breakfast,' Boltfoot?"

"You wait your turn. I'm as hungry as a parson's dog."

The door to Drake's cabin opened an inch or two. Elizabeth poked her face out. Clearly, she was still in her nightgown. She smiled winningly. "Boltfoot, Diego, would one of you go and bring me some breakfast? The sea air has brought on something of an appetite, I am afraid. And for Sir Francis, too, for I am sure he will wake soon."

"Of course, my lady."

Boltfoot looked at Diego. Diego looked at Boltfoot. "All right," Diego said at last. "You go. But bring me some bread, thick spread with butter and strawberry jam."

Inside the cabin, Elizabeth returned to her narrow cot. Her husband was in a hammock stretched between the larboard and stern bulwarks. The hammock swung with the graceful rise and pitch of the ship as she hit wave after wave on her easy, smoking flow westward. Drake snored like a man at peace with himself. Elizabeth's bed was warm and she curled into it, looking up at Francis. He was twice her age. He had circled the world yet there was so much he *didn't* know. In particular, he seemed to know nothing about women and he had no children, either with her or by his late first wife, Mary. Elizabeth was beginning to doubt whether he would ever get her with child. She listened to the aching creak of the English timbers. Sometimes she wondered whether it might not be the prospect of women at home that kept her husband so long at sea.

Richard Young, magistrate of London, knocked softly at the door of John Shakespeare's timber-frame dwelling in Seething Lane. He feared that a heavy pummeling at the door would drive those inside into hiding, which was just what he did not want. He could not afford to tear this place apart as they had done to Lady Tanahill's property. Topcliffe had overstepped the mark on that occasion and angered the Queen. It could not be repeated so soon, and certainly not at the home of one of Walsingham's chief officers.

It was early evening, just after dusk. The street was quiet and dark. That was the way he had planned it. No fuss. Simply pick up the woman and Thomas Woode's children and cart them off. Mr. Secretary, in his great mansion a mere thirty yards down the lane, would be none the wiser and nor would anyone else. Until Mr. Topcliffe was ready to bring the matter of the woman's treason to court.

Jane answered the door. She was in her nightgown, ready for bed. It had been a long day of worry since being woken by Harry Slide early in the morning, followed by the arrival of the message from Master Shakespeare to Catherine saying he was riding west and did not know when he would be back. Jane looked at Young and his companion in dismay. Everyone in London knew Richard Young. It was said Topcliffe had learned every manner of wickedness he could from the magistrate and then added his own. These men were devilish devices cast from the same dark foundry.

Without awaiting invitation, Young and his assistant pushed past her and strode into the hall of the house. They looked about them. "Who are you?" Young demanded. "Are you Catherine Marvell?"

Jane shook her head with vigor. She knew she was trembling but could not control it. "I am Jane. Jane Cawston, sir. I am Master

Shakespeare's maidservant."

"I am Justice Young and I have an arrest warrant. Bring me Catherine Marvell. Produce her at once, Mistress Cawston."

Jane could scarcely think; all she could find to say was, "I cannot, sir."

"Cannot! What do you mean you cannot?" Young was raising his voice now. Jane prayed that Catherine would hear it from her room and find some sort of hiding place.

"She is not here, sir. She was here but she has gone home to York, whence she came and where her family still resides."

"You lie, mistress."

"No, sir. Look about you at your will."

Young glanced at the pursuivant accompanying him. He was short, with a distended belly. The man's face was a mask of bland unpleasantness. Young looked back at Jane. "What of the two children?"

"Both are asleep, sir. They have been entrusted to my care."

"Well, fetch them. They must come into custody with us. They are a danger to the commonwealth and must be kept under close restraint."

Jane's mouth fell open in horror. Without thinking, she moved directly in front of Young. What fear she had was gone like smoke. She was still trembling, but with rage now, not fear. "They are but four and six years old. They are a danger to no one and you will not take them."

Young tried to brush her out of the way. "Stand aside, woman. I *will* take them. The Lord Treasurer himself, Lord Burghley, does approve of taking Papist spawn away for proper education, to save them the contamination of wicked priests."

Jane was healthy and strong from hard work and she pushed herself back in front of Young. She raised her own voice now. She had always been able to make herself heard. Now, she knew, she had to make as much disturbance as she could: anything to delay Young and alert Catherine. "You will have to kill me first. How will that look when Mr. Secretary and the Queen hear of it? Or will you fabricate treason against me, too? Maybe you will even hang, draw, and quarter a girl of four years for high treason. Show me your warrant!"

Agitated, the magistrate drew his sword. He was a man in his late forties, much lined by weather and cruelty, but without the raw physical strength that his confederate Topcliffe possessed. He was a spindly man with a stoop. It was easy for him to inflict torment on men — or women — when they were presented to him in chains. This was another matter. He was painfully aware of the need for subtlety in this arrest, and he lacked Topcliffe's confidence. This serving wench was making things difficult, if not impossible. He looked again at the pursuivant for some kind of support, but there was nothing there. The man would do what he was told, but would not engender any ideas or course of action and might very well balk at the thought of carrying off screaming children.

"Mistress Cawston, I will give you one last warning. You will produce the children now or I will return in force and remove not only the children but you as well. Do you understand? I have the power not only of arrest, but arraignment, and you will be consigned to hard labor in Bridewell. I will see to it."

"Well, sir, take me . . . if you can. But you will *not* take those children while I draw breath."

Justice Young rose to his full beanpole height. Jane could see that he was shaking with anger, just as she was. But she knew now that he could not kill her. Not here, not this day. This was political and he was afraid of the consequences of the arrest not proceeding smoothly. He was afraid, perhaps, of Master Shakespeare or Mr. Secretary.

"Damn you to hell!" he exclaimed, quivering with rage. "I shall see that you suffer for this."

"And I shall ensure that Mr. Secretary, our neighbor, knows what you are about, sir." Even as she said it, she knew it was an idle threat; she could not possibly call on the Queen's Principal Secretary and lay this tale before him; but Justice Young did not know that.

Young turned and marched to the door, swinging his sword, slashing a tapestry, knocking a good flower vase crashing to the ground. At the doorstep he swiveled his head and looked back at Jane with eyes full of menace. Without a word, he buried his sword in its sheath and went off into the night, his assistant trailing in his wake.

Shakespeare woke abruptly, suffused by a feeling of dread. He felt sure he was not alone. The night was dark and the window was draped. He might as well have been blind. Jumping up from the mattress, he tried to gauge his bearings. Recalling vaguely where the door was, he stumbled toward it and pushed it open. Light trickled into the room from a glimmering wall sconce in the hallway beyond.

He looked back into the parlor. Nothing.

Nobody. Just the mattress on which he had been sleeping and some items of furniture, all pushed to one side to make way for him. He shivered and wrapped his arms around his body. Leaving the door open, he went back to the mattress and climbed back under the blankets. He unsheathed the poniard at his belt and clutched it by the hilt in his right hand. It gave him a sense of security. On the floor beside the mattress lay his sword belt. Something did not seem right, or was he just imagining it?

Lying in the flickering gloom, he could not get back to sleep though his body cried out for it. His thoughts whirled around visions of Catherine Marvell and Isabella Clermont. Their faces melded into one and the scent of lust hung over him like an overripe apple in autumn, still moldering on the tree long after the leaves have fallen. He could not wait to see Catherine again, take her again into the sheets of his bed, yet nor could he dismiss the events surrounding the Davis witch and her French whore. Why take an eyebrow? What sort of spell did a witch cast with the short, wiry hairs of a man's brow?

He must have slept again, for he eventually woke with the landlady's hand on his shoulder.

"Master Shakespeare, wake yourself. It will be daybreak soon. Will you take breakfast?"

Shakespeare felt a moment of panic. In his dream he had been at home in Stratford with his mother as she made raspberry tarts — a long way away from all this. And then he recalled where he was. The landlady opened the drapes and the first whisper of daylight etched the glass. He got out of bed and stretched his arms above his head. "I will take some warm milk, if it please you, mistress. And I would be grateful if you would prepare some bread and cold meats to go with me, so that I can be on my way."

Within ten minutes, he was ready to settle up with the landlady and ride on. Through the windows he could see that it was thick with fog outside. He could not wait for it to lift. Herrick might be well ahead of him by now. He reached for his purse at his belt. It was not there. His hand scrabbled for it without effect. So that was what had disturbed him in the night. An intruder had cut his purse away while he slept. All his coinage had been stolen. He looked in dismay at the landlady.

She deduced immediately what had happened. "You have been robbed?"

He put a hand to his forehead. "All my

gold and silver."

Her brow creased. "Are you sure?"

"Unless it came away while I slept. It would be in the sheets."

They went back into the parlor and searched in vain among the bedclothes. "I am afraid I cannot pay you, mistress," he said at last. He was quickly seeing the extent of his predicament. Would she demand something in place of money? His coat or sword, perchance? Would she call the constable? Any delay could be critical.

She touched him reassuringly. "Sir, do not think of the reckoning. I am deeply embarrassed that such a thing should happen under my roof."

"Do you know who might have taken it?"

"Just me and my son, Jake, live here. I would swear on the Holy Bible that it was not Jake. He is a fine boy. I fear it must have been one of the drinkers. Shall I call the constable?"

"I cannot afford to wait. Time is not on my side. But if you will let me go, I will settle the bill with you as soon as I can. This I swear to you. I will pass this way again and you will be recompensed."

The landlady smiled and shook her head. "I will not hear of it, Mr. Shakespeare. Take your food and a little money — what little I can afford — and God speed you."

CHAPTER 39

Harper Stanley lay on his cot, alone in his cabin, in an agony of indecision. Herrick had let him down. If he were to kill Drake, he had to do it now, on this ship, before she docked at Plymouth. There might never be another chance, for when the fleet sailed, he would be assigned a command of his own, away from Drake's flagship. But here, on this vessel, he could strike while the Vice Admiral slept. The problem was the constant presence of Boltfoot Cooper and the black-skinned Diego. They would have to be killed first. A sword to the heart of the one on watch, then a blade to the throat of the one that slept. Inside the cabin, he would first cut Drake's throat, and afterwards he would have to put Lady Elizabeth Drake to the dagger, too. He could not be squeamish about killing a woman, even one as beautiful as Elizabeth. The seventy thousand ducats beckoned. . . .

But could he bring himself to do it? If he was discovered, it would be the end of everything. If only Herrick's bullet had not missed; Mendoza, the Spanish ambassador in Paris, had assured Stanley that Herrick was the best. Well, he had failed thus far.

The night was cold, but Harper was wet with sweat. His cabin was close to Drake's. That was crucial, for he would be drenched in blood and would be found out unless he could clean himself before the deed was discovered. Nor could he allow his clothes to be bloodied: he would have to go naked to the murder.

He clenched his teeth together. He had not come this far to back out now. His father, his mother, every forsaken member of the Percy family, living and dead, cried out to him for this act of vengeance and restitution. Quickly he stripped himself from his clothes. He had a pail of water in his cabin to wash himself after the deed was done. It *could* be done. It *had* to be done. And there must be a culprit, one of the mariners first on the scene, quickly put to death so that his protestations of innocence should die with him.

The hour was midnight. On the main decks, the watch scoured the horizon for the lights of other shipping. But here, belowdecks, almost all were asleep, many having had their fill of brandy. He had his play all worked out.

Naked, his body hunched forward and hairy like an ape's, he stepped into the companionway. Ahead of him, he saw the black, familiar face of Diego, lit by candles outside the door to the great cabin where Drake and his wife slept. Diego was awake, staring straight at him. That was good; it meant Boltfoot was asleep. Stanley smiled at him and, with his left hand, patted his ample belly and scratched his stones, like any man stepping from his chamber at dead of night. He mouthed the word "piss" to Diego and strode toward him, his sword and dagger held close to the back of his thigh in his right hand, just out of sight.

Diego was squatting on his haunches with his back to the cabin door. He rose to his feet with a wide smile as Harper Stanley approached. "Captain Stanley," he said in a low voice.

Stanley was just three steps away from his prey. His hand tightened around the hilts of sword and dagger. "How goes the night, Diego? I needed a piss and had no pot."

Diego laughed. As he did so, Stanley pulled back his right elbow. The blades glinted in the candlelight. Diego's eyes seemed to widen and his hands went out in front of him, trying to defend himself. Stanley lunged forward, thrusting the razor-honed blades toward Diego's chest and heart. Diego slid aside easily, laughing out loud as he did so. The sword stabbed into the hard oak of the cabin door, the dagger clattered to the ground, and Diego's arm went out, clutching Stanley by the nape and pulling his head forward, taking the wind from him as he pushed him hard into the hilt of his own sword.

Boltfoot was behind Stanley, tripping him, pushing him into a heap, curling his arm around from behind and slipping his own poniard up into Stanley's fleshy abdomen, just as he had once killed the sea monster on the banks of the Thames. Only this was easier. He had felt a kinship with the sea beast; he had none with this traitor. His death would bring no regrets.

Harper Stanley grunted and exhaled a long gasp. Boltfoot held the blade in place, deep inside Stanley's body, its tip piercing his heart, just as Stanley had intended to do to all of them.

"Well, sir, Captain Stanley," Boltfoot whispered into his ear. "It seems you were wrong. The ocean wave was not so safe and the Vice Admiral *was* in need of protection."

Stanley's eyes were already dead. A trickle of blood seeped from the small wound in the abdomen where the blade still held him impaled. There was no rush of gore for Boltfoot to contend with. It was a clean kill.

"What now, Boltfoot? Do we wake Sir Francis?"

"I do not think the Vice Admiral would wish his lady to be disturbed, Diego. Let us send Captain Stanley to a mariner's watery grave. The world shall think he killed himself. It is a common enough occurrence. Stepped overboard in a panic, frighted by the Spaniard, no doubt. If anyone is at all interested, that is. Which I think unlikely."

Boltfoot slid the blade from the dead body and wiped the blood on his kerchief. "Come, Diego, look lively. You take his legs. I'll take his arms."

The dead man was heavy but they were strong and hauled him without difficulty to the poopdeck. Diego dropped his end of the body with a dull thud onto the timber and walked out on deck. The watch was some way distant. He signaled to Boltfoot, then returned to pick up Stanley's legs. Quickly they hoisted him onto the deck, then up and over the stern bulwark. With a final push, they sent him into the waves like a stone. They scarcely heard a splash.

"Fish food, Boltfoot."

"I fear he may stick in their craw, Diego. I could not eat traitor pie with relish."

The fog was dense, slowing John Shakespeare's progress to a crawl, yet he plugged on, feeling his way along what he took to be the highway. Only when the fog swirled away briefly could he break into a trot. Occasionally he passed a cart or another horseman going eastward toward London, and it encouraged him to discover he was still on the right road. Yet no one could give him any news of a lone rider answering the description of Herrick. The trail had gone cold.

From the milestones he encountered, he estimated he was halfway to Plymouth by midday. His back caused him pain and his thighs were rubbed to great soreness from the saddle, but he would take no break. He felt he had to make up for lost time, that somehow his quarry was slipping through his fingers, like a wraith or will-o'-the-wisp.

On he rode. At nightfall he was determined to continue, but couldn't. It was simply impossible to make out the road. Better to rest up, replenish his body, then move on. He had passed a large post tavern a mile back and found his way back to it.

The building was well lit and welcoming to a weary traveler. The money the landlady of the White Dog had lent him was just enough for one night.

After a good supper of roast fowl and vegetables, he locked himself in his small second-floor room, prayed, then closed his eyes and slept until dawn.

When he opened his eyes, he knew immediately that the fog had lifted. It was a clear day with a few white clouds. By nightfall, he reckoned, he could be at Plymouth. God willing, he would be in time.

Thomas Woode had resigned himself to death. In the quiet moments between sessions of torture, he made his peace with God and prayed for his children.

Topcliffe had learned nothing from him. He had always believed he had not the stuff of martyrs in his veins, yet he had not been broken by the rack or manacles. What could he tell them, anyway? That a Jesuit priest called Cotton and another called Herrick had stayed at his home in Dowgate? He could tell them no more, for he no longer knew where they were. The tortures now were pointless and driven by malice alone. When Topcliffe or his foul apprentice, Jones, taunted him or threatened him with death, he greeted the prospect with equanimity bordering on joy. Anything to end this torment would be welcome.

He had always imagined the rack to be the worst torment devised by man, but in truth he found it easier to abide than the manacles. It seemed to him that the pain he suffered hanging against the wall must have been almost of the magnitude endured by Christ, and then chided himself for such unworthy thoughts; who was he to place his own suffering alongside that of the Son of God?

He would die here and that did not concern him. It was Grace and Andrew that made him fearful. How would they survive without him? His will contained instructions for them to be put in the guardianship of Catherine Marvell, but what if his estate were to be attainted — made forfeit to the state and let fall into the hands of such as Topcliffe? For this alone, he had to remain silent. He must not sign any confession, whatever the pain.

The stench of the cell no longer caused him any concern. He lay in the filthy straw unable to move. He could not lift his arms to feed himself, so he hardly ate or drank. Nor could he move his legs, which meant he had to defecate where he lay.

Margaret came to him as if in a dream one day. He knew not whether it was light or dark outside, for nothing of the world came into this cramped cell in Topcliffe's house of death. His wife was there with him, burning bright in a haze of gossamer, as light as mayfly wings. She dipped a cloth into cool water and mopped his brow. She kissed his lips and, though no sound came from her, she seemed to say that everything would be all right. *Only endure, and all will be well. Sleep, Thomas, sleep and all will be well. We will be together soon.*

Topcliffe was pacing. He had just come from the Queen's privy chamber and she had asked him, casually, about the Jesuits. "I had thought to have seen them in the Tower before now, Mr. Topcliffe, especially Lord Burghley's cousin Southwell! You did tell me a month since, and I recall it well, that he was as good as taken."

The key, he knew, was the woman Catherine Marvell and the children of Woode. If Woode saw them threatened with torment or death, he would talk like a goodwife outside church of a Sunday. Woode was Southwell's familiar; he would lead the way to the Popish nest of hornets.

"Tell me again, Dick, do you really believe

she was not there, that she has gone to York?"

Richard Young sat at a window seat in Topcliffe's hall. The room was full of the fug from Topcliffe's pipe of sotweed. "I don't know, Richard. I believed it then. Now I am not sure. The maidservant may well have been lying."

"Should we bring *her* in?"

"On what charge? There is no evidence that she is even a Papist. She is well known at the parish church as a faithful servant of our Church."

Topcliffe drew deeply on his pipe and strode back and forth, back and forth. The Queen had spoken half in jest, but the other half was what counted, the half that said: *I am deeply disappointed in your failure in this matter, Mr. Topcliffe; my patience is running dry.*

"Is the house watched?"

Young nodded. "I left my sergeant there and sent another as relief. It is a small house. It is easily watched and would not be difficult to search. If the Marvell woman should venture out, she will be apprehended on the instant."

"Good." Topcliffe had to find the Jesuit, therefore he had to make Thomas Woode talk. Catherine Marvell, stretched on the rack, her pretty face suffused with fear, her lovely joints beginning to crack, would make him tell all he knew. The information would come flooding out. "A thousand deaths to the Pope and all his acolyte demons, Dick, we must go back there. In force and with speed. If the woman is there — and I believe she is — we must take her before the alarm can be raised and before Walsingham or any other can intervene. We must risk his intervention; it is the only way. Once she is in our hands, no power on earth will prize her loose before we have what we want, I promise you that. We must do it, Dick, and we must do it before Shakespeare returns. Walsingham will doubtless be angry. He will see it as crossing a line, Dick, shitting on his doorstep. But I would rather cross him than the golden virgin. Gather a squadron of pursuivants: our ten best men. We go in before dawn."

CHAPTER 40

After Exeter the countryside changed rapidly. Soon Shakespeare found himself on uncompromising moorland. Everywhere he looked, he saw bogs and bleak outcrops of rock. Wild horses roamed free. He passed a gypsy camp where a fire burned with a cauldron perched over it.

He was certain now he was traveling in the right direction. He knew this to be the southeastern edge of Dartmoor, and the beaten track was easy to follow without woodland in which to get lost. At the southern tip of the moor the land finally became more lush and he descended into a wooded valley. He had a choice to make: go directly to Plymouth or first to Buckland Abbey, in case the Vice Admiral had made straight for there.

Where would Drake be most vulnerable? Buckland Abbey might have a large permanent staff of servants who would spot a stranger straightway, but it would be impossible to provide total protection night and day. Herrick could watch from a distance, pick his time and place to kill.

On the other hand, Plymouth was where Drake would spend most of his time. He had a house there, too, in Looe Street, and he would need to be close at hand to oversee the final provisioning and preparation of his war fleet. If Drake was to be at sea within two or three days, Herrick would have no time to lose. Shakespeare decided to head for the old abbey first. He'd alert the servants to the danger and then make for Plymouth, where he could join forces with Boltfoot.

On talking with a parson whom he found striding out beside a river, he got his bearings and turned northwest toward Buckland Abbey, the fine and ancient home Drake had bought from his fellow admiral Sir Richard Grenville with the immense plunder taken from the Spanish carrack *Cacafuego* in the Pacific in 1579. Elizabeth Drake was in her withdrawing room sewing a tapestry when Shakespeare arrived, and sent for him immediately. When he entered he was struck immediately by her pale beauty; she was bathed in light angling in between the stone mullions of a high arched window.

She smiled in greeting. "Mr. Shakespeare, what a delight to see you. But why, pray, are you in Devon?"

Shakespeare was exhausted. He knew he looked shabby. His clothes were torn and coated in mud like a pigman's. His leather boots were clogged with soil and soaked through. "Lady Drake, I seek Sir Francis. I must warn him. The killer sent by Spain has followed him here. There is great danger." He spoke breathlessly, panting with the final exertion of the day's long ride.

"We shall get the message to Sir Francis straightway, but in the meantime we must not have you catching your death of the sweating sickness, Mr. Shakespeare," said Elizabeth. "Please, sit by the fire and warm yourself. Do you have a change of clothes? We must fit you out with some."

Shakespeare ate and drank quickly, for he wanted to get to Plymouth before nightfall. As he devoured the food, Elizabeth Drake told him of Captain Harper Stanley's death on the voyage from Dover. "It is thought he must have jumped to his death, taken by the melancholy, Mr. Shakespeare. No one believes he could have fallen accidentally. Such a great tragedy."

Shakespeare was shocked and disturbed

by the news. He had liked Harper and he was the last man he imagined would have taken his own life. "It is, indeed, a great sadness, my lady. I knew him well." Could there have been more to his death than that, though? Shakespeare needed to speak with Boltfoot urgently.

"But life goes on, Mr. Shakespeare. Weather and winds permitting, Sir Francis is resolved to set sail with the tide tomorrow. He says he must go before the Queen changes her mind, which she is certain to do, as she always does. Tonight the town is throwing a banquet in his honor, which you must attend if you are recovered."

"A banquet? Tonight?"

"Why, indeed. Feasting, music, dancing. Is that such a surprise? The men set sail to do battle with the Spanish tomorrow. I believe they will strike a blow to Spain's heart — attacking where the King's great armada is being assembled, in Cadiz and other ports."

The thought of a banquet filled Shakespeare with dread. Anyone could slip in. And in the milling throng, Drake would be in grave peril.

"If I may ask, my lady, who will be there, do you think?"

"All the great families of Devon, Mr.

Shakespeare. The Grenvilles, all the Drakes — and there are many of them — the Hawkins family, my own cousins the Sydenhams, Raleighs, Carews, Gilberts, Sir William Courtenay and his kin. And then there will be the captains and masters and gentlemen officers of the fleet, the corporation of Plymouth, of course, the important shipwrights and chandlers."

"So everyone will know each other at such an event?"

"Most certainly. And we have another young guest, a charming young Huguenot gentleman from La Rochelle who intends to join the venture. He burns with desire to give the King of Spain a bloody nose."

Shakespeare felt a sudden chill. "What Huguenot is this, my lady?"

"Now, Mr. Shakespeare, I know you fear for my husband's life, but you know he is very capable of looking out for himself, as he has proved on many occasions in these past twenty years. This young man is called Pascal. Henri Pascal. He drank wine with me here in this withdrawing room and I believe him to be exactly what he says he is: a Huguenot fugitive from France who wishes to fight for the Protestant cause. What is more, he is a mariner, so he will serve us quite well. I told him to come to the Guildhall this evening for the banquet, where I shall introduce him to Sir Francis, so that he may sail with him on the morrow. I am sure you can find no fault in that. I must tell you he had letters of introduction from Lord Howard of Effingham, the Admiral of the Fleet. Surely there could be no better recommendation."

"May I see these letters?"

"I am afraid I do not have them. He took them away."

"What shape of a man is this? Is he beardless, tall?"

Elizabeth Drake looked puzzled. "Why, yes, he is."

"And his accent? Is it strongly French?"

"Well, no, he speaks exceptionally good English. A slightly clipped accent, perchance, but that is all."

"Lady Elizabeth, I must ride for Plymouth immediately. I fear you have entertained the man who would kill your husband."

Drake had not believed for a moment that Harper Stanley took his own life. "Come on, Diego, the truth."

The Vice Admiral was in his cabin with Diego and Boltfoot aboard the *Elizabeth Bonaventure,* at anchor in Plymouth Sound, one of Europe's most sheltered deep-water harbors. In the distance they could see Plymouth, a town of squat mariners' dwellings and bustling dockyards, which seemed to be burgeoning day by day as England's maritime ventures grew ever bolder. Drake had been conferring with his captains and had now sent them back to their vessels to prepare for the next day's departure for the Iberian peninsula. "Not an hour is to be lost, gentlemen," he said. "Even now a messenger could be riding from Greenwich Palace with orders from the Queen countermanding our commission. Her Majesty has already changed her mind four times in five days. We must be at sea to avoid that happening again."

It was only with his wife safely out of earshot at Buckland Abbey that Drake felt easy talking of Harper Stanley's fate; he did not want to worry her more than necessary.

"He was coming to kill you, Sir Francis. In fact he was coming to kill all of us. He was naked so that our blood would not drench his clothes. But we knew he was coming." Diego glanced at Boltfoot, who stepped forward.

"I had suspected him for a while. When Sir William Courtenay lunged at you with the blade on the way to Dover, I saw something in Stanley's eyes. He held back, but it was more than that. I could see that he wished you dead, sir. I think he was never what he seemed."

"Well, I have no idea *why* he should wish me dead. I always promoted him and gave him great opportunity for plunder and glory. Was he a Papist, do you think? Perchance we will never know. But I can say this: he was a good seafarer. I would have liked him at my side on this venture." Drake glowered at Boltfoot. "Still, I am sure we can find a replacement. Do you think you could captain a ship, Mr. Cooper?"

"Possibly, Sir Francis, but I would rather be flayed than do so."

"Hah! Still the same mongrel cur, eh, Boltfoot? And don't go about congratulating yourself that you have saved my life. If Harper Stanley had somehow got into my cabin with his sword, I would have cut him down in my sleep. No one bests Drake and certainly not a beplumed peacock like Harper Stanley. Now then, I would like your thoughts, Diego. Look at this chart." Drake jabbed his finger three times at the chart showing the coasts of Portugal and Spain. "We will attack the Antichrist's ships here, here, and here."

There was a knock at the cabin door and

the ship's master opened it. Drake looked up, irritated by the interruption. "What is it?"

"Mr. John Shakespeare to see you, Vice Admiral," the master announced.

Surprised, Drake glanced at the entranceway. "Shakespeare, by God's faith, what are you doing here?"

Shakespeare bowed, then rose, stiff-backed from his ride, to his full height. He was a good six inches taller than Drake and looked down at him uneasily. "Sir Francis, the killer has followed you to Plymouth."

Drake laughed. "You are too late, Shakespeare! Your man Boltfoot and my friend Diego here have already done for him. He lies at the bottom of the Channel even now, with eels swimming into the hole that Boltfoot put in his belly."

"You have killed Herrick? How so?"

"Herrick? They have not killed anyone called Herrick. They have dispatched Captain Harper Stanley, Mr. Shakespeare. The traitor came for me in the middle of the night, naked, like a thief. Diego and Mr. Cooper saved me the trouble of killing him by impaling him on their blades, then dropping him overboard. The world has been allowed to believe that he took his own life. Amusing, do you not think?"

Shakespeare was aghast. "You think Stanley intended to kill you?"

"It is a certainty."

"That is a worrying turn of events, Sir Francis, but he was not the one I seek. There is another man, far more dangerous, sent by King Philip for the price on your head. He is utterly without fear or mercy and has already killed one of my best men, Harry Slide. It is he who shot at you at Deptford. Harper Stanley could not possibly have done that for he was aboard ship, not ashore."

"Then we have two traitors to contend with. Or should I say 'had'? For now there is just the one, which sounds like no danger at all, as we are to sail tomorrow."

Shakespeare sighed. "And what of tonight, Sir Francis? What of the banquet? I must tell you that this Herrick will be there. It would be best if you were not."

"What! Miss my own banquet, Mr. Shakespeare? You jest, sir! The Spaniard would laugh at me and I would die of shame. No, sir, bring on this Spanish killer and I will happily deal with him! But pray tell me, sir, what the devil has happened to your eyebrow? You look most curious without it."

The tension in Seething Lane was palpable.

Jane shuttered the windows as soon as darkness fell, and they spoke in low voices in case anyone listened at the door. They felt besieged.

The confrontation with the magistrate Richard Young had shaken Jane to the core. "I can't work, Catherine, but I have so much to do. There is cheese to be made, linen to be repaired, hose to be darned, preserves to be bottled and stored . . ."

"Jane, stop it. You're not helping."

"If only Mr. Shakespeare were here. I won't sleep tonight for worrying. What if the magistrate comes again? What if he brings Topcliffe?"

Catherine took Jane by the shoulders and made her sit on a bench at the table. "They *will* come, Jane. And that is why you must stop this. Take a deep breath. We must think."

Jane breathed deeply. It did not help. She was worried less for herself than she was for Catherine and the two children. "We have to get you and Grace and Andrew away from here, Catherine."

"Yes. They will come back in force tonight and they are utterly without pity. I must tell you, Jane, they are so soaked in blood that they will think nothing of killing us all. My master, Mr. Woode, could well be dead by now. But even that will not make them falter. They are relentless; their thirst for vengeance will not be slaked even by a death. They will take his children and break them on the Bridewell treadmill as a warning to others."

Jane hugged Catherine and gave her a weak smile. "How can you get out, then? I am sure we are being watched. There is no secret way out. If you try, they will take you straightway in the street. You will be done for."

"Well, we can't simply sit here and wait. There is no hiding place, you say?"

"None that they would not easily discover."

Catherine and Jane were in the small kitchen, amid the pots and cooking utensils. Jane had been making candles and the debris of her work, wax and wicks, lay on the table before them. A helpless silence descended. Upstairs the children slept, unaware of the fate that awaited them.

"I suppose I could try to talk to Mr. Secretary."

"What would his reaction be? Does he not back Topcliffe to the hilt? Would he not turn us over to him?"

They had been over this ground before. Catherine felt sick with dread. This should have been the happiest time of her life, days of honey with a man she loved, but he was gone and there was no way of knowing when — or if — he would return. The message delivered from him to Jane merely said he had to go away west immediately and that he would be gone a few days. Inside the message was another, hastily written on a small scrap of paper, folded and addressed to Catherine. *Would that I had poetic words in me. All I can say is that you are my love and I love you. Hold firm until I return.* It had made the small hairs on her neck stand and a shiver of warmth spread out across her breasts. She had folded the paper again and put it within her bodice.

Jane raised her head suddenly, as if struck by a thought. "Perhaps . . ."

CHAPTER 41

The Guildhall was lit by a thousand candles.

Guests would soon begin to arrive. Shakespeare paced the main hall. He had examined the building in detail, seeking out every entrance, every staircase, every window through which a shot or crossbow bolt might be fired. He and Boltfoot had interviewed and searched every member of staff: the footmen, the cooks, the master of ceremonies, the musicians. And he had put them on alert in the event they should see anything at all out of the usual.

He had left Drake under the protection of Diego; they would, of course, be the last to arrive. Boltfoot, meanwhile, had come ahead, trudging through the cold, blustery streets by the docks, his heavy left foot dragging behind his squat body. He was now positioned by the grand doorway where all the guests would enter wearing their finery. Shakespeare had questioned Boltfoot yet again about his confrontation with Herrick in the aftermath of the shot from the chandler's attic in Deptford. He'd picked at his brain, desperate to find more clues about the assassin and his appearance. "Most of all, Boltfoot, would you recognize him again?"

"I don't know, Mr. Shakespeare. I do not feel confident. I did not get close to him."

"But you are the best hope we have. You must have some kind of impression. Use your instinct, Boltfoot. Look at the men's faces carefully. We know Herrick is clean-shaven and that he is tall. Study any such men closely. Maybe he has stuck a false beard to his face or disguised his height by walking with a stoop. If you have any doubt about someone, however small, take no chances. Stop them and search them. This Herrick will come; it is his last chance."

Shakespeare himself had borrowed a suit of clothes from the butler at Buckland Abbey. It enabled him to move at ease among the throng as people arrived; as a mere serving man he would attract no comment.

The hall was high-ceilinged with fine pargeting and great colored windows, but it was not big and the guests would quickly fill it. As the evening wore on, and the claret and malmsey flowed, it would become increasingly difficult to spot who was coming in or going out, who was bearing arms or advancing on Drake. In such a crush of sweating bodies, a poniard, even a wheel-lock pistol, could all too easily be concealed.

They began arriving at seven of the clock, just as the church bells chimed nearby. Shakespeare took a deep breath. "This is it, Boltfoot. We know he will be here and that he has no fear. The way he walked into Buckland Abbey proved that. If only Lady Drake could stay by the door with you, for she must recognize him better than anyone; she has taken a cup of wine with him in her own withdrawing room. But her thoughts and attention will most certainly be occupied elsewhere."

Boltfoot looked unimpressed. He was convinced that Drake was immortal, that he had signed some pact with the Devil. He had seen him exchange fire with the finest soldiers of Spain, brave arrows and spears flung at him by native peoples the very globe over, walk tall and strong when all others were falling down with sickness in mid-ocean. Whatever happened, he never shed his glow of invincibility; he was untouchable. Could a mere mercenary, a mortal with a wheel-lock sent by Philip of

Spain, do him any harm? Boltfoot rather thought not.

The guests wore glittering clothes, studded with dazzling gemstones. This was not the royal court with its plethora of exquisitely cut gowns, but the clothes were costly nonetheless. Plymouth was a wealthy port. After London, it was the hub of England's trade with the world. Here lived hard, unsentimental men — Hawkins, Drake, and their extensive families, all cousins with one another — who plundered Spanish treasure, who stole men and women from their beds in western Africa and sold them as slave labor in the Indies, who found spices and cloth and jewels from the earth's most far-flung shores to sell in the capitals of Europe. Their wealth, however ill-gotten, shone as gaudily as the night sky in this hall. Shakespeare doubted that there was a single gemstone in the hall paid for other than in blood.

The tables, formed in a great U shape, were bedecked with candles and silver plate. The guests all thronged in the center of the hall, where, after feasting, there would be dancing. In a corner, the musicians played the songs of old England, passed down through Devon's generations for hundreds of years. This was not a time for mournful ballads.

Drake and his lady arrived last, to thunderous applause. He wore a saffron yellow doublet topped by an enormous ruff of fine lace and a cape at his shoulder. The Vice Admiral bowed with a sweep of his cape, and Lady Drake, in her finest blue velvet and cloth of gold gown, curtsied with a radiant smile. They were accompanied by Diego. Drake caught sight of Shakespeare in his butler's livery. "Fetch me a cup of brandy, my man," he said, laughing. He and his wife walked sedately to their seats at the head of the main table, acknowledging the applause and cheering of the guests every inch of the way. He vaulted onto the table with the agility of a man half his forty-six years, puffed out his broad chest, and clapped his hands.

The crowd fell silent. Drake stood, legs asunder, hands on hips, as if he were on the deck of a royal galleon with a fierce northeasterly in his gray-red hair. His eyes shone. He had his audience, his people, where he wanted them: in the very palm of his hand.

"Welcome, welcome one and all. Eat, drink, and be merry, for tomorrow our fleet sets sail into the teeth of the Spaniard's jaws, where we shall blow out his brains and tear his heart from his cowering chest. Let

534

Philip and Santa Cruz tremble with fear, for I will discover them, mewling in their lair, and turn their great towering ships to matchwood. But first let me tell you a little of the ways of this craven prince: he has sent a Fleming for to kill me; a man of dishonor who would kill by stealth for he is afraid to stand in open combat. I am told he will be here tonight. Well, Mr. Fleming, here I am! Draw your pistol, take aim, and fire." Drake thumped his hand against his chest. "Here is my heart. Shoot it to death, by God's faith."

He stood back and looked around the room. The silence was absolute. All eyes were on the Vice Admiral. He cupped his ear with his hand. "Hark, do I hear a pistol being cocked? Mind you come closer. We don't want you to miss now, as you did once before."

An explosion tore the silence. The guests shrieked and ducked down as one, an instinctive reaction to the force of the blast. All eyes turned to the back of the hall, where a man stood holding a smoking wheel-lock. Then everyone looked back at Drake. He stood where he had before, unflinching, hands on hips even more aggressively, chest pushed out until it might seem he would burst his doublet, his face creased into a scornful grin.

Shakespeare pushed his way through the throng toward the gunman. He was about to leap on him when he stopped in his tracks. The gunman, too, was grinning. His red hair and shoulders were covered in the plaster that had fallen from the ceiling, where he had loosed the ball from his pistol. He looked back at Drake, who was laughing loud.

" 'Tis my little brother Thomas, Mr. Shakespeare. He has let off his pop-pop into the ceiling. Would you take him away and lock him up in Plymouth gaol?"

Shakespeare shook his head in dismay. By now the whole room was laughing with gusto until the walls echoed.

Drake clapped his hands again. "Forgive me, Mr. Shakespeare. It was a jest we could not resist. Now let us say grace and give thanks to the Lord for the fare we are about to receive." He clambered down from the table and called on the Bishop to lead them in prayer.

The banquet proceeded in disorderly fashion. The din of laughter and conversation was as loud as a score of anvils being hammered. Shakespeare was worried. He offered to taste Drake's food for poison, but Drake would have none of it. Worse, if the killer had been anywhere in the vicinity when Thomas Drake shot his pistol, he could well have found his way into the hall under cover of the confusion; all the plans to search and examine those coming in could have gone up in smoke.

As the evening grew ever more wild, weapons were produced and mock sword fights staged along the center of the tables. Drunken guests kicked food and silver and candles around like so many pirates. Drake clapped his hands whenever he felt it was time to tell another story. At one stage he called for silence and demanded prayers for his cousin John, a fellow sea captain, captured by natives and then by the Spanish on the River Plate. "Remember, while we eat and drink, my cousin molders in some Spanish hole in Peru. If he could hear me now, I would say 'Keep strong, John! Keep the faith and spit on their saints and relics!' "

The dancing began. Riotous voltas and galliards; not for these revelers the sedate elegance of the pavane. The men threw their ladies high into the air, and occasionally dropped them, sprawling in a drunken heap.

Diego came up and slapped Shakespeare on the back. "I am sorry about Sir Francis's little jest. He insisted on it."

"This is folly, Diego. Drake jests, but this man, this Fleming, will come tonight. He may be waiting in the shadows outside; he may be here already inside. But I tell you, I know he has ridden here and he believes this to be his last chance. I think he is without fear for his own life."

A drunken couple staggered into Shakespeare. The man wore the mayor's chain of office and had his hand clasped to the woman's breast and his mouth at her neck; she had her hand held firm at the front of his breeches. Shakespeare pushed the amorous couple on their way, stumbling around the room in their curious impression of a dance. "Good to see him taking care of corporation business," Shakespeare told Diego. "I fear Mr. Secretary would not approve of any of this."

"Definitely not. But Mr. Secretary does not stand on the deck of a warship driving it straight into the guns of the enemy," Diego replied. "They are enjoying life while it lasts, John. Tomorrow we set sail. This may be the last time you see any of us."

"This is certain fine, Diego, so long as you all *do* set sail on the morrow. Your Vice Admiral included."

The banquet was rapidly descending into a free-for-all. Beautifully prepared food was flung across the tables; ale was drunk from pitchers so that it ran from the mouths of men and women, down the sides of their jowls and onto their fine clothes. Shakespeare watched in despair. All he could do now was stay close to Drake and scour the room for anything untoward, while Diego and Boltfoot watched the doors. Yet men and women were slipping in and out all the time.

Drake broke off from a heated conversation with young Richard Hawkins, son of his old friend John Hawkins. "Enjoying yourself, Mr. Shakespeare? Your brow seems uncommon furrowed tonight." He turned to his wife. "What say you, my lady?"

"I would say, Sir Francis, that you should be thankful for the care that Mr. Shakespeare is taking concerning the preservation of your life. I think you owe him better manners, sir!"

"Hah! Roundly told off. I would rather be cut at by a Spaniard's halberd than feel the edge of a woman's tongue."

Someone shouted "Fire!" It was a word to drive fear into the hearts of stout men. Even those stumbling about with an excess of wine stopped and held still. "Fire! There is a fire!" another voice shouted. Then a roar went up and guests began scrambling for the great doors at the front of the hall.

Shakespeare did not hesitate. He seized Drake by the arm and pressed his hand into Lady Elizabeth's back. "Come with me. I know a better way out. This fire will have been laid by the killer. He will make his attempt in the confusion . . ."

A rush of flame took hold of a gold-and-red French tapestry that hung from a wall. Fire leapt from it into the drapes and up to the beams. Black smoke billowed in the narrow confines of the hall. The scramble of bodies toward the door turned to panic. Women and men coughed and screamed and pushed and trampled.

Drake pushed Shakespeare's hand away from his arm. He grabbed a silver salver from the table and banged it hard repeatedly. "Hear me! Hear me!" he shouted. "Gentlemen stand aside and let the ladies go first. With some order, we will all get out safely. Hear me!"

Suddenly the undisciplined charge for the doorway halted. Even in the most intense heat of fire, men obeyed Sir Francis Drake. Most men did stand aside and those few that didn't were hauled out of the queue by others. The women then proceeded to exit at a brisk pace.

The fire was growing fast, gobbling up

paintings and furnishings, setting light to the beams in the ceiling. Cooks and serving maids began running in with pails of water. Shakespeare realized a few pails was not going to be enough. This was going to be a hard blaze to bring under control. Boltfoot and Diego had emerged from the crush of people and were now back with Shakespeare and the Drakes.

"We really must go, Sir Francis."

"Mr. Shakespeare, we are in your hands. Kindly take us your secret way."

They moved forward. Shakespeare suddenly realized the way he had intended, through the kitchens, was blocked by flames. He turned to the west side of the building, to the corporation's council chamber. There had to be a way through there. The smoke was getting worse; sounds of coughing and choking filled the hall as the fire raged out of control. As soon as they were in the chamber, Shakespeare slammed the door behind them to keep out the flames and the worst of the fumes. They stood a moment, catching their breath, trying to clear their lungs. The faces of eminent Plymouth burghers looked down on them from portraits around the walls.

"How do you fare, my lady?" Drake asked of his wife, touching her arm tenderly.

With her hands, she tried to brush the black soot from her dazzling gown. "It is a great excitement, Sir Francis. I begin to understand why you men are so quick to go to war."

"You have a fine spirit! Think how brave our sons will be."

"And our daughters, sir."

Shakespeare pushed open the door into the council antechamber and stepped through in front of Drake and his wife. Boltfoot followed. At the far end of the room, he could see the side entrance to the building. A group of men was standing around the doorway — serving men and ostlers. "Is the way clear?" Shakespeare called.

"Aye, sir," came a reply. "Come through. We are setting up a pail chain here."

If I were a killer, thought Shakespeare, *this is where I would make my move. This is where I would expect Drake to make his exit and I would attack now.* He drew his sword and signaled to Drake to do the same. "Come, sir, beware. He will be hereabouts. Boltfoot, have your caliver primed and ready."

Drake strode ahead, disdainful of Shakespeare's caution. "Home, Lady Drake, to bed. I have had my fill of this nonsense of Walsingham. I love him as a friend, but I will not be wet-nursed by his nannies."

They moved out into the street. Shakespeare could see now that flames were licking the sky. A great crowd had gathered outside the Guildhall, all standing agog at the blaze. It seemed the whole town had risen from their beds to watch the spectacle or help with the pail chains. Drake ignored them. "You will see better fireworks when I put flame to Philip's galleons," he said to no one in particular, striding through the chill night air.

The walk to Looe Street, where Drake had his town house, took little more than five minutes. Two roistering mariners, who had consumed too much brandy on this their last night ashore, whistled and called at them. "Here, sweets, leave them dodderers and come with us. *We'll* fill yer cunny with honey!" Then they spotted their Vice Admiral and dashed down a side street.

"I recognize that voice," Drake said. "He's bosun on the *Dreadnought.* I'll have him flogged on the morrow for lewdness!"

CHAPTER 42

The Drakes' house was surprisingly modest compared to his majestic mansions and estates in other parts of Devon and London. It was a tall structure, built of stone to withstand seaborne gales. Above the ground floor, jettied chambers overhung the narrow street. Clearly, the crucial thing to the Vice Admiral was its convenience, being so close to the mouth of the Plym and the dockyards, where he had to spend so much time repairing and provisioning his ships.

Drake stood at the steps to the house. "Well, Mr. Shakespeare, you have brought us safe home. You can tell Mr. Secretary that you have accomplished your task like a true and faithful servant. Good night to you, sir." He was about to push open the door when Shakespeare stepped in front of him. He addressed Elizabeth: "Might I just ask you, my lady, did you tell the Huguenot, Pascal, about this house?"

Elizabeth Drake looked flustered. "It is . . . possible. I might have mentioned it. I cannot recall."

Shakespeare lifted the latch to the door. "If it please you, Sir Francis, I will go first. Boltfoot, come with me."

Suddenly Drake's good humor vanished. He thrust Shakespeare angrily aside. "No one but the Queen commands me what to do, Shakespeare. Remove yourself from my way. Lady Drake, let us go inside." He opened the door for his wife. She hesitated, but knew her husband's moods well enough to realize this was no time to try disagreeing with him. Smiling sweetly at Shakespeare and mouthing a silent "Thank you, Mr. Shakespeare," she stepped forward into the house.

Drake followed her and was surprised to find the hallway empty and in darkness.

"I think the staff are out watching the fire, Sir Francis," Elizabeth told him. "Perhaps we might ask our companions to set some lights about the house for us."

"By God's faith, what sort of staff is it that leaves its post to watch a little bonfire, madam? I think you must look to our domestic arrangements before I am next home."

Taking her cue, Shakespeare and Boltfoot

entered the building behind the couple. Boltfoot produced a tinderbox and began lighting candles. Shakespeare pushed on into the house. He had been convinced Herrick would strike at the banquet. And now? If there *had* been a Huguenot called Henri Pascal who just happened to turn up at Buckland Abbey, why had he not been at the banquet to introduce himself to Drake?

The blow came as Shakespeare entered the Drakes' private chamber on the second floor. It came out of the darkness, a crack to the back of the head that felled him instantly. He slumped awkwardly to the floor, his head hitting the foot of the bed as he went down. He felt himself losing consciousness, but he fought the sensation and thrashed out wildly with his arm, which still clutched his sword. Dimly, he heard a sound like a grunt or cry. He rolled sideways across the room and felt the reverberation of a heavy blade stabbing down into the boards where, a second earlier, he had been sprawled.

Shakespeare scrambled farther from the assailant, clawing his way to the other side of a large oaken bed. In the gloom he saw a flickering light, a candle flame, and then heard a gasp. Elizabeth Drake had stepped into the chamber. In the dim, shadowy light he saw a face appear: Herrick. It had to be Herrick. In horror, he saw him grab Elizabeth, his muscled arm encircling her neck and forcing her back. The candle fell from her grasp and the room was plunged back into darkness.

Shakespeare jumped to his feet. His clubbed head felt as if gunpowder had exploded within it. He felt blood trickle down the inside of his ruff collar. He still had his sword in his hand, his grasp firm on the hilt.

Another light appeared at the door. Drake. "What is this?" And then he saw his wife, her neck twisted back, the point of a poniard blade at her exposed throat, pressing into her flesh, blood dripping down onto her velvet gown. "My lady?"

Shakespeare was at Drake's side now.

"Out." Herrick said the word quietly to Shakespeare. He stood scarcely five feet from Drake. "Out or she will die. Not you, Drake — you stay. But the other one, leave now or you will see such a gush of blood from this woman's throat as will sink all your galleons."

Drake nodded to Shakespeare, his face grim. "Leave now, Mr. Shakespeare."

Elizabeth was breathing fast. Her body was rigid, as if the slightest movement would draw the needle-sharp point of the blade into her throat.

Shakespeare stood his ground. "I am going nowhere. My order is to protect you."

In one lightning-swift motion, Herrick flung Elizabeth across the room. In the same movement, he lunged at Drake, poniard raised, with all the force of a bull in the ring. As he thrust forward and down with the blade, he hissed, "So die all heretics . . ."

Drake did not retreat an inch. Herrick's blow descended hard, slicing through flesh and glancing off bone, but it was Shakespeare's left forearm that took the blow, not Drake's body. Shakespeare's right arm came down behind Herrick's neck, the hilt of his sword cracking into the base of his skull and pummeling him to the ground at Drake's feet. Shakespeare stamped his left foot down onto the nape of Herrick's neck. He raised up his sword, now greasy with his own blood, in his uninjured right arm and held it suspended as if about to drive it down through the would-be killer's back.

"No, Mr. Shakespeare," Drake said. "Save that pleasure for the headsman."

As Shakespeare stood over the assassin's prostrate body, Drake went to his wife and helped her from the floor. He took her in his arms with a tenderness Shakespeare would never have thought possible of such a man among men.

"Are you much hurt, Lady Drake?" her husband asked.

"I am sure I shall survive, Sir Francis." She dusted herself down, then turned to Shakespeare, whose arm was pouring blood. "But I fear Mr. Shakespeare will not — unless he quickly has some assistance."

Boltfoot arrived with candles to light the room. Servants were drifting back from the fire and one was sent to fetch the constable. Lady Drake staunched the flow of blood from Shakespeare's arm with a ripped-up shirt of her husband's, then told a maid to summon a physician to look at the wound properly.

Herrick was beginning to come around, but Boltfoot had already bound him and was sitting on a stool, pointing the octagonal muzzle of his caliver at the assassin's face. It was not long before the constable and two powerful assistants arrived, all smelling of the fire they had been helping to douse at the Guildhall. Without ceremony, they carried Herrick out and tossed him onto a handcart. As he was hauled off to the town gaol, his face was a mask of bitter frustration.

"Well, Mr. Shakespeare," Drake said. "Do

you have any more Spanish killers up your sleeve to frighten me with?"

"I trust not, Vice Admiral."

"Good. Then all we have to worry about is the ever-changing tide of our sovereign majesty's capricious mind. Let us sleep now and sail in the morning. With God's help, I vow that we will give the Spaniard such a beating he will wish he had never heard the name of Sir Francis Drake!"

The ships of Drake's fleet sailed with the morning's tide. He was aboard the *Elizabeth Bonaventure*, accompanied by three more royal galleons — *Golden Lion, Dreadnought, Rainbow* — and twenty other vessels. They were manned by three thousand sailors and soldiers, heavily armed and angry, and many tons of cannon and ball. Before weighing anchor, Drake found it in him to say a grudging word of thanks to Shakespeare for his "diligence," then scribbled a final message for Walsingham and handed it to Shakespeare to carry to him:

The wind commands us away. Our ship is under sail. God grant we may live in His fear as the enemy may have cause to say that God does fight for Her Majesty as well abroad as at home.

There was a new urgency about the mission. The latest intelligence gathered by Walsingham had revealed that the Spanish admiral, Santa Cruz, planned to have his armada ready to sail this spring or early summer. Drake's task was to destroy the enemy in her ports or at sea and to intercept and capture the Spanish treasure fleet from the Indies. Failure would mean nothing less than the destruction of England.

Shakespeare stood on the shore with Elizabeth Drake, Boltfoot, and thousands of townsfolk, all cheering and throwing their caps in the air as the brave pennants of the fleet stretched out in the stiff breeze. Elizabeth touched his face. "I am sure my husband has not thanked you adequately, Mr. Shakespeare, but please accept my sincere gratitude. Last night you saved both our lives."

He had thought about it all at length. Despite exhaustion, he had hardly been able to sleep, so fast did his heart beat. The thing that kept coming back to him was that he could have killed Herrick, there and then, helpless on the floor, with one foot on the back of his neck. Like every child, Shakespeare had killed injured birds and hunted squirrels with bows and arrows for their red fur, yet he had never had cause to kill a man and often wondered whether he would have the stomach for it. Well, now he knew.

His left arm was heavily bandaged and supported across his chest in a sling. It was painful, but the cut had been clean and there was no reason to believe it would not heal. A physician dressed it with herbal tinctures to prevent gangrene and told him to drink brandy to counter the loss of blood. The ride back to London would be uncomfortable, but manageable.

Early that morning, Herrick had been arraigned before magistrates and then left to ponder his fate in Plymouth jail until trial, which would be a matter of two or three days; execution would follow swiftly. Shakespeare felt that this was a matter best dealt with locally; Mr. Secretary would not wish to have another Papist martyr paraded through the streets so soon after the execution of Mary Stuart. Anyway, Plymouth butchers could bowel and quarter Herrick as efficiently as the London headsmen.

Shakespeare spent a few hours with the would-be assassin, trying to persuade him to talk. He got little — neither confessions nor denials. Only when Shakespeare mentioned the murder of Lady Blanche Howard did the Jesuit break his silence briefly. Herrick laughed, humorlessly. "You do not think that was *me,* Mr. Shakespeare? Look to your own . . . look to your own."

Shakespeare pressed him but all the priest would say was, "My fate is certain, why should I waste what little breath I have left in talking with you?" Then he turned his back on his interrogator and dragged his heavy shackles and manacles into a marginally more comfortable position. For a brief moment, Shakespeare wondered whether to bring torture to bear; Mr. Secretary would undoubtedly approve. The thought did not last long. Torture repulsed him, as it did most Englishmen.

After Drake's fleet sailed, Shakespeare and Boltfoot took horse for London. On the way, they stopped at the White Dog inn to repay the landlady who had helped Shakespeare when his purse was stolen. He had been handed ten pounds by Drake. "It is a loan, Mr. Shakespeare, to get you home. Not a gift." Boltfoot had chuckled.

The days were growing longer. In a matter of just forty-eight hours the mist had given way to spring sunshine and crisp, clear nights. All the way, Shakespeare thought of Catherine; every mile they rode brought him closer to her. He clung to their one night together and prayed to God that it meant as much to her as it did to him. He would propose to her, of course. Yet he had, too, some nagging fear. Walsingham would not be best pleased that one of his senior officials intended to marry a Roman Catholic; perhaps he would go so far as to dismiss Shakespeare from his employment. Well, if that was to happen, so be it. His love for Catherine Marvell was paramount.

The riders made good progress and Shakespeare decided to take a short diversion to the Thames near Windsor, where he asked the way to the village of Rymesford.

He found the monk that Thomas Woode had told him about huddled in the remains of one of the drying rooms in the old mill. It was a ramshackle, dilapidated place of ancient rotted timbers, and it looked as though it might soon collapse into the river and be carried downstream. Hundreds of birds had made their nests in its beams and rafters and their noise was a cacophony. The old monk was scarce in better condition than the building. His skin was like yellowed parchment, his eyes hollow sockets without light. His old robe, which looked as though he might have been wearing it at the time of the dissolution of the monasteries fifty years since, was little more than rags, hanging from his gaunt shoulders and tied at the waist with frayed strands of rope.

"Are you Ptolomeus?"

The blind monk shied away at his voice like a beaten dog.

A sheet of paper caught in the breeze that blew through the gaping holes where once windows had been and fluttered past the old man. Shakespeare caught the paper. It was blank but it looked of identical quality to the papers found scattered around Lady Blanche Howard's mutilated body in Hog Lane, Shoreditch.

"Ptolomeus, I have no wish to harm you. I am come to talk with you."

The old man's beard was long and pepper gray, as was his hair. He was encrusted with dirt and grime. He sat on his haunches on the floorboards, beside a worn, cast-away grindstone. At his side was a wooden trencher with a few crumbs.

"Boltfoot, give him some food."

Boltfoot limped back to his horse, which was tethered outside the mill, and took some bread and meat from the saddlebags. He brought it back and touched the sightless monk by the shoulder. "Here," he said, less gruffly than usual. "Food. Take it."

The monk stretched out his arms from the folds of his robe and held them together like a tray for the food. He had no hands. Both had been severed at the wrist, and not

555

that long ago, for the scars were fairly fresh. Shakespeare closed his eyes, suffused with feelings of pity and disgust that anyone could have done such a thing to the old man. Boltfoot lay the food on the man's stumps. "I will bring you ale, too," he said.

"What happened to you, Ptolomeus?"

"The law, sir, the law." His voice was surprisingly firm.

"What crime did you commit?"

"Libel, sedition, illegal printing, unlicensed papermaking. What does it matter? My life is done. All that is left me is birdsong and the scraps the villagers bring me. At least they do not judge me. I am content to be judged by God."

"I am right in thinking that you have made the paper scattered about this place?"

"I cannot see the paper, sir. My eyes have been put out. But if you have found it here, I would hazard a guess that it is my work, poor though that is, as anyone that knows about these things will tell you. It is the water here, you see. Too muddy. That and the sad quality of the rags. The ragmen know their worth, sir." He laughed drily.

Shakespeare stood quietly a moment and looked at the devastation around him. This broken man sat in the middle of it, still, like the silent heart of a storm. When you have lost everything and there is nothing left to lose but your life, what is there to fear? Ptolomeus ate some of the food Boltfoot had given him, hunching his head down as he pushed his stumps together around the bread and meat and held it up to his mouth. It was obvious the pain of his amputation had not yet dulled, for his body tensed with each movement and his face was set in a grimace.

Much of the panoply of papermaking was still here. The main shaft of the milling machine was attached by levers to mallets for mashing the sodden rags to pulp. Nearby, there were wooden frames with fine sievelike bases from which the water would drain, leaving a thin layer of pulp, which, when dried out, would become raw paper. There was a press, too, to help squeeze the water from the sheets. But there was no printing press. Where, wondered Shakespeare, had that gone?

"Thomas Woode told me he gave you an old press so that you could print Romish tracts on behalf of seminary priests. Where is it, this press?"

"Gone with my hands, sir. Gone with my hands."

"Mr. Woode told me you would never have printed anything seditious."

"That, too, is true enough. Or so I thought. Others disagreed. They said that *whatever* I printed was illicit; Star Chamber has ruled it against the law to print anything without explicit license."

"Then tell me who did this to you? Was it the town magistrate?"

Boltfoot raised a cup of ale to the old monk's lips. He drank thirstily, then wiped his mouth with his grubby sleeve. "That is good, sir. That is good. Thank you. No, it was not the magistrate, but one of whom you may have heard. He is named Topcliffe and I do believe him to be Satan incarnate."

"Topcliffe?"

"He killed my fellow monk Brother Humphrey. Topcliffe cut him into pieces before my eyes and threw his remains into the river. Then he took my eyes and, lastly, my hands. He put my arms together against a log and removed the hands with one blow of an axe. He left me to bleed to death, but God, in his mercy, has let me live a little while longer."

Shakespeare looked at Boltfoot and saw his own horror reflected. Very little could move Boltfoot, yet the cold brutality of the old man's tale shocked even him.

"You are silent, sir?" the monk said. "Are

you surprised, then, by this demon's handi-work?"

"No. No, not surprised."

"A goodwife from Rymesford tended my wounds and brought sustenance. She still helps me, as do others. Burghley and his like cannot kill our faith so easily, you know."

Shakespeare reached out and touched the monk on the shoulder. Ptolomeus did not flinch. "We will leave you money," Shakespeare said. "But you must tell us what happened to your printing press."

"The money would be a kindness, sir. Thank you. As for the press, Mr. Richard Topcliffe took that, too. He said he had some use for it. I did hear him laugh as he carried it off on the back of my own cart."

CHAPTER 43

John Shakespeare and Boltfoot Cooper rode in silence. They had passed by the great castle of Windsor and were close to London now. The villages that serviced the city with vegetables, livestock, timbers, and ironwork were becoming more numerous and prosperous. It seemed to Shakespeare that London was the center of a great wheel and that these roads in, with their increasing numbers of hamlets and towns, were its spokes. You could hardly turn a corner without spying another church spire against the skyline.

The fields were different, too, better cared for and enclosed than those he had encountered traveling west. They passed through part of Surrey and Shakespeare collected his gray mare that had gone lame on the way to Plymouth; she was hale and in good spirits and he paid the peasant who had cared for her half a crown for his efforts. It seemed fairer than the sixpence he had promised.

The silence between Shakespeare and Boltfoot reflected their thoughts. Each knew what the other was thinking. Shakespeare broke the spell. "It can mean but one thing, Boltfoot," he said at last.

Boltfoot nodded.

"It can mean only that Topcliffe himself printed that tract in Hog Lane. But why would he do that?"

"Justification, Master Shakespeare. To show the Catholics as treacherous."

"Would he go to such lengths?" But Shakespeare knew the answer: what lengths *wouldn't* Topcliffe go to in his mission to destroy every Roman Catholic priest and adherent of the old faith? Surely, a man who could commission a rack and torture room for his own home would be capable of printing a tract to justify more arrests. "Yes," Shakespeare agreed, "yes, he *would* go to such lengths. The tract was naught but a poor copy of 'Leicester's Commonwealth.' It was without meaning and could have had only one purpose: it was a diversion."

They rode on a little way in silence. Then Shakespeare turned once more to Boltfoot. "And that leads us on to another certainty . . ."

"He killed the Lady Blanche."

Shakespeare flinched at the harshness of the words, then said them, more quietly, himself. "Topcliffe killed Lady Blanche Howard."

Boltfoot issued a low noise like a farmyard animal.

"But why did he kill her?" pressed Shakespeare. "Why pick on a Howard, with all the complications that could bring? She may have been a Catholic convert, but even Her Majesty would not brook the murder of her cousin in that way."

"I think he killed her by mistake, sir. Then tried to cover his tracks. I think he tortured her for information, but she died. The relic and crucifix were added later, as were the cuts to her throat and belly."

Shakespeare shook his head. "No. It wasn't a mistake. He planned to kill her all along. He knew he could not allow her to live as soon as he subjected her to torture; if he had set her free the wrath of the Howards would have destroyed him. He planned to kill her and put the blame onto the Catholics by befouling her body with the crucifix and relic, to make it seem like some debauched Popish rite. That fits in with the Searcher of the Dead's findings. He said she had been dead three days and that she was killed somewhere else. The wounds that were supposed to have killed her did not produce enough blood, he said."

And the marks on her wrists, he thought. They could just as easily have been caused by manacles as a rope used to tie her. He had seen similar injuries on Thomas Woode after his sessions against Topcliffe's wall. But what sort of information would Topcliffe be trying to prize from her? The answer was plain: he wanted the same information from Blanche that he was now intent on extracting from Woode — the whereabouts of Robert Southwell. He must have heard of some link between Blanche and the Jesuits; perhaps a servant in Howard of Effingham's household had passed on information, or an informant within the Catholic network. Topcliffe was a man possessed when it came to finding the Jesuit priest. Topcliffe wanted Southwell, and he did not care whom he had to ruin or slaughter to get to the priest. Shakespeare spurred his horse. He had been away from Catherine too long.

Topcliffe, Young, Newall, and a force of their ten most hardened pursuivants came to Shakespeare's house in Seething Lane in the darkness half an hour before dawn.

They tethered their horses a street away, then trod softly toward the ancient house so that none should awake and alert Walsingham. There was to be no alarm, no uproar. This was to be done with precision and silence. Mr. Secretary must awake at dawn or after and be none the wiser of what had happened at his close neighbor's home.

The plan was to go in at lightning speed. Flatten the door with one blow from the battering tree, then advance *without* shouting or mayhem, each member of the force to take one room so that no occupants of the house should escape. Topcliffe looked around him. The street was empty. "Where, Dick, is your watchman? Who is guarding this house?" His voice was a gruff, urgent whisper.

Young looked around. "The idle fool must have gone home. I'll have strong words with him for this."

"God's blood, Dick, you'll flog him raw. Take his skin off. All right, let's go in."

Six men held the heavy tree trunk and swung back and forward once, then back again and brought it forward halfway up the door, close to the lock, crashing it down with one blow.

Topcliffe went in first, closely followed by Young. Then they stopped where they stood, mouths agape at the scene that confronted them.

The hallway was lit by torches and candles and the room was filled with men, twenty or so. Some stood, leaning on swords or holding bows. Others lay back against the walls. One or two puffed at pipes. All wore martial clothes, thick leather doublets like the pursuivants, and they all gazed on Topcliffe and Young with nonchalant disdain.

It was an eerie sight in the flickering light. It seemed that two platoons had suddenly come face to face, both armed and ready to fight, yet one of the armies — the one already there — could scarcely bother to stand up for the battle. Topcliffe at last found his voice. "Who are you?" he bellowed.

One of the men rose to his feet and sauntered forward until he was face to face with Topcliffe. He was a young man, perhaps early twenties, with a short, neatly trimmed beard and dark hair swept back about his ears. "No, sir, who are *you?* And what are you doing in my brother's house?"

Topcliffe spluttered, "You are Shakespeare's brother? What do you do here? I had not expected you!"

"My friends and I are lodging here, thanks to the kindness of my brother. We have been levied from Warwickshire to train with the London militias. We will soon be garrisoned at Tilbury for the defense of the realm, not that it is any of *your* business. And what, pray, *is* your business? It seems you are trespassing and have caused some criminal damage to my brother's door. Are you housebreakers? If so, I shall see you hang for it. It would behoove you well to think on this: my brother is a senior officer with Sir Francis Walsingham."

A vein pulsed in Topcliffe's forehead. He looked at Shakespeare's brother with undisguised rage, then at Richard Young. The magistrate looked nervous and nonplussed. "God in heaven, Dick! Why did your man not bring us word of this?"

Young threw up his hands in red-faced bewilderment. "I don't know, Richard. Perhaps he was afraid of these soldiers."

Topcliffe took in the room. He was outnumbered almost two to one. There was no hope of taking on a band of heavily armed and trained fighters. This was some trick of Shakespeare's, some stratagem to defeat him. "I don't know how this has come about, but I promise you, Shakespeare — you and your brother — that I will be back and you will both pay. I will bring down the wrath of God and Her Majesty on your head. And I *will* get that which I seek."

Shakespeare's brother was a steadfast man with bright eyes and a wide forehead, shorter but more powerfully built than John. His mouth curled into a slight smile. "I think, sir, you rise above your station invoking the deity and our glorious sovereign lady. I suggest you crawl back into your festering little hole and take your brother maggots with you before you are all squashed."

Topcliffe's rage nearly got the better of him. He drew back his hand to strike this impertinent pup on the face, then thought again. Churning inside with fury, he swung on his heel and strode to the gaping doorway. "Let us go, Dick," he said. "Let us unpluck your so-called watchman from his wife's sweaty thighs and give him a beating he will not readily forget."

One of Shakespeare's men sitting on the floor rose to his feet and dragged a cowering fellow up by the scruff. He kicked his breeches and sent him flying toward Topcliffe. "Is this your watchman? Take him. We don't want him."

CHAPTER 44

On arrival in London, Shakespeare rode with Boltfoot to Seething Lane, but instead of going into his house, he went straightway to Walsingham's office to report on the two failed attempts on Drake's life and, finally, the mariner's successful departure for the coastal waters of Spain.

Walsingham's dark brow lightened a shade. He nodded repeatedly. "That is good, that is excellent. You say he is well and that he has definitely left these shores with the fleet?"

"Yes, Sir Francis. All is as it should be."

Walsingham chuckled. "She sent a messenger after him, you know, with orders not to proceed with the mission. You are sure he did not receive these orders in time?"

"Well, if he did receive the Queen's orders, he certainly did not act on them. And he sent you this letter."

Walsingham carefully undid the seal with

a knife and read the brief missive. He folded it carefully and put it on the table. "This is good, John. This is exactly what I wanted. Thank the Lord the Queen's rider did not arrive in time. You have done well, you and Mr. Cooper between you."

Shakespeare allowed the warm glow of praise to wash over him. It did not last long.

"However, John, things are not so happy for you in other regards. A complaint has been laid against you, with certain serious allegations made . . ." Mr. Secretary looked at his chief intelligencer with accusing eyes.

Shakespeare felt the blood rising to his face. An image of Mother Davis and Isabella Clermont, then of Catherine Marvell, flashed across his thoughts.

"Allegations of lewdness, John, and of witchcraft. There is talk of a charge being laid."

"What are these accusations you speak of, Mr. Secretary? And who has made them?" Shakespeare frowned, as if in bewilderment.

"Are you sure you do not know?"

"I can think only Topcliffe."

Walsingham nodded gravely. He paced to the window and looked out on the street. He could just see Shakespeare's modest home farther up the way. It was quiet now, but he had heard rumors of a disturbance there. He turned back to Shakespeare. "Yes, of course. Topcliffe. I warned you, John. I warned you not to allow your personal disputes to disrupt our common cause. I even gave you a warrant to enter Topcliffe's home to interview a witness, did I not?"

"You did."

"And he allowed you to do so?"

"He did. I would say he reveled in showing me his instruments of torture. He seemed very proud of breaking Thomas Woode's body. A man not found guilty of any crime, nor even shown in court."

Walsingham never raged. He did not need to. His whisper was more intimidating than the bear's growl or the wildcat's roar. "John, this is not the time to debate such things. There are matters of more immediate import to concern us. Topcliffe lays this charge against you: that you did go to the sorceress and whoremonger Mother Davis. That you gave of your seed and your face hair to procure a love potion for a spell to ensnare a young woman named Catherine Marvell, a notorious Papist. These are serious charges and Topcliffe says he has possession of the foul items used for the potion." His eyes lifted to Shakespeare's forehead. "If none of this is true, how will you explain the loss of an eyebrow and the discovery of identical hair in the possession of Mother Davis and now in the keeping of Topcliffe? The seed cannot be proved as yours, but alongside your brow, a court would accept it as most compelling evidence. You must know the penalty for witchcraft. As the book of Exodus tells us, 'Thou shalt not suffer a witch to live . . .' "

For a moment, Shakespeare was speechless, then he erupted like a pot left too long to heat. "This is madness, Mr. Secretary! This is all Topcliffe's doing. Yes, I *did* talk with Mother Davis, but only as part of my investigations. Under duress, Walstan Glebe, the broadsheet publisher, informed me that Mother Davis knew details of the Howard killing and that she would contact me. This she did, so I went to see her. I was met by a French whore and taken to the Davis woman's presence. She gave me drink, but plainly it contained some witch's potion, for the next I knew I found myself being *used* most lewdly by the French whore. My arms and legs were fixed motionless, dead as though I had imbibed hemlock. Mother Davis showed me a vial with what she said was my seed and told me I was now hers, that I could never escape her. I fell into unconsciousness and when I next awoke the house was empty and in darkness. I discovered my eyebrow was missing, but I have no recollection of it being removed. That is all I know. Except this: I know Topcliffe was privy to this, because he boasted as such at his house in Westminster. I fear he and Mother Davis are confederates, Mr. Secretary. I would go further and say that I *know* it to be so. The whole charade was designed to ensnare me. The French whore said she was attacked by Southwell but it is not true; her injuries were superficial. It was all part of Topcliffe's plan to save his own neck and put the blame on the Jesuit."

Walsingham watched Shakespeare's face intently as he spoke. Finally he sighed. "This is grave news, John, grave news. You have been a fool, however righteous the cause. But on your behalf, I would say that your story is so preposterous it has the ring of verity about it."

"There is more," Shakespeare said. "Much more. The culprit we look for, the killer of Lady Blanche Howard, is none other than Topcliffe himself."

Walsingham rolled back on his heels. "Topcliffe killed Blanche Howard?"

"It is certain, Mr. Secretary."

"No, John, you cannot say such a thing. Be careful. Be very, very careful. You have made him an enemy already. I am trying to get the charges against you dropped, but if you start throwing wild allegations about, he will most assuredly proceed against you for witchcraft and lewdness. And I will be hard-pressed to defend you, for he will produce witnesses and take you before Justice Young. Of that you can be certain."

"So I am to be damned by the words of whores and murderers while a most cruel killer walks free — is that what you are saying? Is that the England you fight for, Sir Francis?" Even as he spoke the words, he realized he had made a mistake. Walsingham's loyalty to Queen and country was beyond questioning. He could not insult him so and emerge unscathed.

Yet Walsingham did not turn him out, nor did he react badly. Instead, his voice softened. He rang a bell to summon a servant. "Bring us brandy," he said. When the serving man had bowed and departed the room, Walsingham indicated Shakespeare to sit at the table and then took a chair close by himself. "Come, John," he said. "You are overheated and tired after your long journey and you have already rendered your country and Queen a great service. I will forget what you have just said and I will listen to you. If you have proof against Topcliffe, then tell me it. But then you must listen quietly to what *I* have to say."

Shakespeare told him everything: the detail of the crucifix and relic found in the corpse of Lady Blanche and then reported on, however obliquely, by Walstan Glebe in his *London Informer* broadsheet; the full squalid details of his visit to the house occupied by Mother Davis and her whores; the story of the blind monk Ptolomeus and the removal of his printing press by Topcliffe; the certainty that the seditious tract found at the burnt-out house in Hog Lane was printed on this press using paper from Rymesford Mill. "And lastly, there is the motive, Mr. Secretary. Topcliffe is possessed with the desire of a Bedlam madman to capture the Jesuit Robert Southwell. He will do anything to find this priest and bring him to his death. I contend that he believed Blanche, a new-converted Papist, had knowledge of Southwell's whereabouts. He knows only one way to extract information: torture. But he went too far and killed her and then had to cover up his crime. If you have doubts, Mr. Secretary, then talk with the Searcher of the Dead. Everything I have described fits in with Joshua Peace's findings."

Silence. Walsingham stroked his dark beard. His face hung as heavy as a beaten dog's. Finally he spoke. "John, you must listen to me very carefully now. You have had your say. I have heard you out and I must tell you that you do not have enough evidence. Consider, Richard Topcliffe is the Queen's favorite, he has control over the interrogations carried out in the Tower, he is so trusted in his fervor that he has a rack in his home, licensed by the Privy Council, he is Member of Parliament for Old Sarum, and, lastly, he is fighting in his own way for England. This is all fact. On your side, you have the word of a blind, decrepit monk and your own surmise. You have nothing —"

"But —"

"I said listen. You have nothing, John, and that should be the end of the matter. However, you have done an immense work these past days for me and for England. You have saved Drake to set sail against the Spanish armada. I will ignore this sordid gossip about you and some Popish woman named Marvell, for I am sure you would not be so foolish as to embroil yourself with such a person. But I will allow you leeway. You may take your information to Topcliffe and use it against him to secure your own future. Some might call it blackmail; I would call it a trade. You let him know that if he does not drop all charges against you, then you will proceed to tell all you know to Lord Howard of Effingham. That will give Topcliffe pause for thought. He knows that Howard, in his turn, will take your allegations direct to Her Majesty. And that is surely the last thing Mr. Topcliffe wants."

"Why can I not just go straight to Howard?"

"Because John, you will end up dancing at Tyburn and Topcliffe will retire wounded to his estate. And that is not an option that would suit me or you. I need you, John. Just as I need Topcliffe."

John Shakespeare looked around his hall in astonishment. "William? Why are you here? And who, pray, are these soldiers?"

"They are company players, the Queen's Men, and I have joined them, for they were short a man. We are soon to play at the Theatre in Shoreditch, but I think we have already given a fine performance."

"You will have to explain more clearly." Distracted, Shakespeare could think of little save his talk with Walsingham and how to act upon it.

"We have been playing the soldier, John. Do we not look the part?"

"Indeed you do." Shakespeare smiled weakly and at last embraced his brother with his one good arm. He stood back and looked him full in the face. They had not seen each other in two years.

William clapped his hands, and as if waiting for the signal, Jane and Catherine descended the stairway, each holding the hand of one of Thomas Woode's children. Jane and the children were smiling, but not Catherine.

"Topcliffe was coming for them, John," his brother told him. "Jane went out, ostensibly to market, and found me at the Theatre. I came with my friends. Topcliffe battered down the door to get at Mistress Marvell, and the children, but was confronted with us instead. We had been rehearsing for a history with battle scenes and were able to raid the costume box for this attire and the prop box for our weapons. Luckily, we did not need them, for the swords are as blunt as sheep's teeth. Had Topcliffe known we were but players rather than fighting men, he might not have been turned away so readily. But as it was, we had a merry time and shooed him and his cohorts off. I fear, though, that we are out of pocket. The play should have been staged by now."

Shakespeare was not listening. He had eyes only for Catherine and approached her slowly, as in a dream, across the hall. He wanted to take her in his arms but he was conscious of all the people around him. She let slip the hand of little Grace and touched hands with Shakespeare. She saw the sling that held his injured arm, but said nothing of it. She was pale, stiff with tension, and distraught.

"Catherine, I have longed to see you."

"And I you, John. But I can think of nothing but Master Woode. What has become of him?"

Thomas Woode was at the heart of this outrage. Yet how could that be righted with all that Shakespeare knew of him? The gift of an illicit press to a renegade priest, the harboring of Jesuits. There was enough there to hang Woode twice over, and Shakespeare could bear witness against him. But he would not, for Catherine would be implicated, too. And perhaps for another reason: because it would be wrong for the merchant to suffer more, after all he had been through in Topcliffe's strong room. "I am going to Topcliffe this day. I will do what I can." Even as he spoke these words he realized he risked giving her vain hope. There was every chance Woode was already dead. He moved forward, but she flinched and held back. This was not the time, he realized, nor the proper company.

His brother broke into his somber thoughts. "We must away, brother. We have a play to perform for the *paying* public. But before we go, we have a matter that concerns you."

"What matter?"

"The matter of four members of our company who are sorely missed. They arrived here in London ahead of us to ready the Theatre for our coming. After much investigating, we discovered they were taken by *you* while sleeping in a barn."

Shakespeare was puzzled. He knew nothing of any players. "What manner of men are these, pray?"

"You deemed them worthless vagabonds and sent them to Bridewell. They had been near the scene of an infamous murder, I am told, and were considered possible witnesses by you. And now they have disappeared."

Shakespeare felt a stab of shame. "God in Heaven! Yes, of course I do remember them. They were removed from my custody by Topcliffe's men. I tried to find them but could not. I had not realized they were players . . ."

"And does that make a difference in this brave England, John? Are you not thought worthy of protection under the law if you are a mere beggar? Does a player have more justice than a vagabond, or is a knight of the realm better served by jury than a glover's son?"

"William, I am sorry. I will do what I can."

CHAPTER 45

The meeting started badly. They stood facing each other at the forbidding entrance to Topcliffe's home in Westminster. Shakespeare and Boltfoot on the outside, Topcliffe and his boy Jones within the doorway, standing foursquare like bulldogs guarding their territory.

When Topcliffe spoke, it was in a growl. "Mr. Secretary told me you might arrive here, Shakespeare. How fares your Catholic whore? Does she know you have been a jack-sauce with the beguiling Mam'selle Clermont? It is my bounden duty to inform her, I think . . ."

Shakespeare's hand went to his sword hilt, but Boltfoot, whose caliver hung loosely in his arms, restrained him.

"Hah, Cooper! That won't save your master's life. He is at my mercy. And I will see him hang before the week is out."

"No, Topcliffe." Shakespeare shook his

head. "*You* will hang. I know what you have done and I have witnesses. You took Lady Blanche Howard and tortured her because you thought she could lead you to Robert Southwell, the Jesuit. You killed her. . . ."

Nicholas Jones, the apprentice, sniggered.

Topcliffe's arm lashed out and caught Jones full in the face. The boy reeled backwards, blood gushing from his nose. "Stow you, Nick." Jones wiped his filthy sleeve across his face to staunch the blood. He seemed to shrink into his shoulders, like a whipped dog.

"I have all the evidence I need, Topcliffe," said Shakespeare. "Only you could have printed those tracts found at Hog Lane, because *you* were the one in possession of the press."

"That isn't evidence! Who will listen to a dead monk?"

"Ptolomeus is very much alive."

Topcliffe laughed and clapped an arm around the shoulder of Jones. "Is he, now? What do you say, Nick?"

Jones managed to snigger again, though he snorted a spray of blood in the process. He drew a finger slowly across his throat, then flicked it up theatrically toward the ear. "Squealed like a little piglet. I would never have thought a Popish devil would

have so much blood in him, Master Topcliffe." He dabbed at his nose with his sleeve
again and wiped away more blood.

Shakespeare felt a stab of overwhelming
guilt. He should not have left the old monk
to such a fate. But how could he have
known that Topcliffe would return to finish
him off, and in the circumstances, what
could he have done? The only comfort was
that Ptolomeus had clearly been longing for
death; the sadness was the cruel manner of
its arrival. "Trust me, I have enough evidence of your crimes without Ptolomeus.
And I will take it to one who will listen:
Howard of Effingham."

The smile froze on Topcliffe's mouth. He
raised a hand and made an indecisive chop-
ping motion with it, as if he was about to
make a point but had suddenly become lost
as to what that point should be. Shakespeare
saw that he had hit home; that Topcliffe
could see instantly that such a course of action would make things not just difficult for
him, but impossible. The Queen might feign
ignorance of the horrors he did in her name,
but she would not ignore her cousin Charles
Howard, particularly not in relation to the
death of Lady Blanche.

"I see you are lost for words, Topcliffe.
Who *now* has the other at his mercy, pray?"

"I could kill you this very moment."

"You could try, but I doubt that you would succeed. Mr. Cooper is quite handy with cutlass and caliver, as you must know."

Topcliffe stood frozen, disdain writ all across his face. When he spoke, his voice dripped scorn. "Your problem, Shakespeare, is that you are young. You do not have the stench of burning Protestant flesh in your nostrils. You weren't there in the fifties when Bloody Mary and her Spanish droop were burning good Englishmen and women in the name of the Antichrist. All these Papists know is brutality. It is all they respect, so if they poke out your eye you must poke out both theirs, and their mother's and child's."

"So what you do is better, is it, Topcliffe?"

"It is God's will, Shakespeare. That is all. God and Her Majesty. All right, enough. What do you want? Why are you here?"

What Shakespeare wanted and what Mr. Secretary would allow him were two very different things. He wanted Topcliffe taken off the streets, hanged preferably or, at the very least, locked away where he could never again harm anyone. But he had to settle for another trade. The words stuck in his craw to say, but he took a deep breath and laid out his terms. "You will return what is mine, taken from me most foully by your witch familiar Davis; you will never venture to my house again, nor will you molest or interfere with Mistress Catherine Marvell, nor the children in her care, nor my maidservant; you will release Master Thomas Woode this day; and you will tell me where you have brought the four vagabonds from Hog Lane so that they may be given their freedom. In return for these boons, I will not reveal to her family your murderous cruelty toward Lady Blanche Howard. I have, however, left a deposition with a certain lawyer, who will take it immediately to Lord Howard of Effingham should any accident befall me. Do you understand all this?"

"Curse you, Shakespeare, you Rome-squealing little clerk! It seems you have me strapped over a cask."

"It seems that way, does it not?"

Suddenly Topcliffe barked a laugh. "What think you, Nick?" he said to his apprentice. "Do *you* think I can be frighted so easy?" Then he turned back to Shakespeare. "And what would you want with the four Irish clapperdudgeon vagabonds anyway? Perchance you fancy playing girl-boys with one of them? Now you have acquired a taste for Papism and bitchery —"

"They are Crown witnesses and you have cloyed them away illegally."

Topcliffe shook his head. "Nothing illegal about it. I got the mittimus from Mr. Justice Young, magistrate of London. They languish in one of London's most stinking holes. If you can find them, you can have them. As for the traitor Woode, there isn't much left of him to hand over, so I think I'll just hold on to him a little longer. As I recall, the warrant from Mr. Justice Young does allow me yet seven days before I need to bring him to court."

"Then you leave me no option. I will go straightway to Deptford to consult with the Admiral of the Fleet, Lord Howard of Effingham."

"Do that, Shakespeare! You have no evidence against me, not a shred, and you will find yourself in front of the magistrate for lewdness and sorcery before ever I face a court. I will piss on you while you swing."

The door slammed shut. Shakespeare stood in the street shaking. Above him the majesty of Westminster Abbey soared. There seemed to be hope in the air, yet on the cobbled stones there was none. A killer would walk free to stalk London, taking and torturing at will while he, Shakespeare, faced an uncertain future.

Boltfoot Cooper slung his caliver back over his shoulder. "It is time to meet fire with fire, master."

His words knocked Shakespeare from his dark trance. "What is that, Boltfoot?"

"I will hunt down the vagabonds. If need be, I will visit every one of London's fourteen gaols and break down the gates to find them. And you must find the Davis witch and her whore."

"Thank you, Boltfoot. It is good that one of us thinks clearly this day."

As they moved away in the bright spring sunshine, Shakespeare noticed a young woman, fair of face and light-haired, walking toward Topcliffe's door. She was carrying a bundle that he thought to be a baby.

Shakespeare hired a tiltboat from Westminster stairs downstream to St. Mary Overy stairs, then walked a half mile to the street where he had been lured by Mother Davis and Isabella Clermont. He was aware he was being followed by Topclife's apprentice, Jones, and another man, more powerfully built. Shakespeare knew he had little time; Topcliffe would get the magistrate Young to issue an arrest warrant in very short order. Languishing in Newgate, Shakespeare would be helpless to do anything for Catherine or Thomas Woode.

The house in which he had encountered

Mother Davis and her whore stood dark and empty, its windows shuttered and its doors locked. A poster was pasted on the bolted doorway announcing that the building was available to let. As Shakespeare looked up at the blank windows, Jones and his companion jeered at him. "Looking for a wench, Shakespeare? How about a juicy blackamoor? Or you can have my sister for half a crown. She'll spur you on."

A warehouseman passed, pushing along a small handcart, top-heavy with bulging jute sacks. Shakespeare stopped him.

"Whose building is this?" He handed him a penny.

The man, grateful to put down the handles of the cart, looked over at Jones and the other man. "They friends of yours?"

"Anything but."

"Good. I've seen that sniveling little one round here before and I don't like the looks of him. This fine building belonged to a Spanish gentleman, sir. Imported wines from Portugal and beyond. I sometimes helped him when a ship came in. But he was discovered helping Romish priests, sir, and was flung out of the country, back where he belongs."

"And now?"

"And now it does stand empty, sir, awaiting another occupant."

"Does it ever get used?"

"Not to my knowledge, sir. It was declared forfeit by the court."

"Who has the keys?"

"That would be the new owner, sir. One Richard Topcliffe of Westminster, a famous priest-hunter, who has made himself exceeding rich, people say, by drawing the innards from young papists." The young warehouseman laughed.

It was another dead end. Topcliffe had given Davis the key to the building to set her trap for Shakespeare. He had just one more hope. Walking quickly westward along the bank of the Thames, still followed, he made his way to the Clink prison, a long two-story stone building one street back from the river and close to the London residence of the Bishop of Winchester.

Street traders with baskets of pies, cakes, bread, and roasted fowls were busy selling lunch to the prisoners who clustered on the other side of the iron-barred windows, stretching out their hands through the narrow gaps with coins to pay for the food. There was a lot of shouting and bargaining. Shakespeare banged on the heavy door. The turnkey, a small man with cadaverous cheeks and a tongue that continually licked his lips like a serpent, looked at him suspiciously. Shakespeare demanded to see Starling Day and Parsimony Field on Queen's business.

The turnkey leered at him. "They are here, young gentleman, but it'll cost you two shillings to consort with them. Those harlots can charge what they likes, but I want my two shillings first."

"Did you not hear me, gaoler? I said I am on Queen's business."

"And if you will just pay me two shillings, you can join them in lust and it will be worth every last groat to you." Angrily, Shakespeare handed over two shillings. Jones was right behind him in the street and he wanted to get away from him. The other pursuer had gone, probably to take word to Topcliffe and Young. "You do realize, gaoler, that you could very well lose your license for demanding money and turning this gaol into a bawdy house? I am like to report you to the Liberty of Clink for your dealings."

"As you please, sir. And do you think they will do anything that might come between them and their own garnish?" He looked over Shakespeare's shoulder at Jones. "Will you be bringing your young friend, too? Give me another shilling and he can have admittance as well."

Shakespeare handed the gaoler two shillings more. "This is to *not* give him admittance, turnkey. Keep him locked out at all costs."

"As you wish, master. As you wish." The gaoler grasped Shakespeare by the arm of his doublet and yanked him in, pulling the four-inch thick, fortified door closed just as Jones thrust his lower right leg into the gap. The boy yelled with pain as the heavy wood cracked on the side of his knee.

Shakespeare found Starling and Parsimony living like merchants' wives in the best cells in the Clink, two large rooms, next to each other, with feather beds and a goodly supply of wine and food.

"Ah, Mr. Shakespeare, sir," Starling called. "What is your pleasure this fine day? You will see we are well settled in here, happy as two bees in honey."

Shakespeare looked about her cell with some amazement. She had set it up as well as any room to be found in a luxurious trugging house or inn. There were wax candles burning all about and fine linen on the bed. Starling herself looked well fed and rosy cheeked. "I can see you are well provided for here, Mistress Day, but I have come to set you free. On one condition: that you tell me the whereabouts of a whore called Isabella Clermont and her procuress, one Mother Davis."

"Sorry, ducks, never heard of them. Try Parsey. She knows all the game girls."

Parsimony's door was shut. She was just finishing off with a customer. Two minutes later the door opened and a red-faced, well-fed man emerged. He wore expensive courtier's clothes, which he was busy adjusting. He briefly caught Shakespeare's eye and hastily looked away. Parsimony held the door open. "Come in, Mr. Shakespeare, come in. This is a fine vaulting house you sent us to. A wondrous place full of gentlemen of fine birth."

The room was every bit as well appointed as Starling's. "I have come to offer you a deal that will lead to your freedom, Mistress Field."

She laughed. "I am well set up already, sir. And I have forgiven you for sending us here. I suppose we met in difficult circumstances, Mr. Shakespeare. It was a sad day that the lovely Harry Slide was done for. God rest his soul. Harry Slide knew how to make a girl happy. Attended to *our* pleasures as well as his own, which is uncommon in a man of any breeding. He was a good friend."

Starling noted Shakespeare's impatience.

"He's looking for a couple of Winchester geese, Parsey, and he's in a hurry."

"I need to find Mother Davis and Isabella Clermont. Do you know of them?"

Parsimony turned pale. "Know of them? I know of Mother Witch, Mr. Shakespeare. Don't go near her. That woman consorts with demons and Satan himself. She is succubus and incubus and every worm with sharpened teeth and poisoned talons in hell."

"You have had dealings with her?"

"Oh, yes, I've had dealings. She snatched two of our best girls when I was with Gilbert Cogg. Took them in broad daylight and shacked them up with her own lice-crawling punks. That's not right. By the time we found out where they were, they both had the pox, their paps had shrunk from lack of food, they had rat bites on their legs and arms. Looked as appetizing to a man as a baggage of foul-smelling bones. Those girls were worthless to us, sir. Worthless."

"I need to find her."

"And what do I get in return?"

"Your freedom . . . and vengeance on Davis?"

"And the lease back on our house of entertainment?"

"If at all possible. I can't give you any

money."

"Just vouch for us, Mr. Shakespeare."

Shakespeare felt uneasy. But what option did he have? "All right," he agreed. "If you lead me to her, I'll do what I can."

Parsimony smiled. She had nice white teeth. "That witch is like smoke," she told him. "But I will give you a place to try, sir. . . ."

CHAPTER 46

There was a locked door at the back of the gaol into a yard, then more doors through outhouses. The gaoler unlocked them and showed Shakespeare the way into a long, muddy garden, where a pair of pigs were rutting energetically.

At the end of the garden was an eight-foot-high wall. The gaoler thrust an apple-tree ladder into Shakespeare's arms.

Shakespeare scaled the wall easily. There was no sign of Jones. He began loping through the streets away from the Clink, eastward. He was heading for London Bridge to get north of the river. As he ran onto the bridge, he felt the deathly gaze of the traitors' heads bearing down on him from their pikes atop the gatehouse. The heads were boiled in brine so that they might last many months as a warning to others.

Parsimony had mentioned a house in Billiter Lane, not far from his own home in Seething Lane. It was not the sort of place you would expect to find a sorceress and her whores, for it was the heart of the City, an expensive street where traders and their fur-clad wives resided. But perhaps that was the attraction of the area for Mother Davis; she could affect the ways of the wealthy there and gain anonymity.

Past Fen Church, he trotted along the broad sweep of Blanch Appleton. His heart pounded; his lungs dragged harshly at the air. To his left he noticed the huge works that were being carried out on Ironmongers' Hall. Enormous cranes of oak and elm with dangling ropes and pulleys towered over the skeletal structure.

He turned into Billiter Lane and stopped in his tracks. Ahead of him, like a wall of steel and black leather, stood twenty pursuivants, swords drawn, wheel-locks armed and pointed along the street toward him.

For a moment he stood frozen, scarcely comprehending what he saw. He turned to run the other way, but his face met the fist of the chief pursuivant Newall full on. Shakespeare's legs buckled and he fell into the muddy ditch in the center of the street. Then his temple was hit by another blow, delivered by a silver-topped blackthorn, and darkness fell.

He awoke into gloom. His skull hurt in a way it had never hurt before. A heavy, insistent throbbing that made death seem preferable to life. He tried to move and realized his feet were fettered in cramp-rings, fixed solidly into the ground. He was in a cell, lit by a tallow candle in a black iron wall sconce. He looked up and saw Nicholas Jones, Topcliffe's apprentice, smirking at him. "Thought you could get away from Jonesy, did you?" The boy had a pipe in his mouth and belched fumes as he taunted him. "We've got some laughs and merriment in store for you, John Shakespeare, I'll tell you that for nothing. You wait there and I'll just go and tell Mr. Topcliffe that you've come around. No strolling off now . . ." He took the pipe from his mouth and tapped the burning sotweed and ashes over Shakespeare's head.

Shakespeare longed to shake his head to rid himself of the hot embers, but he did not have the strength. His vision came in drifts like snow in the wind.

He collapsed once more into nothingness.

When he woke again, Shakespeare knew he was in a dream. Above him were the warm oak beams of his bedroom ceiling. Sunshine flooded in through the window across the bed in which he lay. He turned his head and winced with pain. At his side, on a three-legged stool, sat Jane, his maidservant.

"Master Shakespeare?"

"Jane? Is that really you?"

"You are awake at last."

He closed his eyes. A feeling of immense fatigue enveloped him. Had he dreamed the time in the cell watched by Jones? Some wicked nightmare? An incursion by demons?

"How long have I been here, Jane?"

"Three days and three nights, master. Thank the Lord you are with us. We feared you might never wake. The blow to your head . . ."

"How did I get here?"

Jane reached out and held his hand. "You were brought here on a cart by Mr. Secretary Walsingham's men. Don't talk now. Let me bring you some light food and drink."

As he came more awake, he became aware of his body: various regions throbbed with a dull ache — his arm where it had been cut by Herrick's blade, his beaten face, his temple. "Walsingham's men brought me here? I believed I was in a cell, held by Richard Topcliffe."

Jane stood from the stool and fussed

around him, smoothing his bedclothes and plumping his bolster beneath his head. "Sir, you have not eaten for three days or more. The physician said you must keep still when you have come around and take food and drink slowly."

Shakespeare raised himself on his elbows. "Jane, enough. I am not a baby to be coddled. Tell me what I need to know."

"You *were* held by Topcliffe, Master Shakespeare. We feared the worst. But Boltfoot went to Mr. Secretary Walsingham and he straightway sent his men with a warrant to free you. When you were brought here, you looked no better than a corpse, sir, covered in blood and filth. Your breathing was so faint I could scarce detect it."

Shakespeare tried to collect his thoughts. He recalled his dash from the Clink to Billiter Lane, coming face to face with the pursuivants, the brutish blow to the face and the crack on the head. Then nothing, except lightning glimpses of Topcliffe's torture room and of Nicholas Jones, his infernal boy.

"Is Catherine here?"

Jane busied herself opening the casement window. "Not at the moment, master, no."

"Where, then, is she?"

Jane's eyes were still averted. She looked

out over the little garden at the rear of the house. Birdsong filtered in through the open window. "She is at her master's home in Dowgate, sir. She has left a letter for you." She handed it to Shakespeare, then hurriedly made for the door.

"No, Jane, wait here."

Shakespeare carefully opened the seal with the knife that always lay on the table beside his bed. The letter, in a fair hand of well-formed writing, was not long but it seemed to take him an age to read.

John, If you are reading this letter, I know that you are recovered, for which I give thanks to God that our prayers have been answered. Yet there is no happy ending to this story. I do not have words adequately to explain how it sorrows me to write you this letter. My master, Thomas Woode, is now at home in Dowgate and I must go to him with his children. He is broken. He cannot walk, nor can he raise his arms and hands even to feed himself. He has been close to death and will never be whole again. I must be nurse to him as well as mother and governess to Andrew and Grace. It is my Christian duty so to do.

You know my love for you, John. You

can have no doubt. For a few short hours we were as one, and I shall, at least, always have memories of that night. But I cannot be yours for their need is greater than ours. Do not be angry with me, nor come after me to Dowgate. I could not bear the pain of saying goodbye to you again.

John, your efforts have brought about the release of my master, for which I thank you. I regret many of the things I said to you and know you to be a good man. I must also thank Jane and your brother and his company, and I will write to them all, for they undoubtedly saved me and the children from a terrible fate.

Forgive me, John.

Yours, in the love of Christ,
Catherine.

After a while, Shakespeare looked up from the letter. He breathed shallowly. "Do you know what is in this letter, Jane?"

"Yes, master." Her voice was choked and she would still not look at him.

"Do you think there is any hope that she might change her mind?"

Jane shook her head. Her tears flowed and she could not speak.

"None?"

She shook her head once again.

"Thank you, Jane. You may go."

She ran from his chamber. He heard her howling like a wounded animal as she ran down the stairs. He crumpled the letter into a tight ball and threw it to the floor. Moments later, he slipped tentatively from between the sheets. He felt unsteady, but he was able to walk across the room and pick up the crushed paper. He took it to the window, where he smoothed it out and read it once more.

CHAPTER 47

"What word from Drake?" Walsingham demanded.

"None. There is nothing as yet, neither good nor bad," John Hawkins replied. "That is how we would wish it."

Walsingham looked unconvinced. "That is not how *I* would wish it, Mr. Hawkins. I would wish to hear that Drake has sailed your ships into Lisbon and set fire to this Spanish armada before it can leave port, for assuredly we are not ready to repel it."

The room was silent. All those sitting around the long table in the library of his house in Seething Lane knew the truth of what he said. England's defenses were woefully inadequate. Should Spain's battle-hardened troops ever land in Sussex or Kent or Essex, they would sweep past the Queen's new-formed militias and descend on London like lions. There would be bloodletting in the fields and towns of England on a scale not known in five hundred years.

Around the table sat Hawkins, architect of the new Navy, Walsingham himself, his secretaries Arthur Gregory and Francis Mills, codebreaker Thomas Phelippes, and John Shakespeare.

"Well, at least we have got him to sea," Walsingham said at last, breaking the silence. "For which we must thank Mr. Shakespeare."

All those at the table nodded in Shakespeare's direction. Mills put his hands together, as if applauding at the playhouse.

"But Mr. Mills, I worry more than somewhat about your intelligence gathering . . ."

Mills reddened. "You do, Mr. Secretary?"

"Indeed, I do. When last this group was convened — *sans* Mr. Hawkins — you gave a report on the events surrounding the murder of William the Silent at Delft. In the main, it was helpful and accurate, but there was one detail which I now know to be dangerously inaccurate. In truth, I would go so far as to call it false and misleading; I sincerely hope not deliberately so. You said that the assassin Balthasar Gérard had an associate and you gave intelligence, purportedly from Holland, that this unnamed man was known for his beating of whores and that he had battered one to death, mutilating her body with religious symbols. Pray, where did you get this information?"

Mills spluttered, seemingly lost for words. His sharp little eyes widened in something like panic as the eyes of all the others in the room lighted on him. "Why, my contacts in the Dutch network, Mr. Secretary."

Walsingham shook his head grimly. "I have taken the liberty of contacting the authorities in Delft and Rotterdam. They do not support your information. Yes, they were certain Balthasar Gérard had a confederate, but there was no suggestion of a link with the murdered woman. What they did find was that this confederate of Gérard was a flagellant and that he employed prostitutes to scourge him. At no time was he known to return the favor. Nor were there religious symbols carved into the body of the woman who died."

"I . . . I do not understand. That was my information."

"Are you certain, Mr. Mills, that you did not receive that information closer to home? From Mr. Topcliffe or his associates, perchance?"

Mills was cornered. Shakespeare watched him. The encounter held the same brutal fascination as a bear-baiting when one of the great bears, Sackerbuts or Hunks, had a dog in its grip, breaking its back between the immense power of its paws. Mills conceded defeat. The Secretary nodded. "He told me he had contacts in Holland that had told him this, master. I confess I should have made certain."

"You should, Mr. Mills, also have wondered *why* Mr. Topcliffe sought you out to bring you this information. It is scarce within his remit." Walsingham turned to Shakespeare. "Do you not agree, John? I think your job might have been a little easier without this false trail laid."

"My apologies," Mills said. He pushed back his chair and stood. "Mr. Topcliffe told me he had certain information on this matter from a priest he had interrogated, but he said I must not divulge that he was the source. It was unforgivable of me to pass on this information without checking or at least explaining its provenance. Please accept my resignation, Mr. Secretary. I have failed you and must accept your derision."

"No, Mr. Mills, I will not accept your resignation. But I will accept your apologies. And I trust Mr. Shakespeare will, too. Let us all learn from this. The *accuracy* of our intelligence is paramount. We must question every scrap of information that comes to us and examine the motives of those from whom it comes. And you must *always* divulge your sources to me. The fate of our nation depends on it. I leave it to all of you to make your own deductions as to Mr. Topcliffe's motives in this case. Now then, let us consider other related matters. Firstly, the question of John Doughty, the brother of Thomas Doughty who was executed by Drake on that far-off shore all those years ago. We know John Doughty had his own plot against Drake, that he wanted revenge for his brother's death, not to mention a twenty-thousand-ducats reward from Philip of Spain. John Doughty was caught and ended up in the Marshalsea. But no one seemed to know what happened to him next, and I believe Mr. Shakespeare wondered whether he might somehow be at large and involved in this most recent plot. Well, I think we can now put everyone's mind to rest on this matter. Mr. Gregory, if you will . . ."

Arthur Gregory stood just as Francis Mills slowly sat down, glad to have the eyes of those present focused elsewhere. Gregory smiled and spoke slowly, trying to cover his stammer as best he could. "I made further inquiries. It s-s-seems John Doughty was taken from the Mar-sh-sh-shalsea to Newgate to await execution s-s-some four years past. This sh-should, of course, have been registered in the Marshalsea's Black Book, but wasn't. Doughty then cheated the hangman by dying of the bloody flux. A mundane end to a sm-sm-small, resentful man. It s-seems fitting that no one knew, nor cared, what had happened to him. Anyway, the one thing we do know is that he played no part in this most recent affair."

Walsingham took over. "So we are left with two men: a Fleming going by a variety of names, including Herrick, and a treacherous sea captain named Harper Stanley. The first of these, Herrick, certainly fits the description of Balthasar Gérard's associate from Delft. I am convinced he was the 'dragon slayer' sent here by Mendoza and Philip to assassinate the Vice Admiral, and he came mighty close to succeeding on at least two occasions. I suspect that we will never know more about him, but that does not worry me. I do not wish to make a martyr of Herrick, which is why I believe Mr. Shakespeare was correct to leave him in Plymouth for trial and execution. As far as I am concerned, the fewer people who ever learn of this attempt on Drake's life, the better. We want our Vice Admiral to be invincible and heroic in the minds of our people. His strength gives us all strength."

"What of Captain Stanley?" Shakespeare put in. "Do we know aught of him?"

Walsingham looked to his codebreaker. "I took the liberty of asking Mr. Phelippes to make a few inquiries while you were recovering, Mr. Shakespeare."

Phelippes breathed on the lenses of his glasses, then wiped them clean on the sleeve of his shirt. The glass was scratched and almost opaque from endless buffings. He did not stand to speak. "Indeed I did. He changed his name to Stanley from Percy. We should have spotted him a long time ago. I talked to some of his brother officers and discovered he was an habitué of the French embassy. Stanley told friends that there was a French gentlewoman there with whom he was intimately acquainted. He came and went at will. I then recalled some intercepted letters from the embassy to Mendoza detailing ship movements. We could never work out who sent them. Those letters were exceeding damaging to England, betraying positions and strengths of our fleet. When Drake or Mr. Hawkins was at sea, Mendoza would know of it within days. I have now compared the hand used in these missives with Captain Stanley's hand, in his papers. They are identical. We believe he sold these secrets for the money

609

and out of resentment for the punishments and disgrace inflicted on his family after the Northern Rebellion eighteen years past. I also believe there is a probability he was linked to the man we are calling Herrick. My theory — and it is no more than such, I am afraid — is that Stanley told Mendoza four or five months ago that if he sent a hired killer, he would provide the assassin with assistance in weapons and access to the Vice Admiral. In the end, when it seemed the plot would fail, he decided to take matters into his own hands. Fortunately, Drake's companion Diego and Mr. Boltfoot Cooper stood between him and success."

Walsingham cleared his throat. "So there we have it. Drake has been saved. For the moment. But keep vigilant and work hard to discover conspiracies in the dunghills of London. This will not be the last of Mendoza's plots on behalf of his prince. Say your prayers, gentlemen, every morning and every evening and ofttimes in between, for truly it is in God's hands now whether England lives or dies." As the assembled rose to leave, Walsingham raised his index finger to Shakespeare. "You stay, Mr. Shakespeare."

When they were alone, Walsingham offered Shakespeare refreshment then began pacing the room, his hands clasped behind his back. Shakespeare watched him in silence. At last Mr. Secretary spoke.

"There is one final matter, John, of which I thought it best to speak with you alone. The matter of Robert Southwell, the Jesuit priest. You haven't found him yet . . . have you?"

"No, Sir Francis," Shakespeare said instantly. He had rehearsed this moment in his mind. Perhaps he *had* met Southwell, but if so he could never be sure, for the priest had never admitted his name.

"Topcliffe believes you *did* meet him. He believes he was harbored by Thomas Woode and his governess, Catherine Marvell, and that you somehow colluded with them."

"That is not true. I have colluded with no one."

"Yet if you did find this Jesuit, you would tell me, would you not?"

"Indeed I would, Mr. Secretary."

"And if you thought that Woode and Mistress Marvell were harboring Jesuit priests, you would tell me that, too?"

"I am sure they are not harboring Jesuit priests, Mr. Secretary."

Walsingham raised a dark eyebrow. "Interesting phrasing, John. The present tense.

Surely you are not learning the Romish art of equivocation?"

"Mr. Secretary?"

Walsingham picked up a paper from the table. "I will let it pass. This time. But you must not deal lightly with these Jesuits, John. This Southwell is our bitter enemy." He showed the paper to Shakespeare. "You see there is a verse here. It is by Southwell. Read it, John, though it turn your stomach. You see he calls Mary of Scots a saint and a rose and a martyr. This is the woman who worked for the death of our beloved sovereign, and he calls her saint."

Shakespeare read the verse. Was this the man he'd met in the knot garden? How had he written such a thing? Surely even Roman Catholics must know Mary Stuart for a scheming murderess?

Walsingham took the paper back from him. "Enough. I will just tell you that this Thomas Woode is known to my intelligencers in Rome, where he has been a generous benefactor of the English college. Let us now speak of other things. Tell me, John, I believe there is a fondness between you and Mistress Marvell? Is that correct?"

Shakespeare breathed deeply. "There *was* a fondness, sir."

"It is finished?"

Shakespeare nodded again; he could not speak.

Walsingham's voice softened. "I am sorry. But it is for the best, John. I understand your sorrow, but it is for the best. Trust me on this; such attachments cannot survive in the present climate, not while you do the vital work you do, not while suspicion and sedition lurk in the shadows . . ."

Shakespeare wanted to shout that it was not for the best, that his heart was broken. He wanted to shout that he would rather be a schoolteacher and married to Catherine than do this job and be without her. But no words would form in his throat.

Walsingham saw his distress and poured wine. "We will talk no more about it. You must have a few days away from your toiling, John. I believe your brother has arrived; spend some time with him if you wish. You have suffered injuries; make yourself whole. But before you take your well-earned rest — and your ride to Plymouth and all that ensued was, indeed, magnificent and much admired by Her Majesty — I have one more task for you. I want you to go to Lord Howard of Effingham and tell him you have solved the murder of his daughter. You are to tell him that the killer was a man called Herrick, who is now executed for that murder and for the attempted murder of Sir Francis Drake."

At last, Shakespeare found his voice. "You are asking me to say something that we both know to be a lie, Mr. Secretary. We both know who killed Lady Blanche Howard."

Walsingham's face tightened. "Do this for me, John. I have had to make excuses for you; I have gone up against a man beloved of our Queen to save you from the weight of the law. We must do unpleasant things sometimes to protect ourselves from an infinitely greater evil. Which of us would be spared by the Inquisition should the Spanish prevail? The answer is none. We seek only those who sow discord. So you will do this thing for me and I promise you that Mr. Thomas Woode and Mistress Catherine Marvell will never be threatened or molested by Richard Topcliffe again. Do you understand?"

Shakespeare nodded.

"Then do it today, John. And God go with you."

CHAPTER 48

Boltfoot Cooper looked uncommonly awkward. He held his cap between his gnarled hands and twisted it as if he were wringing the neck of a fowl.

Shakespeare studied him quizzically. "Tell me, Boltfoot, what happened with your inquiries into the whereabouts of the four vagabonds from Hog Lane?"

"I have discovered them and set them free."

"Really, Boltfoot? That is wonderful news. Pray, where were they?"

"Still in Bridewell, master."

"In Bridewell!"

"They were in none of the other prisons, so I went back there. As I questioned the turnkey he looked increasingly uncomfortable, guilty even. In the end I threatened him with the might of Mr. Secretary — and yourself, of course — and he broke down all afraid and confessed they were still there.

Newall had ordered him to say they had gone. I think it probable there was some garnish involved in the transaction, though the turnkey denies it."

"What! I shall have that cheating, dissembling gaoler up before the aldermen for this. He insisted to me that they had been taken away to another prison. But what of the four men; what is their condition?"

"Poor, master. They had been flogged, set to work stripping oakum, and were half-starved. But all are alive and will recover from their tribulations. I have returned them, well fed and watered, to their company."

"And did you question them about what they witnessed on the night of the fire?"

"I did, and they swear they saw nothing except the fire itself. The chiefest among the four told me that when they saw the fire they rushed to help. They carried pails for two hours until it was doused, then, exhausted, they went to sleep in the stable block. They said it was warmer there than at the Theatre."

"So they did not see a body taken to the house in Hog Lane?"

"No, master."

"And they knew nothing of Lady Blanche?"

Boltfoot shook his head. "Nor did they see anything at all suspicious."

Shakespeare mulled this information. Of course, Topcliffe could not have been sure whether the four men had seen anything or not, but when he discovered they had slept close by, he thought it safest to keep them where Shakespeare could not question them. Where better than right under his nose? "Well done, Boltfoot. You have been a diligent servant."

"Thank you, master," Boltfoot said, pleased, yet making no effort to leave. He began twisting his cap even harder. Any rooster or capon locked by the neck between his powerful hands would be long dead by now. "Master Shakespeare," he said, averting his gaze, "I would ask you a favor, sir, a boon if you will."

Shakespeare sighed. "Do get to the point. I know very well that you want my permission to court and woo Jane, yes?"

Boltfoot nodded sheepishly. "Yes, master."

"Now, why would a pretty young maiden like Jane Cawston wish to be wooed by a truculent, grizzled, stumpy old man of thirty or more like you, Boltfoot?"

Boltfoot's face fell. He looked genuinely hurt. "I am sorry, master. You are right, of course."

Shakespeare clapped his arm around Bolt-foot's shoulder. "You ass, Boltfoot. I jest! Of course you may woo Jane. I am delighted for you both. You're a lucky man and I think her a fortunate young woman. Step out together with my blessings. I will pray that your children look more like her than you!"

Boltfoot grinned. "I will pray for that, too, Mr. Shakespeare. And thank you."

Shakespeare smiled back at him. Bolt-foot's joy threw his own sadness into stark relief, but he could not fail to be happy for such a man. No one could deserve happiness more than Boltfoot. Life had dealt him a rotten hand and he deserved a change of fortune.

"Come, Boltfoot, let us call in Jane and share a glass of sweet wine to celebrate. I have been short of good cheer these past few days. . . ."

The interview with Lord Howard of Effing-ham was painful from the start. Howard was not pleased to see Shakespeare and betrayed no emotion as he listened to the news that the supposed killer of his adoptive daughter had been apprehended and executed.

They stood in the entrance hallway to Howard's great house in Deptford. Shakespeare was not invited farther into the dwelling.

"So that is the word that is being put about, is it, Mr. Shakespeare?"

"My lord, the murderer, a Fleming called Herrick, was executed at Plymouth. He had been attempting to kill Vice Admiral Drake. It is possible he thought he could somehow get to Drake through you. I fear that is why he tried, at first, to become friendly with your daughter. Perhaps she found out too much about him and he wished to silence her."

"Yes, yes. I have heard all this. I believe you did good work, Shakespeare. But I am not stupid, sir, and I have my own beliefs about the murder of Bella. As, I am sure, do you. However, we are all subjects of Her Majesty. It is our duty to accept certain things."

"Yes, my lord."

"So I will bid you good day." He spoke curtly and rose, leaving Shakespeare no option but to leave.

As he stepped out onto the quayside, he felt as though he had betrayed Howard. A murderer had been left to walk the streets and murder at will. Howard knew it, too. It was a solution of convenience, nothing more, and a stain on the country they both loved. And both men would have to swallow the bitter taste of bile brought up from their stomachs.

Thomas Woode felt the cool of linen sheets on his body. It was as if he were floating. If he lay still, there was no pain, but the slightest movement sent tremors of agony through his body.

Catherine stood at the side of his bed, regarding him. Gently she mopped his brow with a muslin cloth dipped in water.

"Thank you," he said, barely moving his lips. "Thank you."

He had been home two weeks now. Improvement was slow. They had no way of knowing whether he would ever walk again or even use his arms, so badly was he injured. His face was haggard and his hair had turned white, yet there was light in his eyes.

"I had resigned myself to death . . ."

"You are safe now. We are all safe."

He closed his eyes and Margaret's face came to him again. Yes, he was safe now. Nothing could hurt him. And yet he knew that something was not right about this. Too many lives had been sacrificed already. It was important that no more should be given up. . . .

■ ■ ■ ■

"Is that it then, Rose? Is that your baby?"

Rose Downie held her baby in her arms. He was so much bigger now, but she knew instantly that it was William Edmund, her "Mund." His blue eyes looked up at her from fat, ruddy cheeks, without recognition. For two months now he had been held by another mother, the woman who stole him from the marketplace when Rose put him down for a minute to argue with the stall-holder.

"He is healthy and fine, is he not, Rose?"

The tears rolled down her cheeks. "He is, Mr. Topcliffe. He is lovely. I had forgot how blue were his eyes. And he is fatter now, much fatter."

"Good. And I can tell you that the other baby — if such a monstrous creature merits the word *baby* — is now back with its real mother. But, Rose, you must remember that you still have not delivered me up the foul priest Southwell."

"I am sorry, Mr. Topcliffe, but he *was* there. I implore you to believe me, sir."

"I do believe you, Rose, but that is not enough. You must stay in that house of traitors until he returns, and then you must get word to me on the instant. For Southwell will be back. Do you understand?"

Rose could not lift her eyes from Mund's face. She kissed his fat pink cheeks and the lids of his eyes. He was blurred by her tears. "Yes, sir, but Lady Tanahill does not trust me. Nor do the other servants. They know, I think, that I did come to you with intelligence of the priest."

"And have there been any visitors since last we spoke?"

Rose shook her head, all the while sobbing and smiling down at the baby. "No, sir."

Topcliffe came to her and clasped her breasts. "You are milking well, little cow; I can tell that your paps are full and heavy with creamy milk. Your baby will feed well."

"Yes, sir."

"Keep looking for priests, Rose. Should I hear of anything which you have not told me, it will be the worse for you. As I have restored your child, so can I remove it. Remember, Rose, you are my creature now. Never try to escape me."

Topcliffe took his hands away from her breasts. Rose held the baby tighter. "I will always tell you everything I know, Mr. Topcliffe. I do swear it by all that is Holy."

"Good. And are you not interested to

know where your child has been?"

"I am, sir, I am. But he looks well cared for, thank the Lord."

"He was with the lady wife of a City merchant. Well-moneyed people, a knight of the realm. I will not disclose their name. The wife was most distraught at the birth of her monster and was turned mad with grief. She did not know you. She just happened to see you with your baby and followed you. When you put the baby down, it gave her the chance she needed and a simple exchange was effected. Unfortunately for her, a wet nurse noticed the difference in the children and gossiped, and when people gossip, I hear it all. You were wise to come to me as you did, Rose. Topcliffe is your man." He reached his hand under her skirts and ran his hand along the inside of her thighs. She did not move away from him. He could do whatever he wanted because nothing else mattered now. She had her baby back.

"Thank you for everything you have done, Mr. Topcliffe. I will tell the world how wonderful you are, sir." Yet somewhere, at the back of her mind, she thought of the baby she had cared for these past weeks and felt a pang in her heart. She prayed it would be looked after well.

"Do that, Rose. Do that . . ."

CHAPTER 49

John Shakespeare reined in his mare at the northern end of Seething Lane and slid from the saddle. He had spent a few days in Stratford and his body ached from the long ride home to London. But at least his physical wounds were healing well. He could use his left arm again and the bruises had left his face. He walked the gray mare into the cobbled courtyard of the mews and handed the reins to the ostler. He gave her a pat and rubbed her ear, then ordered the ostler to bring his saddlebags around and walked the twenty yards to his front door.

Jane opened the door almost as soon as he touched it. "Oh, master, thank the Lord you are home safe!"

"Whatever is the matter, Jane?"

"Nothing, Master Shakespeare, nothing is the matter. But so much has happened since you have been away. I do not know where to start."

"Well, you could start by helping me pull off my boots. I fear they may be glued to my calves. And then some ale would go down well."

Jane's face broke into a colossal smile and then she burst into tears, gathered up her skirts, and ran away into another room. Shakespeare watched her in bemusement, then took off his hat and sat on a three-cornered stool in the hallway to attempt the removal of his boots alone.

He had wrenched off the right one after much tugging and was working the left one loose when he heard the door open and looked up. Their eyes met and held.

"Catherine," he said. It was little more than a whisper.

She stood in the doorway. "Hello, John." She held out a paper. "I bring you an invitation. From Little Bird and Queenie. It says they are opening an establishment of unimaginable luxury and would be honored to entertain you as a guest."

Shakespeare tore his eyes from hers and tugged impatiently at his boot. He did not know what to say. "They helped me with my investigation — pointed me toward Plymouth," he muttered.

"Well then, you must certainly accept their invitation." She noticed his fumblings. "Do you need some assistance, John?"

He laughed and tears pricked his eyes. "Indeed, I do."

She knelt before him and pulled his boot loose with one tug, then held it aloft. "Perhaps you should dismiss that useless maidservant of yours and take me on instead."

"Catherine?"

"Indeed, it is me."

"Thank God you're here."

"Or you would never have loosened your left boot."

She rose from her knees. He thought she had never looked lovelier. Her dark hair shone and he could not help himself reaching out to touch it.

"You may kiss me if you wish, John."

He took her in his arms and their mouths met. She let his boot slip from her hand to the floor, then slid her hands around him and held him to her. "I have caught you now, Mr. Shakespeare."

"Did I fight so hard to escape you, Mistress Marvell?"

"Perchance not, but I have caught you anyway."

"And I you. I hope. Will you marry me, mistress?"

"I will *insist* upon it, sir, for I believe you

have already stolen my maidenhead. And such a theft cannot go unpunished."

"As I recall, you colluded in the misdemeanor."

"Then we are confederates and must suffer our punishment together. Marriage it must be."

"And all for a maidenhead." He held her closer. They kissed again.

At last she stood back. "Well, sir, I see you are as forward as ever. I offered you a kiss, not a feasting."

He laughed. "Catherine, how has this come about? I thought your duty to Master Woode had precluded our match. Has he recovered sufficiently?"

Of a sudden she became serious. "No." She shook her head. "No, he will never fully recover, but we have a plan. Master Woode insisted on it and I can see no barrier to it. Though you may have objections, John."

"What plan?"

"This news should not come from me but from Boltfoot and Jane. They will be seeking your permission to marry. Jane's father has already blessed their union."

"Well, of course I will permit them to marry. But how does that affect us?"

"Master Woode is crippled and needs more help than I can give him alone. I am physically not strong enough to lift him and attend to all his wants. Jane suggested she and Boltfoot might work for him. She does get on exceeding well with the children."

Shakespeare laughed. It was all so improbable. "So we are to do an exchange. Jane and Boltfoot go to Thomas Woode and I get you in return."

"Not a very good deal is it, John? Lose two, gain one."

"Well, no, put like that, it is not at all a good trade. And most like I will have to turn to schoolmastering, for I will of a certain fall foul of Mr. Secretary."

"We will both be teachers, then, for I will still go to Dowgate six days a week to tutor the children. I am, after all, their governess."

"Two and a half to Master Woode, then, and only half to me."

"Do we have a trade, then, sir?"

"Oh yes, dearest Catherine, we have a trade. But Boltfoot still works for me as and when he is needed."

"Let us shake on it like merchants then."

"No," said Shakespeare, reaching for her again, "let us seal it with a kiss instead."

Father Robert Southwell, also known as Cotton, walked the dark early morning streets from his new lodging in Holborn, down toward the bridge. He was on his way to the Marshalsea once more, to bring Mass and comfort to the faithful there. As he approached the river, a gray fog rose, swirling, from the water.

The stooped, cowled figure of a woman hurried past him along New Fish Street. Southwell did not break his stride, but watched her bustle along ahead of him. She was bent over as if she could shrink herself to the size of an ant and not be seen. She walked on to London Bridge and her pace faltered. Slowly she trod along the central walkway through the grand houses that lined most of the crossing. Southwell held back, observing her. She was more than halfway across, just before the Drawbridge Gate, when she stopped. She went to the edge of the bridge and looked down from the parapet on the eastern side. Below her the Thames surged and raced and beckoned.

In her arms, beneath her long cloak, she held a baby. All its body apart from its head was wrapped in sacking. For a brief moment she looked down into its curious, monstrous eyes. Then she slipped a large stone into the sack with the baby. She pulled the sacking over the baby's head and tied it closed with string. The baby screamed from within like a cat.

Southwell froze at the sound. It was a noise he had heard before in another place. He moved toward the woman, but she was already holding the sack with the baby and the stone out over the parapet. Without hesitation, she let it drop into the fast-flowing waters below. For a moment it seemed it might float; the sackcloth billowed over the swell of the water, but then it filled and sank. Tears streamed down the woman's face. She turned, saw the face of the man approaching her, and brushed past him. Without looking around, she hurried back over the bridge. Back to her large house, her expensive tapestries, her clothes of gold and silver threads, her many servants and her rich merchant husband.

The London Informer, May 21st, 1587
BLESSED VICTORY FOR BOLD SIR FRANCIS

Forgive us, dear reader, for the recent absence of this your best-favoured broadsheet, but we have lately sustained an enforced absence. That episode is happily at an end thanks to the gracious offices of that most loyal and upright servant of the Crown Mr Richard Topcliffe, the Member of Parliament for Old Sarum. We are now at liberty to do our pleasant duty as London's foremost harbinger of news and report on a fortunate event. Let us ring the church bells with joy and set bonfires in the streets. A pinnace from the fleet of Sir Francis Drake has this week sailed into Plymouth Harbour, bearing news that the beloved Admiral has gained a victory worthy of being writ in the annals of English history alongside Agincourt, Crecy, and Poitiers. Drake, our greatest English mariner and sometime hero of the circumnavigation, has saved England from attack with a masterly display of daring and seamanship. We have learned that on the evening of April 29th last, the Admiral led a bold raid on Cadiz Harbour, where he fearlessly engaged the King of Spain's vaunted galleons, destroying thirty-one vessels and carrying off six, with a loss of no English ships. The cowardly Spanish put up little resistance. In the most part, they did attempt to flee the man they call the Dragon, so much did they fear Drake, but to little avail. Not a whit afraid, Sir Francis remained triumphantly in the bay for three days, gathering plunder and putting Señor Felipe's ships to the torch. All the while, ashore, the King's soldiers looked on in wonder and durst not counter-attack. Sir Francis's fleet is now believed to be stationed off the coast of Portugal, awaiting the Spanish King's treasure ships and preparing to do yet more grievous harm to his ports and shipping. It is now the great pleasure of *The London Informer* hereby to predict with confidence that Drake has rung the death knell for Philip's Armada and his cursed Enterprise of England. It will not happen, my lords, ladies, and gentlemen. The Spanish Armada will never sail for England. Yet again, Sir Francis Drake has pre-empted the enemy so that we may all sleep abed without concern for the safekeeping of our Sovereign or her people. God Bless Sir Francis Drake. God Save The Queen.

Walstan Glebe, publisher.

A FEW NOTES

Pursuivants: state-employed officers with the power to execute warrants of search and arrest. They were a ragtag bunch of armed mercenaries, often hastily assembled from local people, court hangers-on, legal officials, and even convicts, all made legitimate by wearing the Queen's escutcheon. They were particularly used in hunting Roman Catholic priests and those who harbored them. Christopher Devlin in *The Life of Robert Southwell* describes them as "hounds to whom harrying women was cheaper and more sensational than stag-hunting."

Priest holes: hiding places built deep within the fabric of Catholic houses. The greatest exponent of the craft was Nicholas Owen, a diminutive carpenter and lay Jesuit brother from Oxford, who built many priest holes before being starved out of one himself and dying under torture in the Tower in

1606, staying silent to the end. Owen, who was known as "Little John," was canonized and beatified in the twentieth century. One of the finest remaining examples of his work, which visitors can enter, is at the National Trust property Oxburgh Hall, Norfolk.

Intelligencers: spies reporting to the Principal Secretary Sir Francis Walsingham, who is seen as the father of the modern secret service. His network of agents and correspondents encompassed Europe and the Middle East, yet he was expected to fund the operation himself and was so impoverished at his death in 1590 that he was buried privately at night to avoid the cost of the splendid funeral so immense a figure might have warranted.

Jesuits: members of the Society of Jesus, a highly disciplined religious order founded in 1534 by the Spaniard Ignatius Loyola with the aim of converting heathens to Christianity. They took vows of poverty, chastity, and pilgrimage to Jerusalem (though this was, at that time, impossible). They were known for their unflinching obedience to the Pope and for their care of the sick and destitute. Jesuits soon became the "shock troops of the counter-Reformation" (well, that's the way the Protestants saw them), sending the likes of Robert Southwell and Edmund Campion to martyrdom in England. Elizabeth I and her ministers regarded Jesuits as traitors ready to resort to assassination to restore the Pope's authority. In 1606, the Jesuit Fr. Henry Garnet (who had arrived in England with Southwell in 1586) was hanged, drawn, and quartered having been implicated in the Gunpowder Plot.

Weapons: Firearms were rapidly replacing the medieval crossbow and longbow. The most frightening innovation for monarchs was the wheel-lock pistol, which was replacing the matchlock. Wheel-locks had a mechanism which spun a serrated steel edge against a piece of iron pyrite, sending sparks into the gunpowder, which exploded and discharged the ball or bullet. Previously, with matchlock weapons (including the cumbersome old arquebus, familiarly known as hagbut or hackbut), the gunpowder had to be ignited by a pre-lighted taper, or match. The big advantage of wheel-locks was that they could be held in one hand, be primed and loaded in advance, and be small enough to be concealed under a cloak or in a sleeve. Ornate wheel-locks became the must-have accessory for men of substance, and whole cavalry squadrons carried them into battle, each man carrying two or more primed weapons in their hands and belts. Men commonly armed themselves with swords and daggers (a poniard is a small dagger). Guards carried pole weapons — pikes and halberds. The pike was little more than a pole with a spear head, while the halberd had a three-edged head: axe, pike, and hook.

Whores: It is curious that the seamier side of life flourished so well at a time of great religious fervor. Southwark was famous for its brothels, which the London authorities could do nothing to control, being outside the City walls. Prostitution was illegal but bribery of constables was commonplace. Whores were often called Winchester Geese, as much of Southwark came under the control of the Bishop of Winchester. Other slang names included bawdy basket, callet, drab, punk, hobby horse, stale, strange woman, strumpet, and trug. A brothel madam was known as "Mistress of the Game," and her clients were called "committers" or "hobby horse men." Sexually transmitted disease — the French Welcome

— was rife and, in the days before antibiotics, virtually untreatable (though that didn't prevent early quacks devising and selling so-called cures).

Army and Navy: Unlike the professional Spanish troops, England did not have a standing army. In times of trouble, such as the impending Armada invasion, militias were raised by the nobility from among their tenants and by the great craft guilds. Nor was the Navy a permanent fixture, but thanks to the enthusiasm for privateering of Drake, Hawkins, and others, the English had become great sea warriors. Their ships were designed to be leaner and faster than the towering Spanish galleons, which had an advantage in close combat but were easily harried and outgunned by the English at longer range.

The Privy Council: the rough equivalent of a modern-day cabinet of ministers. During Elizabeth's reign it varied in numbers from ten to twenty. The Queen did not attend meetings, but the proceedings were reported to her assiduously and she had the final say over matters of policy. Generally, she expected her ministers to get on with the day-to-day business of running the country. As well as executive powers, the Council also acted as a court when it sat in Star Chamber (the old council chamber at Westminster). Lord Burghley and Sir Francis Walsingham were the dominant Privy Council men for much of the reign.

Prison: There were fourteen gaols in London. A wide variety of offenses could land someone there, ranging from vagrancy, debt, or fortune-telling to the most severe of crimes. The conditions prisoners had to endure depended largely on how much garnish (bribe money) they could afford to give the Keeper. They were surprisingly open, however, enabling Robert Southwell and other priests to visit prisoners and say Mass. The Marshalsea and the Clink in Southwark were seen as softer options than the City gaols such as Newgate, Bridewell, Wood Street Counter, and the Fleet. Southwell's companion, Fr. Henry Garnet, wrote of feeling "safe from danger" while visiting prison.

Tobacco: Tobacco was *not* introduced to England by Sir Walter Raleigh. Though he sponsored ventures to Virginia in the 1580s, he never went there himself and, anyway, tobacco was probably brought to Europe by sailors — Spanish, Portuguese, and English — as early as the 1560s, when Raleigh was still a boy.

Beasts: Richard Topcliffe and others used the word to refer to the Pope, Jesuits, and the Catholic Church generally, because they were seen as the anti-Christ — "the beast of the apocalypse," from the Book of Revelation, chapter 13.

Printing and newspapers: Some historians believe that half the population of England could read by the end of the sixteenth century. Londoners, particularly, were hungry for news and bought up broadsheets (or broadsides) as fast as they could be printed. Illustrated by woodcuts and often written in ballad form, they would look very different from newspapers as we know them.

ACKNOWLEDGMENTS

I am indebted to the writings of many superb historians, but a few books merit special mention for the assistance they have given me in understanding the late Elizabethan period.

Most important, I would like to pay tribute to *The Life of Robert Southwell* by Christopher Devlin, a vivid biography and history that was first published in 1956 and makes one feel as if the events described happened last week.

Other books I would particularly recommend include *The Defeat of the Spanish Armada* by Garrett Mattingly, *The Confident Hope of a Miracle* by Neil Hanson, *Elizabeth's Spy Master* by Robert Hutchinson, *God's Secret Agents* by Alice Hogge, *The Awful End of Prince William the Silent* by Lisa Jardine, *The Secret Voyage of Sir Francis*

Drake by Samuel Bawlf, *A Brief History of the Tudor Age* by Jasper Ridley, *The Reckoning* by Charles Nicholl, *The Elizabethan Underworld* by Gamini Salgado, *The A to Z of Elizabethan London* compiled by Adrian Prockter and Robert Taylor, *Elizabeth's London* by Lisa Picard, *Shakespeare* by Bill Bryson, *The Master Mariner* by Nicholas Monsarrat, *The Coming of the Book* by Lucien Febvre and Henri-Jean Martin, *The Englishman's Food* by J. C. Drummond and Anne Wilbraham, *Invisible Power* by Alan Haynes, *Palaces & Progresses of Elizabeth I* by Ian Dunlop, *Entertaining Elizabeth I* by June Osborne.

I would also like to thank my wife, Naomi, my brother, Brian, and the Reverend Selwyn Tillett for their invaluable help.

ABOUT THE AUTHOR

After a career in national newspapers, **Rory Clements** now lives with his family in an old farmhouse in Norfolk and writes full-time. When not immersing himself in the world of Elizabethan England, he enjoys a game of tennis with friends, a glass of red wine with his artist wife, Naomi Clements Wright, and village life generally. *Martyr* is his debut novel, the first of a series featuring John Shakespeare. He is at work on his second John Shakespeare novel, *Revenger.*

We hope you have enjoyed this Large Print book. Other Thorndike, Wheeler, Kennebec, and Chivers Press Large Print books are available at your library or directly from the publishers.

For information about current and upcoming titles, please call or write, without obligation, to:

Publisher
Thorndike Press
295 Kennedy Memorial Drive
Waterville, ME 04901
Tel. (800) 223-1244

or visit our Web site at:

http://gale.cengage.com/thorndike

OR

Chivers Large Print
published by BBC Audiobooks Ltd
St James House, The Square
Lower Bristol Road
Bath BA2 3SB
England
Tel. +44(0) 800 136919
email: bbcaudiobooks@bbc.co.uk
www.bbcaudiobooks.co.uk

All our Large Print titles are designed for easy reading, and all our books are made to last.